D1363568

HER LAST
WALK
HOME

PATRICIA GIBNEY

bookouture

Published by Bookouture in 2024

An imprint of Storyfire Ltd.
Carmelite House
50 Victoria Embankment
London EC4Y 0DZ

www.bookouture.com

Storyfire Ltd's authorised representative in the EEA is Hachette Ireland
8 Castlecourt Centre
Castleknock Road
Castleknock
Dublin 15 D15 YF6A
Ireland

ISBN: 978-1-83525-603-9
eBook ISBN: 978-1-83525-602-2

For Lydia Vassar-Smith

PROLOGUE

VALENTINE'S NIGHT

If she could turn back time, she'd never have got into the car. *Never accept lifts from strangers*: the words had been imbedded into her brain as a child, but she was not a child now. She *had* accepted the lift. She hadn't realised she'd been in any danger. Who would, when a woman was driving? And there was a child seat in the back.

It had been after a date for drinks, but she'd felt uncomfortable in her date's presence. Following just two gins, she'd scooted out the rear exit after excusing herself to go to the toilet. Why did he make her feel uncomfortable? she wondered. Probably because he was more interested in commenting on the other girls in the pub, and had thrown a few less-than-desirable comments her way.

Outside, the temperature had dropped. Icy air swirled about her. Of course she'd run out leaving her coat on the back of the chair and her phone, which had died, in the pocket, such was her haste to leave unnoticed. But she had her handbag containing her apartment keys and wallet. She'd slung the strap up over her shoulder, cross-body, and wrapped her arms around her waist, trying to ward off the rawness of the night.

The car had pulled up alongside her just when she'd been thinking of ducking in somewhere warm to restore the feeling in her limbs. The street lamps threw a dour hue downwards and she'd walked in that dim light without fear of threat. Gratefully, she'd accepted the kind offer from the woman, hardly registering the familiarity. What followed was so unexpected that she still could not get her mind to make sense of it. She'd ended up here, wherever *here* was.

She eyed the woman walking around her in an ever-decreasing circle. Lying on the wooden floor, face up, she had a view of the blue denim jeans, the bare feet with nails painted crimson.

What was that noise? She closed her swollen eyelids, trying to figure it out. Nothing was forthcoming. On opening her eyes, she saw the woman clutching a knife as she moved. She wanted to cry out. It was impossible. Her mouth was bound with sticky tape wound around her head.

Water dripped from a tap somewhere. A door opened.

She was no longer alone with the woman and her knife. She could not see who entered, but she heard the woman gasp in annoyance. And then she heard a sound so alien to her circumstances and surroundings that her body went rigid.

A child. Laughing. Close by. In another room? Was the child captive like her? Or were they part of this terrifying ordeal?

Her thoughts were cut short as the woman leaned down on her haunches and tipped her chin upwards with the point of the knife. She looked into eyes so dark they shimmered. And she heard no more.

ONE YEAR LATER

THURSDAY

Mark Boyd waited outside the therapist's office while his eight-year-old son, Sergio, attended his three p.m. therapy session. He had no idea what the conversation was like behind the door, but Sergio usually came out smiling, so it couldn't be too bad. However, once they arrived back at the apartment, the boy's mood drifted into silence, melancholy almost, and Boyd was at a loss as how to deal with it.

Just six weeks had passed since Sergio's traumatic near-death experience, and Boyd had spent every day since then by his side, watching and caring for him. He'd gone rogue during the last murder investigation. Heading off in a blizzard to the north-west of the country on a search for the boy. Despite the fact that he'd found him, there had been recriminations. He'd left without permission, operated outside his jurisdiction and been generally belligerent in his quest. But with the positive press garnered from the rescue, and the fact that Boyd had solved the mystery of the woman who'd died in the car crash, Superintendent Deborah Farrell had let him off with a stern warning and a note on his personal file. He did not care in the slightest. He had his son home safe and that was all that mattered to him.

Now it was time to return to work. The pain of being separated from his son skewered his heart so badly he thought he might suffer cardiac arrest. At least he'd be going back on a Friday, so it would ease them into a new routine.

After the therapy session, he settled Sergio on the couch while he shoved a chicken in the oven to roast for dinner.

'When is Grace arriving?' Sergio asked, tugging a blanket up to his chin, television remote in his hand.

Boyd had asked his only sibling, Grace, if she could come and stay for a week or two until he got settled back at work. Sergio wouldn't be attending school until after February midterm, so he was in the process of finding a childminder. He could no longer depend on Lottie's daughters for that. Chloe had been great, but now that their grandmother, Rose, was suffering from the early signs of dementia, the girls had to keep an eye on her.

'She should be on the seven o'clock bus. We'll pick her up from the station.'

'Will she like me?'

'Of courses she will. Grace is the nicest person I know.'

'I thought Lottie was the nicest person you knew.' The boy looked up from beneath his long lashes, a slight grin on his lips that warmed Boyd up.

'I suppose you could say they are *both* the nicest people I know, besides you.'

'Mm.' Sergio pointed the remote at the television.

About to sit beside his son, Boyd heard the doorbell. He wasn't expecting anyone to call and was hesitant opening the door. He needed time alone with Sergio to explain more about Grace.

He also had to talk to him about school and the possibility of them moving to a new house at some stage. Once he found the right place and secured a mortgage. Lottie and her family had to figure into that scenario, but he had no idea how it would work, if at all. That thought saddened him as he went to unlatch the door.

'Don't stand there catching flies in that open mouth of yours, Mark Boyd, let me in to see my one and only nephew.'

Words deserted him. He tugged open the door, which was prone to sticking on the mat in damp weather, and watched as his sister dropped an enormous wheelie suitcase on the floor before brushing past him.

By the time he made it to the living room, after eventually succeeding in shutting the door with a shoulder push, Grace had divested herself of her coat and was sitting beside Sergio. Wearing a woollen dress, heavy tights and walking boots, she looked totally different from what he remembered. She seemed a lot older than her thirty-three years.

'Grace, this is Sergio. Sergio, this is your Auntie Grace. She's come all the way from beyond Galway to stay with us.'

'Grace is cool,' Sergio said.

'Master Sergio, I've been called all sorts of things in my life, but that's the first time I've heard my name and cool in the same sentence.' Grace looked up at Boyd. 'We will get along just fine. Are you making tea, Mark?'

'Ehm, I've dinner in the oven, but if you want tea...'

'I wouldn't have mentioned it if I didn't want it.'

'I'll put the kettle on.'

In the kitchenette, he recalled just how black-and-white Grace saw the world. Never one to waste words, she uttered aloud what others merely thought. She was her own woman. And he realised something else. How could he have been so stupid? His cramped one-bed apartment was definitely too small for three.

With the kettle boiling, he leaned against the breakfast bar and studied his sister. She wore her hair tied back in a meticulous ponytail with a red satin ribbon. Her cheeks were a little sunken. When had her face become so thin? She caught him staring.

'Remember what I said about catching flies, Mark. You need to be careful.'

'I was supposed to pick you up later at the station. Did you catch an earlier bus?'

'I must have, otherwise how would I be here?'

'Right. And you took a taxi from the station?'

She rolled her eyes and shook her head. To Sergio, she said, 'Your daddy is such a silly billy. I hardly walked, dragging my case behind me, in that weather.'

'You could have phoned me,' Boyd said, aware of the petulance that had crept into his tone.

The kettle whistled. It was impossible to have a straightforward conversation with her. He wanted to call Lottie to ask her to come over and rescue him. But he had to make the tea, then the dinner, and sort out beds for the night. Perhaps having Grace to stay was not one of his brighter ideas.

Katie Parker watched from the top step of the stairs as her mother arrived home from work just after six. Lottie banged the door, shuffled out of her black puffa jacket, balled it up, feathers flying like dust motes in the air, and stuffed it on the floor beneath the overflowing coat rack. She took off her boots, with one foot on the heel of the other so she didn't have to bend down and tug them off. Then she ran her hands through her damp straggly hair, took a few deep breaths and made her way to the kitchen. Another door banged.

'Bad day again, Mam?' Katie said to the air.

She grabbed the banister, stood and made her way into her bedroom she shared with her three-year-old son, Louis. She'd been nineteen when her boyfriend, Jason, was murdered, without knowing she was pregnant. She hadn't even known herself. Louis was adorable. Jason's father, Tom Rickard, loved his grandson, and lodged a regular stipend in Katie's account for him, but she couldn't bring herself to touch it.

The few jobs she'd had hadn't worked out. Childcare was expensive and she regularly found herself unemployed and unemployable. The days seemed as endless as the impossibility of holding down a job.

She flung herself on the bed. Burying her head in her pillow, she yelled into the synthetic foam. It did nothing to relieve her anxiety, but at least she was doing something.

Turning over, she stared at the yellowing ceiling. The roof of the old house had sprung a leak the week after Christmas and her mother couldn't afford to get it fixed. Lottie's guy, Boyd, and their colleague, Kirby, had ventured into the attic and nailed a few boards where the slates had disintegrated. But rain still dripped into her room. Now Louis had a cough and she feared his asthma would spiral. Maybe she should put some of Tom's money towards a deposit for an apartment. No, she needed a proper job. She needed to feel like the real Katie Parker again. She needed a life. And then she realised what was at the centre of her anguish. She missed her dad.

A knock on the door and her mother stood there, holding Louis' hand.

'I can mind this imp tonight. Why don't you go out? Meet some of your friends.'

'What friends? They got on with their lives while mine stagnated.' She hadn't meant to sound irritable, but that was exactly how she sounded. She had pushed her girlfriends away. Dropping out of college hadn't helped. The few dates she'd had turned tail the second she mentioned her son.

'What about that guy you dated for a while last year? I thought it was serious. What happened there?'

Katie's stomach clenched. She sat up and put her hands beneath her to hide the shaking. That had been a disaster. Another reason why she was Katie-no-boyfriends. She forced a smile. 'I'll ring around a few of the girls. And thanks, Mam.'

'You need to cut yourself a break. Life's too short. Getting a job is just one part of life; it shouldn't consume you. It will happen. In the meantime, have some fun.'

'Yeah, but I need to work to earn money.'

'Don't you have money from Tom Rickard?'

'That's for Louis, not for me. What I need is a sugar daddy,' Katie said wryly.

'*What?*'

She laughed at the expression of horror on her mother's face. 'Joking, Mam.'

'Please don't joke about things like that.'

Louis broke free from his grandmother and jumped onto the bed. 'I want a sugar daddy. Please can I have one, because I don't have a daddy.'

Katie needed her daddy too. She caught sight of her mother's unreadable expression.

'It's okay, Louis. Will you help me get ready? I'm going out and Nana Lottie will be minding you.'

'Yeah!'

The little boy leaped off the bed, ran to the dressing table and began waving a foundation brush in the air. 'Magic brush for Mam.'

'I wish,' Katie said as the door shut softly and her mother left her alone.

He packed up the car boot with things he didn't want to have to use, but she constantly told him he had to *be prepared*. Like he wasn't, eh?

'You need to be on the lookout.' Her voice was too high-pitched. Too excited. 'You can't let anyone take you by surprise.'

'I know, I know,' he replied, trying not to let his annoyance coat his words with something she could attack.

'Don't be sharp with me. If it wasn't for me, where do you think you'd be? I deserve your respect, so I do.'

She turned her cheek for the obligatory peck, repulsing him. But rather than suffer another tongue-lashing, he air-kissed her and stood back.

'I think I have everything,' he mumbled, anxious to put distance between them.

'Did you remember the scissors?'

'Yes.' He muffled the groan that surged up his throat. He'd forgotten the scissors.

'You can't be leaving your DNA on the roll if you have to bite the tape off. Have you got the rope in case you need it?'

'Of course.' At least he'd remembered that. 'Can I go now? It's getting on.'

'We do this for each other. You know I love you, don't you?'

Whatever she construed as love, he had a different opinion. An opinion he could never verbalise. Not in her presence. 'I wouldn't be doing this for you if you didn't love me. I'll set off. Don't want to look suspicious.'

'How can you look suspicious when all you look is stupid?' Her mood turned so quickly he wondered how it never tripped her up.

Once inside the car, he breathed heavily with relief. Freedom. A knock by his ear caused him to jump. Her face pressed to the glass, a finger gesturing to let down the window. He did as instructed.

'Bring this. I have a good feeling about tonight.' She pushed a leather pouch into his hand and walked back to the house.

He ran his finger over it and shivered. It was her treasured knife. How did she think of everything? She was so much cleverer than anyone he'd ever met, and that scared him.

With every turn of the wheels stretching the distance between him and the house, he began to relax, sinking into the comfortable leather seat. By the time he reached the corner at the end of the lane and pulled out onto the road, he was light-headed with relief.

A glance at the leather-bound knife on the central console was enough to make him sit up straight and concentrate. This night could be short and uneventful. Or it could be long and bloody. Though he knew he was forever cloaked in her shadow, night was a time for his power to reign without her influence pulsing between his shoulder blades.

The tan was a disaster. If she'd taken her time doing it, it would have turned out grand. She'd applied fake tan too many times to count in her twenty-five years but tonight it had to be perfect and it wasn't. It was a streaking mess.

'Typical,' Laura Nolan moaned at her reflection in the smeared mirror.

Trying not to cry, which would be detrimental to her make-up, she attempted to muster up positive vibes. She'd had her hair washed and blow-dried, even though it broke her heart to fork out the twenty euro she couldn't afford. The effect was worth it, wasn't it? She hoped so. She'd already ruined her silver sequin skirt with tan and had to resort to a pair of dark denim jeans. Her black chiffon top with its diamanté spaghetti straps was okay. She hoped.

Flicking an eyelash with another dab of mascara, she heard a voice behind her.

'Stop fiddling with it. You'll make it worse.'

Laura groaned as her mother revealed herself in the mirror, her face a little askew because of the crack in the top right-hand corner. Small, too thin, with not a grey hair in her fair mane (she could afford the salon, of course), Diana's bracelets tinkled as she moved a hand to fix a stray hair at the back of Laura's neck.

'Don't!' Laura snapped. 'You'll ruin it.'

'Be hard to ruin something that's already ruined, missy.'

'Can you leave me alone? Please?'

'Where are you going?'

'Out.'

'I gathered that. Out where?'

'Why do you care?'

'I want to make sure you're safe. Are you meeting up with a friend?'

'Yeah, for dinner and drinks,' Laura said, to shut Diana up. Her friends had drifted away once she'd got pregnant with Aaron. He was almost four now and she loved him with every bone in her being, but she missed her friends.

'I can't be on call to babysit all the time, you know that?'

'I do, and I'm grateful to you. It means a lot to me.'

Her mother smiled. Laura knew it was forced. 'Just so you don't forget, you have a little boy here who wants to see you when he wakes up in the morning.'

'I won't forget.'

How could she, Laura thought, when Diana was constantly reminding her? How could she when she loved her son so much? *A mistake, a one-night stand, how could you? No condom, not on the pill, how could you be so stupid?* Her mother's words from the night she'd told her reverberated in her brain. She'd had no choice but to tell her. No choice but to drop out of college and lose her grant. To run back home because she could no longer pay the rent. All of that. But Diana had insisted she keep the baby. No daughter of mine (she was the only daughter, as far as Laura knew) will get an abortion. Over my dead body.

She had agreed to help. And Laura had accepted. But she hadn't realised that the help was offered grudgingly. It came with more complaints and caustic words than a day could hold. The proverbial strings attached to that help circled her neck and threatened to choke her to death. But she didn't want to think about all that now.

She pursed her glossed lips, dropped her mascara tube into her cosmetic purse and scrunched the purse into her tiny handbag along with her phone. Maybe tonight she would meet the man who wouldn't mind dating a girl with an almost-four-year-old child in tow. A young woman who still lived with her mother.

One could hope.

———

Why did pubs have music playing so loud? It was only nine o'clock and Shannon Kenny already felt like the band had set up a practice session in her ears. She leaned towards her date to say something; he turned at the same time, their noses inadvertently touching.

He laughed. 'That's an Eskimo kiss.'

At least that was what she thought he said. He could have asked her to marry him and she wouldn't have known.

Trying not to make a tit of herself, and as loudly as she could, she said, 'I'd love another drink.'

'Same again?'

She was able to lip-read that. 'Make it a double,' she said, miming.

While he was at the bar, she studied the broadness of his shoulders and realised his waist looked too small, his legs too short. In fact he appeared totally misshapen. Or was that the effects of drinking on an empty stomach?

It should have been the first warning sign. He'd promised

her dinner in the Joyce Hotel restaurant but then had insisted on pre-dinner drinks in Danny's Bar. And it now appeared he had no intention of leaving. Maybe she should have asked for a packet of crisps.

She glanced around, trying to see someone she recognised. The place was heaving and the band had got louder – if the thrumming in her ears was anything to go by. He was still at the bar, chatting with the girl who worked there. How they could hold a conversation with the resounding din was beyond her. Maybe she should leave. Grab her coat and get the hell out of there.

'I must be getting old,' she told herself, despite having just had her twenty-fifth birthday. Not that long ago, all this was her idea of heaven. But that was before...

'That was then, this is now,' she said.

Shit, she was talking to herself. God Almighty, was this what rehab did to you? You went in with one complaint and came out with a host of new ones. Next stop, the asylum.

Grinning at her own dark humour, she noticed him glance over his shoulder at her. A quick smile before he turned back to the bar. Was he checking she hadn't escaped? More likely he was telling the girl what a big mistake he'd made tonight with his date.

How long could she sit here with him up there flirting while the boom of the band took root in her ears? Not much longer was the answer. But as she stuffed her phone in her bag, he returned with her large gin in a fancy balloon glass, and she decided she couldn't let a good drink go to waste.

———

Laura sat in Casey's on her own. The pub was less crowded than usual. She wondered if she should have phoned Shannon. Not that they'd spoken in almost a year. But sometimes you needed to confide in someone other than your bloody mother.

Her date hadn't turned up. She checked her phone. It was early yet. Plenty of time. She had the correct pub, hadn't she? She scrolled through the app and found the message. Yes. So where the hell was he?

Glancing at his photo, she smiled despite herself. He wasn't half bad-looking. Clicking out of the app, she strained her neck to look around again. No, he wasn't here. She ordered a Diet Coke. He could buy the alcohol when, if, he arrived.

Then she felt a tap on her shoulder. Slowly she turned, hoping it was him, and a warm, fuzzy feeling settled in her chest as she waited for her eyes to meet his for the first time.

But it was just someone trying to get close to the bar to order a drink. She felt her shoulders deflate and her expectation flying away on the expelled air.

———

It was after ten and he was driving around Ragmullin again, being careful to keep to the outer roads, using rat runs through housing estates. He didn't want to be caught on traffic cameras or CCTV in the centre of town, nor the guards to stop and quiz him when he was on a scouting mission. And that was what tonight was about. He was searching for the ideal candidate. The approximate age and build were ingrained in his brain as if etched by a knife on a slate. He knew who he was looking for, even if he didn't yet know who she was. But he had been given enough information to recognise her when he saw her.

He parked in a housing estate, and sat there with the engine off for maybe twenty minutes, keeping his mind alert by recounting the tools he kept in the boot, while ignoring the knife he'd stuck into the glovebox.

If the guards happened to stop him, he had a plausible story:

the taxi light was off because it was broken. Not that he would give anyone a reason to stop him. He felt a tug of excitement. Maybe tonight he would be successful.

He glanced at his phone. Time to move. Turning up the heat to defog the windscreen, he set off once more. If unsuccessful, he'd try again later. He could not leave town empty-handed. *She* would not be pleased.

In the end, Katie had lied to her mother and told her she was meeting friends at Danny's. She'd gone to Fallon's instead and sat on her own at the bar while her sister dished out words of wisdom in between serving customers.

'Join a dating site. I'll set up a profile for you.' Chloe smiled. 'I have one, and that's how I get my dates.'

'You haven't been on one in ages.'

'Hadn't time recently. I worked every hour over Christmas, and before that I was minding Gran. Go on, be a devil, Katie, for once in your life.'

'I was a devil once and look where it got me.' She swirled the remnants of her gin and tonic as if by Louis' sense of magic the glass would become full again.

'Whatever, but you need to get a life. I'm serious. Before you know it you'll be thirty, and then what?'

'I'll still be a mother, still have a little boy and my family around me. Isn't that what's important?'

'Some of it is, but Mam will go off with Boyd to set up a new life for herself. I saw him looking at houses on a real-estate website the other evening. If she moves, what about us?'

'She wouldn't move without us.'

'Maybe not without Sean because he's still at school, but Katie, we're adults. We need to fend for ourselves. To live our own lives.'

'When did you become the wise one in our family?'

A voice rang out from the end of the bar. 'Hey, two pints of Guinness when you're ready there.'

Katie watched her sister pull the pints while still talking.

'It's not wisdom. It's common sense,' Chloe said over her shoulder as she turned to another customer while the pints rested.

Katie mulled over her words. Chloe was right. She had to start living. Holding her phone in one hand, she tapped with her thumb and brought up the app she'd added a profile to earlier that evening. Her finger hovered over the icon as she bit her lip and prayed for some activity. Before she could tap, though, someone crashed into her back. She dropped her drink but saved the phone.

'Oh, I'm so sorry. This place is mental tonight. What are you drinking? I'll get you another.'

'No, it's fine. I was leaving anyhow.' She went to slide off the stool, but his body was blocking her. She could feel the harshness of his denim jeans against her leg. She hoped her tights wouldn't run.

'Can't move,' he said. 'A stag party just arrived. I'm jammed in. Give me a minute.'

Glancing side-eyed at him, she noticed he was a good deal older than her. Not bad-looking, though. Short dark hair and a touch of stubble on his chin that seemed to be by design. His eyes, with tiny lashes, were the tired sort, black-ringed and dilated. Maybe he was on drugs. Maybe he worked long hours. Maybe he was married. Maybe she should go home.

'One minute,' she said.

'If I can catch the eye of that cute barmaid, I'll buy you a drink. And don't say you're leaving. Please? One drink to apologise, okay?' A hand was thrust in front of her. 'Jackson,' he said. 'My mother calls me son, but everyone else calls me Jack.'

'I don't think I'll be calling you son,' she laughed, and it felt good to have a smile on her face. Normally her smiles were reserved for Louis. 'I'm Katie.'

'And what did Katie do next?'

'Huh?'

'Like the book.'

'You've lost me now.' She was having to shout over the din, and the smell of alcohol mixed with perfume and sweat was giving her a headache. Maybe she should leave.

'I know you're thinking of escaping, but I want to buy you that drink.'

'Okay, so. Hey, Chloe?'

He widened his eyes and ordered her a gin and a pint for himself. When Chloe put the drinks on the counter, she gave Katie a less-than-subtle thumbs-up.

He appeared to ignore the gesture and leaned on the counter, having inched his way into a narrow gap. Now that she could see him properly, she thought he could be well in his thirties. Way too old for her twenty-three years. All the same, a free drink was not to be sneezed at.

'You must come here often if you know the names of the bar staff,' he said.

'Is that your usual chat-up line? Or...' She paused. Maybe it would be good if he didn't know Chloe was her sister.

'Ha, you got me there. Is it always this mental?'

'Nah, just leading up to the weekend. Thursday night is the new Friday night as far as I can see.'

'What about we drink up and get out of here? Wallace's is quieter. We can get to know each other.'

'What if I don't want to get to know you?'

'Then we can talk about books. I'd love to tell you what Katie did next.'

She wasn't letting him win that easily. 'Instead, let *me* tell you what Katie did. She said thanks for the drink, went outside, got in a taxi and hurried home to her three-year-old son.'

'Okay. But can I tell you what Jack did next?'

She was surprised he didn't flinch at the mention of Louis. Or maybe he hadn't heard. 'Went up a hill with Jill to fetch a pail of water?'

'You're funny. No. He gave Katie his number, phoned a taxi for her, let her go home to her son, then called her the next day to arrange a night out. Somewhere quieter with good food and wine.'

Gobsmacked, Katie felt like crying. Was she unbelievably lucky to have met a genuinely nice guy? Or was he too good to be true?

Someone else nudged her in the back, and once again she failed to rescue her drink. She watched it drip onto her lap and seep over the counter until Chloe appeared with a cloth, eyeing her intently.

Leaning over, her sister whispered into her ear, 'Don't look a gift horse in the mouth.'

If it hadn't rained, she might never have got into the car with him. He glanced out through the windscreen at the forbidding night-time blackness and the shimmering street lights punctured by silver daggers of rain spearing the earth. Bad night to be out, all right.

She was standing under a tangled wreck of a cheap umbrella while the rain cascaded. So what was he to do but stop and offer her a lift? *She* would be so pleased when he got home.

'Thanks a million,' the young woman said, sitting in and shaking so hard that water flew in all directions. She didn't apologise for the mess she was making, and that irritated him a little. Without looking at him, she glanced at the child seat in the back. It seemed to reassure her. Good. 'Are you off duty? Your taxi light is off.'

'Keep meaning to get it fixed, and forgive me, but the wife forgot to take out the child seat.' He ran a hand over his cultured beard, glad that he'd let it grow.

'I've had a bitch of a night. The wind turned my brolly inside out and I swear to God I was ready to lie down and cry.'

'And what good would that do?'

She shrugged out of her coat, rolled it up and put it in the footwell. 'I'm sorry about the water all over your lovely seats.'

An apology at last. Maybe she had some manners after all. 'They'll dry out, and so will you.'

He snatched a look, amazed at how pretty she was, despite being bedraggled, wet and flustered. Then he looked at her more closely and a quiver of fear ran down his spine. He surreptitiously tugged his scarf up to his mouth.

She shut the door and the interior light went out. As she snapped on her seat belt, he put the car in gear and took off, slowly.

'Where will I drop you?'

'The bridge will do me grand.' She had her head down, wringing out the leg of her flared jeans, despite less than a moment ago being apologetic for the state she was making of his car. Another tick in the negative column.

'I can leave you to your door. No charge. You don't want to get drenched again.'

He thought she might argue, but she said, 'Do you know Redwood Court?'

'Sure I do. And you were going to make me leave you at the bridge? Nothing to be afraid of, sweetheart. I'll even wait until you get inside. Your ma and da might be up waiting for you.' He was probing, but she didn't fill in the blanks that might tell him she lived alone or with friends. 'You in college?'

'Not at the moment. I was in Maynooth. Commute was a bitch.'

'Tough all right. No accommodation there?'

'Too expensive. Can't afford to return as a mature student.'

'Bastards get you every which way. This country is a joke.'

'Suppose so.'

She lapsed into an uncomfortable silence, and he felt he had to fill the space to stop himself reaching out and touching her knee.

'You don't look old enough to be a mature student.' He stopped as the traffic lights turned red at the bridge up ahead. The town was eerily quiet. Anyone who was out must still be in the pubs.

'I'm twenty-seven,' she said haughtily. He knew she was lying.

He drummed his fingers on the steering wheel, waiting for the lights to change. 'What brought you out tonight?'

'Just drinks with a friend.'

'Not much of a friend if they left you to walk home in this.'

'It's complicated.'

'Isn't everything?'

The lights switched to green and he turned left on the bridge, still driving slowly, trying to get his thoughts focused on what he wanted to do with her.

'Hey, that's my turn. Over there.' She pointed to the right, swivelling around, but was restrained by the seat belt. She grabbed his elbow. 'You missed the turn for my estate. Let me out.'

She really was pathetic.

He flung out his arm. His elbow caught her in the throat. She flopped forward, chin drooping onto her chest. Regaining his composure in order to navigate the large roundabout at St Declan's Asylum, he blinked in time with the wipers, breathing in and out in the stagnant air of the car. He smelled her female scent mingling with the raindrops on her clothes, and felt a flurry of excitement in his groin.

Don't look at her, he warned himself. Keep driving. It wasn't that late, he thought, he might still have time to go back and get another. That cheered him up as he drove.

The green glare from the digital clock was imprinted in Diana's eyes. 02:00. Where was Laura? She was really pushing it now. She tried her daughter's phone again. The little witch had it switched off. At least her grandson was asleep. Not a peep out of him. She flung back the bedclothes and made her way down to the kitchen in darkness.

She opened the refrigerator and the light swept an arc over the floor. Grabbing a carton of milk, she let the door swing shut and was once again enveloped in the night.

By feel she got a glass and poured the milk. Thirty seconds in the microwave. Then she went back to bed. Warm milk should help her sleep. Laura was in big trouble this time. Diana sipped her milk propped up by pillows and tried to figure out exactly what she would say to her daughter when she walked through the door.

———

George Kenny pulled back the curtain and looked out at the rainy night. His sister, Shannon, was really getting on his nerves. He couldn't rely on her. He glanced at the time on his phone. 02:15. And she was still out.

He let the curtain fall back in place, reprimanding himself for thinking like his mother used to sound. Three years they'd lived without her presence, and in those years he'd assumed the mantle of mother and father. Because of Shannon's problems last year, he felt there was little he could do now. They were both adults, though she acted like a spoiled child. No point in staying awake worrying about her. She could look after herself, couldn't she?

Tucking the phone under his pillow, he turned over and went back to sleep.

———

The clock ticked over to 2.30. Lottie had heard Chloe come in from work a half-hour earlier. Had she slept through Katie coming home? She'd dozed but hadn't properly slept. The job of minding Louis meant she was on edge. He could choke on a cough in the night. His asthma was getting worse and she knew the damp house was partly to blame.

She wondered if Grace had arrived at Boyd's. She was looking forward to having him back on the team. He'd been around at hers a good few evenings. Sergio loved Sean. Or maybe he loved the PlayStation games more. Sean loved Sergio too, so that was a positive in a world of negatives. Boyd was pushing for them all to live together and Lottie felt it wasn't practical. She humoured him while being non-committal.

Up on her elbow, listening, she thought it would be comforting to have Boyd lying beside her. Life continuously conspired against them. Surely they were due something good soon? But her life rarely delivered what she wished for.

Another glance at the clock. 'Where the hell are you, Katie Parker?'

FRIDAY

Rex didn't want to go to school. He'd had enough of bullies. Ginger this. Ginger that. He'd even thought of dyeing his hair, but his mother threw a wobbly when he suggested it. He wanted it cut short, and she'd clipped him on the ear and said no way. He was only seven, but he knew younger kids who'd at least got a fade. It wasn't too much to ask. His mam had even started tying up his hair at home, it was that long. He toyed with robbing her scissors and cutting it himself. But she'd kill him. The row between his mam and dad last night had been so bad that this morning he'd grabbed his school bag, fixed it to his back and crept out the front door before they were even awake.

It was still dark, not yet six, but he wasn't scared. He was way too early for school. Maybe he could take the day off. Sneak into the cinema that was close to his estate and curl up on a soft seat at the back for the day. If he could sneak in.

A foggy mist lingered over the GAA pitch and it made him want to sit in the middle of it; to let it swallow him up. He glanced up the road at the cinema. Was it a good idea? How would he get in without anyone seeing him? It didn't open until noon. That was a problem. But Rex wasn't one to let problems stop him. Unless it was his mother laying down the law about his hair. Sure what harm could a day off do? A day without taunts.

His mind made up, he turned to his right, away from the school and town, and walked towards the cinema complex. Maybe he'd find out what it was he'd seen last night through his bedroom window.

The barrier was locked, so he hopped over the wall and moved slowly through the long grass. There were a load of shops situated around the cinema, even a coffee shop that sold smoothies. He was mentally counting the change in his pocket when his foot touched something. Making to sidestep whatever it was – probably a dead fox – he couldn't help himself. He glanced down at it.

Two muddy feet. No shoes. A pair of jeans, wet and dirty. Further up his eyes travelled, over the bloody chest, the twisted arms, until they rested on the face. A woman. A girl maybe. It was hard to tell with only the street lights in the distance for illumination. She was so pale. And dirty. Black streaks under her eyes trailed onto her cheeks. And her lips were almost as chalky as her skin.

Afterwards, Rex would wonder why he'd been so calm. Why he hadn't screamed and run away. Instead, his seven-year-old feet were rooted to the wet grass. He took out his phone, which he wasn't supposed to bring to school, and switched on the torch. The scene before him was shocking. Still he remained mute, his tongue stuck to the roof of his mouth. He felt his eyes bulging from their sockets at his terrible find. He could feel them stretching the skin.

He'd seen his granddad dead in his coffin, so he knew this woman was dead. He should call the guards. But he didn't want to have to explain to them, to his parents, his teacher, why he was there at godawful o'clock.

He switched off the torch and sat on his school bag on the wet grass. Cocking his head to one side, he studied her broken body, and wondered who she was and how she'd ended up bloodied and dead at his feet. And then he wondered who had killed her. Would they kill him too?

The twin-spired cathedral dominated the Ragmullin skyline. Nestled in a natural hollow, the houses and shops and factories spread out like the petals of a flower searching for light in which to flourish. The serpentine flow of the canal, with the railway tracks running alongside, circled like a snail trail about to take ownership of all in its path.

A grey fog hung low in the darkness. Rain wasn't far off, as usual. The lakes on the outskirts of the midlands town ensured the weather was damp most of the year, though during summer you might be lucky enough to get warmth for a week maybe, if the weather gods were on your side. But definitely not in late January. Spring couldn't arrive quick enough.

Above the shores of one such lake stood an ancient house that held many secrets yet to be revealed, though a few had been uncovered in the recent past.

Lottie stood outside the house, wrapped in her jacket, which was failing to ward off the chill in the air. Mug in hand, she sipped her coffee. She should have put a jumper on over her long-sleeved white top, and the biting wind penetrated her black jeans. Glancing at her boots, she saw they had already gathered mud when she'd walked from the house to the fence. Normal service so.

It was still dark as she stared out over Lough Cullion from the fence that surrounded her home. Temporary home, she corrected herself. The house belonged to her half-brother, Leo, who lived in New York. He had promised time and again to put it in her name, and one time she believed he had actually completed the paperwork, but on checking with the solicitor she could not afford, she found it not to be the case. Leo was a liar and a crook, despite working for the NYPD.

After a restless night, she wondered if she should move house. Find somewhere to make a home for her family with Mark Boyd and his son. But she had no capital, no savings, no nothing. Was she to be stuck in this rambling old structure for the rest of her life?

She glimpsed through the darkness the lake shimmering in the beginnings of the dawn. Sighing at the beauty surrounding her, chiding herself for not feeling more grateful while simultaneously wishing that for once in her life she could have what she desired. Since her husband, Adam, had died from cancer six years previously, she'd been treading water, sinking and coming up gasping for air. Boyd kept her afloat, as did her children.

She knew she had to think of her family over herself. Seventeen-year-old Sean had exams looming and he wanted to do a gaming course. Private college with astronomical fees. Chloe worked long shifts in Fallon's pub. And then there was Katie, who couldn't hold down a job long enough to have any decent chance at life. Of course little Louis kept her daughter busy, but being stuck in the house was no life for a twenty-three-year-old woman who had suffered so much tragedy. At least she'd been in her bed this morning, though Lottie had no idea when she'd come in.

As she swallowed the last of her coffee, her thoughts turned to her mother. Before Christmas, she'd felt she'd have to make a heartbreaking decision about Rose's care. But during the course of her most recent investigation, she'd come across an old friend of her mother's, and that friendship had reignited dramatically. In an odd sort of way, Betty had energised Rose. Maybe Lottie could delay any decision on her future care. It was still a worry that her mother lived alone, with her dementia bringing its own risks. But like herself, Rose was headstrong and bullish, when it suited her. Betty had gone to Birmingham for a few days to visit a relative, so it remained to be seen how Rose coped.

Tipping the mug over, Lottie recoiled at the lumps of coffee stuck to the sides. Having no patience was another of her failings. Who had time to wait for a kettle to boil? Who had time to stand in the early-morning half-light and stare at the beauty of a lake while bemoaning all the ills in their life? Who did that when they should be on their way to work? Someone who was running out of excuses to hide their rising anxiety.

Maybe she could pull a sickie? Call the boss and say she was dying or something. The thought of ringing Superintendent Farrell for anything other than a search warrant spurred her resolve to get her arse into the station. She turned her back on the beauty being slowly revealed as a new day came into being.

Lottie hadn't even time to park at the station before she had to drive to the cinema complex at Connell retail park. A body had been discovered by a young lad on his way into work. She felt the familiar tug of heartache that accompanied her on such investigations.

After she'd donned a protective suit and booties, she signed the log, walked through the cordons and gazed at the dead woman lying on the grass. She knew this death would necessitate a full-scale investigation, because it was plain to see the young woman had been murdered. When would this stop? Young lives being snuffed out by narcissistic fuckers. She despaired.

Looking away for a moment, she took a deep breath. School buses passed on the main road, and she was glad SOCOs had erected the tent so quickly. Diversions were being put in place, but not fast enough.

She stood inside beside Grainne Nixon, leader of the scene-of-crime team. Green eyes and a tendril of red hair were all that made the SOCO appear human. Kitted out head to toe in protective boiler suit, mask, booties and gloves, Grainne was unusually quiet.

'What do you think?' Lottie asked, her voice breaking the silence in the cramped space.

'A young woman with her life snatched from her before she got to live it. There are some bastards around, aren't there? Why do they think they have the God-given right to take a life? To stub out the existence of another human being. There's no reason for it. It's so unfair.'

'Agree with you on all points. Can you offer me any insight as to *how* she died?'

Grainne kneeled on a steel plate beside the body and pointed out the woman's injuries. 'I'm not a pathologist, but I suspect there are at least three knife wounds. One to her neck, which also has evidence of strangulation. Another on her arm – it may be a defensive wound. Her top is soaked with blood, so I imagine we'll find another to her chest. Which of them was the fatal wound? The pathologist will determine that, but I'd guess a struggle took place.'

The dead woman was clothed in jeans and a flimsy top, no shoes or coat. She lay at an awkward angle, one leg partially under the other, her arms askew, as if she had dropped from a height. One strap of her top was missing, or perhaps it only had the one.

The area where her body had been discovered was close to the cinema, coffee shop and retail outlets on the outskirts of town. The waste ground was surrounded by a stone wall and hedges. The entrance barrier had been secure, so it was feasible that someone had heaved her over the wall and thrown her down on the ground.

'Who found her?' Lottie asked, trying to keep herself detached from the horror inflicted on the as yet nameless woman.

'A teenager. Detective Kirby can fill you in.'

'Okay. Any ID on the body?'

'None that we've found yet, but her purse, her phone even, could be somewhere among the bushes. There's a couple of my lads searching. Have you a team here yet?'

'Rustling them up at the moment. Can you give me anything to go on before the state pathologist arrives?'

'The victim appears to be in her mid twenties, looks fit, so maybe she works out. Her clothes are inexpensive. She wore make-up and fake tan, which has run. Her nails seem clean but they'll be swabbed. Her feet are muddy. No sign of her shoes. Her jeans are zipped and buttoned, so perhaps there was no sexual assault, but that's just an observation. I need to get to work.'

'She has no jacket or coat and her top is light. Where's her outer clothing? Her shoes? Could she have been taken from her home?' Lottie mused.

'I'd say she was dressed for a night out.'

'It was raining last night. You'd imagine she'd have a coat if she was out.' Something to consider, Lottie thought. 'Any idea how long she's been here?'

Grainne widened her eyes, two emeralds flashing disdain. 'You and I both know that it's up to the pathologist to give us an indication of that, and even then it's not in any way definitive.'

'I know, but I need a ballpark idea.'

'Her clothes are wet. Maybe from the dew, but we had a lot of rain last night. Gosh, it's so terribly sad.'

'It is. Thanks, Grainne.'

'Oh, one last thing. The ground around her seems to have been disturbed. Footprints. They're quite small. I checked the guy who found her. His feet are bigger, but we'll examine his shoes. And there's flattened grass over there.' She pointed. 'I had it covered to protect it for evidence.'

'Evidence of what?'

'Don't know yet, but maybe the killer sat and watched her die.'

Outside the tent, Lottie whipped off her mask and inhaled the fresh morning air. She had deposited the protective gear in a paper bag by the time Detective Larry Kirby joined her at the inner cordon.

'Where's the lad who discovered the body?' she asked.

Kirby puffed out his cheeks and ran a hand over his bushy hair in an attempt to control the mass of curls. 'I sent him over to the café. Don't bite my head off yet. Garda Lei is with him. He said he knew the boy.'

'Walk with me and fill me in.'

'His name is Shane Santos. He's nineteen, said his family live in Enfield but he shares a flat beside St Declan's.'

'Go on.'

'He arrived early to open up the coffee shop. Seven thirty. The other shops open at nine, though the cinema doesn't open until later. He makes coffee on the go for retail staff, who usually appear by eight thirty. So he said.'

'How did he get in here? Wasn't the barrier down and locked before our lads had it opened?'

'He jumped the wall.'

'Was it normal for the barrier to be down?'

Kirby shrugged. 'All I know is what he told me. SOCOs took his shoes for testing and said they'll make moulds of the footprints around the body for analysis. He has spare runners stored at the shop.'

'Let's go and see if this Shane can help us.' She sincerely hoped so.

She was greeted by the aroma of freshly brewed coffee. The café was a nice open space with black PVC tables surrounded by white chairs. A long stainless-steel counter stood to one side, and at the end wall a nook was lined with high stools. The shop was unoccupied except for Garda Lei and a teenager. They had takeout cups of coffee on the table, but neither was drinking.

She held out her hand. 'Detective Inspector Lottie Parker. You must be Shane.' Pulling out a chair, she sat. The nineteen-year-old's jet-black hair was cut short and his brown eyes were filled with the horror of what he'd stumbled upon.

'I couldn't believe it,' he said. 'She... she was just lying there like that. Like she fell or was asleep or something. I thought I'd have a heart attack. I'd have chucked up my breakfast, so it's lucky I didn't eat this morning.'

His hands shook violently as he spoke. When he'd finished, he pushed them down on his lap under the table, out of sight, and nestled his chin in the cowl neck of his black sweatshirt as if that might disguise his trembling.

'I'm so sorry you had to witness what you did, Shane. You are a very important witness and may be able to provide us with information that might help us find out what happened to the young woman. Do you think you can answer a few questions?'

'Yeah, sure. Whatever. It's shocking.'

'Did you see anyone else around this morning before you found the body?'

'No one. I swear. It was so awful.'

'Do you know who the dead woman is?'

'Me? Know her? No way. I've never seen her before in my life. Swear to God.' He paused, and ran his hand under his nose. 'But I didn't look too closely. Her eyes were open. She was dead. Oh my God... I'll never sleep again.' He lowered his head, sniffing continuously. Lottie looked from Lei to Kirby for a tissue and received shrugged shoulders in return.

'What did you do after you hopped the wall?' she asked gently. 'After you saw her lying there?'

'I backed up straight away and rushed over to the barrier. I nearly puked then, but I didn't.' He raised his head and eyed her shiftily. A dribble hung from the end of his nose. 'I phoned 999 immediately.'

She wondered why he was suddenly looking defensive. 'Did you?'

'What do you mean?'

Lottie knew all about teenagers, and it was logical to conclude that the first thing Shane might do was whip out his phone, no matter how traumatic the scene. 'Did you take photos?'

His cheeks coloured. 'That's ridiculous.'

'Can I see your phone?'

'No, why?' He backed up, and the legs of his chair screeched.

Garda Lei put a hand on his arm. 'Shane, it's best to be truthful now rather than end up in a world of trouble later. I know if it was me, the first thing I'd do is take a snap of the scene.'

Lottie raised an eyebrow at him, and he gave her a quick shake of his head to let her know he was fibbing.

'It's not a crime, is it?' Shane fished his phone out of his pocket and slid it towards her. 'I was in shock when I found her, but I suppose I always have my phone in my hand and it was a reflex to take a pic.'

'PIN code?'

He told her, and she opened up the phone, going directly to his photos. He had one photo of the body taken a little distance away. Lottie shook her head. 'What were you going to do with it?'

'Nothing. Delete it. I don't know.'

Sure, she thought. 'Did you send it to anyone? Post it anywhere?'

'No. You can check my messages and social media. I just snapped the pic and ran.'

'Did you walk around the body?'

'No.'

'Did you sit and look at her?'

'What?'

'Did you move the body?'

'Are you joking me?'

'Shane, I can guarantee you, joking is the furthest thing from my mind right now.' She leaned closer to the boy. 'This is a very serious situation. I have to tell that young woman's family that she's been murdered, and I need your help to find out what happened.'

'Murdered? God, shit. No. I never touched her. Why did I have to find her?'

She handed him back his phone, along with her card containing her contact details. 'Send me the photo, then delete it. Now.'

'You can AirDrop it.'

'What?'

'You know...' he began. 'Never mind.' With visibly trembling fingers, he did as she requested. 'Done.'

'We need to interview you formally at the station. We'll have to take your fingerprints and a sample for DNA comparison. Okay?'

'I told you, I didn't touch her.'

'All the same, you were in the vicinity. Like I said, you'll be helping us.'

'Sure. Whatever. Can I do it after work? My manager will be in soon and I haven't even swept the floor.'

'I think now would be better.' Lottie worked hard to keep her impatience locked down. The boy was traumatised. 'No premises will be open today. We need to forensically examine the entire area.'

She rose then, and nodded to Lei. 'I'll leave him in your hands.'

Outside, she looked over at the scene and beyond the wall and barrier.

A crowd of onlookers had started to form.

Next the reporters would arrive.

And questions would need answers.

———

He really shouldn't have left the house so early that morning. He should go to school, but wasn't he already in trouble? Rex wiped at the cold tears on his cheeks. Why had he stayed? Why hadn't he run a million miles away from this horror story? But he was still here. Hiding. Watching. Would they know he'd been there, beside her body? That he'd sat and watched her like she was a statue until that other boy had come along? He'd thought there were blue veins on her skin that made her appear as if she was made out of marble.

He'd heard the boy whistling outside the wall in the cold air and had scampered away just in time. He'd almost forgotten his school bag but remembered it at the last minute.

Now the white-suited CSI guys were all over the place. Searching. For him? Did they know he'd been right up beside the body? More tears pooled in his eyes, and he wiped them away with stone-cold fingers.

He watched as the tall woman walked around with a small fat guy, giving him orders before she headed off. It might be a good time for him to leave too. But he couldn't go home and he couldn't face school. Or maybe that was what he should do. Which way was best? Well, he couldn't leave by the main entrance; the guards had it all blocked off. Instead, he'd have to make his way behind the cinema and hop through the gap in the ditch to his housing estate, which backed onto the complex.

Still he waited and watched, not knowing why he couldn't tear himself away. But in his heart he was sure the dead woman was linked to what he'd seen from his bedroom window during the night. And he became very afraid.

11

The shakes rippled through Kirby's hands as he stood outside the coffee shop. He felt the tremble move to his throat and he gulped. The dead woman had unnerved him in a way that even the deaths of two children in their last investigation hadn't. Was it the fact that it brought back memories of the attack on his girl-friend, Amy? Possibly. Amy still had night terrors and was undergoing physio in an attempt to allow her to walk pain-free.

He had an urge to phone her, to see how her morning was progressing. Then he shrugged off his concern. Amy had started a new job the previous week in a solicitor's office in town. Two mornings a week. It had brought some colour back to her cheeks without doing anything to mask the pain she suffered. He could read it in her eyes as if she had it inscribed there in actual words.

At least she was alive, unlike the woman lying on the damp ground inside the crime-scene tent. *Gather all the CCTV from the businesses and the cinema. Find out who she is*, the boss had commanded. That was what he'd do. He headed towards the tent.

Grainne Nixon looked up from her work when he ducked inside.

'Get out, Kirby. You're not even suited up.'

'Shit. Sorry. Just checking if you have anything for me yet.'

'Like what?'

'A name?'

'Wonder Woman isn't mine, and I already told Inspector Parker that there's no handbag, phone or ID scattered around.'

'There's no sign of a coat either.'

'Gosh, I'd never have noticed that without your input, Sherlock.'

Kirby sighed. 'I'm not being smart, I'm observing.'

'You need to be suited and—'

'Any chance you can turn her over.'

'Not until the pathologist arrives.'

'Just a teeny bit.'

'What for?'

'She might have something in her jeans pockets. Her phone, maybe, or student ID.' The victim looked young, but she wasn't a teenager. 'Something to give us a hint to her identity.' He stared at Grainne, silently imploring her to give him a break.

'Get Gerry for me and I'll have a quick look. Okay?'

He rushed outside the tent and nabbed the SOCO who was recording the scene around where the body was located.

Once he had pushed Gerry into the tent, Kirby hunched over at the opening flap and watched as the two SOCOs carefully turned the victim onto her side. Grainne tapped the denim pockets, then glanced up at Kirby. Expectation surged through him. With long-handled stainless-steel tweezers, she eased out a slim card and held it up.

'Bank card.'

Gerry snapped photos while Kirby held out an evidence bag and Grainne dropped it in.

'Thanks,' Kirby said.

He left the bag with her as he exited the tent. He had a name for the victim, but he didn't feel any exhilaration. The poor woman was still dead.

12

He drove the child to school, then travelled home via the cinema complex at Connell retail park. Roadblocks had been hastily erected and diversion signs were being put in place.

They had found her body.

He quickly ticked through the checklist in his head to ensure he hadn't left anything of himself to lead the guards to his door. If he had, he might as well be dead himself. He'd smashed up her phone with a hammer from the boot and thrown it out the window on the dual carriageway. He'd ripped her coat and bag with the knife and scattered them along with her shoes in the ditches on his way home. He'd done well.

It had taken him until the early hours to wash out the car and be sure there wasn't a spot of blood left anywhere. Of course it wasn't scientifically cleaned, but if he was ever to become a suspect, there was other evidence to convict him besides her having been in his car. And wouldn't he have a legit reason to have her in the taxi? He wondered about CCTV. No, he was certain he had avoided it all.

He zapped open the ten-foot-high solid gate and parked carefully in his designated space, then walked slowly around the side of the house, hugging the concrete wall that surrounded it on all four sides. He entered through the back door with his key, having taken off his shoes outside. No point in adding to the tirade that would surely follow. Because *her* car was still out front, he knew she hadn't yet left for work.

'I can't believe you fucked it up,' she said.

'What?'

'Don't act stupid with me. I heard it on the Midlands radio news. A body. You stupid, stupid man.'

He pulled a chair to the table and sat. The aroma of coffee from the pot tickled his nose and the tang of fresh toast lingered in the air. His stomach rumbled, but otherwise he remained silent. He'd learned the hard way that it was best to let her rant and rave; to burn herself out. Everything would be okay in a little while. He only had to wait.

'I specifically asked you to bring her here. What went wrong? And don't dare tell me she attacked you. I've heard that one before.'

A shrug of his shoulders elicited a smack of a tea towel across the back of his neck.

'You're such an idiot. The guards and that CSI crowd will be crawling all over Ragmullin. I wanted her. She was part of my plan. How am I going to get the next one and get rid of the other one now? Answer me that, genius.'

'I-I d-don't know. I'm s-sorry.'

'You bloody well should be. I'm always left to tidy up after your mistakes. I really don't know why I keep you here with me. You know what?' She put up her hand to stop him replying. 'You're a waste of space.'

He watched as she flounced around the kitchen swiping the cloth at the counter, the cupboards, the refrigerator, the oven. At all the inanimate objects that were unable to fight back. And he knew she regarded him as no higher than those objects.

Waiting for her to attack him used to be more terrifying

than when she actually pounced. The fearful anticipation had once made him wet his trousers. Big mistake. Now, though, he was more in control of his emotions, his words and of course his bladder. He knew what was coming, so he could distance himself, place himself on a higher plane and watch the man below him getting battered. It had taken years of practice, but he felt he'd eventually mastered it.

She circled, and circled. Stopped behind him. He took a deep breath in case she punched him in the ribs. She'd once broken one and wouldn't allow him to go to the hospital. But this time her fist came down on his shoulder, taking him by surprise, and he yelled. So much for the higher plane.

'Get out of my sight.' Her voice whistled, piercing the air around his head.

He resisted rubbing his shoulder. Not that rubbing it would do any good. It would take hours for the pain to subside. He was hungry and would have loved to grab a coffee. But he knew better than to delay. Scuttling out the back door, he put on his shoes and walked to his shed at the bottom of the walled garden, where he'd stay until she calmed down. Until she allowed him back inside.

13

At the station, Lottie dumped her coat on the back of a chair and sat at an empty desk in the general office. She looked at the photo that Shane Santos had taken. Studying the young woman with her long wavy hair, she mourned the life so brutally snatched away. She thought of a family waking up this morning to find she hadn't come home, of the turmoil Lottie would visit on them with the news, and then the ensuing public scrutiny of the woman's life. These thoughts caused her chest to tighten.

Boyd joined her and sat on the edge of the desk. He put a Bean Café coffee by her hand.

'Hey! Welcome back, Boyd. You're a lifesaver.'

'My middle name. Good to be back.'

She sipped the coffee, grateful for the sugar he'd put in it, and turned the phone towards him. 'Know her?'

'The body found this morning? No, I don't.'

She stood and made her way to her office. 'Check if any calls came in about missing persons.'

'Your coat.' Boyd passed it to her and followed her inside, where he grabbed her hand, pulling her close. He smelled good and his face was relaxed. 'You need to take it easier, Lottie. You're killing yourself.'

'And someone killed that poor woman. I have to do my job.'

'Pace yourself, then. Don't go twenty-four-seven like you usually do on a big investigation. I'm serious.' She smiled, and he seemed to grab onto that. 'Hey, how about dinner tonight? On me. We need some alone time and you need some down time.'

They were still engaged and had almost succeeded in getting married not that long ago, but fate had intervened and they had begun to drift, through no fault of Lottie's.

'What about Sergio?'

'Grace arrived. His favourite auntie.'

'His only auntie.' Lottie smiled. 'When is he going to school?'

'After the February mid-term. A few weeks yet.'

'How are you all coping in your small apartment?'

'It's a nightmare. I'm house-hunting.'

'I was thinking the same thing this morning.'

'Thought you were thinking of getting a loan to renovate Farranstown House?'

'Renovate? It needs to be gutted. Anyhow, I don't own it, Leo does, so I'm not going down that road.'

'We discussed this before, and I firmly believe we should get a house together. Pool resources. There's this show home on a new estate, Pine Grove, that we should look at and—'

'Missing persons, Boyd?' She tapped the keyboard to awaken her computer.

'On it. And I'll ring the estate agent about that house too.' He winked as he left, and Lottie felt warmth tingling in her stomach.

She set about organising a murder team. With limited resources, that was her first major job of the morning. When Kirby bustled into her office, she hoped he had good news.

'She had a bank card on her,' he panted. 'I contacted the bank. Got an address and a photo emailed over. It's her.'

'Good work. Any family?'

'Yes.'

'What about CCTV?'

'Some of the businesses had cameras but I doubt they'll be of any use. As far as I could see, there was nothing trained towards where the body was found.'

'Once door-to-doors are organised, gather whatever footage is out there. McKeown can trawl through it. The super will be on my back, so I need everyone on this. I'll get Boyd to come with me to break the bad news to this poor girl's family.'

She knew Kirby was disappointed at being left behind, but Boyd was the more senior detective. Plus she wanted to spend time with him.

14

'We have to close down the site next week, John,' Patrick Curran said. Receiving no response, he nudged his colleague's arm. 'Are you even listening to me?'

John Morgan had heard what the site manager said, but he didn't want to listen. When he'd secured the job on the building site, he hadn't realised how much it would improve his sense of self-worth. Plus there was the bonus of getting the foreman job. He was proud of this achievement; perhaps for the first time in his life he felt he was someone important. Workers asked his advice and he readily dispensed it, relishing giving orders and watching in awe as the latest phase of the housing estate took shape under his commanding eye. He even had a notion that he was first in line for the site manager's job when Patrick headed to Canada during the summer to spend time with his daughter.

'What do you mean by close the site?' At last he found his voice.

'Have you been listening to me at all, lad?' Patrick's jowls wobbled as he slammed his fist on the rickety Formica table that served as a desk in their prefab office. 'You think you're the be-all-and-end-all here, don't you? Well, bucko, let me tell you, no matter how good a job you do, it counts for nothing in the end. It's money that matters. Money.'

'What are you talking about?' John scratched his head, a bit lost. He'd always been paid on time and the wages were good. As far as he knew, there'd been no rumours of anything amiss.

Patrick shoved his hard hat back on his head and ran a grubby hand through his thinning hair. 'In Cafferty's last night I heard that the boss man has capital problems. Can't get any more business loans, and those he has might be called in. Bottom line, we can't pay for concrete or blocks or wages. And because of that, the site is closing at the end of next week.'

John leaned against the wall for support. 'But if it's just pub talk, how can you know for certain?'

'I phoned the boss this morning and he confirmed it. I'm only passing on the bad news. I'll have to tell the rest of the crew later. Just letting you know now.'

John shook his head frantically, a surge of fear and anger clashing under his ribcage. 'You can't be serious. Most of the houses in this phase have holding deposits. We have to finish them. And people are already living in phase one... We can't just lock up and walk away from a half-finished estate.' He felt his emotions turn to panic, which rose in his chest as quickly as a golf ball leaving a tee.

'We have to. It's probably only temporary, until the fat cats release more funds. Don't worry. There's plenty of work around.'

John gulped loudly, trying to dislodge the ball of panic. He didn't like the thought of begging other builders for a job. He wanted to stay here. He'd believed GC Construction was a sound firm. He'd definitely not heard any rumblings about money troubles.

'Are you serious?' He just about got the words out.

Patrick nodded his head slowly. 'Very serious. I'm sorry, lad. This place locks up next Friday, this day week, and I don't know when it'll reopen.' He stood, slapped John on the shoulder and went out into the chilly air.

With the draught entering through the open doorway, the gas heater fizzled and died. John felt an icicle filtering through his chest and freezing his heart.

He thumped the fragile wall with his fist and wasn't surprised to see it wobble and the maps stuck there flutter. He had to talk to Gordon Collins. He couldn't let his job disappear. No way. He needed to be on the site. He needed to be busy. He couldn't go back to the way he was a year ago. He had invested too much of himself in this job; he couldn't let it die. Gordon Collins would sort it. He always sorted it.

15

'If I told you once, I'll tell you again, sit the hell down.'

George Kenny squirmed at the sound of his own voice. He didn't like shouting at Davy, but his sister hadn't come home and he was worried. She was good with her two-year-old nephew. Today, Davy was covered in blister-type spots and unable to go to day care. Trust his partner, Niamh, to head off to Lanzarote on a winter holiday with her girlfriends and leave him to mind their son. And he'd missed his early-morning slot at the gym. As if to remind himself, he flexed his muscles and threw back his shoulders.

'Shannon might sit with you for an hour later on.' If she appeared home, that was. 'Would you like that?'

Davy shrugged. He slapped the spoon into the cereal, then did it again. Milk splashed out over the table. The child went to turn, and his elbow caught the bowl, upending it onto the floor.

Counting silently, George said, 'Go watch the telly.'

Davy didn't need to be told twice.

Alone with the mess, George slumped onto the chair and tugged fluff balls from his black jogging pants with one hand while scrolling on his phone with the other. Why was his life such a fucking mess? Literally a mess.

Facebook had a grainy photo taken at a distance showing garda activity out by the cinema. He glanced at the comments. Most had simply put a broken-heart emoji. One post caught his eye. A woman had been found dead. He looked at the kitchen clock, which was always fifteen minutes fast.

Clutching the phone to his chest, he raced upstairs and barged into Shannon's room. She had definitely stayed out all night. The phone felt like a dumb-bell in his hand, as if what he had read weighed it down. He sat on her bed and rang her number again. Not a sound. Battery dead? Phone lost? Left behind in a pub? He sent her a message and waited for the blue ticks to tell him she'd read it. Nothing.

He ran back down the stairs and paced up and down the hall, knocking into the coat stand, upending it. He hadn't the energy to pick up the coats, so he kicked them with his bare feet into the corner and made his way to the messy kitchen. 'Baby Shark' blared from the sitting room. Davy could watch what he liked for now. Automatically George began clearing up the spilled cereal, keeping one eye on the clock and wondering if he should report his sister missing.

He should probably message her friend Jess in case she'd kipped on her couch. An unsettling shiver had taken hold of the little hairs on the back of his neck. No matter how drunk Shannon got, she usually let him know where she was staying. Usually, but not always, he reminded himself. However, he had a nauseating sense that something was terribly wrong.

He clutched his phone, unable to dislodge the increasing sense of foreboding.

'Where are you, Shannon?'

Then the doorbell chimed.

There was still no word from Laura. Her mother had caught fleeting bouts of sleep throughout the night, which had increased her anger. It was now replaced with a sense of unease.

She'd got Aaron dressed and fed, and as the time ticked on, she became increasingly worried. Whenever Laura stayed out late, she always rang or texted. Always. And never had she not come home. Not that she went out often.

The doorbell rang and she felt a rush of relief. Laura was home. Forgot her key. Thank God. *I'm going to kill her*.

She opened the door ready to berate her daughter, then stopped.

'Good morning. Diana Nolan?' The tall woman on the step was wrapped in a dark jacket.

'That's me. Sorry. I thought you were my daughter. How can I help you?' Diana's anxiety flared as the two strangers looked at each other before the woman faced her.

'Would it be all right if we came in? I'm Detective Inspector Lottie Parker and this is Detective Sergeant Boyd.'

Diana felt the blood drain from her body. She clutched the door to remain upright. 'It's about Laura, isn't it? Something's happened to her. She always rings or texts. She's a good girl. Where is she? What's happened?'

She led the two detectives to the kitchen because Aaron was in the sitting room. By their sombre faces she knew they hadn't good news for her. Feeling numb to her core, she slumped onto a chair and waited for whatever they had to say.

16

The house felt claustrophobic. Too much of everything in the kitchen. The lingering odour of burned toast hung in the air, while breakfast dishes lined the draining board.

Lottie pulled out a chair and sat. Boyd stood by the door, his overcoat open, hands shoved in his trouser pockets. Diana sat opposite Lottie without offering tea or coffee.

'Okay if I call you Diana?'

The woman nodded, face sombre, eyes ready to spill.

'I'm so sorry to have to give you bad news, Diana. The body of a young woman was discovered this morning. There's no easy way to say this, but I'm afraid we have reason to believe it's your daughter, Laura.'

Diana gulped and shook her head slowly. 'No, it's not her. It can't be. Honestly, it's not Laura.'

'I regret to say we believe it is your daughter. You or someone close to the family will have to identify the body, but we received photo ID from her bank. I'm awfully sorry, but in cases like this there are no words I can offer. Just to say you have my sympathy and we will do everything in our power to find out who did this.'

'Did what? What happened to her?'

It seemed Diana had not heard the early-morning news. 'Her body was found in the grounds of the cinema at Connell retail park. I'm afraid she suffered a fatal assault.'

'That can't be true. What would she be doing out there? That must be a good mile outside of town.'

'It's about a kilometre and a half from here. Was she out last night?'

'She went into town. With a friend, she said. I was here with her son. I hardly slept, waiting for her to come home. I thought maybe she'd met someone...'

'Her son?' Boyd took his hands out of his pockets. He pulled out a chair and sat beside the weeping woman.

'My grandson. Aaron. He's nearly four.'

Lottie exhaled. Not only had a mother lost her daughter, a little boy had lost his young mother. Goddammit. 'You said Laura went out last night. Do you know who she was meeting?'

'She just said a friend. I think. God, I don't know. She was secretive about things like that.'

'Where did she go?'

'One of the pubs, I presume. Not that she went out that often. Not since Aaron... Now that I think of it, she did say something about going for a meal.'

'I'll need her friends' names and details. One of them might be able to help us fill in the blanks.'

'I... I don't think she had many friends. Things had been difficult for her since Aaron came along.'

'Who was she meeting, then?'

'I've no idea. I never pried too much. I think I got on her nerves enough as it was.'

'Did Laura work outside the home?' Boyd asked.

'Yes. In Lidl. Checkout and shelf-stacking. She dropped out of college when she got pregnant. Ruined her life, so it did.' She must have caught Lottie's look, because she added, 'I don't mean

it that way. Aaron is a sweet boy and I love him to bits. So did
Laura. I just wish she'd gone back to college and then she could
have set herself up in a decent career.'

Lottie had thought the same thing about her Katie.

'Had she a laptop?' She'd love to see Laura's calendar. It
might give them some idea if she had a date. Her online activity
could also help.

'No laptop. She kept her life on her phone, like all the
young ones.' Diana raised her chin. 'You have her phone,
haven't you?

'Unfortunately, we haven't found it. I'll need her number
and we'll try to trace it. Did she have a handbag with her?'

'Yes. A tiny thing. Only held her phone, a few cosmetics
and a bank card. Not that she had much to spend... You said
you got her details from the bank. How did you manage that?'

'Her card was in her jeans pocket. No handbag. No phone.'

'I can't get my head around all this. Are you sure it's Laura?'

'Yes, I'm afraid so. When did you last hear from your
daughter?'

'She was in her bedroom finishing her make-up. We had
words. The state she left the bathroom in.' Diana dropped her
head as if realising how inconsequential it was now. 'Our relationship was strained to say the least. But isn't that always the
way when mothers are disappointed with their daughters'
choices?'

'What choices made you disappointed? Her decision to
keep her son?'

'No, that was my decision,' Diana said, sadly. 'I wouldn't
allow her to give him up. She loved her child. She was a brilliant
mother to Aaron. It was our relationship that wasn't the best. I
was too hard on her and... now she's gone.' She folded in on
herself and sobbed loudly. Lottie could see that the woman was
horribly broken. 'I want her home. I want her back. I'm so sorry
for everything I ever said to her and it's too late to tell her.'

'What about Aaron's father?'

'I don't know who he is. Laura never said, though I probed enough about him. He was never on the scene. I'm a widow myself. Not long after Laura was born. And now she's...' Her sobs blotted out her words.

'Diana?' Lottie said. 'Can I look at her room, please? I won't remove anything unless I deem it essential to our investigation, and if there is something I need, I'll ask you first.'

'Sure.' Diana waved her hand towards the door. 'Upstairs. Can you tell me how she died? Did she suffer?'

'We need to have a post-mortem in order to answer your questions.'

As Lottie stood, a little blonde-haired boy scampered into the kitchen.

'Nan, where's Mammy? Is she at work?' Then he seemed to notice the two strangers standing there and leaped up onto Diana's lap.

'I'll have a look upstairs so,' Lottie said, and she nodded at Boyd for him to stay in the kitchen.

17

'Where the hell do you think you're going at this hour of the day?' George shouted before Shannon had one foot over the threshold.

She ducked under his outstretched arm. 'Couldn't find my key.' She had no idea where she'd left it. Now she'd have to get one cut. More expense. And her head was swimming.

'You missed work again. They phoned me wondering where you were. I was about to call the guards. Jesus, Shannon, you can't keep this up. You need to slow down.'

'What? And be piss-boring like you? Feck off, George. I need a shower.'

'You need to grow up. You promised you'd help me out with Davy this week. I was trying to work from home while minding him.'

'He's your kid, not mine. I didn't head off for a two-week holiday like Niamh did, so shut it.'

'Where are you even getting the money for these nights out?'

'I have a rich boyfriend.'

'Pull the other one.'

'Believe me or not, I don't care.'

He grabbed her arm as she put her foot on the stairs. 'I can't go through all this again.'

'All what?' she shouted over her shoulder.

'You and drink, and... I think you're using again. Are you?'

'Chance would be a fine thing.' Looking into his sad eyes, she knew his concern was genuine and immediately felt like a bitch. He was only three years older than her, but he was ageing by the day. She noticed a thread of grey had appeared in his dark hair. And he was forgetting how to dress. The faded T-shirt and baggy joggers did nothing for him. 'George, I'm not using. I had a few drinks. Stayed with a friend. Lost my key. Now I'm home. Once I have a shower I'll look after Davy for you. Okay?'

'Sure.'

'Put the kettle on. I'd kill for a cup of coffee.'

As he made his way into the kitchen, she breathed a sigh of relief. Her brother was good to her. Too good. But she couldn't stop to think about it. She needed to shower and have her coffee and a nap. Then she'd be ready to do it all over again.

18

Lottie felt a twinge of despair as she entered Laura's room. She'd left Boyd downstairs comforting Diana and the little boy. He had a way with people, especially those who had suffered trauma. An ability to display compassion better than she could. She was one of those people who tended to keep everything locked down tight. Too tight.

The sparsely furnished room had a mess of clothing flung everywhere. A small table doubled as a dresser with a scattering of make-up brushes, tubes and bottles. Nothing expensive. Nothing to point to a boyfriend who bought Laura gifts.

Besides the Lidl uniform lying in a bundle on the floor, along with other discarded clothing, she found underwear and tops in a drawer, and jeans and hoodies hanging in a free-standing IKEA wardrobe with the door removed. Or maybe it had fallen off.

With gloved hands she flicked through the young woman's clothing, mainly from Penneys, like her own girls' clothes. She found no pieces of paper with notes or anything to point to what had happened to Laura. Nothing beneath the mattress and pillows, or under the bed. No laptop or other electronic devices.

Before returning downstairs, she glanced into the other bedrooms. The little boy's room was nicely painted, with boxes of toys neatly stacked at the foot of the bed. She closed the door, sadness crushing her heart. The poor child. The bathroom was small and clean, though she could see a streak of tan on the shower door and around the plughole. Diana would no longer have to fight with her daughter over leaving a mess behind. The banality of that made her even sadder for the decimated family.

Back in the kitchen, she laid a hand on Diana's shoulder and squeezed it gently. 'We'll contact you about...' She struggled with what to say in front of the little boy about his mother's body having to be identified. 'When we need you, we'll contact you. Okay?'

'Okay.'

'Here's my card if anything crosses your mind that might help us. No matter how insignificant you think it is, let us know.' Boyd joined Lottie at the door as she continued. 'And don't talk to reporters. Please. We'll appoint a family liaison officer to keep you informed of all developments before anything is released to the media.'

'Let yourselves out. I don't think I can stand. But we don't need anyone. We're fine on our own.'

'All the same, I think it would be helpful for you to have someone here for a few days.'

The woman bowed her head with a tissue clasped to her nose.

They let themselves out as instructed.

———

For what seemed like hours after the two detectives left, but was probably only minutes, Diana sat with Aaron on her knee, stroking his hair. It was so unlike the child to be this quiet. It was as if he knew something terrible had happened; something they couldn't talk about. He didn't ask about Laura and he fell asleep where he sat.

She felt like her heart had been ripped out of her. A void grew in her chest, threatening to pull her into the darkness. She found it hard to get her head around the fact that her daughter would no longer be bustling in the door like a whirlwind, dropping shopping bags with cheap clothing as she went.

And what of Aaron? What would become of him? Diana knew she could look after him, but he was only four and she had a life to live too. No, stop, she warned herself. Don't be selfish. She wondered why she didn't feel profound sadness, just this emptiness. Then she realised she was numb from the shock. There was no handbook to tell you how you should act or react. Here she was, suspended in time and space, with a child sleeping in her arms.

A shiver shook her body out of its numbness. She tried to visualise what the days and weeks ahead would look like. She hadn't any friends, so there wouldn't be callers with Tupperware tubs of food. But there was another thing that worried her. The invasion of their privacy by the media. And when the papers tired of Laura being a murder victim, mightn't they start in on her own life? If they did that, they might find things to write that wouldn't be nice. Old stuff. Unsavoury stuff. She couldn't bear that for Aaron. Or for herself.

But before the papers got wind of any scandal, she was certain the guards would find out. One thing she was sure of: they would not find out from her.

19

'Who were you on the phone to?' Lottie asked Boyd as they climbed the steps into the station.

'An estate agent. I realise we have this murder investigation, Lottie, but could we squeeze in at least a half-hour this afternoon to look at the show home at Pine Grove?'

'Are you for real?' She tapped her ID against the pad and headed up the stairs to the office.

'Just a quick look. Charlie says it's the only time she has free. Three thirty. Today.'

'And what's wrong with tomorrow? Or next week? Or when we find Laura Nolan's murderer? And who the hell is Charlie? Shit, Boyd, it's your first day back.'

'Humour me, for once.' He opened the door and let her in by him. 'Charlie's the estate agent. It'll only take ten minutes.'

'Thought you said half an hour.'

'Don't be pedantic. Please, Lottie.'

'I'll see.'

'I have to let them know.'

'You go. I might not be able to get away.'

'I want us both to see it.'

'Boyd,' she turned to him, 'leave it for now.' Speaking to the others in the office, she asked, 'What's the latest?'

Kirby said, 'The super is holding a press briefing at three and wants all the available information before then. Preferably a suspect. Her words, not mine.'

'She doesn't ask for much,' Lottie said. 'We've only just broken the news to the victim's mother. She's in complete shock. I'll need an FLO. Garda Brennan, that's you.'

'Ah, boss, I can't.'

Lottie raised an eyebrow.

Martina Brennan had isolated herself following their last major case, when she'd made an error that could have been more costly than it was. And then there was all the hassle over her doomed affair with married Detective Sam McKeown.

'I messed up last time, boss,' she said.

'Get back in the saddle,' Kirby said. 'It's the only way.'

She gave him a side-eye filled with derision. 'You do it then.'

'I'm not trained. You are.'

'So is Detective Lynch.'

'She's on holidays,' Lottie said, hoping to dispel further aggravation. 'And Garda Lei isn't fully trained yet.'

He raised his head. 'I don't mind doing—'

Lottie tugged off her jacket. 'It's Martina's gig. End of story.'

'Sure,' Martina said, her mouth turning down in disgust.

'What else have you lot found out while myself and Boyd were with Laura's mother?'

Kirby stood. 'She worked in Lidl. I had a chat with her manager on the phone. Laura was well liked. A good worker. Punctual and friendly. I'll call over there later to see if I can discover anything else.'

'We need to identify who she was out with last night. Her mother, Diana, seemed to think she was meeting a friend, possibly for dinner, but then she said Laura had no friends. She gave me Laura's phone number. Where's McKeown?'

'Late again,' Kirby said.

The door opened behind him. McKeown came in and sat at his desk.

'The very man.' Lottie laid a sheet of paper in front of him. 'This is Laura Nolan's phone number. See if you can find where and when it was last used. And anything else that might help us. We need to track her movements last night.'

'Will do.'

'Kirby, you go chat with her workmates and manager. Then see if the bank will release her card activity. If not, prepare a warrant.'

'Sure thing, boss.'

'Someone must know where she was. Someone knows how she got to where her body was found. Did this mysterious dinner date, if there was one, drag her there and kill her? Or was she attacked while walking home? We need all the CCTV you can get, McKeown.'

'It would help if we had some idea of where she was last seen.'

'I agree, that's why you all need to work quickly on this. How did she get to the retail and cinema complex? Did she walk? Who was she with? I want to know.'

'That's quite a walk from her home, or from town for that matter,' Boyd said.

'I'm brainstorming here. Have you any bright ideas?'

'No, sorry. She could have been killed anywhere and her body dumped there.'

'It was a vicious attack,' Kirby said. 'Could have been personal, the way she was stabbed. Someone she knew?'

'Personal or random, we haven't one clue to go on yet.' Lottie turned back to McKeown. 'Check all available CCTV around that area for last night until we can trace her movements prior to her body being found, and pinpoint any other relevant security cameras. If you find anything or anyone suspicious on the footage, work backwards from there. It will help us to track her.'

'I'll do my best,' McKeown said.

'Has Shane Santos been interviewed yet?'

'Yes,' Kirby said, 'and I've checked his alibi. He's in the clear.'

'Thanks. I'll ask the super to put out an appeal for those who attended the late-night cinema showing to come forward. In the meantime, interview everyone who was working there and whoever locked the barrier.'

'That's a tall order,' McKeown said, running a hand over his shaved head. 'We don't even have a time of death.'

'I'll contact Jane and see when she's scheduled the post-mortem.' She turned to Kirby. 'Has she arrived at the scene yet?' Although Lottie didn't get on well with a lot of people, she admired Jane Dore, the state pathologist.

'She wasn't there when I was leaving, but she had been summoned.'

'I'll follow up with her. It might be no harm seeing if we can find out who the father of Laura's son is. Diana claimed she had no idea and I didn't think it was appropriate to press her. Garda Brennan, you might be able determine if she was being truthful. You're more diplomatic, more subtle than I am.'

'Sure.' But Martina didn't sound sure at all.

20

The shed was his refuge within the fortress she'd made of their home. His escape from reality. With only himself and his plants for company.

He loved to pot seeds and watch them sprout and grow. Potatoes were his favourite. He had two shelves of seed potatoes. Once he was sure there'd be no more frost, usually in March, he would bring them out to the field that backed onto their property and sow them. If she allowed him.

The flowerpot beneath him was eating into his skinny arse. He eyed the fold-up chair in the corner. It was covered in cobwebs, so he wasn't going to sit on that. He'd sprayed the shed to get rid of the little buggers, but they seemed to materialise like ghosts to taunt him.

'That's what I'll do,' he said aloud. 'You won't get away from me again.'

He rooted through a wooden cupboard searching for the bug spray. It pained him to have his work consigned to the shed. He'd have loved his own greenhouse. She'd said he wasn't good enough to have one. Another of her methods of humiliating him, just like she humiliated anyone she didn't like who came in contact with her. He wasn't innocent in all this, but it gave him comfort to know none of it was his fault.

———

She lay on the hard, narrow bed. She no longer had any concept of how long she'd been held here. Weeks? Months? She had no idea, but it seemed like a year. She'd fallen into their routine, which meant waiting to be summoned downstairs to work.

Straining her ears, she listened. The house was quiet. That was good, wasn't it? But she'd heard the argument that morning and heard him slamming the door of his shed, where he went to nurse his wounds. Pathetic man.

There was no chance of escaping, of opening the front door and running away. The house was surrounded by high stone walls and trees. She assumed it was located out in the country-side, somewhere no one except the householders ventured. His shed was wooden, with a long corner window. He could see her if she attempted to go out the back door. Not that she'd tried. All the windows in the house were bolted shut and seemed to be triple-glazed. As for the front door! It had multiple locks and huge steel bolts.

What she couldn't figure out was why they wanted her, why they kept her. Okay, so she did some housework for them, but that was used as a humiliation tool, as was taping her mouth. What was their ulterior motive? Because she knew in the depths of her soul that she hadn't been brought here just to wash dishes.

If she hadn't been so nosy, if she'd left the past where it belonged, this never would have happened.

She'd learned over the time she'd been held here that it was unwise to ask questions. A beating would ensue. Her meagre food would be withheld. Her bony body bore testament to that. So she remained silent. The will to fight had been knocked out of her. That defeat made her more despondent than all the punishments she'd endured.

21

'And like I told you on the phone, Mark, phase two of Pine Grove will be finished by the end of the summer,' Charlie Lennon said, directing all her attention towards Boyd.

The estate agent was probably in her mid forties, but looked not a day over thirty. Tall, with shimmering dyed blonde hair tied into a carefree ponytail that Lottie suspected was anything but carefree, she wore a tailored green trouser suit and was very beautiful. Lottie didn't like her.

'Is the show home for sale?' Boyd asked, overenthusiastically.

Lottie wanted to thump him to shut him up. Instead, she buried her chin in her jacket collar, wishing she hadn't come along. It was madness leaving a hectic investigation for this. Boyd's eyes were glowing, and she fought the urge to drag him away. Don't get so bloody excited, she thought, we can't afford this house.

'Sorry.' Charlie's mouth drooped slightly. 'Already sold. The new owners are still in London, but they'll be moving here in the next six months. It's great to have access to it, as it helps us sell houses off plan for the next phase.'

Lottie hadn't wanted to see the show home at all. And leaving while Superintendent Farrell was doing the press briefing mightn't be the best idea Boyd ever had. She was well aware that seeing the house would plant a seed of discontent in her.

'Three bedrooms upstairs and another downstairs that can double as an office. You both could work from home. The broadband is excellent in this area. Let me show you this...' Charlie marched ahead, hips swaying, her voice drifting along behind her.

Lottie shrugged a shoulder at Boyd, whose face was a picture of excitement.

'It's perfect,' he said.

'For you and Sergio perhaps, but what about my brood? We'd need to build an extension. And work from home? Where did she get that idea from?'

'I may have told a white lie when I booked the viewing. No point in scaring her off saying two detectives are interested in buying a house on this estate.'

'What estate, though? The second phase has barely started.' Lottie felt like digging her heels in on this argument. The house was too small, full stop.

Reluctantly she followed him into the kitchen, where Charlie had spread drawings over the quartz countertop. Everything was sparkling whites and greys. The units were a light grey, the walls white. Good luck with that, she thought, visualising Louis running around with chocolate-smeared hands or, God forbid, a Sharpie marker. Sliding glass double doors led out to a miniature patio area surrounded by a matchbox-sized garden with a neat lawn. It could be AstroTurf, it was so perfect. This was not the house for them.

Her heart sank when she saw Boyd leaning over the drawings, pointing and asking questions, getting even more excited with whatever Charlie was telling him. Was this a losing battle?

Her inner dialogue highlighted the negatives. It was too expensive, too small, too new and way too white. She'd become used to living in dilapidated Farranstown House.

'There's a lot of white and grey,' she murmured.

'Oh, don't worry about that,' Charlie enthused. 'You can choose your own colours. And it's not grey, it's cashmere.'

'Thought cashmere was a wool sweater.'

Charlie smiled, her perfect teeth glinting under the recessed lighting. Lottie wondered if she'd flown to Turkey for them. The teeth, not the lights. With the commission she earned on this estate alone, she could probably afford to have her dental work done at home.

'I can show you upstairs, or would you like to have a look around on your own?' Charlie winked. Lottie stifled a groan.

'We can manage,' she said sourly, and turned on her heel towards the stairs.

'Why are you so crotchety?' Boyd joined her. 'What's not to like about the house?'

Without answering, she entered what she assumed was the main bedroom. The furnishings seemed top-of-the-range, designer stuff maybe. It all made her feel like mussing up the immaculately hotel-styled bed. Or lying on it, for a few minutes' sleep.

'Can you imagine having to take all those cushions off the bed every night? You'd have to stack them on the floor and then restyle them in the morning. Who has time for that? I hardly have time to hop in the shower, never mind make the fecking bed.'

'It's a show home, Lottie. They do these things to make it look chic.'

'Chic? That a new word for you?'

'Come on. Have an open mind.'

'Oh, it's very open. I can see only enough room for your side of the family. Where do you think Sean and Chloe would fit?

Not to talk of Katie and Louis. And I'd need space for my mother to stay over occasionally.'

'Sounds like you want a house for the Brady Bunch.' Boyd opened a door she'd thought was a cupboard, to reveal an enormous, blindingly white and chrome en suite.

'Wow,' she said, genuinely stunned. 'It's amazing.' And it was. The floor-to-ceiling tiles were white with grey grout. 'The shower looks like something out of the Kennedy Space Center.'

'You been there?' he asked, a smile in his words.

'You know what I mean, smart-arse.'

She edged out by him and found another bedroom. It was bright and airy and decorated for a child. She could imagine Louis in here, playing on the soft carpet without fear of getting splinters in his knees from ancient floorboards. But three bedrooms, four if you counted the office, was not enough space. Sergio needed his own room, plus her three and her grandson. And one for herself and Boyd.

'Let's go,' she said, when he'd finished opening doors, salivating at the beautiful rooms.

'I want to hear what else Charlie has to tell us.'

He bounded down the stairs.

She stood on the top step clenching her teeth.

22

Armed with a colourful brochure and a price list, Lottie eventually succeeded in dragging Boyd away from the mesmerising Charlie.

On the footpath, she said, 'It's too small. Too expensive. It's not us.'

He was staring back at the house. 'Oh, there's a garage. I missed that when we arrived. We could convert it into an extra bedroom.'

Lottie couldn't help the roll of her eyes. 'Your minutes are adding up by the second, and Superintendent Farrell will be on the warpath if we don't get back.'

'Hey, Charlie,' he called as the estate agent began to lock the front door. 'Can we see the garage?'

'I totally forgot about it. We can enter it from the utility room. I don't have the outdoor key.' She led them back inside. Lottie trailed behind like a reluctant, moody child.

'Give me a minute until I find the right one.' Charlie jangled a bunch of keys.

'Boyd, let's go. We're way too busy for this and it's not suitable.'

'Aha! Got it.' She waved the key and unlocked the white door. 'It fits a family car and can hold the overflow stuff from your shed.'

'Our shed?' Lottie whispered in Boyd's ear.

Charlie flicked on the light, then stumbled backwards, her hands flying to her mouth. 'Christ Almighty!'

Lottie shoved past her to see what had made her cry out. 'Don't touch a thing. Go back into the kitchen, Charlie. Now.'

'I don't understand,' the estate agent cried. 'What is that?'

'Go back!' Lottie commanded the stunned woman. With her hand still clasped to her mouth, Charlie retreated. 'What the hell, Boyd?' Lottie crowded at his shoulder in the small space.

'He hasn't been here long. There's no smell.'

'But he's dead, isn't he?' Charlie said from the kitchen. 'I better call the guards.'

'Will you tell her or will I?' Lottie asked him.

'I'll get gloves and stuff from the car,' he said, 'and call it in.'

As Boyd left, Lottie maintained her vigil inside the door and surveyed the scene. The garage was empty except for the male body, which was lying against a wall in a corner to her left. She was sure it was a male despite the head being slumped towards his chest. He was dressed in workmen's overalls and muddy black safety boots. His fair hair was cut short. She fought the urge to rush over and lift his head, but his statuesque stillness told her he was dead, as did the small pool of blood that had seeped out from beneath him.

They'd just found a body in Boyd's dream home.

Waiting for the team to arrive, she moved back into the gleaming kitchen. Charlie sat on a high stool at the island.

'Do you know who it is?' Lottie asked.

Charlie gulped. 'I'm not sure. He could have worked on the site, couldn't he?'

'You tell me.'

'I didn't see his face, just his clothes. Maybe you should talk to the builders.' She chewed on a piece of gum Boyd had given her to help calm her down.

'We will talk to them. Did you check over the house before we arrived?'

'Yes, but not the garage. I never even thought of it before Mark asked to see it.'

'Have you had many viewings here recently?'

'You're the first in a couple of weeks.'

'Really? I thought there was a shortage of houses at the moment.'

'Shortage of *affordable* houses. These are at the high end of the market. I was hoping to sell a few off phase two plans, but it's all a bit dead at the moment. It usually is in the winter, especially after all the expense of Christmas.' Her eyes widened and her mouth formed a perfect red lipsticked O. 'That poor man. His family. Do you think he might have had a heart attack while working here?'

'I thought this house was finished.'

'Of course. Silly me.'

'There doesn't appear to have been a break-in. Who else has keys besides yourself?'

'The site manager. The foreman too, I expect. And the developer, of course. Gordon Collins. GC Construction.'

'What's the name of the site manager?'

'Patrick Curran. Nice man.'

Lottie made a note. 'Did you disarm the alarm before we arrived?'

'No, it's not in use until the new owners move in. No need really. The interior designer supplies the furniture and other decorative stuff and then moves it on to her next show home.'

'Has this designer a key also?'

Charlie shook her head. 'She's never around once her job is complete. When she needs the key to clear out the house, she asks Patrick or myself.'

'Do you know the site manager well?'

'A bit. I liaise with him from time to time. He's my contact here.'

'Okay. When did you last see or speak with him?'

'Earlier today. I called him to let him know I had a viewing. That's you two.' She glanced at Boyd, who'd come back into the house. 'You never said you were detectives when you phoned.'

He blushed slightly, but recovered quickly. 'I'm sorry about that, but I thought it best not to mention it.'

'You should be grateful that we were with you when you opened the door,' Lottie said.

'If it wasn't for you,' Charlie eyed Boyd, 'I might never have opened it at all. Now I'm going to have nightmares for the rest of my life.'

23

Jane Dore, the state pathologist, arrived shortly after the forensic team. Once she'd finished her preliminary examination of the body, Lottie walked with her to the hall. Out of Charlie's earshot.

'It's great you got here so quickly.'

'I was finishing up with the victim from this morning,' Jane said. 'I was still in Ragmullin.'

'And our man back there, can you tell me anything?'

'Male, mid to late twenties. Single wound to the back of his head. Blunt-force trauma.'

'Why all that blood?'

'Cracked his skull. Didn't die immediately, though he was immobilised. In fact I'd say he had a slow and painful death. I'll know more once I conduct his post-mortem. And don't ask me how long he's been dead, because I don't know. The heat in here played its part. How can people live in such warm houses? It's way too hot.'

'Maybe tell that to Boyd. He's thinking of buying one. Hence why we were here.'

'Well, lucky for you. Another couple of hours lying undiscovered and the body would have been smelling to high heaven with flies buzzing like an orchestra.'

'What's your take on the death of Laura Nolan? The young woman who was discovered on the cinema grounds this morning.'

'Stabbed three times, also signs of strangulation. And before you ask, I can't yet see anything to connect the chap here to her.'

'Time of death for Laura?'

'Hard to tell. She was out in the elements. I might know more when I examine her at the mortuary.'

'Thanks, Jane.'

The pathologist disrobed from her protective suit at the front door, where a tent had been erected. Lottie watched her disappear into the dark afternoon.

Back in the kitchen, Charlie seemed to have recovered somewhat from the shock and was all business again. 'How long do you think it will be before you remove him? The body, I mean.'

'It'll take as long as it takes. You'll need to be formally interviewed. Fingerprints and DNA. That sort of thing. When can you call to the station?'

'Now, if you want. I have no more viewings scheduled today. And it might be best to do it before the real shock sets in.'

Here was a woman with her head screwed on, Lottie thought. 'I'll phone ahead and have someone waiting for you so that you won't be delayed unnecessarily.'

'I appreciate that.'

Once Charlie had picked up her belongings and left, Lottie returned to the garage. Boyd was deep in conversation with Grainne, the SOCO team leader.

'Find anything to help us?'

Grainne's green eyes and Boyd's brown ones looked at her above their masks.

He held up an evidence bag. 'Phone. We'll need the PIN, but Techie Gary should be able to unlock it.'

'We need to know who the victim is first,' Lottie said. 'Let's find the site manager.'

Outside in the fresh air, she waited for Boyd.

'You took your time,' she said. 'Did you have a good conversation with Grainne?'

'Yes, great. She is a font of information.'

'Does she know who John Doe is and how long he's been dead?'

'No, but she knows a lot about buying a new house. She said—'

'Feck's sake, Boyd, I don't care what she said about buying houses. There's a murdered man in there.'

'Okay. Right. No need to get your knickers in a twist.'

She was about to reply when an agitated man tried to bundle his way through the cordon. Garda Lei was fighting a losing battle attempting to restrain him.

'What's going on?' Lottie asked.

Lei fixed his hat and the man slumped against him in defeat. 'He says he's the site manager and entitled to know what's going on.'

'Patrick Curran?' Lottie enquired. She could smell what she thought was cement from his donkey jacket, which was dusty beneath a yellow hi-vis vest. He had a hard hat on his head over a beanie. He pulled both off and tucked them under his arm.

'That's me. What happened? I heard someone died. Is it true? Who is it, do you know?'

His words ran into one another, while his fingers raked through his hair, causing dust to billow about him like fireflies. Worry lines were etched around the eyes hollowed in his grey face. She felt a moment of pity for him.

'Patrick, I'd like a chat with you.' She gently took his elbow and led him to a waiting garda car.

'Who is it? Can you tell me that at least?' He walked alongside her.

When she had him seated in the car, she leaned on the open door. 'Is there anyone missing from the site?'

'Oh shite, it's not one of my lads, is it?'

'We don't know who it is yet.'

'Good Lord, but this is shocking, so it is. You know that a lot of the lads are going to be let go? We've been instructed to halt work on phase two from the end of next week. Shutting up shop for the foreseeable. Boss man said it's until he decides what's best. He can't be losing any more money. That's what he said.'

'And the boss is Gordon Collins?'

'That's right. Big shot, in his own mind.'

'Would you be able to look at a photo of the dead man for me? It's not particularly pleasant.'

He wiped a grubby hand with nails caked in dirt across his mouth. 'Show me.'

She swiped up the photo she'd hastily taken with her phone. Grainne had been holding the man's head between her hands and he appeared to be asleep. If only. She turned the screen towards Patrick Curran.

'Ah no. Don't tell me it's him. For fuck's sake.'

'You know him?'

'Aye. God rest his soul, poor bugger.' He blessed himself and Lottie noticed his eyes water.

'Who is he, Patrick?'

'John Morgan. Young lad. With us less than a year. Great bricklayer. Promoted to foreman recently. Did he fall or something?'

Or something, Lottie thought. 'When did you last see him?'

'Things have been hectic. I suppose I saw him this morning. I've been off site a lot today. Had a meeting with the boss. Christ on a bike, this is going to damage potential sales even more.'

His concern for his colleague had been quickly replaced with thoughts of his job, she noted. He pulled his shoulders back and made to stand. She stepped back to allow him out of the car.

'I'll need John's contact details. Next of kin. That sort of thing.'

'In the office. Everything's there.' He pointed to the cabin situated halfway down the unfinished site, behind a chain-link fence.

'Garda Lei will accompany you. You'll have to come to the station to make a full statement.'

'I'll do anything to help. Poor fecker.'

Lottie watched as Lei walked off with Patrick. The site manager, his shoulders hunched, seemed to have aged a decade in the few minutes she'd been speaking to him.

She turned to find Boyd.

'Our dead man has a name. John Morgan. He was the foreman on the site.'

'Well, that was kind of obvious.'

'That he was the foreman?'

'That he worked here. His clothes and all.'

'Did you ever consider becoming a detective, Boyd?'

'No need to be sarcastic. I was only saying...'

'Forget it. Ask your fan club in there to get the forensic report to me asap. We have to move on this before the trail goes cold.'

'You mean Grainne? Lottie, why are you resorting to conversing in clichés?'

'Boyd?'

'What?'

'I mean this in the nicest way possible, but could you ever feck off?'

24

Jane Dore sat in the cold, sterile surroundings of her cutting room in the Dead House. The body of Laura Nolan lay on a steel table. It had arrived while she'd been at the Pine Grove house, and she'd got to work as soon as she returned.

She made her way around Laura's naked body once again. Her clothes had been inspected, bagged and tagged. Samples had been taken to be sent to the lab, but even under a microscope she hadn't found any trace of semen on the clothing or underwear. Perhaps when she opened the body it would tell her a different story. Still, the fact that the young woman had been fully clothed pointed to little or no sexual assault.

She examined the body head to toe. Besides the three stab wounds, there was bruising on her neck. Studying the discoloration, Jane was sure that partial strangulation had come first, followed by the knife wounds. She could see that the young woman had applied fake tan recently, and her nails were gel. She swabbed beneath each, taking the samples to inspect under a microscope before they too were transported to the forensics lab. Under the right index fingernail, she found what looked like a tiny deposit of clay. There was also a trace on the girl's neck.

Had it come from the ground where she was found? Once it was analysed, its source should be clearer.

She scraped and swabbed, then inspected the stab wounds and found they had been administered without hesitation. The killer had struck each site cleanly once. In and out. Had the neck wound been to hide the strangulation? Perhaps, and it was likely the arm wound happened as Laura tried to defend herself following the strangulation attempt. This wound was to the back of the girl's lower right arm. Definitely a defensive action, Jane concluded. The chest wound was the final one. She'd have expected some hesitancy here, but the knife appeared to have struck cleanly through the clothing. She noticed fibres in the wound, and to the naked eye they matched what Laura had been wearing.

Turning, she looked at photos of the site where the young woman had been found. Little blood.

'Where did he attack you, sweetheart?' she murmured. She was certain that Laura had already been dead or dying when she was left in the grounds of the cinema complex at Connell retail park.

———

Lottie had hardly had time to catch her breath on the drive to the Tullamore mortuary. Now she watched as Jane detailed Laura Nolan's post-mortem, grateful to the pathologist for pushing the girl up the list.

'He tried to strangle her,' the pathologist said. 'She may have lashed out in defence, and he stabbed her lower arm. The stab to her neck was perhaps to hide evidence of the attempted strangulation. There would have been a lot of blood, and it would have sprayed the killer. The final stab was to her chest. Upwards thrust through her clothing. He was either smaller than her if standing, or they both might have been seated.'

'Could she have been in a car?'

'It's possible. What makes you say that?'

'Just that if she was a passenger, it would account for the right-hand side of her body having the most injuries.'

'That might be the case, but *might* is the operative word. You have to find the evidence.'

'So,' Lottie mused, 'I'm looking for a car with a vast amount of blood in it. Though it's probably been forensically cleaned by now.'

'Or a scene somewhere close to where she was found with, as you say, a vast amount of blood.'

'Anything else?'

'I found dirt, like clay, under one of her nails and a trace on her neck. It's gone to the lab. SOCOs also took samples from the ground around the body. And they made casts of the footprints found there.'

'This clay,' Lottie said, 'when will we have the results of that analysis?'

'As soon as they have it, I'll have it, then you'll have it. These things take time.'

'I know, I know. Have you found anything at all with DNA?'

'So far I've swabbed her neck and all her fingernails. They had gel extensions, so if she scratched him, there will be something there. Enough for DNA? Let's wait in hope.'

'Anything else of note?'

'You see her stretch marks? She'd had a pregnancy.'

'She had a little boy. He's almost four.'

Jane paced around the table. 'So sad. I hate to see young lives destroyed like this.' She gazed at the body on the stainless-steel table. 'Laura had her whole life in front of her. A son to love and raise. All of that has been annihilated in one night. Why? And who by? You have to find this person, Lottie.'

Lottie nodded. 'Have you looked at John Morgan's body yet?'

'He hasn't arrived. I did a quick examination at the site. We have to inspect his clothing and all that, but outwardly the only wound I noticed was the blow to the back of his head. Crushed skull. Considerable force. My initial observation is that he didn't fight back. So he may have been taken by surprise and hit from behind.'

'Killed where we found him?'

'Most likely.'

'Do you think it's two different murderers?'

'I can't say until I examine the body here. But if it is two killers, you might need to call in assistance. Don't be afraid to ask for extra hands on deck.'

Lottie felt her jaw drop. 'What do you mean?'

'Tracking one murderer is difficult enough with the resources you have, but trying to get a handle on two...'

'I get it. I'll see how things pan out. Send your reports asap, then I'll know what I'm dealing with. And Jane? Thanks for doing this so quickly. It really helps.'

25

He'd seen it on some late-night television show, God only knew what the name of it was. Something about romance and acting outside of your comfort zone. But as Kirby scattered rose petals over the bed, he felt like a right twit. Come morning, he would have to gather them up again. Still, he admired the effect, and the new duvet cover looked fresh and smooth, even if it was cheap.

He wanted to make Amy feel special because she'd gone through such a difficult time. If nothing else, this would make her laugh.

Sweating by the time he'd finished lighting the last candle, he heard her arrive home. He closed the bedroom door softly and went down to greet her.

'How was your day?' He kissed the top of her head.

'Grand. It came and went. I'd kill for a glass of wine.'

'Oh, don't do that or I'll have to arrest you.'

She laughed. 'That's so corny.'

Leading her by the hand, he brought her into the kitchen, where he'd been cooking a curry before he'd gone upstairs to decorate the bedroom.

'Smells...' She paused. 'Is it burning, Larry?'

'Goddammit to hell.' He whipped the pan off the hob. The curry sauce, which should have been a creamy yellow, was burned brown. The chicken pieces had shrivelled to black dots like buttons on a coat. The rice had melded into a soggy mess.

Switching off the appliances, he scratched his head. 'I wanted to do something special for you. Looks like it's a mega failure.'

'It's the thought that counts. We can order in. The table is fab, though.'

He felt heat flush up his cheeks. He'd set it with new plates and cutlery that he'd got at half price in the Guineys January sale, and he'd sprinkled a few rose petals across the table too. Despite all that, he felt like a grade-A dope.

She pulled out a chair and sat, wincing.

He sat opposite her. 'Want me to take off your brace?'

'I need my pills first. Would you be a pet?'

'Your wish is my command.' He filled a glass of water and fetched her pills from the cupboard. As she swallowed them, he noticed dark rings circling her eyes. 'Is the new job taking too much out of you?'

'It's tiring, but I need it to keep me sane. I was going bananas looking at the same walls day in, day out. And Larry, I really appreciate all this.' She swept her hand out over the table. 'What will we order?'

'I'd love a McDonald's.'

She laughed. 'That's what we'll have then. Ring it in, and while we're waiting, you can take this cursed thing off my leg.'

'With pleasure.'

Kirby smiled. Maybe tonight wouldn't be a total disaster.

26

He'd sat in his shed, on and off, for most of the day, after he'd scoured the inside of the car and scrubbed himself for the third time. He thought about the man who'd been murdered on the building site. Waiting for the release of his name. Nothing had been leaked so far. He was fearful, and that angered him.

He had to park all that and direct his rage elsewhere. First, though, he had to think where he'd gone wrong with the young woman they'd found at the cinema complex. After much deliberation, and ten pots planted with seeds from little packets, he reached the conclusion that *she* was right. He had to watch them for a longer period before he took them. He had to listen to her and take direction from her. She wouldn't like him to make a big fucking mistake again.

One thing he was sure of, he had to be aware that the next one might fight back like Laura had. The news app gave some of her details. Laura Nolan. Age twenty-five. So she *had* lied about her age. Bitch. And she had a son! That had never been in the equation. Just as well he'd killed her. If he'd brought her home, there would have been hell to pay when *she* found out about the child. As it was, she'd shouted at him for ten full minutes before she'd run out of breath.

'They are all prostitutes,' she'd said. 'No one cares about them. They fade from the front page quickly, and if the media isn't harping on about them, then the guards won't put in the effort. They will be forgotten about. Like the other waste of space we have here. No one missed her. But Laura had a child! Are you totally stupid or what?'

He didn't remind her that she'd had a hand in selecting Laura. Why didn't *she* know about the kid? It wasn't all his fault, was it? He kept that thought to himself.

He got into his car and drove into town. He could smell the bleach. Despite that, he doubted he had got rid of every last speck of blood. He had to be even more careful now. He parked, got out and locked the car, then headed towards Fallon's, where all the young ones hung out.

It was time to stalk the next prey.

————

Shannon Kenny held a bottle of Coors Light in her hand while her friend Jess guzzled a pint of Orchard Thieves. Fallon's was busy by 9.30, it being Friday night and all, but they'd found a nook that afforded them a view of the pub.

'And you left him there?' Jess said, putting her glass down. 'You walked out on your date last night?'

'He was a flirt. Eyeing up the woman behind the bar and ignoring me. I've had enough of that shite.'

'Jealous boots.'

'I didn't give a shit, to be honest.'

'Did you get paid at least?'

'I didn't even get the promised meal. He was a cheapskate.'

'That's so not on, Shannon. Did you read the small print? Isn't it in the terms and conditions that you get fed?'

'Stop messing, Jess. It wasn't funny. In all honesty, I was kind of scared.'

'Maybe you should take your name off the site. Try dating the old-fashioned way.'

'I want one with money.'

Jess lifted her pint and pointed it towards the bar. 'A few fine things sitting up there.'

'You'd shag one of them? They're ancient.'

'They're the ones with the money.'

'And don't forget, they're the ones with the wife and four kids at home.'

Jess leaned her head to one side. 'Divorced, maybe?'

'Divorce means baggage. Suitcases full of it.'

'What about your man at the end of the bar? On his own. Nice eyes. I caught him watching us a minute ago.'

'You can hardly see his face, let alone his eyes.'

'Quit moaning, Shannon. Let's have fun.' Jess drank more cider. 'Where did you stay last night if you didn't go home?'

'Karen's. She didn't mind. Can't say the same for George when I arrived home this morning with no door key.'

'Your brother is a nutter at times. What did he say?'

'More like what he didn't say.'

Jess licked her lips. 'Don't look now, but your man at the end of the bar is kind of cute. I like the ones with beards.'

'Will you stop? I bet he's one of those with a trunk full of baggage.'

'I wouldn't mind seeing his trunk!' Jess laughed.

Shannon had to smile. Her friend was a tonic, but even so, she felt a moment of jealousy. Jess had a natural beauty, whereas she herself had to shovel on the foundation and fake tan, and her hair was a fucking nightmare. Still, she had to admit she looked good on the agency's website. It had cost her a small fortune to get a make-up artist to work her magic. But it'd be worth it, wouldn't it? Her saviour was probably out there right now, staring at her face on a screen, his millions burning a hole in his pocket. That thought made her feel better before her mood took a downward spiral.

'Jess, did you hear about that girl's murder?' She tugged her short skirt towards her knees, feeling suddenly vulnerable.

'Oh God, yes. Horrific. Twenty-five, same as us. Did you know her?'

'Kind of. Hadn't talked to her in a long time.'

'And she had a kid.'

'Shocking.' Shannon wondered if she should remind Jess where she'd first met Laura Nolan. A filament of unease threaded itself between her vertebrae, and she shivered.

'Don't look now,' Jess said, 'but he's actually staring at us.'

'Who's staring?' She was glad the conversation had shifted.

'Your man at the bar.'

'That's such a cliché.'

'A what?'

Jess wasn't the sharpest knife in the drawer, but Shannon loved her. She was one of the few friends who had stood by her when she'd gone through all that shit last year. She sipped her Coors Light and dampened down the urge for a hit of something stronger. No, that had broken her family before. She couldn't go there again.

'Which of us is he staring at?' She forced jollity into her tone.

'Don't know. He's kind of all right, if you ask me.'

'I *didn't* ask you, and stop staring. You're encouraging him.'

'Get down off your high horse, Shannon, and—'

'Horse. What? Where?'

'You're so mean.' Jess stared into her near-empty pint glass. 'Another?'

'Why not? When we're out, we're out.'

———

He thought the young one behind the bar was kind of cute, but she seemed to have her shit together. Anyhow, she didn't fall into the prostitute category, nor was she on the list. The two sitting over in the nook were a different story. One pure blonde and pretty as hell. The other a little darker and made up like a kid at Halloween. The target. He got out his phone and tapped into the site just to be sure he was right.

There she was, looking like an A-list film star. Shannie. What sort of a name was that? He tapped into her profile. Twenty-five. Or was her age as fake as her name? Didn't matter. She was on the list, so that was good enough for him. He was glad he'd picked Fallon's to check out first. Saved him bar-crawling, looking for her.

He called over the young one who was serving and ordered another Heineken Zero to keep his vigil going. The night might be worth it after all. Then he remembered he'd been told to watch for longer. How much longer? That, he had not been told.

———

'That guy at the bar sent these over,' Chloe said as she placed the drinks on the table in front of the two women.

'Another cliché,' Shannon said.

Jess handed Chloe their empties. 'Tell him thanks a million.'

'He asked if he can join you.' Chloe looked dubious.

'Sure.' Jess shrugged.

'No way,' Shannon said.

'Personally, I'd decline,' Chloe said, but still she waited.

'It'd be a laugh.' Jess nudged her friend. 'Go on.'

Shannon leaned forward. 'Tell him thanks for the drinks, Chloe, but we're on a girls' night out.'

Chloe winked and went back to the bar.

'Spoilsport,' Jess said.

'Don't forget a girl our age was murdered in town last night. That lad up there could have killed her.'

Jess feigned shock. 'Did you ever think of writing a crime novel? You've a great imagination.'

'Shut up. I don't like being picked up by strange men.'

'But you can go out with a stranger from the agency?'

'They're vetted. He's not. He could be... the Yorkshire Ripper for all we know.'

'Isn't the Ripper in jail or dead or something?'

'You know right well what I mean.' Shannon shoved her phone into her bag. 'Let's go somewhere else. I'm not comfortable with him buying us drinks when we don't even know him.'

'I like men buying me drinks, especially when I'm almost broke. Stay.'

Shannon bit the inside of her lip, considering the dilemma. Was she actually an idiot for declining a free drink? For some unknown reason the man at the bar was causing warning signals to flash through her brain. Leave, she told herself.

'No, come on, Jess. I'm broke too, but I sneaked my brother's card into my bag. I'll get you a shot in Danny's. Deal?'

'You know George will go apeshit again. Feck it. Deal.' Jess's eyes brightened even more than normal.

As they left the pub, Shannon noticed her friend wave to the bearded creep sitting at the bar.

She couldn't get out of there fast enough.

27

Kirby had eaten two Happy Meals and a McFlurry while Amy had a burger and fries. They'd been mainly silent during their meal. Kirby felt unable to burden her with the distress of his work. But the murdered young woman swam around his skull the whole evening, and he was only half listening to what Amy was saying, never mind what the new Netflix series was about.

'What? Sorry, Amy, I was miles away.'

'That's what I'm talking about.'

'I'm so sorry. The new investigation isn't the nicest thing to talk about over a McD's and Netflix.' He realised they were still sitting at the kitchen table, from where they could see the television through the double doors to the sitting room.

'I was saying maybe we should book a holiday.' She must have seen the look on his face, because she added, 'I'm not talking about next week.'

'God, I don't know when I last had a proper holiday. Like going on a plane to a different country kind of holiday. It sounds amazing. Let's do it.'

She clapped her hands like a child. 'Oh, great. Where will we go?'

'Anywhere, as long as we're together.'

'You know what? You're just a romantic at heart.'

And then he remembered. 'Fuck. Shit.' He flew up the stairs, with Amy struggling on her bad leg behind him.

'What's wrong, Larry?'

He threw open the bedroom door and was greeted by a plume of black smoke. He flicked on the light, drew back the curtains and flung open the window.

'Oh my God,' Amy said. 'What have you done?'

With his eyes watering from the smoke, he started blowing out candles. Two, in jars, had burned down to the end and were the cause of the black smoke. When he had them all extinguished, he looked in despair at the walls.

'This is a nightmare,' he said. 'The whole room will need redecorating. I'm so sorry.' He sank onto the now blackened duvet as the smoke dwindled out the window. 'It was supposed to be a romantic surprise for you.'

'You are too sweet, Larry Kirby.' She leaned into him, her head resting against his shoulder. 'We can sleep in the spare room tonight.'

'You go ahead. I want to make sure there's nothing left to ignite. I'll clean up the kitchen too.'

'Forget about the kitchen. Tomorrow is another day.'

'I've to find the murderer of a young woman tomorrow. No, I'll clean the kitchen and head to bed then. Don't fall asleep before I get there.'

'I've no intention of falling asleep.'

When he had the room half decent and the kitchen fairly clear, he switched off all the lights and headed up to the spare room. Before he even pushed in the door, he heard her soft snores, rising and falling.

And despite everything, it was the sweetest sound in the world, because it meant that he was no longer living his life alone.

28

Lottie's favourite place at home was outside. She stood at the fence and stared at the lake through the muted darkness. Stars glinted in the sky, and it would be a romantic scene if she hadn't that ball of anger lodged in her chest. After a few moments, the cause of her annoyance appeared at her elbow.

'Lottie, we need to talk about the house,' Boyd said.

'Oh, you mean the house where we discovered a murdered man's body?'

'That's just the show home.'

She turned towards him, leaning back, her arms on the damp paling. 'We can't afford to buy anything in that estate and the houses aren't big enough.'

'We could make one big enough.'

Moving away from the fence, she clenched her fists in frustration. 'You can't honestly be harping back at renovating a garage in a new house, can you?'

'I spoke with the site manager, after he made his statement, and he said we'd be buying off plan so it's only a matter of changing the garage into a room. Simple. Very little extra cost if we do it before a block is laid.'

'But they're closing down the site.' Shaking her head, she made to walk by him, but he caught her elbow.

'At least discuss it with me.'

He was so close she could smell the desperation on his breath.

'Even with the garage converted into a room, there's not enough space, Mark.'

'There could be.'

'What do you mean?'

'Your girls are adults. Chloe is working. Katie works when she can. They should get their own place. Together, with Louis.'

She turned her back on him, squinted up at the stars. All she saw was a red mist of rage floating over the sky, blotting out the twinkling celestial bodies. She both loved and despised him in that moment. *You couldn't be more conflicted, could you?* She was fed up arguing with herself. So she let fly at him.

'How dare you! How fucking dare you, Mark Boyd.' She swirled around again and stepped into his space. 'You want to split up my family so you can play happy families with me?'

'For God's sake, I didn't mean it the way it sounded.'

'What *did* you mean, then? Huh? Tell me exactly what you meant.'

'It's just that you have to accept they're not kids any more. They're adults and can't be sponging... I mean living off you for ever.'

'I thought I knew you. I really thought I knew your very soul, Mark. How wrong can a person be?' The red mist grew darker, and she felt powerless in its depth.

'Please, Lottie, I'm sorry. Honestly. It's just that I'm stressed with Grace being at mine as well as Sergio. I need her help while I'm at work, but there's no space.'

'You should have thought of that before.'

'I just thought that a new house would be perfect,' he insisted. 'With both our incomes we could get a mortgage and—'

'I want you to leave, Mark. Now. Go home and buy the fucking house for yourself and Sergio. And you know what? There's enough room for Grace there too without converting the garage. You can even park your car in it. Please just leave me alone.' She could taste tears at the corners of her lips and realised she was crying.

He put out a hand and touched her arm. She shrugged him off and marched back to the house, slamming the door as hard as she could.

After he'd left, she sat at the table waiting for the kettle to boil.

Twisting her hands together, she stared at her engagement ring, the one she'd eventually consented to wearing. The single diamond sparkled under the fluorescent light. With uncontrolled anger still coursing like a hurricane through her veins, she tugged at it until it came off. As the kettle whistled unanswered in the background, she put the ring in the centre of the table and sat staring at it for a long, long time. Then she put it back on and made her tea.

———

Katie had opened the window to air her room, which smelled of damp and the alcohol she'd spilled on her clothes the night before. She'd forgotten to put them in the wash and they lay in a crumpled heap on the floor. Louis was in Sean's room, probably watching his uncle play some online football game. She should put him to bed, but she wanted to relax in the few peaceful alone moments.

Standing at the window, she spied her mother and Boyd out by the fence. Were they arguing? She leaned forward, earwigging. It was rare to witness a full-blown argument between them. She pulled back quickly, stung by the words she was hearing. There didn't seem to be any malice in what Boyd was saying. It was the vehemence in her mother's reply that stunned her.

Backing away from the window, she picked up her dirty clothes and sat on the bed with them bundled in her arms. She mulled over what Boyd had said. Was it true? Should she and Chloe move out and let their mother get on with her life? She was so caught up in her own woes that she rarely considered Lottie as a separate entity. She needed to assess her life, her future. She was twenty-three, with a three-year-old son. Her future held... what? She deserved better than this. She had to be proactive with her life, or it would pass her by.

The smell of alcohol from the clothes was disgusting. She recalled when it had been spilled. When she'd met Jackson. She grabbed her phone. She could call him to see if he wanted to bring her on that dinner date he'd mentioned. That'd be doing something proactive.

Without hesitation, she tapped his number and listened to it ringing, praying that he'd remember her. Then praying that he wouldn't answer so she could hang up and forget all about it. Daft idea anyhow.

'Katie,' he said, just before she disconnected. 'I knew you couldn't resist me.'

She laughed and felt the tension leaving her body. 'Jackson. About that dinner...'

29

Shannon was drunk. Scuttered, George would say. Shit. She didn't want to think how she was going to pay him back what she'd spent on his bank card. She'd waved Jess into a taxi outside Danny's. She knew it'd cost another ten euro on George's card to get home, so walking was her only option.

Buttoning up her teddy coat and snuggling into the warmth of the collar, she slung her bag over her shoulder and set off down the street. It was bloody freezing, and her skirt was way too short and her tights too thin to protect her legs from the sharp breeze. She looked over her shoulder at the taxi rank, but it was now empty. Fifteen minutes, maybe twenty in these heels, and she'd be home.

When she reached the bridge, she turned left heading for Cairnbeg, her terraced estate. Nearly there. Another five minutes. She wouldn't have to pass the cinema complex where Laura's body had been found. That was good. She couldn't bear to think of her lying out in the cold all night, dead.

The lights of Cairnbeg beckoned. Almost home. But she had an unsettling feeling that someone was following her. Glancing over her shoulder, all she saw was the sparkle of the canal as it flowed slowly under the bridge. Keep walking. Don't look back. She stumbled on her heels and put out a hand to the wall of a house to steady herself. Damn it, she was so drunk. George would throw a hissy fit. As she turned into the estate her laboured breathing eased a little.

Had she imagined she was being followed? Or had there really been someone skulking behind her in the dark, walking in her footsteps. She was now among the lights and houses and gardens. Still a shiver of terror rattled her to her core.

Nearly home.

She was safe.

Almost...

———

He was walking a good distance behind her. Then she looked back and he slid into a doorway before she saw him. Her pace remained steady. She wasn't running. That was good. But she looked like the whore she was, in that fucking fluffy pink coat. All long legs and narrow sharp heels. A whore called Shannie. For God's sake.

Keeping well back, out of sight of her nervous glances, he watched as she turned into the estate. His car was parked at the pub. How could he snatch her and get her back there? He'd made a mistake offering to buy them the drinks. That had spooked her. Still, he'd followed her and her friend into Danny's. The bustling crowd there had helped him remain hidden. And when they'd left, he was able to follow unnoticed.

Now he hung back and watched and waited to see which house she entered. Then he'd decide what to do next.

———

Without turning on a light, Shannon sneaked the bank card back into her brother's wallet where he'd left it on the kitchen table. She had one foot on the bottom step of the stairs when she heard him speak from somewhere in the depths of the house.

'You are some bitch, Shannon Kenny.'

Through the open sitting room door, she saw her brother seated on an armchair in the semi-darkness. The floor lamp beside him burst into light as he put his foot on the switch.

'What are you doing in the dark, George?' She didn't move.

'What are *you* doing, more like?'

'Heading up to bed. You okay?' Still she did not move.

'Had a nice time on my money?'

Shit. He knew. 'I'll pay you back. I'm sorry. I'm skint.'

'Not find a fancy man to bail you out, then?'

'Will you stop? Look, I'm wrecked. We can talk in the morning.'

He jumped out of the chair and in an instant was in the hall, grabbing her arm and pulling her off the step.

'You promised you'd help with Davy. But then you disappear and I can't work or get to the gym. Then you have the cheek to steal my bank card. You are some muppet.'

She exhaled with relief. He was mad, but not so mad that he couldn't make her smile.

'I'm sorry. How is Davy? Has the chickenpox eased?'

'Like you care.'

'He's your kid, but I am concerned.'

He returned to the sitting room, where he flopped onto the armchair again.

She followed, though she really wanted to remove her make-up, fall into bed and sleep away the thought that someone might have walked home in her shadow.

'Shannon, you need to get a decent job,' he said. 'You spend more than you make and then you spend mine. We have bills, utilities to pay. I'm sick of being the responsible one around here. You swan out to the pub and come back when you feel like it. Where were you last night? I was sure you were that girl they found dead at the cinema. Then you waltz in the next morning without a care in the world.'

'Told you. I stayed with Karen. But listen, George, I think someone followed me home tonight. I had the weirdest feeling and—'

'Nothing to do with being drunk, was it?'

'Will you stop? I had feck-all to drink.'

'My online banking tells me different. Shannon, you have a problem. Did you buy drugs tonight? Was all the money I spent on your rehab a waste?'

'You sound just like Mam used to.'

'And look what you did to *her*.' He jumped up. 'I didn't mean that, Shannon. I swear.'

'But you thought about it enough that it was on the tip of your tongue.'

She edged back into the hall. She felt a lump in her chest. George was right. The strain of her habit had killed their mother. Well, cancer took her in the end, but what Shannon had done while on drugs had to be a cause of the stress she'd suffered. George often reminded her of it, before he became contrite.

'I'm sorry, sis. Go to bed,' he said. 'I've to catch up on my work in the morning and I need you to care for Davy.'

She nodded. As she turned to climb the stairs, she thought she saw a shadow move outside, through the glass panel in the door. Must be the drink, she told herself, but in reality it cemented in her head the idea that she had been followed home.

Upstairs, she abandoned the idea of taking off her make-up. She just wanted to sleep.

30

He was still smarting from the argument with Lottie when he got back to his apartment. His overcrowded apartment. Grace was using his bed. Sergio was asleep in the fold-out bed on the floor. Boyd was consigned to the couch again. Twisting and turning wasn't going to bring sleep. At two, he got up. He made a sandwich from the chicken carcass he'd cooked the day before.

He could not believe Lottie's vehemence earlier. What was stoking her fire? Two murders weren't helping. He got that. Beneath her anger he sensed insecurity. Fear, maybe. But fear of what? Why wouldn't she talk it out with him?

'Talking to yourself is the first sign.'

He twirled round on the high stool to see Grace in the bedroom doorway, a red dressing gown tied tightly at her waist.

'Jesus, you scared the shite out of me, Grace. What is it?'

'I want to know what has my brother up at two in the morning. It's Lottie, isn't it?'

He wasn't going there with Grace. 'It was my first day back at work. A young woman was found murdered this morning. Then we found a man murdered this afternoon. I'm overtired.'

'Ever think of quitting?'

'Quitting?' He was horrified. 'What do you mean?'

'Your job. Give it up, Mark. It's not good for you, and definitely not good for Sergio.'

He wanted to verbally lash out, to ask what she would know about having a son, but held his tongue. 'I just needed something to eat. Go back to bed.'

'You left that chicken out of the fridge. It's probably reeking of salmonella by now.'

'It's cooked. It's fine. And there's nothing left on it now.'

'Don't come crying to me if you're vomiting in the morning.' She turned on her heel and went back to bed.

He felt like crying all right. Grace had sounded so like his dead mother. He realised how much he missed having that strong west of Ireland matriarch in his life. Then he did cry.

———

The wind woke Lottie at two in the morning. She shot up in the bed as another smash and crash happened outside.

She noticed she'd forgotten to close the curtains such was her anger with Boyd and his attitude to her family. Had she overreacted? Possibly. She knew what he'd meant, but didn't want to hear it. Yes, her girls were young adults, but she was their mother and she would care for them as long as they needed her.

Another crash outside.

At the window, she peered into the ebony night. There were no stars or moon now. Wind and rain pelted the glass. Pulling on a hoodie, she made her way down the unlit stairs. In the kitchen, she switched on the outside light and unlocked the back door. She stuck her head outside. A storm was blowing in from the lake, and rain fell in torrents. She peered at the ground, where she found the source of the noise. Broken slates lay on the concrete path. Hearing a creak from above, she ducked back inside just in time as another slate smashed to earth.

Shit.

She locked the door and made her way upstairs and into Katie's room, where they'd had the leak over Christmas. Sure enough, she heard the drip of water from the ceiling. Katie was sound asleep, so she didn't put on the light but waited for her vision to accommodate the light from the landing. Then, in the corner, she noticed the ceiling bulging with water.

Leaning against the wall, she hugged her body, shivering. Maybe Boyd was right. It was time to bite the bullet and find a decent home to live in.

She fetched a bucket from the kitchen and brought it back upstairs. Placing it beneath the drip, she went back to bed. There was nothing she could do at this hour; only hope for the best and pray the worst stayed well away from her home and her family.

31

She was still up at 2.30 a.m. when he parked out front and switched off the ignition. The light shining through the gap in the front-room curtains was a warning. He knew what awaited him. He'd failed her, but there was an extra bounce in his step as he let himself in the front door. He could take what she meted out, because in his cold heart he knew he had not failed himself.

'Well, any luck?' She was staring over his shoulder as if something or someone was looming behind his back.

'It's too soon. Guards are everywhere. Outside pubs and on street corners. Patrolling in squad cars.'

'That's all your fault, moron. Why are you so late? Why didn't you just turn around and come home?'

This was the tricky bit. He could lie to the whores, but he found it difficult to lie to the woman standing in front of him.

'I wanted to scout around. To see if there was any area of town the cops had forgotten to patrol.'

'And?'

'A few places, but nothing good for my mission.'

'*Our* mission, you lug. Ours.'

'Sure. You're right. I think I'll turn in.'

'That one needs to go soon.' Her tone was sharp and stopped him leaving the room.

'I thought she was doing okay.'

'Okay? Are you blind? She's a disaster waiting to happen. She has proved impossible to bend to my will. Just when I think I have a breakthrough, she goes and does something stupid.'

'Maybe you need to give her more time to adjust to her circumstances.'

'She's been here long enough.' She paused. Dangerous, he thought. 'And what circumstances would you be referring to?'

She continually confused him when she talked like this. Why couldn't she just say what she meant? Why couldn't he tell her what he thought? What he felt?

'I see you have no answer, because you are a stupid, stupid man. God knows what I did in a previous life to be lumbered with the likes of you and—'

She was cut off by the sound of a muffled shriek from upstairs. She lashed out and clipped him on the ear. 'I'd need the patience of a saint with you lot. The patience of a saint...'

Her words trailed up the stairs behind her. He rubbed his ear as he filled the kettle for a cup of tea. She had sucked all the energy out of the room and his motivation had fled with it.

He was trapped.

32

SATURDAY

The overnight storm had eased to nothing more than a sharp breeze and intermittent showers as Lottie reached the station. Her mood had disintegrated into narkiness by the time she marched into the incident room. A leaking roof, a falling-out with Boyd, as well as two murders to solve, and she was at a loss to know which way to turn. Detective Maria Lynch usually kept the incident boards up to date, but she was off somewhere hot and sunny with her family. Lucky Maria.

As her team trickled in for the morning briefing, Lottie paced in front of the sparsely populated boards. One held Laura Nolan's photograph, crime-scene images and information about her murder. The other held a photo of John Morgan with even less data.

'Who is supposed to be updating this?' She swivelled on her heel, hearing it crunch on something underfoot. Looking down, she saw it was the heel itself that had given way. She slammed it back in place.

Garda Lei raised his hand like a shy schoolchild. 'Me, boss.

But I have to collate information before I can post anything practical. We're still doing interviews out at Pine Grove.'

'Have you anything to report?'

'Not really. Regarding Laura's murder, there are no witnesses except for Shane Santos, who found her body. He's given his statement, but he was there after the event so there's nothing new from that angle. In her press briefing the super asked for public assistance with dash-cam footage and the like. Nothing has come in yet.'

'Okay. Anything to add to John Morgan's board?'

'As I said, we're still interviewing residents and the site workers. We conducted house-to-house in the area. There are twenty-nine houses occupied, but most of the residents are out at work during the day. Two work from home, but their offices are at the rear of their houses. No one saw or heard anything unusual. Said the only thing they normally hear is the building going on in the phase two development.'

'Did Patrick Curran make a statement?'

'The site manager?' Boyd said.

She hadn't noticed him sliding into a seat at the back of the room.

'You met him,' she said. 'What did he have to say besides trying to sell you a house?' Damn. Why couldn't she keep her mouth shut?

'He was in shock. Couldn't believe anyone would hurt John.'

'Did you locate John's next of kin?'

'His parents are divorced and he had no siblings. Currently we have no contact details for either parent. Curran couldn't find anything on his file, but he said to talk to Gordon Collins. We have yet to interview him. John lived in a bedsit on Main Street. The keys were found on his person and a search was carried out there, but nothing suspicious was found. We took in his laptop, and his phone, which was in his pocket with his keys. They're with Gary now to see if he can find anything.'

'Detective McKeown, you were to look into tracing Laura Nolan's phone. Anything to report there?'

'The provider requested a warrant. As we only have the number and not the device, I tasked Gary with finding out what he could. He determined that the phone ceased working close to the vicinity where her body was found. I sent a team back out to do another fingertip search of the site. Hopefully they'll find something this time.'

'It was searched yesterday and nothing was found. After last night's storm, I doubt we'll find anything today. Has anyone got any good news? Where's Kirby?'

'Here, boss,' Kirby said as he entered. 'Sorry I'm late. Had to help Amy this morning. Her leg is acting up again.'

Lottie counted to ten in her head. Okay, it was Saturday and day two in the investigation, but her team looked bedraggled and unfocused. She supposed she appeared the same. She straightened her back. 'Come on, guys, we need something. A twenty-five-year old is not an island. She has to have friends and a social media presence. McKeown? Anything?'

All she could see was the top of his shaved head as he bent over his iPad, tapping furiously.

'Wait. Just a minute,' he said.

She did. The sounds in the room washed over her. The clinking of the old rads, Kirby's heavy breathing. The hum of laptops. McKeown's iPad.

When he raised his head, he had a smile on his face. 'You won't believe this, boss.'

'I haven't time for—'

'Laura Nolan was listed on a modelling website.' He turned the iPad around so the others could see.

She made her way across to him and he handed her the device. Laura's image, head and shoulders, depicted a beautiful young woman, eyes shining bright and hair swept seductively behind one ear, resting on a bare shoulder.

'Right One Modelling,' she read. 'Is that local?'

'Might just be a website.'

'Someone took her photo. Someone posted it with her details. Someone has a base, even if it's an attic or a shed. What else can you tell me about the site?'

McKeown left his iPad to one side and pulled his laptop towards him. 'The photographer's name and logo are imbedded on the bottom right of the photo. Greg Plunkett. It's a relatively new modelling and photographic agency in town. It might be worth a shot. I'll just check Facebook.' He tapped away. 'Shit. There's a closed group here with Plunkett as administrator.'

'And?'

After a few moments, he said, 'It looks to me like some sort of escort agency.'

'Really?' Lottie racked her brain to figure if this was illegal or not. 'Has this photographer got an address?'

'He has an office in Barrack Lane.' McKeown turned the laptop around so she could see the screen.

'Send me the details. Boyd, you're with me on this.'

'Hey, I found it,' McKeown said petulantly. 'Shouldn't I go?'

'Don't "hey" me, Detective McKeown,' she said.

'Apologies.'

'You need to dig into this Greg Plunkett and find out if his modelling is a front for sex workers.' She marched back to the front of the room. 'Also, Garda Brennan is at Laura's house. Join her there and as diplomatically as possible see if the mother knows about the modelling or if Laura was with an escort agency.'

He nodded, but his face told her it was the last place he wanted to be. Tough.

'Kirby, go back to the building site and get more information on John Morgan. I can't meet the super without something to tell her.' She looked around. 'You go too, Lei, and continue with the door-to-door and the site workers. Populate the board. I can't be looking at empty spaces with the photos of two murdered people staring at me.'

'Sure, boss,' the two men said.

'Anything from forensics? Those small footprints around Laura's body?'

'Nothing yet,' Boyd said.

'What about the dirt under her nails? Has the lab reported back?'

'Not yet. It was only yesterday and—'

'Kirby, follow up with the lab, and SOCOs too. Boyd, are you ready? We're going to grill this Greg Plunkett.'

33

He had shaved off his beard. The girl had seen him last night and he couldn't risk being recognised by her the next time. He sat at the kitchen table and watched the young woman robotically serve up breakfast. She was too thin and fragile-looking, not that anyone would notice. She never went outside. Lack of vitamin D, maybe.

He felt as if something dreadful was about to happen. He used to regularly have feelings of foreboding, but it had been a long time since the darkness had fallen like a weight behind his eyes.

He slipped his phone out of his pocket and tapped the news app. He closed his eyes, hoping there wasn't anything in the first few posts about the dead woman. When he opened them, he glanced at the headlines. She'd been demoted to the second level of interest. The first report was about the death at the Pine Grove housing development.

A tight grip of fear seized his chest and he struggled to breathe. Tapping into the story, he brought up the image of a house encircled with garda tape. Scrolling, he read quickly. The body had been found in a show home. A labourer from GC

Construction. No name yet. But he knew who it was. He'd known when he'd first heard reports yesterday.

He shut off the phone as the girl placed a plate in front of him.

The fried eggs had broken on the pan and looked like a flat, greasy omelette. He rarely showed aggression in the house, especially when he was due to work. But he couldn't help himself. All the years of suppression, of bending to *her* will, suddenly rose like a torrent, and he lashed out at the captive woman and screamed.

———

The strangled sound that came from his lips caused her to drop the spatula on the tiles she'd spent an hour scrubbing at six o'clock that morning. Grease splashed up on the cupboard doors and micro dots stained her legs. Hurriedly she picked up the offending article just as he lifted the plate of food and flung it at the wall behind her. She ducked automatically, though her reflexes of late had been slow. Too long cooped up in a small space. Too long with her mouth taped shut. Too long being forced to be subservient.

Shrinking against the stove, she dared not glance behind her at the mess streaking the wall. She kept her eyes focused on him. He tore at his hair and smacked his cheeks with his ugly fingers. She had been terrified since the day she'd been brought here, but this development caused her to be petrified. Her legs were like jelly, her hands trembled and she wanted to cry. She feared he was spiralling out of control.

'What are you looking at?' he snarled. 'Clean up this pigsty before she comes back.'

She cowered, expecting a blow. But the back door opened and shut as he retreated to his shed.

Lowering her shoulders, she exhaled with relief. At least he hadn't hit her. She'd fetched a cloth to clean up when she heard the front door. Terror shot through her all over again.

The woman was back.

34

Lottie suspected Greg Plunkett was more than a photographer. McKeown had emailed her further information that he'd uncovered.

'It seems to be a front for escorts,' she said.

Boyd said, 'I figure the ladies working for Right One are not sex workers, but they still accept money to accompany a man on a date. Selling sex isn't illegal, only paying for it. Very grey area.'

'Let's see what Mr Glamour Puss has to say.'

'Who?'

'Greg Plunkett.' She glanced at the image McKeown had forwarded. 'His photo looks like it was cloned from a Hollywood A-lister website. Probably airbrushed.'

She turned her phone with the photo towards him before stopping at a door halfway down Barrack Lane, which was located at the back of the town. The office was huddled in between a bike shop and a gift shop.

'You'd miss it if you weren't looking for it,' Boyd said.

She leaned on the brass doorbell and waited.

'Might be no one here on a Saturday,' he added.

An intercom beeped and an echoey voice asked, 'Have you an appointment?'

'I'm Detective Inspector Parker. I'd like a word with Mr Plunkett.'

'Sorry, but he only meets people by appointment.'

Lottie had had enough bullshit for one week. 'You can let me in to see him now or I'll return with ten squad cars to arrest him, and I'll make sure everyone knows what your office stands for.'

Boyd was shaking his head, a warning to cool it, but she had a dead woman lying on a slab in the morgue whose family needed answers.

The door buzzed open and they entered. Directly in front of them was a wooden staircase with a red runner up the centre. The walls were painted black, for God's sake. Quelling the urge to raise an eyebrow, she climbed the stairs, followed closely by Boyd.

The corridor on the upstairs landing led to a glass door with a desk behind it, where a pretty young woman sat applying mascara to what Lottie could only describe as fake lashes.

Flashing her ID badge, she said, 'Mr Plunkett? Is he here?'

'We only work a half-day today. He said to give him a minute or two. Take a seat.'

'I'll stand, thank you.' She would not be intimidated by Plunkett making her wait. Boyd sat in one of the faded navy velvet chairs. So much for a united front.

She paced the small space. The walls were bare, painted black like the hall, so there was nothing to look at, no reading material on the small glass table. Wouldn't a photographer have his photos on display?

'How long have you been here?' she asked the young woman.

'I start at nine, so not that long.'

'I mean, in this job.'

'Oh, sorry.' The woman zipped up her cosmetic bag and lifted a keyboard from her lap to the desk. 'About a year. Greg is a fantastic photographer. The girls love working with him.'

'I'm sure they do,' Lottie muttered, then smiled sweetly. 'Do you find much work for them, once they have their photos taken?'

'We help them compile a portfolio and provide work contacts. It's all very exciting.'

'Have you modelled?'

The girl blushed beneath her make-up. 'A bit. Nothing glamorous. But I love working for Greg.'

'Inspector Parker?' Plunkett walked towards her, hand outstretched. At least he hadn't approached Boyd first, because if he'd made that mistake, her temper would have spiked. 'You asked to see me?'

'I did. Can we talk in your office?'

'Of course. Cathy, pull up my diary. I need the list of locations for today's shoots.'

'Certainly,' the girl said, fluttering her fake eyelashes. Help me, God, Lottie thought.

She studied Greg Plunkett. His clean-shaven jaw was as sharp as his grey suit, but she felt his affability was strained. Trying to be nice? Maybe. And she concluded that his photo had not been altered. He was a handsome man, short fair hair and startling blue eyes.

As they entered his office, she wasn't impressed by its ordinariness. A small desk with a laptop on top, a chair behind the desk with another two chairs in the corner beside a filing cabinet. No photos on these walls either. Nothing to entice a young woman into modelling. It had to be a front for something else.

'What can I do for you?' He sat behind the desk, indicating the other two chairs. Boyd sat in the corner. Lottie remained standing.

'Are you aware that the body of a young woman was found yesterday?'

'I read about it online. Awful business.'

'How does this modelling agency work?'

Confusion knitted his brows. 'Why would you want to know that?'

She wasn't about to give him too much information. Laura's name had yet to be released to the media, but Twitter was at work. Anyhow, she wanted to see what he'd reveal first. 'It's part of our investigation. That's all I can say for the moment.'

His eyes jumped from hers to Boyd's and back again. She waited him out. The silence in the small space bore down on her shoulders like a heatwave. She wished she'd taken off her coat.

'Has this dead woman something to do with my agency?'

'You tell me.'

'I don't even know her name.'

Maybe he did or maybe he didn't, but she told him anyway. 'Laura Nolan.'

He pursed his lips and ran a finger along his chin, face like chalk. 'Name doesn't immediately mean anything.'

'You took her photograph.'

'Did I? I take a lot of photographs. I have over fifty young women and some young men registered with my agency. Let me check.' He fiddled with a laptop and eventually raised his head. 'Sorry, but this Nolan woman is not registered here.'

'Maybe you should check the names registered with your other agency?'

'What do you mean?' His eyes had taken on a cold, piercing glare.

'You also operate Right One Escorts.'

'What?'

'We found Laura's photo, taken by you, on that site.'

'If she paid for a photo shoot, I have no control over where she posts the pictures.'

'Come on, Greg. Quit the bullshit. Laura was brutally murdered. You took her photo. You run this modelling photography lark as a front.' She hoped he didn't ask her to prove it, because she didn't have the time for all that.

'It's just a dating site. It's not illegal.'

'I never said it was.'

He closed his eyes and squeezed the bridge of his nose before saying, 'What do you need?'

'Any records you have to do with Laura Nolan. And your employee database.'

'Cathy out there is the only staff I employ.'

'Really? How do you pay your escorts? You must have a register or database.'

His mouth dropped open. 'I... I... This is ludicrous.'

She tapped the floor with her toe and waited him out.

'Okay, okay. I register the girls on a consultancy basis. No wages.'

Bingo, Lottie thought. 'I see,' she said calmly. 'But you must know who these "consultants" are?'

'Look, they're not really consultants, just... companions, but I still can't give out their details without a warrant. GDPR and all that.'

'And all that,' she scoffed. 'What if it's one of your models who was brutally murdered?'

'I still can't give you anything.'

She decided to change direction. 'When did you set up your business?'

'Must be a year ago.'

'Why did you delve into the escort line of work?'

'I told you, it's just dating, and it's more lucrative than trying to find jobs for models.'

'More lucrative for you? Or the "companion"?'

'For everyone. It's beneficial to those who don't like online or traditional dating and those who don't want to form a commitment. We match the client to an appropriate woman. And then they date. End of.'

'Really? End of?'

'Yes.'

'That sounds like you are prostituting these women. You're nothing more than a modern-day pimp, Mr Plunkett.'

His face reddened so quickly she feared he was about to have a heart attack. It took a few moments before he calmed himself in the stuffy silence. 'I've done nothing wrong. I'd like you both to leave. If you have any further questions, you may direct them to my solicitor.'

Lottie extracted a slim file from her bag and slid a photo across the table towards Plunkett. 'Recognise her?'

He didn't look down. 'I said, you need to go through my solicitor.'

'Look at the photo, please.' It galled her to plead, but she couldn't leave empty-handed. And Boyd was as good as useless sitting mute in the corner. 'You took that photo.'

Plunkett briefly looked at the image, then concentrated his eyes on his lap. He gulped, and she knew he recognised the woman in the photo.

'Is that her?' His voice was devoid of its earlier swagger. 'The woman who was found dead yesterday?'

'Do you know her?'

'I remember her now. I took her photo a few months back. She wasn't really interested in the work involved with modelling. She said she was hard up for money as she needed a deposit to apply for a mortgage, so I told her about other options available to her here.'

'What else can you tell me about her?'

'I already told you, I can't give out personal information.'

'She's dead. I have to catch her murderer. I need your help.'

'Okay, so. She went on a date. Two nights ago. It was her first time.'

'Who was this date with?'

He scowled. 'You know I can't share that without a warrant. If you give me a minute, I'll get Cathy to print off Laura's information for you.'

'Ask her to email it to me too.' She passed over a card with her work details.

He went out to the reception area, card in hand.

Lottie turned to Boyd. 'You're too quiet. Have you nothing to contribute?'

'You're doing a good job getting under his skin. I didn't want to break the flow.'

'You're just great.' Sarcasm laced her words and he caught it.

'I was observing Plunkett. He's cagey as hell.'

Plunkett returned and handed a single typed page to Lottie. 'That's all I have.'

'I could have got that from her mother.'

'Well, now you can compare this to what her mother tells you. I'm sure there will be discrepancies. Young women have been known to provide me with false details.'

'I'd have thought you'd have to verify them?'

'As much as I can, but I'm not running a detective agency.'

Lottie bit back her retort. 'What can you tell me regarding Laura's date from two nights ago? Who was he and where did they meet?'

'I'm repeating myself here, but I honestly can't say who she was matched with, sorry. And I've no idea where they went.'

'How do you get paid?'

'I get a retainer.' He paused, hand in the air. 'You could check her bank account. See if any extra money was paid to her from the client. But I don't get involved in that sort of thing.'

'What would this extra money be for?'

'I'm sure you can use your imagination, Inspector.'

'Is it a regular occurrence? These extras?' Her stomach roiled. If this was the case, it pointed towards the women being more than just escorts, and if so, Plunkett was in the shit.

'Not that I know of.'

She glanced at the page with Laura's details and was unable to see anything she didn't already know. A wasted exercise. She really needed to know who Laura had been with the night she died. She'd have to get that warrant.

Boyd hung back while she went to the door. He picked up a business card from the desk. 'How do you advertise your escort... I mean dating agency?'

'My website has an enquiry tab. I also run a closed Face-book group. You send a message requesting to join.'

'So when you accept someone onto this Facebook group, you allow them access to the site?'

'No. The Facebook group informs them about the Right One website. There's criteria and an online application, which comes to me.'

'I must give it a go. I've tried everything to meet a nice woman. I miss having someone to take out for a meal, to chat with, to share with. This is the first time I've come across Right One. The circumstances are tragic, but I'm glad to have met you, Mr Plunkett.'

Boyd held out his hand and Plunkett shook it warily.

Outside, Lottie jumped into the car and kept her head down. 'That was priceless, Boyd. You were brilliant.'

'You think I was joking? I can't get you to agree to go for a meal, so I thought, why not try—'

'Drive the bloody car, Boyd.'

He laughed as he set off, and despite the enormity of their investigation, she had to laugh too.

35

Garda Martina Brennan was on the verge of withdrawing her name from the FLO database. She had messed up on her previous assignment, and here she was with another young child throwing her anxious glances. How long could she stand it?

The doorbell went. Hopefully not reporters. Diana opened the door, and a familiar, unwelcome voice reverberated from the hall.

Sam McKeown. Probably checking up on her. He could feck right off. With that thought, she watched him walk into the sitting room and sit on the large recliner armchair. Laura's mother remained by the door, eyeing him, then turned her attention to Martina.

'Your colleague wants to ask me some questions. Would you mind taking Aaron to the kitchen for a snack?'

Yes, I would mind, Martina wanted to say. She needed to hear what McKeown had to say first-hand. But she had no option but to take the youngster's hand and lead him from the room. She left the door ajar, hoping she'd catch the gist of the conversation.

When Martina left the room with the little boy, McKeown exhaled a soft breath, easing the tension from his body. Things were so strained between them recently that you could cut the air with a knife. He indicated for Diana to sit opposite him. The woman looked tiny, almost folded in on herself in the large armchair. Like a child. A grey pallor drained her face.

'I'm so sorry about the death of your daughter. We are doing all we can to find whoever did this.'

'Like what?' Her voice was just a whisper as she choked down tears. 'Tell me what you're doing.'

'We have a number of leads. That's why I'm here.'

'Go on.' She rooted up her sleeve for a tissue.

'You need to brace yourself, because you might not like what I'm about to say and I apologise in advance.'

'Detective, just tell me what you came here to say. Nothing can be worse than finding out my daughter was murdered.' There was steel in her tone that made McKeown shiver.

'Right. Okay.' He felt like a shit, but there was nothing for it but to blurt it out. 'Did you know Laura was registered with a dating agency? An escort agency.'

'What? I don't understand. Don't be silly.' Diana stretched the tissue between her hands and it ripped down the middle, sending dust motes into the air.

'She was signed up with Right One Escorts. It's like being paid to go on a date.'

'That's crazy. My Laura? She wasn't a prostitute.'

'I'm sure she wasn't. It's not like that.'

'What *is* it like then?' Her voice had a sharper edge to it and the tissue had disappeared back up her sleeve, leaving fragments floating to her knee.

'The agency matches her with a client and they go on a

date. No strings or anything. Usually just dinner and drinks. She'd get paid for it.'

'And you know this how, Detective?'

'Research. My boss, Detective Inspector Parker, is meeting the person who runs the agency as we speak.'

'Well, I knew nothing about it. You must be mistaken.'

'Laura never mentioned anything about it?'

'Not a word.'

'She never said who she might be meeting the other night?'

'No.'

'Any other time?'

'Never.'

'And you had no idea she was entertaining dates as an escort?'

'Will you stop?' Diana hauled herself out of the chair and stood looking down at him. 'My Laura had a little boy. She worked hard to make ends meet and I helped where I could, but hand on heart I know my own daughter, and she would never have sold herself for money. I think you should leave now, Detective.'

She seemed unnerved and despite her grief he thought she might be lying. Or hiding something. About what, he had no idea.

'We want to find the person who killed your daughter. Please, if you know anything, you have to tell us.'

'All I know is that my daughter is never going to walk through that door again. I have to bury her in a dark grave and I have to rear her son. Your job is to find the bastard who did this to us.'

He rose and leaned against the door while she turned her back to him at the front window. 'Can you at least tell me who the father of your grandson is? We need to rule him out of our investigation.'

'I can't tell you because I don't know. She didn't even have a regular boyfriend, as far as I knew. Aaron was the result of a one-night stand and Laura was four months gone before she realised she was pregnant.' Diana swirled back towards him. 'She told me she had no idea of the name of the father and I doubt he's even aware that he has a child.'

'Okay, that's fine. Thank you. I'm sorry for upsetting you, but one last thing. Do you know a Greg Plunkett?'

He kept his eyes on her and witnessed the little blood in her face drain away.

'No, never heard of him. Is he... is he Aaron's father?'

'Not that we know. Are you sure you don't know him?' McKeown asked.

'I don't, and it'd answer you better to be out on the street, knocking on doors, finding my girl's murderer, rather than harassing her grieving mother.'

He felt he had to press further, or maybe try a different angle. 'A man was murdered yesterday, Diana. Out at the Pine Grove development. It's that new housing estate being built by GC Construction. The murdered man was John Morgan. Have you ever heard of him?'

Diana sank into the armchair once again. 'Someone else was murdered?' Her voice was brittle. 'Is it the same killer? The same bastard who killed my Laura?'

'We don't know. It might not be connected to Laura at all, but we have to explore everything.'

'So this madman might kill someone else?'

'We can't jump to conclusions. As I said, Mr Morgan's death probably has nothing to do with Laura's. I only wanted to know if you'd heard of him. I can show you his photo.'

He took out his phone and scrolled through. 'This may not be pleasant to look at, but I'd appreciate it if you'd give it a quick look. Then I'll leave you in peace.'

She nodded half-heartedly. He approached, holding the

phone out to her. She took it and bit her lip tightly. After a cursory glance at the photograph, she handed back the phone.

'Sorry.'

'You never saw him with Laura?'

'No.'

'She ever mention John Morgan, or the Pine Grove estate?'

Gulping loudly, Diana said, 'Laura once talked about moving into a house with her son. But she was turned down for a mortgage because she hadn't enough saved. She may have mentioned the new houses at Pine Grove. But all that was over a year ago. Before... Anyhow, it can't mean anything, can it?' She broke down again, searching frantically for the shredded tissue.

'I'm not sure, but thank you.' McKeown pocketed his phone. He felt like a total bollox now, and had probably crossed a line, but he was determined to get facts.

As he left her sitting there, with more questions than answers, McKeown was full sure Diana Nolan had been economical with the truth.

36

The morning sky had brightened up a little, though a chill air penetrated his heavy jacket. Kirby doused his cigar, secreted it in a pocket and wiped his hands on his trousers. He had parked at the Pine Grove outer cordon and walked past the show home, now encircled with crime-scene tape. Activity was high, with SOCOs continuing their work following a break for the night. He thought of entering the house to see if Grainne had anything new to report, but decided he'd best continue to the site office to do what he'd been tasked with.

Cars were parked in the driveways of some of the houses, but it was eerily quiet with no one about. It felt like a ghost estate. Even more so as he walked through the gate in the chain-link fence leading to the partially built scaffold-surrounded houses.

The site office was housed in a cabin to the rear of the building site, and Kirby bemoaned the fact that his shoes were now saturated with muck. He knocked on the door, and without waiting for a reply, turned the handle and entered.

A burst of heat greeted him. A Superser gas heater blew out hot air, and he instinctively loosened his tie. The space was cluttered, the floor muddy. Drawings and plans, with curling corners, were taped to the walls. A man and a woman sat either side of a desk overflowing with papers.

'I'm looking for Patrick Curran,' Kirby said.

'That's me,' the man said, without rising. His eyes were bloodshot; his hair stuck to his sweaty scalp. A man who'd had little sleep.

Kirby introduced himself and waited.

Curran ran his fingers up and down his chin. 'Lucky to get me today; we don't normally open the site on weekends. But sure there's nothing normal about today anyhow.'

The woman stood and held out her hand. 'Charlie Lennon. Estate agent. I was just discussing with Patrick what our next step might be.'

Her grip was warm and firm. No wilting female caricature here.

'Good to meet you, Charlie.'

'I can't say the circumstances are ideal,' she said, and moved to stand by a wall.

Curran leaned over the desk to shake Kirby's hand. Callused and hard, in stark contrast to Charlie's. 'Any word on what happened to John?'

'We're following a number of leads. I'd like to ask you a few questions.'

'I made a statement, isn't that enough?' Patrick curled into the uncomfortable-looking office chair.

Charlie picked up a coat from the back of a chair and a large leather handbag from the floor. 'I made my statement too, so I'll leave you to it. We can go over the plans on Monday, Patrick.' She nodded to him and dipped her head at Kirby as she walked to the door. A blast of cold air entered the space as she stepped outside. It disappeared when she shut the door.

'How can I help you, Detective?' Curran's voice rasped with tiredness. His nose was bright red. From a night of hard drinking? Kirby knew all about that and was glad he had Amy around to moderate his life.

'We're finding it difficult to get a handle on the murdered lad, John Morgan. I'm hoping you can fill in a few gaps, Mr Curran.'

'It's Patrick. I'll try, but I hardly knew the poor sod. He'd been with us less than a year.'

'Where did he work before that?'

'I sent his CV over to the station. Didn't you get it?'

'The details on it are sparse, to say the least.'

'Mind if I smoke?'

'Only if I can.'

While Patrick fumbled a cigarette from a crumpled pack Kirby found his cigar in his pocket. As they both lit up, acrid smoke filled the small space. Patrick leaned back and slid open a small window behind him. Kirby welcomed the chill air and waited for the other man to fill the yawning space with words.

'John Morgan was recommended by the boss man,' Patrick said. 'Gordon Collins.'

'Was that unusual?'

'I've worked for Collins for nigh on ten years and he's a good man. I'd never question anything he says or does.'

'Is that why you didn't question his recommendation?'

Patrick flicked ash to the floor and inhaled another drag. 'John turned out to be an excellent worker. No complaints from me. He got promoted to foreman. Did a good job. Such a loss. Only a lad. It's hard to believe he's gone.'

'Bit young to be a foreman, wasn't he?' Kirby recalled that John Morgan was twenty-six years old.

'He had great experience in Australia. He worked in the mines there for two years. No job too hard for him.'

'We need to locate his family.'

'I think his parents were divorced and his mother lives

abroad. Not sure where his dad is. He never talked much about his family.'

'Girlfriend? Boyfriend?'

'He seemed to be a bit of a loner.'

'Unusual for a young man not to have any friends. Did he play sports? Hurling, football? Anything?' Kirby was grasping at the proverbial, and Patrick knew it by the narrow eye he shot at him.

'I know as much as you, Detective.'

'Really?'

'I shared this office with him. But he was all work. No personal talk out of him at all.'

'This his desk?' Kirby pointed to the small square table behind him.

'He didn't even have a drawer, so you won't make any earth-shattering discoveries there.'

Kirby doused his cigar and went over to the desk. He flicked through the papers on top and searched around on the floor. Like Patrick said, no earth-shattering discovery.

'He wasn't a ghost,' Kirby said.

'Did you search his flat?'

'Yes. The keys were in his pocket.' Kirby recalled the sparsely furnished bedsit. They'd found nothing helpful on his phone either. 'He must have had a life outside of work,' he said, half to himself.

'If he had, I didn't know about it.'

'What happened to your previous foreman?'

'Retired.'

'Were any of the workers here aggrieved when John was promoted?'

'Not at all. No one wants the responsibility any more. You can talk to them.'

'We are in the process of their interviews.' Kirby scratched his scalp. No one on the site had anything useful to offer. John Morgan was definitely a fucking ghost.

37

As Kirby left the site office, a silver Range Rover pulled up at the chain-link fence. He watched as the door opened and two feet shod in what looked to him like designer wellingtons swung out onto the ground. The man who followed the feet was tall and slim, dressed in denim jeans with a green wax jacket swinging in the breeze over a checked shirt. A hand went to the black fedora on his head. Here was someone who wanted to impress, Kirby thought, or was at pains to portray someone he was not.

He approached Kirby, and after the detective showed his ID, the man removed his hat, revealing dark shiny hair cut as sharp as his sapphire-blue eyes. He was younger than Kirby had first thought. Early to mid fifties, perhaps. Tanned skin, but not leathery. Long fingers gripped the hat to his chest with one hand while he proffered the other.

'Gordon Collins,' he said, gripping Kirby's hand firmly. 'Welcome to my flagship project, about to go down the drain.'

'Detective Larry Kirby.'

'This about young John Morgan? I can't get my head around it.'

You and me both, Kirby thought. 'Can I have a word?'

'Is Patrick in there?' Collins pointed to the office with his hat.

'Yes.'

'My car, then. Patrick is a nosy fucker.' He turned his back on Kirby and climbed into the jeep.

'Nice leatherwork,' Kirby commented on the cream livery as he sat into the warmth.

'A pain in the arse to keep clean. How can I help you, Detective?'

'Tell me about John. I believe you recommended him for the job here.'

'I did.'

'How did you know him?'

'Through his mother, Brenda.'

'Oh. Right.'

'It's not like that.' A sly smirk crossed Collins's face before his lips turned down. 'A business acquaintance.'

'We haven't been able to unearth any next of kin.'

'I'm not surprised. Brenda is a private woman.'

'I want to make contact with her. She has to be informed about her son's death before his name is released to the media.'

'She already knows. I phoned her.'

'Hmph,' Kirby snorted. 'We need to call on her in an official capacity.' He didn't like Collins's smugness. 'I'd appreciate it if you could give me her number and address.'

'I can, but she lives in London.'

'Right, I still need it. Do you know her well?'

'She bought one of my houses. Her intention was to relocate here within the year.' Collins peered through the windscreen at a point somewhere in the distance. 'I doubt that will happen now.'

'Because her son is dead or for some other reason?'

'I think she intended living here with John until he got his life sorted.'

'Was there something wrong in his life?'

'No, I don't mean it like that. I meant until he got settled.'

'He wasn't settled?'

'You're twisting what I'm saying.'

'Forgive me, Mr Collins, but we are finding it difficult to obtain any information about John. I'd appreciate your help.'

'Look, I gave him a job as a favour to his mother.'

'You do know her well then?'

'Just casually. Met her in London when I was at an investment conference there. She's in banking.'

'Okay. Go on.' Kirby wasn't at all sure that Collins was revealing the full extent of his relationship with Mrs Morgan, but he didn't want to stop his flow.

'John had been in Australia with his dad for two years, working in the mines. Back-breaking work. He made good money but gambled it away. As I said, I met Brenda at a conference. Listened to her story and she asked if I could give her son a job. She vouched for him and he turned out to be an excellent hire.'

'Have you any idea who would want him dead?'

'No. Unless a gambling debt came back to haunt him.'

'An old one, or something more recent?'

'He promised he was finished with all that. I had no reason to doubt him. Patrick never brought anything to my attention.'

'Patrick didn't mention the gambling to me at all,' Kirby said.

'Then I believe John was over it.'

'If not a gambling debt, can you think of anything else?'

'His mother asked the same thing on the phone and I'll give you the same answer. I can't think of any reason why someone would kill the lad.'

Kirby stared out the windscreen at the muddy site. 'He seems to have been a loner.'

'From what I know, he found it hard to make friends and kept himself to himself. A hard worker, he went above and beyond what he had to do. He got on with his colleagues. It's a shame that the good die young.'

'So they say.' Kirby held out hope for a long life for himself. 'John walked into the foreman's job pretty handy. Was there any pushback from the rest of the workers here?'

'Not that I'm aware of. Patrick didn't mention anything and no one came to me to complain.'

Scratching his chin, Kirby wondered if there was a question he should be asking, but he couldn't think what it might be.

'You can email or text Mrs Morgan's details to me.' He handed over his card.

'I'll do it straight away.'

'And John's dad, how can we contact him?'

'You should ask his mother that question. He might still be in Oz.' Collins turned noisily on the leather seat to face him. 'My firm is in financial difficulty and I'm in the process of closing down the site. Temporarily, until cash flow improves. Don't try to link John's death to my money troubles.'

Kirby put his hand on the door, ready to exit. 'We'll do what we have to do.'

'I warn you, though, Brenda is a very powerful woman in the financial world. You'd do well not to cross her, and I know she will want her son's killer brought to justice. Sooner rather than later.'

'Thanks for the heads-up.'

Once he was out of the jeep, Kirby lit his cigar again. Running a hand through his wild, bushy hair, he walked slowly through the unfinished part of the estate until he reached his car. He felt more confused than ever.

———

Gordon sat in his Range Rover for ages after watching the detective walk off puffing on a cigar. He noticed a cement lorry arriving to pour foundations. Had Patrick not got the bloody memo? All supplies were to be cancelled.

He jumped out and clamped his hat onto his head. At the cabin door, he halted, turned and glanced over at the work that had been completed – and the work yet to be done once he got his finances sorted. But in an instant, all that paled as he thought of John Morgan. The boy had been a good worker. True. And he'd taken him under his wing. But his mother was a bloody nuisance. Brenda had lived in his ear regularly, wanting news about her son. Was he gambling? How was he doing at work? He wasn't the lad's father, for God's sake. But he'd mentored him as best he could. He had never wanted a son. Too much bloody trouble. He adored his daughters.

He entered the office to take his frustration out on Patrick, who rarely talked back. Just what Gordon needed.

38

As she washed down the kitchen, she felt the presence behind her. She didn't turn round. Kept her concentration on the wall. On her hand holding the damp cloth.

'What did you do to my tiles?'

She couldn't answer even if she'd wanted to, which she didn't.

'Answer me!'

Now she faced the woman so she could see her duct-taped lips.

'Oh, for heaven's sake. You're totally stupid. Just like him.' The woman marched forward and tore the tape away, causing a painful tingle on her cracked lips, then stood and scrutinised her.

'It was an accident,' she croaked.

The woman ran her finger down the wall and smelled it. 'Eggs. You threw eggs at my wall, didn't you?'

'N-no. Y-yes. S-sorry.'

'You *will* be sorry when I finish with you. Clean it up. I want it sparkling and smelling of lemons. Do you understand plain English?'

'Y-yes.'

'Well then, why are you standing there with your gob hanging open? Get to work.'

The young woman returned to her task. Reaching into the sink with the cloth, she felt a sharp pain on the back of her head as the woman struck her forcefully. She wanted to cry out, but instead she bit down on her lips until they bled. When the presence disappeared from behind her, she rinsed the cloth and got back to work.

She wondered if she would ever escape, but that was the wrong thought. She had to concentrate on *when*, not *if*.

39

It was almost eleven a.m. when Shannon woke up. Her thumping head and the ache in her stomach was the result of consuming too much alcohol and not enough food. Easing her feet to the floor, she averted her eyes from the tangle of clothes strewn around the room. A glimpse at the mascara-streaked pillow told her she had fallen asleep without removing her make-up.

And then she remembered.

The uneasy feeling of being followed home.

She thought of phoning Jess to tell her about it, but then remembered Jess would be at work. Work!

'Oh no,' she groaned. George was so annoyed with her that he hadn't woken her for work. Another sick day wouldn't go down well with her manager, much as she hated working as a cleaner in the hospital. Maybe she should check in with the escort agency to see if anyone had been matched with her.

She scrambled around under her pillow until she found her phone. Dead. With aching limbs she searched for the charger. Still in the socket on the wall. She plugged in the phone and waited. As it came to life, she saw the day and date appear. Saturday. No work. Thank God.

Curling up on the bed, phone in hand, she was unable to dislodge the feeling she'd had on the way home last night. And then there was that shadow outside the front door. Should she tell George? No, she'd have to pay him back first. She was afraid to ask him what she owed. No doubt he'd throw the figure around throughout the day.

Once the phone had enough charge, she watched the screen light up with notifications, missed calls and messages.

'What the hell?' She opened her eyes wide, wondering what was going on.

The notifications were from Facebook and Instagram. But the missed calls and messages were all from Jess.

She read through the texts frantically.

John Morgan was dead. How? When?

She scanned the rest of Jess's messages. They mainly consisted of questions. *Where are you? Answer your phone? Did you hear? Reply asap. Come on. Is it the John you knew? He's dead. Murdered.*

She reread the last message.

Murdered.

Her hands shook uncontrollably. She dropped the phone on the bed. What was going on? The only thing she knew with certainty was that she was terrified.

After showering and looping her hair in a messy bun, Shannon dressed in a fresh pair of jeans and a white knitted jumper. She pulled on her socks and boots, and grabbed a rain jacket from the back of the bedroom door before making her way downstairs.

'The dead has arisen at last,' George said when she entered the kitchen.

'Thought you had work to catch up on.'

'I'm minding Davy, seeing as my drunk sister who offered to help is hungover.'

'You could have called me.' She slipped a slice of bread into the toaster.

'You think I didn't try? You were dead to the world. I did everything except throw a basin of cold water over you.'

'Okay. Sorry. I'm not going out tonight.'

'Where are you headed now?'

'To meet Jess.'

'Really?'

'Yes, really.' She flicked the switch on the toaster and the bread popped up, still limp. Without waiting to butter it, she bit off a corner and chewed. 'Did you hear any more about that girl's murder?'

'Only what's on the news.'

'Jess said someone else was killed. A man.'

'I read that online. Some builder out at that fancy new development. Pine Grove.'

'That's going to be a fab estate when it's finished. I'm going to live there one day. Did it say who it was or what happened to him?'

'No name yet. Why? Do you know him?'

'How would I know if I know him, Einstein, if I don't know his name?' She wondered how Jess had the name if it hadn't yet been released. Probably all over Twitter.

'God, you really need to give up the drink. You're like ten bags of cats with a hangover.'

'I'm just hungry.' She turned to leave. 'I'll get a chicken fillet roll at the garage on my way into town.'

'Do me a favour, seeing as you spent all my money last night.'

'What do you want? A double chicken fillet roll?'

'No, take Davy with you. You told me last night you'd mind

him, and I have work to do or I'll be fired and then we're fucked.' He pointed to his laptop on the table.

'But he's sick.'

'A few goes on the swings in the park might perk him up. It's not good for a kid to be cooped up all day.'

'If you lend me a twenty, I'll take him with me.'

'Jesus, Shannon, I'm not made of money. I'll get his coat.'

'Money first.'

He flicked through his wallet. 'I only have a fifty.'

She snatched it from his hand. 'I'll bring back the change. Promise.'

———

After the plate-throwing incident, he couldn't relax in his usual safe place. He got in the car and left the house just as *she* arrived home. Good, because he was unable to face her. Not now. Not after all that had happened.

An invisible magnet drew him to Cairnbeg, the sprawling housing estate he'd been in the night before. He parked on the opposite side to the house where he'd seen her enter and eased back the seat, scooting down out of sight.

After a while, the door opened and out she came. A childish bobble hat on her head and a purple rain jacket. What was she waiting for? Come on, pretty girl, let's get going, he thought.

She stretched back her hand, and that was when he saw the stroller.

'A kid. Another one with a kid! Do they all have fucking kids?' When his breath fogged up the windscreen, he realised he'd been talking aloud. Could his life get any worse?

He kept watch as she made her way through the estate. Follow her? Yes. In the car? No. She could be going somewhere he couldn't drive. On foot, then.

He found his scarf on the back seat and locked the car.

Tightening the scarf against the sharp mid-morning breeze, he fell into step behind her. She was walking slowly, so he eased his pace. If she glanced behind her, who would she see? A man with a hat pulled low over his forehead, a scarf up around his mouth. His jacket was black, nondescript like his trousers.

Maybe he could catch up. Make small talk. Find out what made her tick. No, keep your distance and don't make a mistake. His thoughts echoed what *she* would say, and that enraged him. He clenched his fists in his pockets and walked as slowly as he could without appearing more suspicious than he supposed he was already.

———

Sitting on the cold bench in the park, Shannon kept her eyes focused on Davy. His spots had died down a little and she hoped the contagious phase had passed. Plus, she didn't want anyone commenting on his chickenpox. Jess could be insensitive at times.

Checking her phone again with one eye on the boy, she found that there was no update from her friend since she'd texted to say she'd meet her. About to put the phone away and get up to push the child on the swing, it rang. She gazed at the caller ID. What was *he* ringing her for? Everything was supposed to be done through the web portal.

'Hi,' she said tentatively.

'Shannie. I've got a date for you. Tonight. Interested?'

'Sure. Hope he's loaded. I'm bloody broke.'

'He knows you're not to pay for anything. I'll send him your number to make the arrangements.'

'Why not do it through the portal?'

'Bit awkward at the moment. Did you hear the news?'

'About what?'

'The woman who was murdered. The guards are all over it,

but you've nothing to worry about. It'll blow over in a day or two.'

'What are you talking about?' A creeping itch spread up her spine and settled at the nape of her neck. Fear. 'Why would the guards be on to you?'

'I didn't say that. Don't worry your pretty head. I'm dealing with it. Have a good night tonight.'

He rang off before she could quiz him further. He'd referred to the murdered girl, Laura Nolan. She'd met her last year. And what about John Morgan? If Jess had got the name right. Was his murder linked to Laura's? Did that mean she was in danger too?

She glanced up to see Davy dangling from the monkey rings by his little hands.

'Jesus Christ, Davy! How did you get up there?' She ran towards him.

'Nice man helped me.'

'What man? Davy! What man?'

'He's gone.'

'Where?' She looked all around but saw no one else.

'Push me on the swing now.'

'Where is the man?'

'Don't know. Push me?'

'Sure.' She lifted him down and brought him to the swings.

The little hairs on the back of her neck refused to lie down. She had the same feeling she'd had last night.

She was being watched.

40

The young guard was trying hard to be friendly and helpful. Despite that, she was getting under Diana's skin like a pulsing pimple. She wanted space and peace.

'Martina, would you bring Aaron out for fresh air? Just to get him out of the house. I'm not up to it.'

The bloody guard refused. 'I'm sorry, Diana. I have to stay with both of you.'

Was she afraid of separating them? Had she an ulterior motive? Diana didn't have to feign a headache to escape, because her head was already thumping.

'I'm going to lie down, then.'

'I'll bring you up a cup of tea,' Martina said.

'No, I want to close my eyes for a half-hour. You okay with Aaron down here?'

'Erm, yeah. Sure.'

She didn't look sure at all, but Diana couldn't worry about that. She needed headspace.

In her room, she flung herself on her unmade bed, wanting to scream. Crying and screaming worked for some, didn't it? She felt lost in a sea of putrid uncertainty. That detective with his questions had totally unnerved her. Why had she mentioned Laura being turned down for a mortgage? Would they investigate that further? If so, what would they discover?

And what about that other murder? John Morgan. And Laura as an escort? What the hell was that about? Was it even true, what the detective had said? He'd have no reason to lie to her. It must be true.

Had Laura got herself involved in a den of iniquity?

Like mother, like daughter.

———

While Boyd was busy drafting a warrant to obtain access to Greg Plunkett's database, complaining that it'd be difficult to haul a judge off a golf course on a Saturday, Lottie talked to McKeown.

'How did it go with Diana Nolan?'

'Not great. She's on edge, which is to be expected with the shock of her daughter's murder. But I sensed she was hiding something. Then again, I could be wrong.'

'Martina might get her to open up.' Lottie thought for a moment. 'You don't think Diana killed her own daughter, do you?'

'No, nothing like that, even though she has no one to corroborate her alibi. She was minding her grandson that night. She's thin as a whippet. No way she'd be able to haul Laura's body to where she was found. Plus, Laura would have had no difficulty overpowering her.'

'She could have had help. Motive, though?'

'None that I can think of.'

'And she's left to raise Laura's son,' Lottie said, 'so I doubt she'd have killed her.'

'She did mention that Laura was turned down for a mortgage. She was looking to buy a townhouse.'

'Greg Plunkett said she needed money for a deposit. Where was she looking to buy?'

McKeown looked at Lottie earnestly. 'Diana said she mentioned Pine Grove.'

She pulled up straight. 'What? Where we found John Morgan's body. Could their murders be linked?'

'Different MO. Just a coincidence.'

She thought he was probably right. 'I suppose it's the only new development around town at the moment. But you'd think she might have looked to rent somewhere first, or get on the council housing list.'

Kirby walked in as she settled behind her desk.

'The very man,' she said. 'How'd you get on?'

'Met the developer, Gordon Collins. He's one swish guy. You should have seen the jeep he's driving. Swear to God it has cream leather seats and him in and out of building sites.'

'What did he have to say?'

'John Morgan's mother, Brenda, asked Collins to give John a job. The mother lives in London. Big in banking over there. I did wonder how Collins came to know so much about her and the family. The father is in Australia – years now, according to him – and that's where John worked before developing a gambling addiction.'

'Really?'

'Collins says John was clean, but there might be something there. I for one know how hard it is to kick that particular habit.'

'Okay. I'll have to contact the mother and inform her of—'

'Collins already told her.'

'What?' She shook her head. 'London, you said?'

'Yep, and he confirmed that she'd bought a house from him.'

'Did you get her contact details?'

'Yes.' He forwarded her what Collins had sent him.

'Anything else?'

'I'll look into John's gambling. Maybe he relapsed and was killed over a gambling debt.'

'Maybe. I wish Lynch was here. She's great at trawling through bank details.'

'Boyd isn't too bad at it either.'

'Request a warrant for John Morgan's financials and see what turns up. The mother might give her consent, but no harm working on it just in case. And while you're at it, draw up one for Laura Nolan's finances too. Get digging.'

'Right, boss.'

As Kirby left her office, Boyd appeared in the doorway waving a sheet of paper. 'I have the warrant drafted for Plunkett's database.'

'Bring it to the super. She can read over it before it goes to the judge.'

'Do you think his operation is a matter for the vice unit?'

'Probably, but we need to investigate if he's involved in murder first. If Farrell mentions it, fob her off. We need to keep it under our control for now.'

'If you're sure?' He turned to leave.

'Boyd?'

'I'd like you to call on Charlie Lennon, the estate agent.'

His face brightened, and she felt bad about dousing his enthusiasm for a new home. 'Not to buy a house. I need to find out what she knows about Gordon Collins and the Pine Grove set-up.'

'All the workers have been interviewed, and from reading back over the interview notes, it appears no one had a bad word to say about John Morgan. That said, none of them had any dealings with him outside of work or knew what he was really like.'

'I'd like to get a handle on Patrick Curran and Gordon Collins. See if your Ms Lennon can throw any light on them.'

'*My* Ms Lennon? Come on, that's not fair.' He'd disappeared before she could apologise. Since when did Boyd become sensitive to a bit of banter?

She stared at the phone number for Brenda Morgan and tried to formulate the questions she needed to ask the grieving mother. The main question being, who would want to kill her only son?

41

Cafferty's was unusually quiet when Boyd arrived to meet Charlie Lennon. The estate agent was seated at a small table. He gave her a wave when she noticed him. Her smile seemed to brighten her white blouse in the relatively dim corner. He ordered a house special sandwich and sat across from her, wondering how he was going to eat such a large sandwich without making an arse of himself.

'Glad you could make time to meet me at such short notice,' he said.

'You're lucky to get me. I came into the office to check something. I only work a half-day on Saturdays.' She put down her sandwich and dabbed her lips with a napkin, then straightened the knees of her dark blue trousers. 'You didn't give me any hints, but I'm excited to know if you might be buying in Pine Grove.'

He felt his cheeks flush. Time to set her straight, he thought, as his sandwich arrived along with a pot of tea.

She continued to talk. 'With interest rates sky-rocketing, and even though it's hard to negotiate on a new house, I'm sure I could get the price reduced a little, if you're dead set on it.'

'Eh, I'm still not sure. The building work is being halted next week, so there's no rush, is there?'

'It's a temporary glitch. Happens all the time. Cash flow and boring stuff. Best to have your name on the list with a holding deposit.'

'I'll think about it.' He poured his tea and added a drop of milk. 'Charlie, I asked to meet you to discuss John Morgan's murder.'

She cradled her mug of aromatic coffee, ran her tongue around her teeth and looked at him. 'So you're not interested in buying in Pine Grove after all?'

'I have a lot to consider and I need to talk to the bank, but I haven't ruled it out.' As he spoke the words, he knew they were true.

'I don't think your partner was too impressed.'

Therein lay the problem. 'It's just that we're what you'd call a blended family.' He thought about that for a moment. Were they even a family, blended or not? 'I promise I'll get back to you once we reach a decision.'

'Right.' She placed her mug on the table. 'What do you want to ask me about in relation to the murder?'

'I'm aware that you didn't recognise the body at the time of the discovery, but did you know John Morgan?'

'I didn't recognise him because he was dead. It's in my statement. I may have seen him on site, but I knew nothing about him.'

'Okay. What can you tell me about Patrick Curran?'

'Why do you want to know about Patrick? Tell me, Mark, is this even proper procedure, interviewing me here?' She swept her hand around the pub.

'I think you might be able to help me. An interview in a sterile environment doesn't always yield results.' He sipped his tea, ignoring the oversized sandwich beginning to sag on the plate.

'Does that mean anything I say can't be taken down and used in a court of law? Or whatever the wording is.' She smiled brightly.

'Correct.' Then he thought about it. What if she revealed something critical to the investigation? But they had nothing much to go on yet, so if she imparted a nugget of useful information, it was better than nothing. 'I asked you about Patrick Curran.'

'I only know him in a professional capacity.' She grabbed her mug once again.

'Is there anything I need to be aware of?'

'Patrick is a good family man, from what I hear. Great to deal with. There. Nothing for you to concern yourself with. Try pinning the murder on someone else.'

'I'm not pinning anything on anyone.'

'Seems like it from where I'm sitting.'

The glint had departed from her eyes, and even her teeth had lost their sheen, probably from the coffee she'd been drinking.

'I'm sorry, Charlie. I thought that as you're a person looking in from the outside, maybe you could help. I apologise.'

She abandoned her coffee, wrapped the remains of her sandwich in a napkin and slipped it into her bag. The only sound was the monotonous drone coming from the television behind the bar. Boyd looked at his own sandwich. His stomach rumbled, but there was no way he could get a bite without dropping half of it down his shirt. He should have asked for a knife and fork.

Eventually, her hand on the strap of her bag, eyes penetrating, she said, 'I'm waiting for you to ask me about Gordon Collins.'

'Go on then, what can you tell me about him?'

'Collins is the polar opposite of Patrick. He struts about like a fucking arrogant peacock. Sorry for the language, but I can't stand the man.'

'Did he do something to you?'

'It's just his self-important attitude.'

'Tell me more.'

'He's married, but separated – maybe divorced, I don't know – with a rake of daughters. All of whom he idolises.'

'How do you know he idolises them?'

'He had this fancy Christmas party once. Invited a load of business people, including the owner of the agency where I work. I was delegated to attend. Watching Gordon Collins in his home, with his brood of fawning girls, was eye-opening. None of the posturing or chest-puffing he usually goes on with. And even though they're separated, if he kissed his wife once on the cheek, he pecked her twenty fucking times.'

Boyd smiled. He thought the swear word sounded alien on her lips. 'Was it for show?'

'Most likely.'

Checking his notes, he said, 'He lives in a fairly mediocre house, doesn't he?'

'It's deceptive. Quite big now that he's renovated it. All glass and shit overlooking Ladystown Lake. Anyhow, all I know is that he's shutting down the site for a while until he sorts out the money issues.'

'And John Morgan? He seemed to be a loner. It's early days, but we can't locate anyone who knew him outside of work.'

'Can't help you there. Sorry.'

'I appreciate you talking with me, Charlie.'

'That's fine, even if you got me here under false pretences.'

'I never mentioned what I wanted to discuss,' he said earnestly.

She smiled, and the light returned to her face. 'You know where to find me when you make your decision on the house.'

She tugged on a warm wool coat and snaked a fleece scarf around her neck. After the door shut softly behind her, Boyd remained enveloped in her perfume.

42

'It's bloody Baltic in here. Did Mother forget to order the oil?' Chloe went to the hall and grabbed a fleece from the over-flowing stand.

'The roof leaked. Again.' Katie stirred a mug of tea. 'Probably cold air coming through it.'

Chloe flicked on the kettle to make herself a cup of tea. From the sound it made, it was clear it was empty. 'Jesus, Katie, you could have put in more water than just enough for one cup.'

'Sorry.'

'Where's Louis?' She filled the kettle and switched it on before sitting on the edge of the table, where she studied her older sister.

'He's upstairs with Sean,' Katie said. 'On some FIFA game.'

'That kid is too young for gaming.'

'It's a kids' game. Sean said Louis is better at it than he is.'

'Too much screen time isn't good.'

'And what would you know about it, Chloe?'

'Whatever. I'm not getting into a row over this.'

'Fine by me.'

Chloe leaned down closer to her sister. 'Instead, I want all the juicy details about this Jackson guy.'

'Kettle's boiling.'

'It's not.'

'Will be in a minute.'

'He's that good, eh?'

'What do you mean?'

'If you don't want to talk about him, that means you like him. But remember what happened with the last guy and—'

'Don't!' Katie held up her hand. 'I'm not going there.'

'Okay. But I want to know what this Jackson is like. Are you bringing him home to meet Mother?'

'Are you for real? And the kettle *is* boiling this time.'

With a sigh, Chloe jumped off the table and set about making the tea. 'Want another one?'

'I'm fine.'

'A word of thanks wouldn't go amiss in this house.'

'Thanks, then. I get five minutes' peace in the day. Leave me alone, will you?'

Chloe stirred the tea bag, then held it against the rim of the mug with the spoon, squeezing it. She needed a strong cup. She hadn't slept great, and another long shift at the pub loomed. Despite that, Katie worried her. They fought like cat and dog most of the time, but she didn't like it when her sister became morose. 'You know you can talk to me if—'

'Are you deaf? I said I want a bit of peace.' Katie jumped up. 'Jeesssuuuss!' She dumped her mug in the sink with a clatter and stormed out of the kitchen.

Shivering in the ice-cold room, Chloe wondered if, in this lifetime, they could ever be friends as well as sisters.

The back door opened and Granny Rose struggled in with a bulging shopping bag.

'Gran! Let me help you. What are you doing here?'

'That's a fine welcome. And who are you, young lady?'

'I'm Chloe,' she said with a groan, knowing further explanation was necessary. 'Your granddaughter. I lived with you for a while last year to look after you. Remember?'

'I don't need anyone looking after me. I'm capable of minding myself, thank you.'

'Of course you are. What's all this, Gran?' Chloe lifted the bag onto the table and started taking out groceries. A slap on her hand halted her.

'Leave that alone, missy. They're mine. Are you stealing from me as well as lying? I'll report you to Peter.'

Chloe leaned against the table. She'd never known Grandfather Peter. He'd died when her mother was a child. 'Can I help you with these groceries?'

A shock of confusion flitted across Rose's face and the elderly lady's eyes misted over. 'I'm in the wrong house.'

'Not really. This is your daughter Lottie's house.'

'Is it?'

'Yes, Gran. Listen, can I drive you home to your own house? I'll light the fire and get you settled.'

Rose continued to stare at her surroundings. Chloe's heart contracted when she noticed a tear break free from the corner of her gran's eye. She hugged Rose and led her to a chair.

'A cup of tea will do the trick.'

'Chloe, isn't it? My old brain is all muddled.'

'Don't worry about it. I'm like that in work. Two pints of Guinness become three Budweiser in the time it takes me to turn around to the taps.'

Rose nodded distractedly and wiped her eyes. 'It's cold in here. Did your mother forget to order oil again?'

Laughing while she made the tea in a pot the way her granny liked, Chloe said, 'Yeah, Gran, something like that.'

43

Boyd found it difficult to recognise his own apartment when he let himself in after work. It might have been tiredness fogging his eyesight from the long day, but he suspected Grace had been busy. The last time he'd given the rooms a good cleaning had to have been before he'd been in Spain with Sergio.

He went to hug his sister, who, disliking human touch, shrank away from him.

'Thanks, Grace, you've done a massive job with the place.'

'I had great help.' She ran her Marigold-encased hand over her forehead, streaking it with what looked like grease, then pointed to Sergio. The boy was dusting the window ledge. 'My nephew is a topper.'

Hugging Sergio, who didn't baulk at touch, Boyd said, 'Did you have a good day with Auntie Grace?'

'It was interesting.' The eight-year-old handed him the dusty cloth. 'Can I watch television now?'

'Certainly.'

'Not yet, he can't. He has to finish his task.' Grace rushed over. She swiped the cloth back and stuffed it into the boy's hand. 'You're almost done.'

'Mama had a cleaner in Malaga,' he said softly, lowering his head to the job.

Boyd blew out air. Sergio rarely mentioned his dead mother. And in truth, Boyd avoided that conversation. He hoped Grace had kept her mouth shut about his ex-wife, though if the question was put to her, she would answer truthfully.

'Both of you have done an amazing job. What about a takeaway to celebrate?'

'Takeaway?' Grace looked horrified. 'I cooked a perfectly good beef stew. Sergio devoured it. Your plate is in the oven.'

Busying himself with searching for a knife and fork in the rearranged drawer, Boyd said, 'How long are you able to stay, Grace?'

'Is that an underhand way of saying you don't want me here?'

'God, no. Not at all. I was only—'

'Don't forget it was you who asked me to come and help you out until you got a childminder for Sergio. Are you changing your mind?'

'No, no. It's great to have you here. Cooking and cleaning for free.'

'I never said I'd do it for free.' She divested herself of the gloves and put them in a basin of water to soak. Then she took an inhaler from her pocket and took a few puffs. 'I have a life, Mark Boyd. But I want to help out my only sibling. We're all that's left of the Boyd lineage, except for Sergio, and he's just a boy. It's only right that we do things for each other.'

'I'm a bit cash-strapped,' he confessed. 'I'm trying to figure out how to come up with enough finance to buy a house.'

'I'm not talking about money. But if you need some, we can sell Mam's house.'

'It's your home, Grace. You live there.'

'No I don't.'

'What do you mean?' He almost dropped the hot plate as he

slid it out of the oven with bare hands. She'd moved the oven gloves from their usual place in the pot cupboard. God only knew where he'd find them.

'I'm getting married. I've moved in with him.'

'Him?' Boyd placed the plate on the breakfast bar and waited while his sister fussed with a table mat to protect the surface.

'Bryan.' She spelled it out.

'What?' Totally confused now, he raised his arms in a plea.

'With a Y not an I.'

'Oh. And who is Bryan when he's at home?'

'At home where?'

'It's an expression.'

'Why do people talk in riddles?'

Boyd wanted to know so much about his sister's life. 'Where did you meet this... Bryan with a Y?'

'No need to be smart.'

'Sorry.'

'We met online.'

'How? You don't know how to do technical stuff.'

'There is nothing technical about signing up to a dating site.'

Sergio giggled in the living room, which was only separated from the kitchen by the breakfast bar. 'You are a dinosaur, Papa.'

'Apparently so.' He opened the cutlery drawer again, still muddled with the rearrangement. He found a fork. It'd have to do. Pulling up a stool, he began to eat. 'Tell me more.'

'Don't talk with your mouth full.'

'Sorry. I want to know about this man you're going to marry.'

'It won't be a traditional wedding. I'm not into wearing white and carrying an oversized posy. Wildflowers for me. I'm going to pick them from the cliffs.'

'When is it?'

'The flower-picking?' She smiled and brushed flyaway hair behind her ears.

'Now who's taking the piss?'

'Language.' Grace never swore.

'Go on, tell me all. By the way, this is delicious.'

'Thank you.' She sat on a stool opposite him, apparently pleased with the praise. 'Bryan is sixty-four.' She must have noticed his incredulous expression. 'No need to worry about the age difference. We get on well together. I'm helping him on his farm.'

He gulped down a mouthful of stew, hoping he wouldn't say the wrong thing. 'Where is the farm?'

'Five miles from Mam's house, may she rest in peace. He has seventy acres. Enough sheep and their wool to make ten mats.'

'Why do you need ten mats?' Sergio asked from the sofa. He had the television on with the sound down low.

'I'm going to have a big house. Bryan's house is too small. He had plans drawn up to extend it.'

'And when is the wedding?'

'June.'

Boyd nearly choked. 'This June? That's not too long away.'

'We have February, March, April and May to get through first, so it's not tomorrow.'

Was she making a joke? He reckoned she was deadly serious. Grace didn't joke. Well, she used not to joke.

'Why am I only hearing about this now?'

'You never asked.'

She was right there. He'd been so caught up in his own life, he'd rarely contacted her. Not until he needed her. 'I'm so sorry. I should have checked in with you more often.'

'You should have.'

'When can I meet Bryan?'

'He works on the farm from six in the morning until seven in the evening, daily. He goes to the pub Saturday nights and Mass on Sundays. So you can find a time to suit.'

Not sure what all that meant, he decided to leave it there. 'This stew is really excellent.'

'You should know by now that anything I do, including cooking, is always to a high standard.'

'I know.' And he hoped Grace's sixty-four-year-old future husband, whom he'd never heard of until a few minutes ago, understood her too. He could not sit by and watch his sister get hurt.

———

The house was like an ice box. Lottie felt the cold air hit her in the face as she shut the front door behind her. She shrugged off her boots, hung up her coat and made her way to the kitchen, hoping it would be warmer than the hall. Fat chance. But she forgot the cold when she noticed Rose sitting at the table.

'What are you doing here, Mother?' She immediately realised that her words sounded wrong. 'I mean, it's great to see you, but it's late.'

'If it's that late, you shouldn't be out. Where were you till this time?'

'Working.'

'Where?'

'At the station.'

'Was your father...?' Rose stopped as if suddenly realising she was living in the wrong era. 'Oh. This head of mine. Sorry. I confuse everything.'

Lottie watched as her mother fiddled with a spoon, stirring it in an empty mug, and rushed to sit by her side. 'Are you all right? Stay here tonight. Or I can go over to yours. Would you like that?'

'No, no. I'm fine.' Rose stared at her, an opaque glaze filtered over her eyes. 'I don't know why I'm here.'

'You brought groceries, Gran,' Chloe said, appearing from the utility room zipping up her coat.

'I think they were for myself. Or maybe not.'

Putting her hand over her mother's to still the futile stirring, Lottie asked gently, 'Have you eaten?'

'I think so. Maybe.'

'I'll find something in the freezer. Fish and chips sound okay to you? I'm starving.'

'A chicken casserole wouldn't go astray. I'll make one for you tomorrow.'

'That'd be great,' Lottie said, catching Chloe's eye-roll. It was likely Rose might not remember this conversation in ten minutes, let alone tomorrow.

'I'm off,' the girl said, and pecked her gran's cheek.

'Where's Katie?' Lottie asked before Chloe escaped.

'Getting ready,' she said, as she stood halfway out the door.

'For what?'

'Going out.'

'Where?

'You better ask her yourself. I got my head bitten off.'

'Who's going to mind Louis?'

'His idol, Sean. Bye.' The back door shut softly as Chloe left.

Lottie looked at her mother and the messy kitchen and wondered where to start. As she set about turning on the oven, Sean walked in, Louis in tow.

'Hi, Mam. You're home early.' He swung Louis up in his arms before settling the boy on a chair at the table. 'Can I help you?'

'Sure, but I reckon you're looking for something,' Lottie said with a grin.

'Good guess.'

'Throw the chips on an oven tray and ask away.'

'Niall wanted me to go over to his house for a while. Are you home for the night to mind Louis? Katie's going out and Chloe has work.'

'Suppose so.'

'Great. Can I do anything else before I go?'

'Did you eat?'

'Yeah. Me and Louis had Pot Noodles, didn't we, bud?'

'Yeah, they're nice and gooey.' Louis looked up adoringly at his uncle.

'Go on, then, and don't be too late.' Lottie shooed her son out with a tea cloth.

'Why is everyone late?' Rose asked, taking Louis up on her knee. The boy squirmed to be released, but his great-granny held fast.

'Food in twenty minutes,' Lottie said, searching for scissors to open the bag of frozen Donegal Catch.

44

He knew he should forget about the young woman now that he'd seen her with the child in the park, but for some reason his mind could not move on. She was on the list, and her looks and body filled him with a primitive need. Not skinny and scrawny like that yoke in the kitchen. But then that girl had been a lot different when she'd first arrived. It wasn't his fault that she had deteriorated. It was *hers* – *she* who ruled the home with an iron fist.

He didn't feel sorry for the scrawny one, but at times he felt sorry for the child. Not that he or the kid knew what was going on beneath the surface of *her* skin. She was an enigma; a Jekyll-and-Hyde character. A chameleon. She metamorphosed (a big word he'd found in the dictionary and he liked the sound of it) into one person to those outside, modifying herself into what she thought was expected in different environments. And he still wasn't certain he knew the real woman beneath her strange veneer.

A knock on the shed door shunted him from his musings. He hid his beloved dictionary back behind a flowerpot. Another knock. Soft and timid. He opened the door to find the young girl there. What age was she? He barely remembered. Probably seven or eight. Maybe even nine.

'Magenta, what do you want?'

'You have to come in. Right away. Urgent.'

'I'll be there in a minute.' He put out his hand to caress her soft curls, but she leaped backwards as if he'd scalded her with a hot iron.

'You have to come now!'

He watched her run as if the wind was blowing her back inside the house, the bare soles of her feet visible as she moved. Her leggings were too short and her T-shirt too thin. But the kid was not his responsibility. He just did as he was told. Like get his arse inside before *she* came out.

With a weary slump of his shoulders he locked the door behind him and trod in the little girl's footsteps, wondering what fate awaited him this time.

———

Curled up on her bed, Shannon shivered. She was acutely aware that it was fear turning her blood cold.

A sniff of cocaine would fix it. No, she couldn't start that again. A dangerous habit that had spilled out of control when her parents died. But she'd kicked it in rehab, good and hard, and she never wanted to go back inside those intimidating doors again.

She thought of Davy in the park earlier that day. She knew the boy could not have got up on the monkey rings on his own. Who else had been there? She was baffled, because she'd seen no one.

She'd stay in tonight and go out tomorrow night. But she had no money, and her next pay cheque wasn't due for a week.

Her phone buzzed with a message. Unknown number. Then she remembered the call she'd received in the park.

Maybe she would have a night out after all without having to spend a cent. With someone who could help her forget the fear stalking her brain. Because she was certain someone was *actually* stalking her.

———

The argument was still ongoing. The one-sided argument. *She* was commanding the kitchen, waving her hands, slapping them against her thighs, her face animated, her hair wild.

'And don't fuck it up. I can't be dealing with ineptitude.'

He scratched his head. She often spoke with big words. Trying to confuse him, he assumed. He wasn't sure what ineptitude meant, but it couldn't be anything good. He'd have to look it up in his dictionary.

'I'll do my best, like I always do.' It was a rare occasion that he talked back to her, but he'd about had enough of her, even though he could never escape.

'Obviously your best isn't good enough, is it?' Her voice was a snarl and he instinctively ducked. She had no weapon in her hand, though her fists were just as lethal. He'd learned the hard way. 'Have you packed the essentials?'

'You know I have.' He bit his nails as his nerves frayed.

'Are you being intentionally obtuse with me?'

'What?'

'Stupid.'

He was lost now, so he just shook his head.

'You better not be, or I might just lose my temper, and you wouldn't want that to happen.'

'I'll head off.'

'Don't arrive back empty-handed.'

'I won't.'

He made his way successfully out to the hall without getting a thump on the ear. He tied a scarf around his neck and began to zip up his jacket. Magenta was sitting on the bottom step, eyeing him. The likeness to *her* unnerved him, and he caught the zipper in his jumper, snagged a thread. She laughed and scampered up the stairs. He gave up on the zip and left. At least he'd get a few hours' peace away from the house. Excitement built within him as he pulled out of the driveway.

Tonight he would not fail.

45

The bastard had texted and arranged where to meet, and then hadn't showed up. Shannon felt like sinking to the ground and crying like a baby. Instead she called Jess.

'I'm out and dateless. The bastard didn't turn up. Please, Jess, come out.'

'I'm wrecked. In bed already. Sorry, hun. Another time.'

Shannon hung up and eyed the inviting door to Danny's while mentally counting the few euros in her purse, with even less in her bank account. She couldn't go on stealing from George. She needed the escort money, if only to get by. It wasn't fair. Life wasn't fair.

She needed another drink. To help get rid of her disappointment. But she hadn't even the price of a half-glass.

She pushed herself away from the pub wall and began her slow walk home.

———

He couldn't believe his good fortune when he saw her walking down the street. Alone, again.

The night was sepia-dark. A forbidding sky heavy with unshed rain blocked out the moon and stars. The street lights cast ochre glints on the tarmac, and he hoped it might rain. Soon. Now. Then he would have a good reason to stop and offer her a lift.

He felt an urge to stop anyhow. To take her and keep her for himself. To not bring her home to *her*. Could he do that? Maybe. But where would he keep her? No way he'd get her into his shed unnoticed. The kid regularly found his key and entered his private domain, where she often destroyed his little plants. He liked to think it was just a kid being a kid, but he sensed evil lurked in her heart too.

He looked over his shoulder at the child seat in the back. His safety net. It would make her feel safe, especially as she had a child herself. And therein lay the flaw. A woman with a child going missing would cause a bigger stink than a woman with no attachments. Not that he knew much about her family life, but she appeared on an escort site, so that told him she might not have a partner and needed the money. That was why she put herself out there. He was certain she hadn't seen him in the park. And he'd approached the kid before realising he might be making a huge mistake. He'd disappeared before she'd seen him. Who would believe a little kid anyhow? They were always making things up.

He drove down the street ahead of her. She had on that awful pink coat and an umbrella in her hand. Would she recognise him? No, he'd shaved off his beard.

He drove slowly and checked the side pocket in the door. To be sure that all he needed was at his hand. He knew the route she'd take, so he drove on ahead of her until he reached a CCTV blackspot. He pulled into an opportune space. Maybe the gods were aligning in his favour for a change.

In his rear-view mirror he watched her approach. He lowered his window.

'Going to rain, love. Can I give you a lift?'

'Nah, nearly there now.'

'It's no trouble. I'm just heading home. Bad night. Was supposed to meet someone and they never turned up.'

She had stopped, glanced into the car, noticed the child seat in the back. Good.

'Same story for me.'

Her face looked cold and miserable. Perfect.

'I've to go out to the cinema, if you're going that way? No bother if you're not.' He knew right well that was the direction she was going, though not that far.

She peered behind her, down the quiet street, and the first drops of rain fell onto her nose. 'Sure, why not. Don't want to be drenched, and this will be useless.' She smiled as she waved the folded-up umbrella. Pink, like her coat.

He held his breath. She stalled for a moment, before walking around and easing into the passenger seat. Superlative, he thought, using one of the words he'd found in his dictionary. It suited the excitement he now felt in his gut. *She* would be so happy with him. And then he felt sad. He couldn't keep her for himself.

'I'm Shannon,' she said.

'Like the river?' He was proud of himself for making glib conversation.

'Suppose so. Though I'm not travelling as far as that.'

That confused him, but he waved it off as he pulled the car out onto the deserted street.

'Where to then, river lady?'

Laughing, she said, 'Cairnbeg Terrace. Drop me at the head of the road.'

'Sure thing. Who's the twat who abandoned a lovely young lady like yourself?' The gormless attitude was second nature to him. Or maybe it was his real nature. Who cared?

'Just an online date thing.'

'The worst sort.'

'Exactly. Hiding behind a screen like a vampire.'

He had no idea what she meant, so he just nodded. The lights changed. Cairnbeg was close. He'd have to act fast.

'Do you mind if I swing out by the cinema first? I'm late to pick up my eldest. He was at a movie.'

'You can drop me here instead. It's fine.'

He sped past the turning. 'Won't take long. He's only fifteen and the movie was for over eighteens. You know what kids are like. Then again, you're too young to know.' He felt elated at his easy lies. Then he wondered if he'd made a mistake. Hadn't he said he'd been in town to meet someone?

She squirmed a little on the seat but didn't go for the door handle to jump out. Clever girl. It was locked anyhow. He didn't want a repeat of the Laura fiasco.

'Oh,' she said. 'I think the cinema might still be closed. Because of the murder.'

He slowed at the entrance, to make it look like he had intended going there. 'Shit, you're right. Crime-scene tape is still up. Where did the lad go, if not to the cinema?'

'Probably went to a friend's house. Look, can you drop me back? I really need to get home.'

'What's the hurry? You'd have been out longer if your date had turned up.'

'Yeah, I know, but I have to get home to Davy.'

'Davy's your husband? Partner?'

'My... my son.'

In the lights around the cinema complex he noticed the first dawning of fear skitter across her face, and she clutched the umbrella tight in her fist. That could be a small problem. She was thinking she'd made a mistake and he had to act fast.

'Okay. I'll drive round the ring road and bring you back that way. Okay?'

'Suppose.'

'Great. I might see my lad hanging around. I'll kill the pup when I find him.' He stifled a snigger. He'd quite like a pup to kill, because he didn't have a fifteen-year-old son. And there was no way he could let this girl die either. He had to get her to his home in one piece. Otherwise, he may as well move into the shed full-time.

46

Rose's friend Betty had arrived home from Birmingham and agreed to stay with her for the night. Lottie dropped her mother and the bag of groceries at her house. By the time she returned home, her brain felt as scrambled as Rose's must be.

Louis was asleep in the child seat. She unbuckled the straps and lifted him into her arms without waking him. Once she had him inside and tucked up in bed, she made herself a cup of tea and sat at the kitchen table, still in her coat. The room was cold and she hoped the tea would warm her. Her thoughts were awash with family issues when she knew she should be taking time out to go over the investigations in the stillness of the night.

She needed to talk to someone who understood her and her family. She wanted to talk to Boyd, but his recent words still stung sharply. There was no way she could ask her kids to fend for themselves, no matter what age they were. They'd lost their dad while they were teenagers, and in effect she'd also been lost to them for the few years after Adam's death. She'd had to be mam and dad, and she still had so much to atone for.

Slipping her phone from her pocket, she tapped his name

and waited before hitting call. Should she? Would it end in another war of words? He'd been grand at work, but this was personal.

Just as she decided not to call, to finish her tea and go to bed, her phone rang. Boyd.

'Great minds, and all that,' she said.

'Just wanted to see how you're doing.'

'I could do with a hug.'

'What has you so melancholy, besides having two murders on our watch?'

'Mother.'

'Is she okay?' He paused.

'She was here earlier. Very confused. Thank God Betty is back. She's staying the night with her.'

'Do you think Rose's condition is getting worse?'

'Hard to say. She has some lucid times, when she realises she's forgetting things. And other times she's back there in another time. It's tough to watch, Boyd.'

'Can I do anything to help?'

'Not being a bollox about my kids moving out would help.'

'I'm sorry. Okay? I've apologised and I won't mention it again.'

'Thanks, but in a way you're right. The thing is, I can't abandon them.'

'No harm in wanting something for yourself from time to time.'

'Sergio and Grace are your only family. You would never desert them if someone asked you to, would you?'

He inhaled deeply before he replied. 'I didn't ask you to desert anyone, Lottie. I feel it might be impossible to find a place suitable for our blended family. That's all I meant.'

She was grateful for his contrition. 'We could renovate Farranstown House. I can ask Leo for a loan. Or a contribution, seeing as the bastard still legally owns the place.'

'I think you'd be mad to put money into that house without having full ownership. Why don't you take a trip over to New York and talk to him? Iron it out, once and for all.'

'Have you forgotten we have two major investigations on at the moment?'

He laughed. 'I didn't mean you should hop on the next flight. It's something to think about.'

'Okay.'

'Don't think about it tonight. Get some sleep.'

'I will. Thanks for the chat.' She sipped her now cold tea before adding, 'Oh, I meant to ask, how is Grace getting on with Sergio?'

Boyd gave a wry laugh. 'I think Sergio is growing weary of her constant orders and cleaning. But I treasure the time they spend together. He needs a mother figure.'

'And you think your sister can provide that?'

'Good God, no. I meant you. He needs you in his life. I do too.'

'I get all that. Honestly, Mark, I do.'

'Did I tell you Grace is getting married?'

'No! I'm so happy for her. When?'

'In the summer. Knowing Grace, she'll have it organised to a T. Now you get to sleep.'

'Thanks again.'

'Love you, Lottie Parker.'

At one time she'd found it so difficult to utter those words in reply, but she'd got over herself, because she knew in her heart that she did love him. Most of the time.

'Love you too.'

She hung up, put her mug in the sink and switched off the light. As she made her way up the stairs, she hoped Chloe was safe at work and Katie was safe wherever she was, whoever she was with. They're adults, she thought, but at the same time they would always be her little children. And for some reason, a worm of fear was squirming in her chest as she undressed and got into bed. She twisted and turned, but she could not sleep.

47

Katie wasn't sure Jackson was who he claimed to be. Then she thought that he hadn't really claimed to be anything in particular. He'd fudged about, saying he was in the entertainment industry. She wasn't letting it go.

She raised her wine glass to her lips without drinking. Rasco's restaurant was now empty except for themselves and the manager, who was throwing tired looks their way.

'Entertainment?' She raised an eyebrow. 'That's such a wide spectrum. Are you an actor, film-maker, photographer to the stars, or what?'

'Or what, maybe.' He winked, but she didn't like his attitude. Maybe this was a big mistake.

'Well, you were such a smooth talker chatting me up in Fallon's, but now you're dodging my questions. That makes me think you have something to hide. Have you?'

'We all have something to hide. I'm sure you do.'

'No, I told you straight up I'm the mother of a three-year-old. That's something most women might keep hidden in order to get a date.'

'But you weren't looking for a date, were you?'

'In fact, I was. My sister told me to get a life, and that's what I was trying to do.'

'By sitting at a busy bar on your own, chatting to no one except the pretty barmaid.'

'That was my sister.'

He grimaced. 'I've put my foot in it now, haven't I?'

'You're good at dodging questions.' She drained her wine and stood. 'I'd like to leave now. Maybe you can lose the act for a few minutes to drive me home. If not, I'll get a taxi.'

'Hey, Katie. Sit down. I'll explain.'

'These guys want us to leave. Let's split the bill and go.'

'I'm paying, and I'm driving you home. There's a murderer out there somewhere. Who's to say he's not a taxi driver?'

'You sure know how to make a girl feel safe,' Katie said drily.

She fetched her coat from the stand by the desk while Jackson keyed his PIN into the card machine. This had been a big mistake. She wasn't sure she even liked him any more. She should just keep going out onto the street and hop into a taxi, but what he'd said about the murderer had scared her a little. She'd have to let him drive her home, and then she was done with him and all men for the foreseeable.

Life was too short to waste on shitheads.

————

The shouting was still going on downstairs. Rex put his hands over his ears, then his pillow over his head. He was terrified. Afraid they would divorce and he'd be like Conor in his class, having to go to his dad's at weekends and live with his mother during the week. It was the fault of this house. He'd loved their old house, so why did they have to move here? It wasn't nice. And he still had no friends.

He thought of the woman he'd found by the cinema. He'd heard her name was Laura. She'd looked so sad lying there, with that blood on her clothes and her bare feet all muddy. He felt sorry for her. He hoped someone had put a blanket over her to keep her warm.

He shot up in the bed at that thought. She couldn't be hot or cold. She was dead.

He ran to his window and raised the blind so he could look out. There was no one there now. The woman was gone. The tent was gone. It was like she'd never been there. Maybe she hadn't. Maybe his mind had played tricks on him.

Another shout from downstairs made him jump back into bed and pull the duvet up over his head. He didn't know whether to be more scared of what was going on inside the walls of his house or what was outside them.

48

SUNDAY

'Shannon?' George Kenny burst into his sister's bedroom to discover it empty. It was hard to know if the bed had been slept in due to the state of the room. Clothes had been dropped across the floor and on the bed. Cosmetics littered the dresser. The odour of fake tan hung in the air like a wet rag. 'Goddam you, sis.'

He thundered down the stairs. Davy sat at the table, dipping his spoon into a bowl of Cheerios without milk.

'Sorry, kid, I'll get the milk.' George rushed to the refrigerator.

'Are you working, Daddy?' the little boy asked.

'I'm supposed to be catching up, but your Auntie Shannon let me down again.'

'When is Mammy coming home?'

'Soon.' George poured milk on the kid's cereal and made a coffee for himself.

'Yeah! She's getting me a football kit.'

'I'm not sure she'll get to the shops.' Niamh's WhatsApp photos had all been taken in pubs.

'She promised,' Davy whined, splashing the milk everywhere.

'Eat up and I'll get you settled with something on Netflix. How about *SpongeBob*?'

'Hate it.'

'I better put some calamine lotion on those spots. Are they itchy?'

'Don't want lotion.'

Davy let his spoon fall into the cereal and stomped up the stairs like a baby elephant. It reminded George of when he and Shannon were little. She was usually the one doing the stomping while he tried to keep the peace with their harried mother. Shannon had always been the one to let the side down. George was fed up being the good guy. There would be a massive row when she arrived home.

He put the bowl and spoon in the sink. He'd deal with his sister soon. She had outstayed her welcome. It was time for her to find a place of her own. A place where she could upset no one but herself.

49

Tiredness was eating into her bones and every muscle felt like it was being gnawed by a rat. Lottie switched off the engine and got out of the car.

Shading her eyes from the watery early-morning sun with her hand, she looked around. The field to her left was awash with crows, as if a black blanket had been thrown across the waterlogged earth. She said hello to the couple of gardaí who had arrived before her.

Garda Lei was tying crime-scene tape to a tree protruding from the ditch. He turned round as she approached.

'Oh, Inspector, you got here quickly. Another nightmare. I really don't know what—'

'What have we got?'

'Female. Deceased, God help her. It's awful. Some people... What's the world coming to at all?'

'Garda Lei?' She had to stop him or he would go off on so many tangents you'd need a map to get him back on track.

'I believe she was murdered.'

'What makes you reach that conclusion?'

'Bloodstained clothing. She may have been stabbed. Plus

she was dumped in a field. No coat or shoes. Hardly natural causes, if you ask me. Not that I—'

'Who discovered the body?'

'A farmer. He was herding cows into the field because he had to repair their barn. He'd already opened the gate when he noticed the bird activity. He was quick-thinking, to give him his due, kept the cows back while he went to investigate. Thought it might be a fox or badger ravaged by a dog but turned out to be much worse. That's what he said when he phoned it in.'

She surveyed the adjoining field through squinting eyes. The birds seemed to be lying in wait for a second chance at the body. 'I'll have a look now, so.'

'You'll need wellingtons. Have you got any?'

'No, but feck it, I have to see what we're dealing with. Any missing person reports?'

'Nothing new that I've heard, but I'll check back at the station. SOCOs have been alerted. You might want to call the pathologist yourself, or will I do that?'

'I'll call her. Finish up with that tape and put up a secondary cordon, maybe halfway down the road. Do both ends when more reinforcements arrive. Only authorised personnel allowed entry. And keep an eye out for drones. We need a tent over her too.'

'All in hand.'

She slipped a pair of protective gloves on over her cold fingers. The body wasn't far from the edge of the ditch that lined the road. Similar to how Laura Nolan's body had been left. But this location in the townland of Drinock was around five kilometres from the outskirts of Ragmullin. Fields all around, with the town on the horizon. Through the morning mist the town's cathedral spires spiked the sky in the distance. If she was dealing with the same killer, did the choice of location mean something to him? And how did he transport the bodies? There were no tyre tracks in the wet grass beneath her feet.

The body was covered with a sheet of plastic.

'Lei?' she called over her shoulder. 'Where did that plastic come from?'

'Farmer had it in his jeep. He thought it might keep the birds away.'

'Hmm.' She hoped it hadn't destroyed any potential evidence. But he was probably right to try and protect the body from further avian carnage.

She stopped before she reached it. The two uniforms who had been standing guard moved to one side to let her through. Noses blue with the cold, they tipped their caps. She nodded in solemn greeting.

It felt odd to be the first detective on the scene. She usually arrived to the hustle and bustle of activity from detectives and SOCOs. This morning, it was her private domain. She felt a fissure of distrust in her ability to remain professional as she lifted the plastic sheet from the deceased's face.

The dead woman was unknown to her. Her face had a bluish-grey tinge. Not long dead, experience told her, but it could still be eight or nine hours. So young. Mid to late twenties, maybe, though in death it was difficult to judge age correctly.

She swallowed the bile that had risen from her stomach on seeing the evidence of the birds' activity. Pecks in the skin, here and there. Eyelids shut, with no marks around them. She was grateful they had not got that far, and thankful for the farmer's quick thinking in covering up the body. He had definitely done the right thing.

Biting her lip, she squinted at the dead woman's hair. It was shorn short. Shorn was the only word she could think of to describe it. Ragged ends, odd lengths. Unwashed. She filed away these initial observations to return to later. She peeled down the plastic covering and gulped away her rising anger. Red-hot anger.

There appeared to be a single stab wound to the chest, just below the victim's breast. The pathologist would tell her more, but there didn't seem to be any other injuries on the painfully thin body. Unless they discovered more when she was turned over. Through the light material of her ripped and blood-soaked grey cotton shift dress, Lottie could see protruding ribs. She glanced at the woman's hands, forcing herself not to take hold of one of them to comfort her. The bones of her thin wrists and elbows stuck out and her stomach was distended. Her legs were like two hawthorn sticks. Thin, dirty and bare, as were her feet.

'What happened to you, pet?' Lottie whispered. 'Who did this to you?' She was aware that she was referring to more than the knife wound that had ended the girl's life.

Carefully she replaced the plastic sheeting, hoping the tent would arrive soon. She rose to her feet and scanned the surrounding terrain. She could make out a criss-cross of boot prints. The farmer's and the initial gardaí who'd arrived on scene, she surmised. Were the killer's prints there somewhere too? She didn't notice any small prints like there had been at the site where Laura Nolan had been found. But SOCOs would check.

She allowed her thoughts to return to the face beneath the plastic. Eyes closed. Mouth slightly open. A spectre of pain and horror. What had the girl seen in the last moments of her life? What pain had she endured in the weeks or months prior to that? Lottie bit down on her lip again so that she wouldn't cry. She was certain something awful had been done to the young woman in the time before her murder. She'd have to wait for the post-mortem, because she knew this body had a lot to say.

50

George thought the guards might tell him to wait forty-eight hours. Forty-eight hours, my arse. He'd go to the garda station and fight to be heard. He'd have to bring little Davy with him. The silence from Shannon's phone had freaked him out. Hadn't a girl been murdered already? His mind was in overdrive and all thoughts of evicting his sister disappeared. Where was she? Okay, she'd stayed out the night before, but she'd come home early enough the next morning. Swore she wouldn't do it again unless she called him first. Was he overreacting? Maybe, but some internal switch had been flipped and he sensed he had cause to worry.

The small garda reception area was hot and smelly. The bench inside the door was free, but he had no intention of sitting there or anywhere else until he got answers. He marched up to the counter, keeping a tight hold on Davy's hand. He knocked on the glass and waited for the tired-looking older guard to make his way from the small open-plan office behind the front desk.

'I want to report a missing woman. It's my sister. She's about this height and—'

'Right, son. Take your time. What's your name?'

'George Kenny. What's yours?'

'Garda Thornton. Will you fill out a form for me?'

George swayed from foot to foot. 'I'm really worried. That woman was murdered the other day, and now Shannon hasn't come home.'

'Okay. Does she often do that?'

'Do what?'

'Not come home?'

He sucked in his cheeks. Lie? Or tell the truth? Maybe somewhere in between. 'She's had issues in the past. But her best friend hasn't heard from her either and now her phone seems to be dead. She nearly always comes home in the morning if she stays out the night before.' Shit, he'd said too much.

'Nearly always, you say. What about other times?'

'Look, Garda Thornton, I know my sister, and I know there's something wrong.'

The man seemed between two minds on what to do. George could see experience in his eyes and demeanour. He figured that waiting was better than having an outburst.

'Okay,' Thornton said at last, 'I'll take the details. Have you a photograph? I'd also recommend you put a post on social media. Did you try contacting her that way?'

'She hasn't been online since yesterday.'

'And that's unusual, is it?'

'Suppose so. I can ask her friend. She would know.'

'We can have a word with her, if you like?'

'Yes. Please do.' For the first time since he'd burst into Shannon's empty room that morning, George felt his burden was being shared.

'What's her phone number?'

George checked his phone and rattled off Jess's number. Thornton gave him a form to fill out and ushered him into a tiny room to the side. He put Davy on his knee, took the pen from the guard and began to enter what he knew about his sister. He hoped it was all for nothing. He sincerely hoped Shannon was safe. But some strange feeling tangled up his gut and a veil of dread drifted over him. He'd felt the same way the morning his mother had died.

In his heart, George knew that Shannon was anything but safe.

———

It took an hour to get all the relevant personnel on site, and Lottie didn't leave until Grainne and her SOCO team were in place. On the face of it, it seemed they could be looking for the same person who'd murdered Laura. That was based on the stab wound, and the fact that the victim had been left out in the open. But she hadn't noticed defensive wounds or strangulation marks on the girl's neck. Jane Dore said it would be at least another hour before she could get there. Lottie left Kirby in charge and headed back to the station. She grabbed a takeout coffee and a can of Diet Coke from the Bean Café on her way.

Boyd was at his desk. 'I'd love a coffee. Smells divine.'

'You can have the Coke. Where were you earlier?' She was unable to mask her annoyance.

'Calming the waters between Grace and Sergio. When I told her I had to go into work today, she wrote a list of chores for him and he rebelled. First time I've seen his temper. Then she wanted to bring him to Sunday Mass before threatening to head back to Galway. Anyhow, tell me about the body.'

'It's so sad, Boyd.' She sat on the edge of his desk, coat still on, and sipped the coffee. 'She looks about the same age as Laura Nolan, maybe a little older. We have no idea of her identity. No bag, or bank card in a pocket like Kirby found on Laura. No pocket, even. She was wearing a horrible grey dress.'

'Wait a minute. Thornton sent up a missing person report that came in earlier.' He tapped the keyboard and the scanned report appeared on the screen. 'Shannon Kenny. Lives at Cairnbeg Terrace with her brother George and her nephew Davy. Last seen at eight last night before she went out. And—'

'Is there a photo attached?' She placed her coffee cup to the side, jumped off the desk and leaned over Boyd's shoulder. He smelled good.

'Thornton has finally figured out attachments.' He clicked the icon and the photo opened up.

'I don't think she's the dead woman.' Lottie didn't know whether to be relieved or not. Identifying the victim quickly would have speeded up the investigation. On the other hand, this Shannon was likely to walk into her home any time soon. She hoped. Quickly reading over the report again, she said, 'It says she's done this kind of thing before.'

'Yeah, but Thornton thought it best to take the statement, seeing as we now have two dead women in the same age bracket.'

'Keep it on our radar, but she's probably sleeping off a hang-over somewhere.'

'Hopefully that's all.' Boyd closed down the screen. 'What do you want me to do now?'

'Check in with McKeown and see if there's anyone who can tell us something about Laura Nolan's movements Thursday night. We need to get on top of that investigation.'

'Do you think it's the same killer?'

'Hard to tell. Single stab wound but no strangulation. She was malnourished. It's like... I don't know...'

'What?'

'The way she looked, the way she was dressed. Not normal. It's like she was starved. Does that sound ridiculous?'

'I haven't seen her body, so I can't say.'

'Head out there and see for yourself. Find out what Jane thinks. I've to meet John Morgan's mother shortly.'

'I think you should hand over his murder investigation to someone else. It might be muddying the water for us. We should concentrate on Laura and this new victim.'

'You could be right. I'll decide after I meet Mrs Morgan.'

51

Brenda Morgan had refused to set foot in the station. A compromise was reached to meet in the Joyce Hotel.

When Lottie entered the noisy bar, Brenda stood. Her face didn't match her company website photo, which had given Lottie a false sense of the woman. She was no more than five feet tall, bone-thin, dressed in a dark navy dress that swathed her body in folds, like a shroud. Her skin was corpse-white, hands like birds' claws, and platinum-grey hair to her shoulders, so straight she might have ironed it. Only fifty-five, but such was the sorrow on her face, she could pass for seventy.

'I'm sorry for your loss, Mrs Morgan.' Lottie reached out her hand. Brenda's grip was sweaty and flaccid, and she sat as quickly as she'd stood.

'It's Brenda.' A clipped tone. 'I can't say it's a pleasure to meet you, given the circumstances. What are you doing to find out what happened to my son?'

Lottie pulled out the low-seated chair and sat. Her legs were too long and she wanted to stand again. 'We have a full murder investigation under way.'

'What has that yielded?'

'It's early stages. John's body was only discovered Friday afternoon.'

'And? Today is Sunday. I don't want excuses. I want facts.'

So be it, Lottie thought. She had to speak above the din of crockery and cutlery and chatter around them, without being overheard. 'We've been unable to establish who might have killed your son, or why.'

'The why could be because my son was a gambler. He may have owed someone money.'

'If that was the case, why didn't he ask you for help?' From her hurried research, Lottie had established that Brenda was wealthy.

'Inspector, my son had an addiction to gambling. I helped him in the past but then I realised that all I was doing was facilitating his habit. He agreed to rehab early last year. I thought he'd kicked his habit after that, but I've been proved fatally wrong, because now he's dead.' She produced a handkerchief from the small black bag on her lap and dabbed her eyes.

'Had he asked you for money in the last few months?'

'No.'

'From our investigation so far, we haven't established any recent gambling. He had few friends, only work colleagues. He lived in a small bedsit that was immaculately clean.'

'I raised him to respect other people's property. Maybe I should have spent more time teaching him to respect himself.'

There was pain behind Brenda's words and Lottie felt the mother's anguish. The hard persona was just that. A persona.

'Had you visited John since he came to Ireland?'

'No. My job takes up a lot of my time. I asked him to come to London at Christmas, but he said he'd rather stay here.'

'Alone?'

'I presumed he had friends.'

'When did you last speak with him?'

Brenda closed her eyes, thinking. When she opened them,

they were filled with unshed tears. 'Christmas Day. A Face-Time call to wish each other a happy Christmas. He looked well. No sign of drug use.'

'Drugs?' Lottie hadn't heard this angle yet.

'He smoked a bit of weed now and then. I doubt he was into anything stronger. Did the autopsy show up anything?'

'Samples have been sent to the lab for toxicology analysis.' Lottie paused and studied the sparrow-like woman before her. There was no sign of the formidable character Mr Collins had mentioned. 'You asked Gordon Collins to give John a job. Why was that?'

'John needed to be kept busy, especially after his stint in rehab. He's a good worker. His father,' she pursed her lips before continuing, 'can testify to that from John's time in Australia.'

'How did you come to know Gordon Collins?'

'He was in London at a conference. He was trying to secure funding for a contract to build a new office block in Canary Wharf. Said he was expanding.'

'Did he approach you?'

'Yes, but his other capital seemed wobbly. My bank refused.'

'Was he annoyed or upset over it?'

'Not that I heard. I only met him while he was attending the conference. I hadn't any reason to sit in on the meetings.'

'Did you know him before that encounter?'

'No, but I'd read his portfolio. He was definitely on shaky ground financially.'

'You still asked him to give John a job, though?'

'I saw an opportunity and I took it.' Brenda sipped her coffee before continuing. 'I knew John would be of benefit to Collins as a labourer.'

'Seems Collins's company is in a lot of trouble. He's temporarily closing down the Pine Grove site next week.'

'Where John's body was found? I've bought a house there.'

'Is there anything else you can tell me about Mr Collins?'

The cup clattered onto the saucer. 'Did Gordon Collins kill my son?'

'We have no evidence to suggest it.'

'But he could have, couldn't he? To get back at me for not making more of an effort with my bank when he asked for funds.'

'That seems a bit extreme.'

'You have to look into him.' Brenda's voice had reached a screech.

'We're looking into everyone associated with John's job. When did you last speak with Collins?'

'He phoned me about John's death. Before that it must have been a week ago. He requested an update on his latest application. I had no news to give him.'

'How did he seem?'

'Normal. Friendly, if anything. He told me John was an asset to his team. I meant to ring John that night to tell him, but I regret I never did.'

'Is there anyone you can think of who would want to harm your son?'

'As I said at the outset, it could be someone connected to his gambling habit, but it's far more likely to be Collins. You need to—'

'We will look at all angles. Thanks for your time, Brenda. I'll keep you informed of any developments.'

'When is John's body being released?'

'We need you to formally identify him. Once the pathologist has concluded her examination, it should only be a day or two, I imagine.'

'I have to organise his funeral.'

'Will his father be coming? I'd like to interview him.'

'I don't talk much to Christy, but I told him about John.'

'What happened to break up your marriage?'

'Is that even relevant?'

'Not sure,' Lottie admitted.

Brenda appeared subdued, almost dazed, when she eventually spoke. 'Another woman. He fled to Oz with her and then dumped her. Or maybe she saw the light and dumped him.'

'I'll have a word with him anyway.'

'He'll sing John's praises. The boy could do no wrong in his father's eyes.'

'And *did* he do wrong?'

'His gambling would have been noticed earlier if my ex-husband hadn't been so blind. He could have gone into rehab sooner.'

'I'll need the name of the facility.'

'I'll send it to you.' Brenda stood and slipped her arms into her coat sleeves. 'I'm staying here until I can have John's body cremated. I want to bring his ashes back to London. I need to keep him close to me.'

The unspoken words were clear. Brenda knew she should have kept her son close to her when he was alive. And that broke off a little bit of Lottie's heart.

52

The field was mucky rather than muddy by the time Boyd arrived. He'd checked in with McKeown, who had nothing new to report on the Laura Nolan murder investigation.

He fetched a pair of wellingtons from the car boot and put them on. Stuffing his hands in his pockets, he walked on the steel plates that led to the tent covering the body. The state pathologist was just finishing up her visual examination.

'Detective Sergeant Boyd,' Jane said, formally. She removed her mask outside the tent. Her face was grave. 'Female, mid twenties, single stab wound to the chest. Severely malnourished. Signs of incarceration.'

'Really?'

'Yes. There's some sort of residue around her mouth. I'd hazard a guess at duct tape, but don't quote me until I run tests. It's possible that the tape was wound around her head. There are clumps of hair missing at the back of her head and behind her ears.'

'Holy shit.'

'As I said, I'll know more later. It could be tomorrow morning before I get to do her post-mortem.'

'Can you tell me anything about the wound?'

'Not much. It's a single stab. If I was pushed, I'd say the killer knew what he was doing. Like Laura's. But you need to wait until you get my preliminary report before broadcasting that nugget to one and all.'

Jane whipped off her protective suit and made her way down the steel plates. He watched her leave before ducking his head inside the tent.

The dead woman was definitely not Shannon Kenny. He recalled the photo supplied by her brother and compared this mental image with the body on the ground. Maybe if she wasn't so emaciated, the victim would have some similarities to the Kenny girl. They were both Caucasian, about the same height, age and hair colour. But there the similarities ended. This poor unfortunate had been badly treated. By whom and where, he had to find out, and he hoped that in doing so, he would find her killer.

———

Shannon had no idea where she was or how she'd got here. Her head throbbed with pain and her memory was hazy. She'd been out in town. Hadn't she? Waiting around outside Danny's. Why? Her date hadn't shown up? She couldn't recall. Then she'd been walking. Yes, something about walking home. Damn. It was too fuzzy. Was she stoned, or drunk? George is going to kill me, she thought with a cry of shame.

Shivering, she felt as if she had a fever. She was on fire. She tried again to see where she was, but there wasn't a chink of light getting in anywhere. A well of horror swirled in her stomach and she felt she was going to be sick. She tried to turn on her side but couldn't.

A cough wrinkled its way up her throat, but it couldn't come out. It was stuck there in her mouth, choking her. Swallowing it, she breathed through her nose. She realised that her lips were tightly secured. Were they taped shut? What the fuck?

Must get it off, she thought, but she couldn't move her hands. With rising trepidation, she found they were bound, as were her feet. Where the fuck was she?

As her fever raged, she was certain she was hallucinating. It was all a nightmare. She closed her eyes, hoping that when she opened them again, she'd wake up in her own bed.

Her inner voice told her that the nightmare was real.

And worse still, it had only just begun.

———

He'd done what *she'd* asked. And she still wasn't happy. Was she ever? Giving out like a woman possessed. Maybe she *was* possessed.

This morning she'd slapped Magenta and caught her by the ear, almost severing the lobe from the soft flesh on her neck. He normally bore the brunt of her anger, both verbally and physically. This was a new level of violence. She'd noticed spots on Magenta's neck and threw a fit about her having to miss school the next day. After she'd gone out, he'd told the little girl to go to bed and he'd check on her later.

Hugging his arms around his body, he rocked as he sat on the upturned flowerpot. His safe haven didn't feel particularly safe today. What had he done wrong? Where had he slipped up? He had to have done something erroneous (another word from his beloved dictionary) for her to be so annoyed. Maybe it had to do with the woman's kid. The boy he'd seen with her in the park. Did *she* find out about the brat? No way. There was nothing on the news yet about them. Not even about the latest body. He'd been clever dumping her in a field, and it'd probably be days before she was found. He'd spied the crows in the trees and knew they wouldn't take long getting fed.

It all provided some breathing space, though he had no space or peace in his head. His brain was clouded over with the fear that he'd done something wrong. What could it be? And how had she found out?

Retracing his steps in his head, he was certain he'd been careful. Avoided areas with CCTV and traffic cams. Lurked in the darkest corners. Even where he picked her up was a security camera blackspot. If his abduction of Shannon was without errors, was it to do with the disposal of the other one?

He stood and began potting seeds, but it was pointless. He itched to make a weapon, to find something to strike *her*. She kept the knife sheathed and hidden, only taking it out when he was on a mission for her. He'd have to think of something.

He wanted to talk to Shannon. Such a gorgeous name. Like the river, fast-flowing and free. But he could not be caught. *She* could return and surprise him. He had to allow more time to elapse.

Waiting and sweating, he counted down the minutes. Then he locked his shed and went into the house.

53

Lottie sat in the incident room beside Boyd and Kirby. She related the conversation she'd had with Brenda Morgan.

'Do we know if John did any jobs on the side?' Boyd asked. 'Maybe he'd worked on someone's house extension or something for cash in hand. And if it wasn't up to standard, perhaps he was killed because of it.'

'That's quite extreme,' Lottie said.

'People murder for a lot less,' Boyd countered.

Lottie tapped her finger on the desk. 'Is there anything to connect John Morgan's murder to that of the two women?'

'Can we even link the two women's deaths to each other at this stage?' Kirby said.

'We need the post-mortem report on the latest woman.' Lottie stood and stretched, arching her back. 'If the weapon used was the same in both instances, then we can link the murders. We should look into their personal lives to see if they're connected in any way.'

'We don't even know who the second woman is,' Boyd said, 'so there's no way we can investigate connections between the two.'

'Then we'd better identify her quickly.' Someone had pinned the victim's death mask photo to the board. Lottie studied the emaciated face, while speaking over her shoulder. 'What about missing persons?'

'I had a quick look by inputting her description,' Boyd said. 'But it's vague, and nothing pinged back at me. She doesn't look familiar to me anyhow.'

'Nor to me,' Kirby said.

'Maybe we should show her photo to Laura's mother,' Lottie said. 'She might recognise her.'

'If she was local and missing for some time, we'd have known about her.' Boyd was at his obstructive best today.

'We have to exhaust all avenues,' she countered.

'Right then, I'll send it to Garda Brennan and she can ask Diana Nolan.'

'Tell her it's sensitive. We don't want to freak Diana out.'

'As if the murder of her daughter hasn't already done that.' Boyd shoved back the chair and left the room.

'What's eating him?' Kirby asked.

'God only knows.'

Lottie continued to study the dead girl's photo. She was so raw-boned she could have been twelve. It was strange that there was not one iota of information about her. From Jane's preliminary examination at the scene, she'd reported that the woman had possibly been restrained and starved. Why hadn't she been reported missing? Shannon Kenny was missing a few hours and already her brother had been in.

She leaned closer and whispered to the photo, 'Who are you? Why has no one missed you?'

———

Diana Nolan bit at the skin tag on her thumb. She tapped a foot on the floor and tried not to scream. The young garda was so annoying. Constantly making tea and sandwiches. Diana had no idea where the bread or milk was coming from, because Martina never seemed to leave the house.

She wanted to go out in the fresh air without having to make up a bloody excuse. Another day cooped up with nothing but memories of Laura everywhere was sure to send her stark raving mad.

Feck it. She ran downstairs, grabbed her coat from the hook and wriggled into it. Once she had her grandson zipped up in his, she stuck her head into the kitchen.

'Martina, I'm taking Aaron out for a walk. He needs air. We need a break.'

'I'll go with you.' The garda must have seen the cloud travel over Diana's face, because she added, 'If you want me to?'

'I don't mean to be rude, but I need a break from you as well. Won't be long. And really, I think you'd be better off back at the station helping with the investigation. You'd be more useful there than making unwanted cups of tea here.'

'If you don't mind waiting for a moment?' Martina had her phone in her hand. 'I want to show you a photograph. It's sensitive.'

Diana felt her stomach roil. 'Show me.'

'I must warn you, it's a photograph of a dead woman.'

'Do you think she's connected to Laura?' Diana felt her heart race in her chest.

'I just need you to look at it if you can and—'

'It can't be any worse than viewing the body of my own poor girl.' Diana gulped and closed her eyes momentarily before taking the phone from Martina. When she opened them, she glanced down. Her heart rate quickened. She shook her head quickly and handed the phone back.

'Do you recognise her?'

Diana couldn't answer. After another head shake, she took

Aaron's hand and the stroller from the hall and was outside before the guard could object.

She strapped him in securely and set off, walking briskly. She had no destination in mind; she just wanted to be away from the cloying memories and the thought that Laura's death was all her fault. And then there was that photograph. Dear God, what had happened to her? She pushed it to the back of her mind. She had to think of her own situation first.

It hadn't always been just her and Laura and Aaron. No. As she walked, she felt tears flood her eyes. Memories she'd hidden so deep she had almost forgotten them began to resurface. But here she was back in Ragmullin, and she'd lost Laura. Her daughter had grown into a beautiful, intelligent, vibrant young woman. And somehow even though she knew it was her fault, she couldn't help blaming *him*. If he'd taken responsibility all those years ago, she wouldn't have had to leave then. Why had she ever come back to this godforsaken place?

'Can I get some sweets in Tesco?'

The little voice broke through her reverie. Wiping away her tears, she leaned over and gripped his hand. 'Sure, Aaron. We can get all the sweets you want.'

She would have to leave everything behind. She'd done it before and she knew what she had to do now.

First, though, she needed a plan.

———

With nothing yet on the second dead woman, Lottie decided to do what she could about John Morgan.

She called the landline number Brenda had given her for her ex-husband's work in Australia. She was put through to his boss, who confirmed that Christy Morgan was indeed on site and gave Lottie his mobile number.

'I heard about his son. Awful business.'

'How is Christy taking it?'

'Badly. I didn't want to let him work, but he assured me it was best to keep busy. He said he'll need time off when the funeral is organised.'

'I'll contact him later. Thank you.'

When she hung up, Lottie wondered where to turn to next. Gordon Collins maybe. The site manager, Patrick Curran, had been cleared, but she still had to talk to Collins herself.

54

He was surprised when *she* arrived home not long after she'd left. It made him fearful.

'I can't believe what you did,' she snarled. 'You practically laid a trail to our front door. What were you thinking? It's all over the news. You fucking eejit. I told you to bury her body miles away from here. You couldn't follow a simple instruction, you moron. What will I do now?'

A shrug of his shoulder elicited a smack on the back of his head. It actually felt better to be physically attacked than the verbal abuse she expelled in his direction.

'Answer me!'

'I messed up. But the truth is, she's dead. She can't talk. There's nothing for you to worry about.' He cowered then, because he rarely stood up for himself.

'Nothing to worry about? How can you be so stupid? There could be DNA or a fibre or something on the body. What if they link her back to here? To us? They'll find out who she is and when she disappeared, and... and then what?'

'I don't know.' He wondered why she was so flustered. He'd never seen her like this.

'When they identify her, and they will, they'll discover where she was last seen and who she was seen with. Ring any bells in that skull of yours now?' Her face flared red, her hands curled into fists and he continued to cower like a poor dog about to be struck.

'Oh, I see.' And he did. He straightened up a little. Shit. She was right. Again. He had totally fucked up this time. He watched as she extracted the knife from its sheath and wondered if he would survive the day.

Instead of lashing out, though, she marched around slapping the flat side of the blade against her thigh, working herself into a frenzy. 'I'll have to spend ages figuring this out because of you. It's all right for you. You can sit on your arse in that fucking shed all day, doing sweet fuck-all, leaving me to sort out the messes you make. I don't know why I bother with you, you useless sack of shit.'

Her words wounded him. He knew he wasn't any great shakes, but he did have a job. He was a driver and a gardener. He usually did his work before she left and after she came home. It meant there was always one of them in the house to make sure nothing went wrong there. A thought struck him as she banged the front door behind her: how come she trusted that he would not run? Maybe because he had nothing, and nowhere else to go.

———

She took deep breaths in the car. She had to calm herself. Driving helped her to decompress. It wouldn't do to draw suspicion her way. Not that she could be linked to anything that had happened. She was clever. She kept her hands clean. And she had an escape plan along with her fall guy if everything went pear-shaped. Which was looking more than likely.

How could he be so stupid? Then she realised that was the

reason she'd kept him. He bowed to her every whim and rarely asked questions. She had such a hold over him, and the thought of this filled her with a power so great she almost had an orgasm in the front seat of her car.

As she pulled away, she looked up. Magenta was staring at her from the top window. She gave the child a chilling smile. As if things weren't complicated enough, she knew she'd have to keep a close eye on her.

She'd spent her life looking over her shoulder, and it seemed that she now had to look at those she'd surrounded herself with too.

55

McKeown had taken over from Boyd and Kirby to complete the warrants for the Right One database and the financial records for Laura Nolan and John Morgan. Superintendent Farrell had insisted on changing some of the wording, and it was taking forever to find a judge who was free to sign them. While he waited, agitation gnawed at his gut.

He had to be doing something. The wheels were turning too slowly. With little or no evidence in any of the murders, they had no real suspects. He pulled up the footage they'd received from the cinema and retail businesses at the complex. He'd already gone through it, but there had to be something he'd missed. No one could leave a body out there without being captured on some sort of security camera. Then he remembered they'd just been sent footage from the football club located across the road from the entrance to the retail park.

The recording started little over an hour before the body had been found by the café worker. He watched, eagle-eyed. And that was when he saw the child – was it a boy? – walking along the footpath and stopping at the wall before climbing over and disappearing.

McKeown stamped his foot on the ground, banging his knee on the underside of the desk.

'God Almighty!' He rubbed his knee, more in excitement than pain. At last. Something.

He rechecked the tapes from the businesses in the complex, but they were all located around the corner from the cinema. At the front there was nothing to see after the cinema had been shut at eleven and the gates locked. Why not? Laura's body had to have been left there some time after everything closed for the night. Maybe the football club had footage from earlier that night. The tape he'd been sent began at six a.m. Or they might have cameras with different angles. He lifted the phone and called the club caretaker.

'Did you see the weather that night?' the caretaker grunted. 'We had a power outage. Must have been caused by the heavy rain.'

'You have nothing before six a.m.?'

'Nah. I came in and reset the trip switches.'

'Any other cameras?'

'There's one at the rear. It faces our car park behind the clubhouse. Not much use to you. All were down.'

'Thanks anyway.' McKeown hung up.

The killer had been inadvertently lucky. It was too much of a stretch to think he had caused the power outage himself, wasn't it? But they couldn't take the risk of ignoring the possibility. He called the electricity company and got confirmation that the power had been out at that location for a number of hours.

He rewound the tape to the little boy with the school bag on his back.

'Who are you, son? Can you tell us anything?'

This was a development. He'd have to inform the boss. An alert would be issued for the boy. And then he had another thought. Why was a young child out alone at that hour of the morning?

———

'What's your name?' the little girl asked as she licked soup from her spoon.

Shannon stopped in the middle of the floor, hands loaded with dirty dishes. They must have been on the table since breakfast time, because cereal had set rock hard to the bowls. The man, his face dour and down, had let her out of the room. Without a word, he'd pointed to the mess, gone out the back door and locked it.

Her memory was beginning to return. A scene had flashed in front of her in full technicolour when the man had entered the room and flicked on the light switch. It came to her in movie frames. He had given her a lift last night. She'd got into his car. Willingly, it seemed. And then... what? He hadn't looked scary then, but now he did.

Another scene flashed up. She'd tried talking to him, begging him to let her out of the car, but he'd struck her with the back of his hand. She must have passed out. She recalled waking up as he parked the car. Then he'd clamped a cloth to her mouth and she remembered nothing else, until now.

Was she supposed to clean the kitchen? If only she hadn't such a raging fever. She felt like she was about to pass out. Glancing at the little girl, she estimated she was about seven or eight. Scarecrow-looking. Angry spots had erupted on her face. Chickenpox, like Davy had. Maybe she should try to make this child her ally. To help get her out of here.

'My name is Shannon,' she offered, surprised she could talk. She tasted the gum from the tape on her lips.

'Like the river.'

'Something like that. But I'm not free to flow like the river. I'm trapped. I really shouldn't be here.'

'Do you not like us?'

'It's not that. This is not my home. That man abducted me. Do you know what that means?'

'Yeah, I'm not stupid. I can read past age twelve. You should be glad to be here. We're nice. We're a good family. I hope you last longer than the last one. She was no use.'

Shannon felt her knees buckle. She put the dishes down on the counter before she dropped them. 'There was someone else here before me?'

'Yep.'

'Where is she?'

'I'm not supposed to talk to you.'

'But... when did she leave?'

'She was here yesterday and now you're here.'

'What was her name?'

'I'm not supposed to tell you anything. You're very nosy. You won't last long.'

'Won't last long?' Shannon gripped the edge of the table. 'What do you mean?'

'Stop asking me questions,' the child snapped, sounding too grown-up for her age. 'You're making my head ache and my spots itchy.'

'What's your name?' Shannon was desperate.

'Stop asking questions!' The girl slammed the table with her fist. 'I have to finish my soup and go back to bed to rest.'

'*Please.* You know my name, it's only fair that I should know yours. I won't let on that I know it. I promise.'

The girl sighed and threw the spoon on the table. 'They call me Magenta. Now leave me alone.'

She marched out of the kitchen and up the stairs, leaving Shannon shivering. Terrifying thoughts cascaded over her about what might be going on.

After a moment, she put the dishes in the sink and turned on the tap. While the basin was filling up, she peered out the window.

The garden was surrounded by large trees and a massive wall, like a fortress She guessed the house was located in the countryside. She couldn't see any sign of life or other houses. The wooden shed caught her eye. It was where she presumed the man had gone.

'Who are you?' she mumbled.

Then she heard the water flow from the sink to the floor. She turned off the tap and wondered how she could escape.

56

Jess hadn't wanted anything to do with the police, but George had begged her, almost on the point of tears. They weren't treating Shannon's disappearance seriously, he'd said. What if she'd been murdered? What if...? He'd droned on and on, and was so insistent that she'd ended up accompanying him to the station.

The detective had agreed to talk to her, mainly to shut up George, who was verging on hysteria and terrifying Davy. He'd insisted on Jess seeing a detective rather than a uniformed officer. When he began mouthing off about how his sister might have been murdered, they'd relented.

'I'm Detective Kirby.' The man pulled in his stomach to allow himself enough space to sit at the scratched table. Jess noticed that the table was bolted to the floor. Was this where they brought criminals to interrogate them? She wished it was over. 'How can I help you, Jess?'

'That's Shannon's brother out there in reception. George Kenny. He's already reported Shannon missing, but he thinks you're not taking him seriously.'

The detective flicked open the thin manila file he'd brought

in with him. 'I can assure you we take all incidents like this seriously. I have the missing person report here. What can you
add?'

'Probably nothing, but I was out with Shannon Friday
night. That's the last time I saw her, though we did speak on the
phone last night.'

'Okay, first tell me about when you last saw her. Anything
unusual that you can remember.' He opened a notebook, apparently ready to jot down points. This made her even more
nervous.

'There was this guy at the bar in Fallon's. I thought he was
cute with a beard and all, but he gave Shannon the willies.'

'The willies?' The detective smiled. 'I know what you
mean, Jess. Continue.'

'We had a few drinks in Fallon's before heading to Danny's.'

'This guy at the bar, what's the story there?'

'He sent drinks down to our table and asked if he could
join us.'

'Did you know him?'

'Never saw him before in my life. He kind of freaked
Shannon out.'

'Do you think she knew him?'

'No, it was just that she had a bad feeling about him. Well, I
think that's all it was. Shannon can be secretive. I rarely know
what's going on in her head.'

'Go on.'

'That's all really. We left him there at Fallon's and went to
Danny's Bar. Afterwards, we were going in different directions,
so I got a taxi and she walked home.'

'Okay. You said you spoke to her on the phone yesterday.'

'I texted her a few times yesterday morning. To tell her
about the murder at the building site. I was to meet her in the
park, but she messaged to say she had to head off. And then she
rang me last night saying she was out again for a date but he

hadn't turned up and she was at a loose end. She asked me to meet her for a few drinks. I was bushed and broke. We'd had two nights in a row and no way could I do another. Anyhow, I was already in bed when she rang.'

'Where was she?'

'I think she was outside Danny's.'

'Did she mention the guy from Fallon's again?'

'Not a word.'

'Did you think he was suspicious?'

'He was just being nice.'

'You mentioned she told you on the phone she'd been stood up. Do you know who she was meeting?'

'No, but it was probably some guy from the agency.'

'Agency?' The detective sat up a bit straighter.

'Oh shit. Don't write that down. Her brother knows nothing about it.'

'About what?' He leaned in closer.

She could smell his woody deodorant and figured he used it to mask the sour odour of cigars. Knitting her fingers together, she took a deep breath. George would kill Shannon if he found out, but feck it, he was the one who'd dragged her here. 'Shannon was registered with an escort agency.'

The detective sat with his pen poised over the notebook. 'What agency?'

'Is it important?'

'It might be.'

'Ehm... It could be called Right One.'

'Right One? Are you sure?'

She knew she could fudge it, but it was probably best to be honest in the circumstances. 'Yes, I'm sure. It's a dating thing.'

'Did Shannon get many dates this way?'

'A few. But more often than not she was stood up or they turned out to be pricks.'

'Did you know Laura Nolan?'

'Me?' Jess was confused. Was she being interrogated? What had Laura Nolan got to do with Shannon disappearing. 'No, I didn't.'

'Did Shannon?'

'She knew of her. Ehm, I'm not sure how.'

'Mm. Okay. Let's back up a bit. You said you were texting her yesterday about the murder at the building site. Did you or Laura know the victim? John Morgan?'

'I didn't, but the name sounded familiar. I remembered I'd heard Shannon mention him before.'

'She knew him?'

'Ehm, I suppose so.'

'*How* did she know him?'

Jess shrugged and said nothing but she knew the detective was about to put words in her mouth.

'Was he registered with the agency, do you think?'

'I don't know.'

'Could she have dated him?'

Jess felt as if she'd walked into a minefield. If Shannon was just hung-over somewhere, she'd never forgive Jess for blabbing. But if she was in trouble, Jess knew she had to tell the truth.

'She met him in rehab. Cuan Centre in Delvin. About a year ago.'

'Shannon Kenny met John Morgan in rehab?'

'Yeah.'

'Go on.'

Jess picked at her nail, keeping her head down. 'She told me about him because they helped each other in that place.' She looked up at the detective. 'But I don't think she'd seen him since she left.'

'What was she there for?'

'Drug addiction. Her mother died a few years ago and Shannon went through a hard time. George discovered she was taking cocaine and pills. He gave her an ultimatum. Get help or get out.'

'So she went into rehab. For how long?'

'About two or three months. I don't think she's taken anything other than alcohol since then. And she's holding down her job at the hospital. She's with the household staff there.'

'You're sure she knew John Morgan?'

'All I know is she mentioned he was nice to her in rehab. She was lonely and he listened to her. So yes. She knew him.'

'Did they date?'

'I don't think so. It was more a friendship. Kindred spirits, she called it.'

'And you say you don't know if they met after she left?'

'I have no idea.'

'Thanks for that information.'

'Is it important?'

'It could be. We need to find out who she was meeting last night and if he was from the Right One agency.'

'She never told me the names of anyone she met that way. I gathered they were all a bit older and had money. That's all I know.' Jess thought maybe she should have been more inquisitive about what Shannon had been up to. But surely it was no more dangerous than meeting someone through a dating app. It might even be safer, because the men were vetted. Shannon had told her that.

The detective stood awkwardly. 'Thank you for all your help.'

'I'm really worried for her.'

'Do you think she's in trouble?'

'Shannon's unpredictable, but she'd contact me no matter what state she was in. Her phone appears to be off or it's out of battery.'

'Okay. We have her number. I'll get someone to determine

where the phone was last used and take things from there.
Thank you, Jess.'

57

Kirby sat at his desk reading over his notes, scratching his head. Who was this Shannon Kenny, with her connections to two murder victims? Laura Nolan was registered with the agency, and John Morgan had been in rehab with Shannon. Were those connections important, or were they just coincidences? The fact that Shannon knew John Morgan from her stint in rehab was interesting. Had she met him since then? Whatever about that, the Right One agency needed another look. He decided to pay Greg Plunkett a visit.

He went to Barrack Lane and rang the bell. There was no answer. Of course, it was Sunday. Damn. One more try.

Keeping his finger pressed on the bell, he waited. No one responded. Back in his car, he searched for a cigar in the glove box. Amy was constantly hiding them, telling him they were bad for him. Usually he just smiled, knowing he had a secret stash, and when the coast was clear he'd go out to the garden for an illicit puff.

He was giving up on his search when a shadow from across the road caught his eye. A man had come out of the Right One office. Kirby recognised him from his photo and watched as he tightened a tartan scarf around his neck and made his way on foot down the street.

Plunkett stopped beside a car illegally parked on double yellows. He took a parking ticket from under the wiper and stuffed it in his pocket without looking at it, as if this was a regular occurrence. The lights flashed as he hit a key fob. He slid into the Toyota something-or-other. McKeown would know the make, bastard. Nothing too flashy. Business mustn't be that great in the photography/modelling/escort business, Kirby thought. Or maybe he wasn't looking to attract attention.

He waited to see which direction Plunkett would head, but the man remained seated in his car, staring at the steering wheel. Nothing for it but to have that chat now.

Plunkett literally jumped in his seat at the knock on the window. Kirby indicated with his hand that the man should lower it, then leaned down, resting both elbows on the opening.

'Mr Plunkett, can I have a word?'

'Who are you?'

'Detective Larry Kirby.' He held up his ID. 'Just need to clear up a few things. Can I sit in? Or shall we head up to the station?'

Plunkett nodded towards the passenger seat. 'Be my guest.'

Once he was settled on the cold seat, Kirby twisted his body to study the man. Plunkett was shaking. 'Is there something wrong? You look scared.'

'You'd be scared too if a fa... a detective accosted you, wanting "a word".'

He even did the air quotes. Gobshite.

'I didn't accost you. You've nothing to be afraid of if you haven't done anything wrong. Have you?'

'Of course I've done nothing wrong. This is harassment. Two of your colleagues already talked to me. Isn't that enough? What more can I tell you? It's tragic about poor Laura, but I had nothing to do with it.'

'Tell me what you know about Shannon Kenny?'

'Shannon?' Plunkett's eyes widened and his hands faffed about in the air, seemingly flustered. 'Why are you asking about her?'

'It's my job to ask the questions.'

'All right, I know of Shannon. So what?'

'How do you know her?'

'She's one of my girls.' Plunkett's face reddened. 'I mean, she's registered with my agency.'

'When did you last see her?'

'Ages ago. We only speak on the phone. Message online. Work stuff.'

'And when did you last speak with her?'

He seemed to relax, planting his hands on the steering wheel. 'Yesterday. Mid morning, I think it was. I wanted to see if she was interested in meeting someone new. She'd been with a guy earlier in the week who didn't treat her well, so I believe. Because you lot had been talking to me, I decided to speak to her first before putting someone else her way.'

'I'll need that person's name.'

'First tell me what's going on.'

'In a minute. That bad experience she had the other night, what happened?'

'Nothing much really.' Plunkett blew out his cheeks as if deciding what he should say. 'She's a bit of a drama queen. Said the guy promised her dinner but they only had drinks and he was flirting with everyone. She's a beautiful young woman and should be making something of herself.'

Kirby figured Plunkett knew nothing of Shannon's troubled past. He kept quiet about it. 'I'll need that guy's details. Did Shannon agree to the date last night?'

'She agreed that I could forward her contact details. With you lot snooping around my website, I felt it was better not to have contact made through it.'

'Did this date go ahead?'

'I've no idea. I sent her number to the guy and heard nothing back.'

'Don't you check in to make sure the girls are okay after these dates?'

'They're adults. They don't need hand-holding.'

'After all that's happened, maybe they do. You could be putting these young women in harm's way.'

'What do you mean? Has something happened to Shannon?'

'She's been reported missing, and Laura Nolan is dead. Two of your *girls*, as you call them. It might be no harm if you paused your business for the time being. At least until we can guarantee the safety of the young women.'

'Shit. Shannon is missing? How? I spoke to her yesterday. She can't be missing.'

'We need your full client list, with the names of those Shannon had most recent contact with. We're in the process of getting a warrant signed, but it'd be a great help if you could supply them without one.'

'Sure. But Cathy is off and she knows it better than me. She can send it tomorrow.'

'I'm certain you can do it today.'

'I'll go back in now and see what I can do.'

'Appreciate it.' Kirby handed over his card. He lumbered out of the car and leaned on the roof while Plunkett got out and zapped the car locked.

'I have nothing to do with what's going on,' he said. 'You have to believe me.'

'Just send me on those names. Oh, and by the way, you need to provide an alibi for Thursday and Saturday nights.'

———

Unable to locate the boss, McKeown parked his discovery about the young boy on the CCTV footage while he had another look at John Morgan. He had Pine Grove doorbell footage to check but for now he needed a change from that sort of work.

Brenda Morgan had accessed her son's online banking and emailed over his bank statements. He went through them and hit on a transaction from a London bank, presumably his mother's. The next day the money went out to Cuan rehab. The boss had mentioned Cuan, but he felt he'd read about it somewhere else. Where, though?

He clicked open tabs on his computer and found it. He sent it and the bank statement to the printer. Dragging the pages as they completed, he burst into the boss's office. Still empty. He was debating phoning her when Kirby ambled into the room, huffing and puffing.

'Hey, Kirby, where's the boss?'

'God only knows. Why?'

'Have a look at this.' McKeown settled on the edge of Kirby's desk while the other detective took a quick look at the statement.

Kirby took off his coat. 'So? We know Morgan was in rehab. And his mother paid for it, so that's not news.'

'But have a look at this.' McKeown handed over the second page. 'Note who is the largest donor to Cuan.' He smirked as he watched Kirby read.

'What about it? He donates to charity. It's a tax thing. No big deal.'

'But Gordon Collins is in financial difficulties. Why was he donating to Cuan?'

'Is it even relevant?'

'I think it's very relevant.' McKeown eyed his colleague. 'Hey, you know something, don't you? Spill.'

Kirby puffed out his cheeks. 'The missing woman, Shannon Kenny, was in Cuan for around three months last year. She met

John Morgan there. And, like Laura Nolan, Shannon was on that Right One website.'

'Holy shit.' McKeown thought of the connections they were making. 'What if Laura Nolan was in Cuan rehab too? That would definitely link the victims.'

'But what about the woman whose body was found this morning? And there's no evidence to point to Shannon Kenny being a victim yet. She just hasn't come home after a night out. It's not the first time she's done it.'

'Come on, Kirby. We already have three murders. You have to admit it's suspicious.'

'How do we go about finding out if Laura Nolan was ever in rehab?'

'I can ask her mother, but first we need to tell the boss. Where is she?'

'God knows. Might be a family emergency.' Kirby scratched his head. 'Where's Boyd, come to think of it? I'll phone their mobiles.'

'We also need to see how Gordon Collins fits into the mix with these charitable donations.' McKeown stalled, starting to doubt the significance of his find. 'Thing is, they were above board.'

'How did you find out about them?'

'I remembered I'd seen something about Cuan when I was checking up on Collins. Googled the article and up comes the bold Gordon in the local paper handing over a cheque,' McKeown said. 'I'm trying the boss again.'

58

Lottie kept thinking of the most recent dead woman. She felt a rising sense of hopelessness about how she'd spent her last days. She imagined all sorts of scenarios. None of them good.

The large gates slid open, and Boyd parked outside the seemingly modest two-storey red-brick house overlooking Ladystown Lake. A lawn bordered the short driveway. No flowers, but plenty of trees. She had phoned Collins and arranged to meet at his house. He surprised her by opening the door before she had pressed a finger to the bell.

'I have cameras,' he said, by way of explanation. 'Come in. You can leave your shoes there if you like. Underfloor heating.'

She glanced at Boyd, and he shrugged. She shook her head. No way was she taking her boots off. She followed Collins down a narrow corridor. He was even taller than Boyd, and he had to bend his head as he led them through a door into an extension at the back of the house.

'Oh my God,' Lottie said, astounded by the scale of the room and the view. The house seemed to be cut down into the earth, a box of glass walls framing the lake. Everything here was new, and definitely not modest. Totally different from the front of the building. Deceptive.

'Tea? Coffee?' Collins asked.

'Coffee, if you're having one yourself,' Boyd said.

'Yes, coffee would be good.' Lottie squeezed her fingers into her palms in an attempt to calm down. Collins was grating on her nerves. Maybe it was the money oozing out of the grey granite floor and the white quartz countertop or perhaps it was just the glorious heat beneath her boots.

When they were seated at the table by the glass wall, Lottie sipped her coffee, hoping it would be horrible. It was delicious. She glared at the industrial-sized coffee machine. She must be getting old if she was jealous of a fecking coffee machine.

'So, you wanted to talk to me?' Collins said expectantly.

'You spoke a few days ago with our colleague, Detective Kirby. I wanted to follow up on that.'

'John's murder was such a tragedy. I still can't believe it happened in one of my new houses. And in the very one his mother had purchased. She had intended to return to live in Ireland. Doubt she will now.'

'Do you have any notion as to why John was murdered there?'

'Is the location relevant?'

'Mr Collins—'

'Please, call me Gordon.'

'Gordon, three people have been murdered over the last few days and one of them was your employee. His mother told me he attended rehab last year. Now I find out it was a facility to which you make large donations.' She was glad of McKeown's hurried call supplying this information.

'I make a lot of donations.'

'Why do you donate to Cuan in Delvin?'

'I just do.' He gulped down his coffee.

'I doubt you're the type of person to stick a pin in a map and say, yep, today I'll give two hundred K to Cuan.'

'Okay.' His body slumped a little. 'Not many people know this, but I had an addiction problem in my twenties. Alcohol. I spent a few months in Cuan. It helped me enormously, even though back then it was a bit of a dive. When I can, I make a donation. It's tax-deductible.'

That figures, Lottie thought. 'Have you visited it in recent years?'

'What has that got to do with anything?'

'Answer the question.'

'I don't know what your point is, but yes, I visited it to present my annual donation, last February.'

'Are you aware that this is where John Morgan was resident for a time?'

'I suggested the facility when his mother asked me.'

'You seem awfully pally with Mrs Morgan.'

'Brenda is a business acquaintance. Nothing more.'

This was going round in circles. Lottie changed direction. 'I'd like to show you photos of two women. One of them is deceased in the photo. Are you okay with that?'

'Why do you want me to look at them?' He seemed to catch Lottie's cold stare and added, 'Okay, show me.'

'I want to know if you recognise either of them.' She showed him Laura Nolan's photo first.

He shook his head. 'I don't know her, but I did see her mentioned on the news. May she rest in peace.'

Lottie slid the second photo across the table, keeping her eyes firmly latched to Collins.

'This is the girl we found dead this morning.'

A tinge of green appeared on his face, and his eyes widened. She hoped he wasn't about to puke.

'Do you recognise her?'

His voice was low as he uttered a strangled 'No.'

'It seems to have affected you more than Laura's photo.'

'Because this is a photo of a dead person.'

'Laura is dead too.'

'You know what I mean. Please, take it away.'

'You never saw either of these young women when they were alive?'

'I don't recall either of them.'

She couldn't be sure if he was telling the truth, but something was off. 'Are you married, Gordon?'

'Not that it's any of your business, but I'm separated. I've five daughters in their teens and twenties. They live with their mother in Dublin.'

'So you get to enjoy all this luxury on your own. Seems a waste.' Lottie knew she was being unprofessional, but frustration had got the better of her. 'Have you a girlfriend?' She felt Boyd kick her ankle in warning. But she had an odd feeling about Collins and she didn't like it.

'Inspector, you're out of line.'

He was correct, but she kept going. 'I'm just curious. Do you use the services of Right One? It's some sort of dating agency, for escorts.'

The green tint had fled his face and now it burned bright red. His hands twitched as he stood and brought his cup to the sink area. She assumed there was a sink there, but she couldn't see it. Probably hidden behind a sliding panel.

Boyd inclined his head towards her and she shrugged. She had no idea what was going on either.

Collins turned round. He leaned against the fancy countertop, kicked off his suede slippers and crossed his legs at the ankles. She noticed he was barefoot and thought guiltily about her own muddy boots trailing across his terrazzo floors. Maybe she should have taken them off like he'd suggested.

'Detectives,' his voice was low and level, 'what I do in my private life is of no concern to you. A young man who worked for me was murdered on my property. I don't know why, nor do I know what happened to those poor unfortunate women. I kindly ask you both to leave my home. Any further questions can be put to my solicitor. I'll forward you the details.'

They had been dismissed. Lottie didn't like his arrogance and opened her mouth to retort, but Boyd stood and spoke before a word could leave her lips.

'Thank you for your time, Mr Collins,' he said. 'We appreciate it. If we have further questions we will contact your solicitor.'

He walked to the door, but Lottie remained seated.

'Do you know a Shannon Kenny?'

'No. Who is—' Collins shut his mouth as if remembering his statement about solicitors.

'Have it your way.' She stood. 'If it becomes relevant to our investigations, I will see you at the station.'

59

Kirby spent an hour calling the men on the list sent over by Greg Plunkett. There would have to be face-to-face follow-up on the few of them who'd met with Shannon and Laura. But for now, he couldn't find any holes in their alibis. Where did that leave him? He went back over his notes and decided to talk to George Kenny about Shannon's stint in rehab.

George ushered him into a cluttered sitting room with a little boy asleep on the couch. 'Have you news of Shannon?'

'Not really. I wanted to ask you about her time in rehab.'

'So now you think she's a junkie and won't investigate?'

'I never said that. We are taking it very seriously.'

George lifted a stack of laundry from an armchair and offered the seat to Kirby. He'd have preferred to remain standing, but George perched on the edge of the couch so he sat also.

'How long was she in rehab for?'

After a pause, Shannon's brother said, 'A few months. I gave her an ultimatum. She was missing work. Drinking all the time. Doing drugs. My mother's death went hard on her, you see. I had to do something. After rehab, she was grand, but recently she's slipped back into old ways. No drugs but drinking a lot. She was heading for a downward spiral. Maybe I was too tough on her. Maybe she did run away.'

'Have you checked if any of her belongings are gone?'

'There doesn't seem to be anything missing. Her suitcase is still here.'

Kirby looked at the little boy. 'This is quite delicate and I'm not sure if you know or not, so don't explode.'

Kneading his fingers into the palms of his hands, George nodded, preparing himself. 'What is it?'

'It's come to our notice that your sister was... She seems to have been registered with some sort of an escort agency.'

George blew out his cheeks. 'I didn't know, but I suspected she was up to something.'

'How did you suspect it?'

'She had feck-all money but could still go out and have a good time. She took my bank card from time to time, even did that the other night. But deep down I knew she couldn't be funding all her nights out.' He looked at Kirby, his eyes imploring. 'Do you believe she's with one of those men?'

'I've checked out those we know about and they all appear to have watertight alibis. Unless she met someone not on the agency's database.'

'Have you checked the pubs? Their CCTV?'

'It's early days, George.'

'You need to give this all your attention. That other girl who was murdered, Laura Nolan, she's taking precedence in your investigation, but what if Shannon... What if...?'

'Don't jump to conclusions. There's something else I wanted to ask you. It's about her time in rehab.'

'Go on.'

Kirby felt sorry for him. He looked deflated, as if all the fight had been sucked out of him with a paper straw. 'Did you ever hear Shannon talk about a man called John Morgan?'

'Morgan? Isn't that the guy who was found dead at Pine Grove?'

'Yes. Did you or Shannon know him?'

'I didn't, but I don't know about Shannon.'

'Did she mention anything about him when she was in rehab?'

George squinted at Kirby. 'The name means nothing to me, other than I heard it on the news. I can't remember Shannon ever mentioning him. Is it important?'

'It might be nothing, but she appears to have been there when he was. It's probably a coincidence, but I'll need details about her stay, to check it out if it does become important.'

'You mean, if she's been murdered too?'

'We have no evidence of that. You're sure you don't know who she was meeting last night?'

'I didn't even know she'd gone out!'

'Okay. Can I have a quick look in her room?'

'What for?'

'To see if I can find any clue as to where she might be.'

'I'll bring you up there.'

Kirby followed George and couldn't help feeling sympathy for one so young having so much to deal with.

———

The pain in her chest was like an irritating itch and Shannon wanted to scratch it like mad. She was back in the room, the tape over her mouth and her hands bound. What type of set-up was this? It was bizarre. Nothing made sense. A house, with a child, where she was some sort of servant? What was that all about? So far she hadn't been sexually assaulted, not that she could remember, but that might change in the days ahead.

Days? What was she thinking? She couldn't stay in this house, prison, whatever it was. She had to get out. Get home.

Wouldn't George miss her? Or would he think she was back on drugs? If so, he'd want nothing to do with her. He'd told her as much after she'd finished her stint in rehab. Don't do it again, he'd said, or you're on your own. And she'd kept clean, hadn't she? But even though she hadn't touched hard drugs or prescription pills, she was drinking too much. The thought made her yearn for a vodka and Coke. To blot out the unimaginable situation into which she'd landed. And she needed a shower. She smelled so bad. Would they allow her to bathe? She hoped so.

Her thoughts were all over the place.

Rehab. That had been so difficult, but John had made it worthwhile. He was cute and funny while being serious behind it all. He'd told her he had a gambling problem and smoked a bit of weed. He was determined get back on his feet, find a good job and make a better life for himself. That was what he'd said, she remembered now, and that was what she'd wanted too. But somehow she'd succeeded in fucking it all up.

And John? Was he really dead? Murdered? It made no sense. He'd been harmless.

She gazed into the darkness for a long time, afraid to fall asleep and knowing she couldn't sleep anyhow. She didn't even know if it was day or night. She was in a living nightmare.

60

McKeown had had enough of office cabin fever, so he headed to Diana Nolan's house. He felt better suited to talk to Laura's mother rather than asking Garda Brennan, who was as thick as two ditches since he'd broken up with her.

He almost did an about-turn when he saw Martina's grumpy face at the door.

She brought him inside. 'Are you checking up on me?'

He reckoned she was still sore over her last FLO mistake. 'Don't be silly. I need to talk to Diana.'

'She went for a walk with her grandson. Should be back soon.'

'How long is it since they left?' He sat at the small kitchen table and rubbed a hand over his shaven head. He was uncomfortable being in close proximity to Martina. She was sexy as fuck and that was what he wanted to do whenever he was close to her.

'About an hour ago,' she said. 'Diana can come and go as she pleases. I'm only here to support her.'

'You don't have to convince me. I know how the family liaison system works.'

'What do you want with her?' Martina stood as far away as she could in the tiny kitchen, which was still close enough to touch his elbow.

'I need to find out if Laura was ever in rehab. It's come up in the investigation. It seems that John Morgan and Shannon Kenny, who appears to be missing, were in rehab at the same time, in the same place.'

'Appears to be missing? She either is or isn't.'

'She didn't come home from a night out, so it's possible she might not be missing. It's suspicious because she was also on that escort website, same as Laura.'

'That's an interesting connection.'

'It is, and she was in Cuan rehab centre last year, same as John Morgan. What makes it even more interesting is that Gordon Collins, Morgan's employer, makes an annual donation to Cuan.'

'You have been busy. But it's all circumstantial, isn't it? This Shannon might be okay.'

'Possibly, but we have three dead in the space of a few days, cause enough to treat her disappearance as a priority. If Diana confirms that Laura was in rehab too, then we have another link.'

'What about the woman who was found dead this morning? Any developments there?'

'Appeals have gone out for information, but we haven't identified her yet. Next step is to issue her death photo to the public, but I don't think the boss is too keen on doing that. Not yet, anyhow. Would you ring Diana? I need to talk to her and get back to the office.'

With a groan, Martina called the grieving mother. 'No answer.'

———

The Aroma Café was quiet, which suited Diana. Aaron happily traced a chip around the pool of ketchup on his plate while she sipped her second cup of frothy milky coffee. She'd heaped three sachets of sugar into it, hoping that the sweetness would clear her head.

A plan. She needed to come up with one, and fast. With the garda ensconced in her house and others dipping in and out asking questions about Laura, Diana knew it'd be more difficult to disappear.

'When is my mam coming home?' Aaron interrupted her futile thoughts.

'I told you, sweetheart, she's gone to stay with the angels. She's happy in heaven.'

'Is she not happy here with me?'

'She is... was. But she wants to be able to look down on you from the clouds and care for you with the angels.'

'Why can't she care for me here?'

How did one convince a little boy his mother was dead? Diana was at a loss to find the right words while her own heart was shattered. The image of angels and fluffy clouds would not satisfy her grandson for long. 'I don't know, honey. Please eat your chippies and let me think.'

'Think about what?'

'Stuff.'

'I want to go home and play with my toys.'

'Soon. You have to eat all your chippies first.'

Her phone vibrated on the table and skittered away from her hand. Martina. Again. Could she not allow her a little time to herself? She could feck right off.

'Would you like to go on holiday with me, Aaron?'

'To the seaside?'

'Maybe.'

'Can Mam come too?'

Diana groaned. This would be so much more difficult than she had imagined. There was no way she was waiting around for the guards to pin Laura's murder on her. She needed to go home for their passports. That was when it hit her. Aaron didn't have a passport.

61

Lottie was developing an irritating itch about Gordon Collins. He had no clear alibi for John's murder because they didn't have a definitive time of death. In and out of the site all day didn't constitute an alibi. And when Kirby told her Shannon had spent time in rehab along with John Morgan, she wanted to see Cuan's records.

'We haven't enough for a warrant,' she said.

'Maybe a trip out there would work?' Boyd said.

'I would have asked Collins about Shannon had I known more. Now that I've awoken the solicitor demon in him, there's no point going back to him until I have evidence that he's somehow involved.'

Kirby chomped on the end of an unlit cigar, like a cow chewing the cud. 'If we could identify the dead woman, it might help tie things together. She has to have been killed by the same man as Laura.'

'I agree,' Lottie said. 'There's no way we have two killers stalking the young women of Ragmullin.'

'Stranger things—' Kirby began.

'Don't,' Lottie and Boyd said simultaneously.

She studied the board of photos. The room was silent except for the hum and rattle of the radiators struggling to generate heat. 'What did you make of Plunkett, Kirby?'

'He's a bit up his own hole. Enough of a twat to make him a murderer? I don't know. He seemed on edge, but that's to be expected. His *girls* are being murdered. And what he's doing is verging on illegal. He should be investigated by vice and—'

'The murders take precedence. Go back to him with the photo of the latest victim. If she turns out to be registered with his agency, then we rip his place apart. Did we get access to his database?'

'Yes. He sent it without need of the warrant. I called the relevant men to confirm their alibis and then gave it to McKeown to go through it.'

'Where is he?' Lottie asked.

'He went to Redwood Court to find out from Diana if Laura was ever in rehab. Should be back by now. I'll give him a call.'

'We should go ahead and publish the photo of the unidentified victim,' Boyd said.

'You know I hate having to do that.'

'What about her DNA? It needs to be checked to see if it throws up anything.'

'Too soon for that, but we do need a starting point. I'll talk to Farrell again about the photo.'

Kirby ended his call. 'McKeown's on his way back. Diana went out over an hour ago. To clear her head, according to Martina. She's not back yet and not answering her phone.'

'She probably needs the headspace,' Lottie said, though she had a jelly-like feeling in her stomach. Was that all Diana wanted? Headspace. Or was she meeting someone? Had she had something to do with her daughter's death? 'Where's Laura's son?'

'With Diana.'

'Ask Martina to check if she took any belongings with her. Just to be sure. Then do a background check on Diana.'

As Kirby got back on the phone, Lottie caught Boyd's eye. He had that look.

'What?'

'I know we need an identity for the woman found this morning,' he said, 'and Shannon Kenny might yet be okay, but we should draw up a graph of anything and everything that links the victims to each other. Are we missing something? Something crucial.'

'We're missing John Morgan's murder weapon, for one thing,' she said.

McKeown arrived and filled them in. 'I'm sure Diana Nolan only wanted to escape from Martina's sour—'

'Enough,' Lottie said. 'Anything else to report?'

'Regarding Shannon Kenny, I found her on CCTV outside Danny's Bar. She was on her phone. Must be when she called her friend Jess. Then she pocketed the phone and headed off down the town. Alone.'

'Check out CCTV from Fallon's for Friday night. A guy with a beard.' She told him what Jess had said, and the time. 'Have you accessed any other footage along the route she'd take home?'

McKeown checked his iPad. 'I almost forgot. I discovered this young lad on CCTV from the clubhouse across the road from where Laura's body was found.' He angled the screen to show Lottie the still he'd taken from the footage.

'What time was that?'

'After six a.m. They have no other footage because there was a power outage.'

Lottie examined the image. 'The child climbs over the wall and into the grounds of the cinema complex.'

'Who is he?' Boyd asked. 'Why is he out at that hour of the morning?'

'And why has no one brought him in? Laura's case is on all the news channels and social media outlets. The super has taken part in countless media briefings.'

'Maybe the kid hasn't told anyone,' McKeown said. 'Maybe he didn't even see the body.'

'Show me the actual footage,' Lottie said, and braced herself.

The furniture in the superintendent's office was shining. The smell of polish caught the back of Lottie's throat as she explained about the boy on the CCTV footage.

'It's a grainy image and he does nothing.' Deborah Farrell smoothed down her clip-on tie.

'I know, but this is important. That little boy was on the site before Shane, the barista, discovered Laura Nolan's body. SOCOs found small footprints there. They must belong to the child. We need to put out an appeal for him.'

'First you want to issue a death-mask photo to identify a woman's body and now you want to paste an innocent child's image all over the media. Do you even know what you're doing any more, Inspector Parker?'

'Look...' Lottie paused. 'We have numerous investigations on the go. Boyd is drawing up a document as we speak outlining how the cases intersect. The unidentified woman whose body was discovered this morning has a stab wound similar to those on Laura Nolan's body. It's possible they were killed by the same person. I'll have more information once the post-mortem is carried out. And—'

'Hold it right there.' Superintendent Farrell held up her hand and settled forward at her desk. 'Weren't there signs that this latest victim had been incarcerated?'

'Yes, according to the pathologist when she was at the scene. Jane has yet to—'

'And it seems likely Laura Nolan was abducted off the street or from a pub, seeing as she was out Thursday night.'

'Yes, boss.'

'How can you link her to a woman who may have been incarcerated somewhere for however long? You haven't even got confirmation that the wounds were caused by the same weapon. Come back when you have more.'

'But we can't identify her. We need the public's help.'

'Her body was only discovered this morning. We have issued an appeal for information via my media briefing and social media. Someone might yet come forward. Run her DNA, chase the pathologist and come back to me when you have the post-mortem report.'

Lottie decided to pedal back. 'About the child. We have footage of him climbing over the wall close to where Laura's body was found. We need to identify him. If I draw up details, can you make a plea for him to come forward?'

'You think a kid watches my press briefings?'

'His parents might recognise him and bring him in.'

'Show me what you've got.'

She felt a twinge of apprehension. All she had was the grainy footage, but she ran it for Farrell.

'I want a very good reason why I should make this public.'

'We need to talk to him. He looks no more than seven or eight and that's concerning. We have no footage of him coming back over the wall. He may have entered the housing estate that backs onto the cinema complex. I don't think we can ignore his presence at the scene.'

'Do a house-to-house then.'

'We're flat out as it is, and I haven't got enough people for that unless you can allocate me more.' Lottie knew Farrell would be thinking of costs and overtime without adding any more personnel to her spreadsheets.

'Send me the best image you can grab from the footage and I'll consider it.'

'Thanks, boss.'

'And Parker?'

'Yes?'

'Find that missing Shannon Kenny woman before she ends up dead like the other unfortunates.'

Lottie escaped out the door. In the corridor, she leaned against the wall to catch her breath. She was glad Farrell hadn't mentioned John Morgan's murder, because she had absolutely nothing to tell her.

62

Martina sent a hasty text to McKeown once Diana and her grandson arrived home.

'You were gone a long time. Where—' She clamped her mouth shut as Diana threw her a look that said, *If you utter one more word I'll thump you.*

When she'd hung up the coats and folded the buggy into the corner, Diana switched on the television for the boy and began rifling through the cabinet drawers.

'Can I help?' Martina offered.

'No, it's fine.' Diana pulled open the next drawer.

Martina settled on the arm of the chair where Aaron was sitting with his legs under him, remote in hand. 'What are you looking for, Diana?'

'My daughter is dead and you lounge around here, good for nothing but making tea. I'm fed up with it. I don't need you here. I'd like you to leave.'

Stunned, Martina stood. 'If that's what you want, but first I think you need to sit down, relax a little and have a cup of tea. I'll switch on the kettle.'

Rising to her feet, Diana took a step towards her. 'If you

make another cup of tea in this house, I will throw it at you. I don't need tea. I don't need you. All I need is my daughter back home, and Aaron needs his mother. Please, just leave us in peace.' Tears glistened in her eyes as she turned back to the cabinet.

Martina supposed she'd have to leave, but she was loath to do so as the woman was in an obviously distressed state. 'Okay, but do you mind if I have a cuppa myself first?'

'I don't care what you do once you leave me alone.'

'You all right there, Aaron?' Martina turned to the child. 'Would you like a juice box?'

'Leave him alone,' his grandmother snapped. 'I can look after him.'

Martina glared at the older woman's back. Surely she couldn't get any angrier if she posed McKeown's question.

'There is one thing I'd like to ask you.'

Diana threw her hands in the air and kicked the drawer closed. 'If it means you'll leave me alone, then go ahead. Ask away.' She folded her arms, but unfolded them just as quickly, as if the action had unbalanced her. She leaned against the cabinet.

'My colleague Detective McKeown called while you were out. Something came up in the course of the investigation into John Morgan's murder, and we need to know if you can confirm whether there was a connection to Laura.'

'What do you mean? What sort of connection?'

Martina took a breath to keep her annoyance at bay. 'Was Laura ever in Cuan rehab?'

'Rehab? Whatever for?'

'I don't know. Alcohol? Drugs?'

'Are you trying to tarnish my daughter's reputation now? Is that your game. Victim-blaming.'

'God, no, not at all.' Shit, she was doing this all wrong. 'We just need to know if Laura was ever in rehab. That's all.'

'Didn't sound like it to me. What are you playing at?'

'Nothing. It was a straightforward question.'

'No it wasn't. It was couched in blame and shame. My Laura had nothing to be ashamed of.' Diana's eyes travelled to Aaron, and Martina found herself feeling sorry for the boy but also angry at what she assumed were diversion tactics by his grandmother.

'All I wanted was a simple yes or no. We are trying to rule in or out potential links between the victims.'

'You're persistent.' Diana hesitated before continuing. 'I was not Laura's keeper.' She pushed herself away from the cabinet. 'Can you just leave me in peace now?'

'Sure, okay. But I'd say Detective McKeown will return to talk to you.'

'So be it.'

As Diana resumed ransacking the drawers, Martina ruffled Aaron's hair and left the room. She fetched her coat. Once outside, she stood for a few moments breathing in the fresh air and expelling the feeling that had caught up inside her. Diana Nolan was definitely hiding something.

———

Hearing the front door close softly behind the departing guard, Diana sank to her knees on the carpet.

'Are you okay, Nana?'

'Just taking a break, sweetie.' She rested her head against the cabinet and exhaled a long, exasperated breath. She shouldn't have been so rude to Garda Brennan. After all, the woman was just doing her job, trying to get answers. Diana wanted answers too. But she didn't want her private life uprooted, laid bare for the world to see. There were too many undesirable aspects of her past that should remain buried.

She knew she should have expected this level of scrutiny

with Laura's murder. But she'd had years of comfort lulling her into the proverbial false sense of security. She could not take any further risks. Her priority was to protect what was left of her family. She had to act. Now.

Sitting on the floor, phone in hand, she googled how to obtain a child's passport. She'd find her own eventually, but first things first, she had to get Aaron one.

Tears started to gush from her eyes as she read the details. It was impossible. She was not Aaron's legal guardian. There would be a minefield of legalities to overcome. Affidavits and the like.

She dried her tears to the sound of the *Mr Bean* cartoon on the television. If they couldn't escape abroad, they'd have to either sit it out here or else flee somewhere locally until it was safe to return. Paranoid or not, she felt she had to leave Ragmullin.

63

With the lines on Boyd's graph criss-crossing in mostly illogical patterns, and nothing clear coming to light, Lottie decided to drive out to the rehab facility. Cuan was a long-established addiction rehabilitation centre, and she was hopeful of getting some answers there.

It took her twenty minutes to reach it. She liked the rural aspect of the location. The building had been *in situ* since the 1960s, even though it had been partially burned down and rebuilt.

As she waited by the intercom to gain entry to the building, she found the darkening evening peaceful. The only sound was the murder of crows roosting on the bare branches of a large oak tree to the side of the building. The trundle of a tractor starting up somewhere caused the birds to rise as one and swarm the sky like a swirling black blanket. She shivered and pressed the intercom again.

After giving her details, she was admitted into a hallway. The cramped space had tired tiled walls and floor. It was like an ancient bathroom, and it was even colder inside than outside.

The reception desk in front of her was encased in Perspex, the only nod to modernism.

'How can I help you?' The woman looked to be in her fifties, her face creased in tired furrows with eyebrows severely plucked and painted back on. Her name badge said *Mona*.

'Hi, Mona. I'm investigating a serious crime and would like some information on residents who were here about a year ago.'

'I doubt we can give out that information. Privacy is paramount for our clients.'

'I get that, but one of your former residents was murdered this week. I'm sure you've read about it. Seen the photos and all that.'

'Oh God, I heard the news. How awful. May she rest in peace.'

She? Lottie tried not to let the surprise show on her face. Did Mona mean Laura? If so, it would need to be confirmed. She had to be careful how she continued her quest.

'I hope you can see a way to help me find justice for her.'

Mona straightened her back and a steely glare replaced her sympathetic expression. 'What do you mean by that?'

'I want to rule Cuan out of my investigation. Who do I speak to about this?'

'I don't know what *this* is yet.'

God Almighty. Was the world made up entirely of stonewallers? 'I need confirmation that the victim was a resident here.' What she really wanted to know was if Laura had been resident at the same time as John Morgan, but she couldn't just blurt out her question. Mona would clam up.

'Irene might talk to you. Irene Dunbar. She's the manager.'

'Right. Will you let her know I'm here?' It was like pulling teeth while standing on eggshells. Lottie swallowed down her impatience.

'She's not normally here on a Sunday, but she came in for a few hours today. I'll give her a buzz.'

While Mona punched in an extension number, Lottie noticed how bare the hall was. Even the receptionist's booth had nothing on the walls, and her desk held only a computer and phone.

'Irene says she'll squeeze in five minutes for you. Wait there.'

I'm going nowhere, Lottie thought. She checked her phone to make sure no one was trying to reach her. Then she scrolled through her recent photos and debated showing one to Mona. No harm in trying.

'I'd like to show you a photograph to see if you recognise who it is. Okay?'

'Sure.'

'I should warn you, the person in it is deceased.'

'Oh, I don't think I have the stomach for that.' Mona paused, then took a deep breath. 'Well, I'll try.'

Turning the phone around, Lottie studied the woman's reaction closely. Mona paled and scrunched up her eyes, her eyebrows meeting in the middle. 'It can't be... Sorry.' She turned her head away from the image and glanced behind her and back again. 'Sorry. I'm so sorry.'

With that, a door opened to Lottie's right and a tall, elegantly dressed woman approached. 'I'm Irene Dunbar. Come this way.'

With a last imploring eye at Mona, Lottie pocketed her phone and followed the high-heeled clip-clop down the tiled corridor.

After formalities were dispensed with, Irene Dunbar, the Cuan manager, seated herself primly behind an old wooden desk with a green leather insert. A bundle of manila files were piled up on the floor, as if the woman had cleared the desk for Lottie's impromptu visit.

'Okay if I call you Irene?' Lottie said, trying to get comfortable on the hard chair.

'That's what everyone calls me. You do know I can't give out any personal information without a warrant, and even then it would need to be carefully worded.'

Jesus, she was going to be a worse pain than Mona. Lottie explained about the recent murders without mentioning any names. 'It's come to my attention that the victims spent time here last year. All I want is confirmation of that fact. It may assist my investigation or it may have nothing to do with it.'

'Who are you enquiring about?'

'Firstly, I know John Morgan was a resident in Cuan last year. His mother told me. Then there's Laura Nolan...' She let the name hang there, hoping Irene would bite.

'And?'

Shit, Lottie thought. The woman's face was impassive, but was that a twitch at the corner of one eye? 'I believe Laura was also here for a time. I just need to confirm the dates. Was it while John was here?'

'I can't comment. I explained that.' Irene's tone implied that Lottie was stupid. Try again.

'You can confirm that Laura was here, just not when?'

'It was you who said she was. I didn't confirm or deny it.'

Could she throw the receptionist under the proverbial bus? She didn't want to, but needs must. 'Mona said Laura had been resident here.'

Irene's face reddened, but she quickly regained her composure. 'Mona had no right to say anything of the sort.'

'So we have established that Laura Nolan resided here for a time. If I give you some dates, I know you won't answer, but can you just nod if they match Laura's time here?'

'Good God, Inspector, this is more like an episode of *Line of Duty* than real life. Off the record, okay?'

'Okay.'

Irene folded her arms, then unfolded them as if she didn't know how best to present herself. 'As she is deceased, I can confirm that Laura Nolan was here for one week last year. I recognised her name and photo on the news. I can't give any more details other than to say that her week was during the time John Morgan was here. Is that all?'

She stood. This irritated Lottie, who remained seated, but it suited her at the same time. She wanted to catch the manager off guard. She whipped out her phone and tapped the photo icon.

'Do you recognise this woman?' She held the phone just far enough away that Irene had to lean over the desk to view the image.

'Good Lord!' Her hand went to her chest dramatically and she dropped back onto her chair. 'Is she... is she dead?'

'I'm afraid so.'

'What happened to her?'

A name, Lottie silently prayed, drop a name. 'She was murdered. Her body was found this morning. Dumped in a field with only birds for company. Awful.'

'Oh my God.' Irene removed her spectacles. She wiped the lenses with the hem of her white shirt before replacing them on the bridge of her nose.

'We can't begin a proper investigation into this young woman's death until we identify her. We know nothing about her, only that someone murdered her. I need your help.'

Finding a tissue up her sleeve, Irene wiped the corner of her eye and blew her nose. 'It's Aneta Kobza. She worked here as a caregiver, early last year. Maybe for a month or so. I can't remember how long. One day she didn't turn up and never returned. I tried her phone, but it was dead. I figured she'd gone home to Poland. I put her behaviour down to bad manners when she left without notice. She was a good worker. And they aren't ten a penny, I can tell you.'

'I'd like to see her personnel file. It might be helpful.'

'As she's deceased, I suppose I'm not breaking any confidentiality laws. Give me a minute.'

Irene rose slowly from her chair, as if the life had been drained from her body. A tinge of sympathy for the woman was quickly replaced by anticipation when she returned with a slim manila folder. It didn't contain much. A one-page job application, including an address at Hill Point apartments in Ragmullin, and a photograph pinned to the inside cover of the file.

Lottie gasped. 'Gosh, she was beautiful.'

'She was indeed.'

Seeing the young woman photographed in life, smiling with her hair flung back, brought a lump of anguish to her throat. The similarities to Laura were subtle. Same hair colouring. Pretty features all lined up in a perfect face. A face and body that had been emaciated and abused since then. The poor girl.

'There's not much information here. No references from any other job in Ireland before she worked at Cuan?'

'No, she'd only arrived the week before she started here, if I'm remembering correctly. She had the proper work visa, all above board. The reason I remember her is that I had to bring her into my office on one occasion.'

'For a reprimand?'

'Not really. She had what I can only describe as a mini breakdown in the common room.'

'What happened to cause her to become upset?'

'I don't know. She refused to tell me anything other than to say her period made her emotional. I sent her home early. I didn't even write it up, as no one was hurt or anything like that.'

'But still you remember it. Why is that?'

Irene hesitated before exhaling, as if she knew she had no choice. 'I have a very clear recollection of it because I was conducting an open-day tour of Cuan for our financial donors and prospective donors. The health service reduced our funding, so it was really a funding drive. The last thing I needed was a disruption.'

'Donors? Was one of them Gordon Collins, of GC Construction?'

Irene flushed and nodded. 'He goes public, so there's no harm in confirming he is a donor and was here that day.'

'Would Aneta have come into contact with him or any of the other donors?'

'I don't see how.'

'Did they tour the common room?'

'Yes, but... her outburst came later.'

'What was the outburst like?'

'I wasn't present at the time, but it was reported to me. She suddenly started to shake and cry, for no apparent reason, and had to be escorted out by another staff member.'

'And she came to work the next day?'

'Yes, for a day or two, I think, but then she just... disappeared.'

Lottie felt stunned. 'And you didn't think to report it?'

'Like I said, I assumed she'd gone home to Poland.'

'Didn't you connect her outburst to her disappearance?'

'I had no reason to.' Irene paused. 'What happened to her?'

'I intend to find out. Can I take this file?'

'Sure.'

'I'll need a list of everyone who was on the premises the day Aneta had her outburst.'

'You'll have to get a warrant.'

'I'll get it.'

'I'm sorry I can't be more helpful.'

Sure you are, Lottie thought. 'You have been helpful. I now have an identity for the latest victim.'

'Do you believe they were all killed by the same person?'

'It's a possibility.'

'Are the killings connected to Cuan?'

'Another possibility. Irene, I'd appreciate it if you kept all of this under wraps until I know what and who I'm dealing with.'

'Of course. The last thing I need is anything unsavoury being linked to Cuan.'

64

It was dark by the time Lottie pulled up at Hill Point apartments. Her stomach growled in protest. It was past the time to go home and cook dinner, or have it cooked for her if she was lucky. But she felt she was on to something. It might turn out to be nothing, but a gnawing in her belly that wasn't hunger kept her going.

The apartment door was opened by a young woman who told Lottie she'd been renting it for the last nine months. She knew nothing about the former tenant.

'Try the caretaker,' she said, 'Nick Carter.'

'Was the apartment cleared out when you arrived?'

'Yes. Refurbished and painted. I could still smell the paint, but it faded after a few days.'

'And nothing belonging to the former tenant remained?'

'Not a thing. Even the furniture was brand new.'

'Thank you.' Lottie went back down the stairs wondering if the caretaker was still around. The office was on the ground floor, beside the dentist's surgery. She knocked and was surprised when the door opened. A stocky, sweating man was zipping up his bomber jacket.

'Mr Carter? I'm Inspector Parker. Can I have a quick word before you leave?'

'Sure. Walk me to my car. The wife rang to say my dinner is on the table, and if I'm not home in the next fifteen minutes, she'll chuck it in the bin.'

'Really?'

'I wouldn't put it past her, she's been so contrary recently. She hates the winter. I hate the winter. Dealing with burst pipes all day long. Do people not realise that in this weather you need—'

'Sorry, can I stop you there?' She realised he was the type of man to moan about his wife and life until she ran out of time to ask questions. 'I wanted to ask you about Aneta Kobza. She lived in apartment 5C last year. Do you remember her?'

'Let me think. 5C. Little Polish girl. Very pleasant. She'd paid her deposit and an advance for the month, think it was up to the end of last February, but I'd have to check. All cash, that's why I remember her. Then she upped and left without a goodbye or a thank you.'

'She left suddenly?'

'You could say that. Dishes in the sink, clothes in the wardrobe. Must have met a lad. Or hightailed it back to Poland.'

'But why would she leave her clothes behind in either scenario?'

'How would I know?'

'Were you not curious?'

'Look, Inspector... Parker, is it? Ha! Like nosy parker. Very good. You should see the state some people leave the apartments. Hers wasn't too bad. It had been earmarked to be redecorated anyhow.'

'Was there any sign of a struggle? Or anything to say she might not have left voluntarily?'

'I'd have called you lot if there was.'

'What did you do with her belongings?'

'Dumped whatever looked like crap. I must have packed the rest into her suitcase and stored it in lost and found.'

'Where is this lost and found?'

'A room behind my office. It's cleared out annually.'

'Are her belongings still there?'

'Should be.'

'I need to see them.'

'And I need to get home for my dinner. I can't afford a divorce and I'm bloody starving. Come back tomorrow.'

'Please, Nick. I believe Aneta was murdered. It's imperative that I get access to anything belonging to her right this minute.'

'Murdered? Holy God. What is this town coming to at all?' He glanced at his car, apparently debating which was the easier option. An irate detective or an angry wife. With Lottie standing in front of him scowling, he made the right choice.

'Come on then, but you can talk to the wife and tell her why I'm going to be late.'

The caretaker opened the office and walked to a door located behind a steel-legged desk. No computer, only an old-fashioned ledger. He searched for a key on a clanging bunch he'd taken from his pocket. The light came on automatically when the door opened.

'Should be in here someplace,' he muttered.

She was astounded at the array of belongings stacked to the ceiling. 'I thought you said you cleared out the room annually?'

'I do. This lot accumulated over the last twelve months. Some people won't pay for removers, recycling or refuse. They leave behind what they don't want to bring with them. Pain in the hole for me, excuse the expression.' He made his way through the narrow space, checking the boxes on either side.

'Aha, here we are. One suitcase belonging to Miss Kobza.'

Lottie was amazed he'd found it so quickly. 'You said you

dumped other things she left behind. Would you have a record of what that consisted of?'

'No way. Sure haven't I enough to be doing. It wouldn't have been much anyway – probably tatty ornaments. As far as I know she arrived with only this suitcase.'

'Okay. I'll need to take it with me.'

'Be my guest.'

The case was made of red material, with wheels. Good. As she went to drag it, she realised it was missing one wheel. Shit.

'Hold your horses,' Nick said. 'This box seems to be hers too.'

The cardboard box showed signs of nibbles, and Lottie shivered. Her phobia of those four-legged creatures caused the hairs to shoot up on the back of her neck. 'Would you mind carrying it out to my car?'

'You'll be wanting to come home with me and eat my dinner next,' he said with a grin. But he took the box and followed her out. She wouldn't mind some of his dinner, come to think of it.

After they'd loaded the case and box into the boot, she shook hands with Nick. 'Thank you for your help.'

'No bother at all. Glad to help the force.'

'Why didn't you report Aneta missing?'

'Inspector, people do a runner all the time. You'd be mired in paperwork if I was to report all the goings-on here.'

'What was she like?'

'Haven't much memory of her. Saw her the day she arrived. Handed her the keys and Bob's your uncle – not that I know if you have an Uncle Bob or not. She didn't come to my attention at all.'

'If you think of anything, call me.' She handed him her card.

'Sure will.' He pocketed the card and made his way to his car.

She sat into hers and watched him drive off. She had an

identity for the murdered woman discovered that morning, and some of her possessions. Now she had to find out when and from where she'd disappeared. Was it possible she had been held somewhere for almost a year? And why had she been murdered now?

With three people dead and Shannon Kenny still missing, was it just one murderer she was searching for? Time would tell, and she didn't have any more time today. She needed to get home and eat.

65

Katie had driven Rose back over to Farranstown House late in the afternoon. She lit the fire in the large draughty sitting room while she began concocting a dinner from the meagre provisions in the cupboards and freezer. She needed to have a serious conversation with her mother. Her gran was not doing well and Katie figured she needed full-time care. It was dangerous leaving her on her own.

With chicken goujons in the oven and potatoes boiling on the hob, she had her head in the freezer looking for peas when she heard the clang of the doorbell. Wiping her hands on a dirty tea towel, reminding herself to put on a wash, she went up the draughty hall to answer the door.

She felt her jaw hang open, unable to utter a word.

'Hi, Katie. We need to talk.'

At last she was able to form words. 'Christ Almighty. What are you doing here, Jackson?' She kept the door only partially open and leaned against it.

'Can I come in? Please.'

'But how did you find out where I live?'

'I dropped you home last night. Remember?'

'Oh, right.' She knew how Rose felt now. She hardly recalled the drive home after their argument at the restaurant. 'Suppose it's all right, then. Be quiet, though, my gran is resting in the sitting room.'

'Will I take off my shoes?'

Katie smiled and pointed at the grubby floor. 'What do you think? I'm in the kitchen with Gordon Ramsay.'

'Will I be safe in Hell's Kitchen?' He followed her through.

She closed the freezer door, deciding on a tin of beans instead of peas, and switched on the kettle. 'Coffee?'

'Sure, thanks.' He seated himself at the table and rolled his finger over and back on a crumb. 'I'm sorry I was such a dick, Katie. I really like you and it makes me sad for us to finish with a row. I like your company. I even like your son.'

'You know nothing about my son.'

'I like you, so I know I'll like him.'

'Leave Louis out of this conversation.'

'I just want to apologise. I've had such a stressful time lately, but it was no excuse for being an idiot with you. I'm so sorry.'

'The food was nice, though.'

'It was, until I ruined the evening.'

She made two mugs of coffee, and sat beside him. 'I feel a confession coming on.'

'This is difficult. I believed that if you knew the real me, you'd run a million miles.' He flashed her a forlorn smile of perfect teeth. Made her wonder how much it would cost her to have her own teeth straightened.

'All right. Out with it.' Just then she heard the front door slam. 'Great. Not. Mam is home from work. She doesn't know how to shut a door quietly.' She stood up and began wiping down the table. Why was she nervous? Did she not want her mother turning her nose up at her boyfriend? Was he even her boyfriend? She didn't know what to think.

Lottie marched into the kitchen dragging a suitcase

unevenly behind her. 'I smell spuds burning. Did you let the water boil off them? Is that Gran's car outside? Is she okay?' She noticed Katie's visitor and stopped. 'What the hell are you doing in my house?'

She let go of the suitcase and it toppled over on its three wheels. Katie held her breath, ran to pick up the pot of spuds and watched Jackson, his face ashen, leap to his feet.

'Inspector Parker?' He turned to stare at Katie. 'She's your mother?'

'*She*'s the cat's mother,' Lottie said, marching into his space. 'I asked what you're doing in my house.'

Katie broke out of her stupor. 'He came to see me. How do you know Jackson?'

Lottie laughed. 'Jackson? That's a good one. Are you a jack of all trades then?'

'I have to go.' He edged towards the door. 'Sorry, Katie.'

'Not so fast, Greg,' Lottie said.

'Greg?' Katie didn't know what was going on. But hearing her mother's tone, dripping sarcasm and disdain in equal measure, she knew it wasn't going to end well.

'Greg Plunkett,' Lottie said. 'Markets himself as a modelling photographer to entice young women into his lair and then sets them up as part of his dating agency, which is really an escort agency.'

'That's absurd,' Katie said derisively. In reality, she was still reeling from the fact that he'd lied about his name. She watched her mother round on him.

'Oh, so you haven't told my daughter what you do?'

'You have it all wrong,' he mumbled, his hand on the door. 'I'm leaving.'

'Without giving Katie an explanation? Have you tried to coerce her like you did Laura Nolan and Shannon Kenny?'

'What? No, and I don't coerce anyone.'

'And what about Aneta Kobza?'

'Aneta who?'

'Don't play the innocent with me, Mr Plunkett. Your business is nothing short of a prostitution racket and you're the pimp.'

'You're insane!'

Lottie pulled out a chair and sat. Katie tipped the pot into the sink, potatoes and water, and switched off the oven. Her mother could starve, because she was being insensitive at best and obnoxious at worst. Did she not realise she was still standing there listening to those awful accusations?

Lottie must have seen the look on her face, because she said, 'Check on your grandmother. I need to have a conversation with Greg here.'

He opened the door. 'I'm leaving. You have no right to talk to me the way you just did. I've been cooperative with you from day one. I've a mind to report you.'

'And I've a mind to lock you up. You're trespassing in my home.'

'I let him in,' Katie said. 'So you can forget about trespassing.'

The door behind Greg pushed in and he moved to one side. Rose stood on the threshold, looking all around. Her hair was matted to her scalp and a sheen of perspiration lined her forehead.

'What's all the shouting about?' She waved her arms. 'I want to go home.'

Katie rushed over and took her arm to lead her back to the sitting room. 'Will you help me stoke the fire, Gran?'

'What fire? Is the house on fire? I smell burned spuds.' She pointed at Greg. 'Who are you?'

Katie took her gran's hand to lead her out, and glared at him thinking that that was a very good question.

———

There was shouting coming from somewhere in the house. Shannon wondered what was going on. She felt so ill and her skin itched all over. A wave of nausea travelled from her stomach to her throat. If I get sick now, I'll choke, she thought. Her mouth was bound with tape again. She had to escape from this hellhole. The little girl, Magenta, might be her way out. But how? Was she as evil as the adults? Who were these people?

She groaned, twisting over onto her side. The door opened and a shaft of light pierced the ink-black room. She blinked and tried to see who had entered, but her eyes were as sore as the rest of her body. She couldn't even cry out.

66

Lottie watched Greg shuffle from foot to foot in his shiny leather shoes. He could have left after Katie and Rose, but he'd remained. Did he think he was safer answering questions here without caution than at the station? She'd find out.

'Sit down.'

He sat at the table, folding his arms. She sat opposite him.

Taking out her phone, she scrolled and then turned it towards him. 'Know her?'

'What? Who is that? Is she dead?'

'Yes.'

'I don't know who she is.'

Lottie scrolled to the last image on her photo app. The photo she'd taken from the personnel file at Cuan. 'This is her alive.'

He scrutinised it. 'I can't say I've ever seen her before and that's the truth.'

She sensed he was sincere, but with McKeown having access to his database, it would be easy to check. That was if Aneta had used her real name.

'Can I leave now?' he asked.

'What are you doing with my daughter?'

'I didn't know she was your daughter. I met her at Fallon's the other night. We had a few drinks and I took her out for a meal last night. That's it. She's a lovely person and I like her. End of.'

'I don't think it's anywhere near *end of*. Stay away from her.'

'Don't you think that's for Katie to decide?'

She had enough on her plate without interfering with her daughter's love life, but she didn't like Plunkett or his business. No matter what she did, though, she'd incur Katie's wrath.

'Go on, get out.'

When he'd left without another word, she ran her hand through her hair. A headache was taking root and she was starving.

Katie returned with Louis wrapped up in his jacket and with a small rucksack on his back. 'I'm taking Gran home. We're staying the night with her.'

'We need to talk.'

'Not now, Mam. I can't take much more of your interference. We can talk tomorrow. Come on, Louis.'

Lottie watched them leave, without even a kiss from her grandson. She was about to switch the oven on when Sean loped in. 'What's for dinner?'

'I'm about to rescue these goujons. I'll throw on a few chips and call you when it's done.'

'You okay, Mam?' Sean asked.

'No, but am I ever?'

'Good point. How's the case going?'

She looked at the suitcase, then realised he meant the investigation. 'Going round in circles. Be a star and bring in the cardboard box from my car.'

'Sure.'

She spread frozen chips on an oven tray and put them in to cook. Glancing at the mess of potatoes in the sink, she was about to clear it up when Sean deposited the box on the table.

'Do you want me to watch the chips?' he said, pointing at the oven.

'Not at all. I'll give you a shout when they're done.'

She made a coffee for herself after he strode out. Sipping the hot liquid, she considered the box. 'I hope to Jesus nothing jumps out,' she said, grimacing.

———

Magenta hated it when they fought, which was all the time. Her head ached and she scratched her spots.

'It has to be chickenpox,' the woman said. 'That school is an incubation hub. Why do you always bring home germs? You're useless. Like him.'

Magenta had to agree about him.

'It's like a pox on all your houses, as Jesus said,' the woman continued.

Magenta wasn't sure Jesus had said that, but when *she* spoke you had to believe her. She was charismatic that way, while also being the cruellest person Magenta could imagine. Would she turn out like her? She supposed she would. She felt like twisting her heel on his head until he could no longer shout in protest. Yes, she supposed she was more like *her* than like him. Was that a good thing? Maybe.

She tried hard not to squirm like he had done. But the slap across the side of her head put paid to any bravado she could muster. A second slap sent her sprawling across the floor. An anger she rarely allowed to erupt burst through her body like a swirling froth and she could not stop the words spilling from her mouth.

'I hate you, you bitch. You keep me here like those women he brings home to you. I hate both of you!' She got up off the floor and fled before another slap arrived.

On her bed, she scratched the spots until they bled.

And then she felt better.

67

Setting down her mug, Lottie opened the box flaps warily and stood back. Just in case. When she was satisfied no living thing was in it, she leaned over and peered inside. At first glance it appeared to be full of leaflets and brochures. She wondered why the caretaker would have packed these up, seeing as most of Aneta's possessions had been dumped.

She slowly extracted them one by one. Some were in a foreign language – Polish, she assumed – but one colourful brochure in English caught her eye. Cuan rehabilitation facility. Settling back on the chair, she wondered if she should pull on protective gloves. Might be best. She got a pair from her bag, then picked up the brochure again. The image painted was of a fun-filled, bright environment to *help people regain their life*. It didn't marry up with her memory of her visit earlier.

Printed in the centre of the brochure was a compendium of photographs. Peering closely, she hoped to see someone she recognised, to give her a clue as to who had killed Aneta. She recognised two people, Irene Dunbar, and Gordon Collins, but the others didn't mean anything to her. She closed the brochure and picked out another. This one was more familiar. Pine Grove housing development.

Why had Aneta got this brochure among her possessions? Didn't young people browse everything online nowadays? But she didn't know what Aneta had been like, so there was no point in mulling over those sort of questions.

Deciding to ask Boyd to help her go through the stuff, she groped around the table for her phone. She smelled burning. Smoke billowed from the oven. The chips. Shit.

Boyd arrived within half an hour. By then both she and Sean had fed themselves on salvaged chips, goujons and a tin of beans. She'd even cleared the sink and wiped down the counters.

'Something's burning,' Boyd said as he came in through the back door.

'Don't start.'

'Whatever.'

'Jesus, you sound like Sean. How's Grace?'

'Had a row with her. Don't ask. She'd try the patience of a saint.'

'But you're no saint, Mark Boyd, are you?'

He scanned his eyes around the room, and she knew he was checking they were alone. 'Sean here?'

'Yep.'

'Pity.'

'Why? Were you intending to ravish me in my own kitchen?'

He laughed. 'I'd settle for a hug.'

'Me too.'

She snuggled into his arms and relaxed. She could fall asleep like this, such was her exhaustion. Sensing his kiss on her ear, she pulled back. 'Boyd, my hair is manky.'

'Don't care.' He nuzzled deep into her throat, then tracked to her mouth.

She welcomed his lips on hers, but her eyes wandered towards the table. 'This isn't what I called you over for.'

'Oh, and I thought you couldn't live without me and wanted to tell me you'd agreed to buy a house in Pine Grove.'

'I mentioned Pine Grove on the phone, but not for that reason.' She filled him in on what she'd learned from Irene Dunbar, and her visit to Hill Point, then indicated the two brochures on the table. 'There's one for Cuan, which I can understand as Aneta worked there. But this one is for Pine Grove.' She held it up. 'Why would she have it?'

'She might have got it from John Morgan while he was in Cuan, but I've really no idea. Was she intending to buy? Maybe she had money we don't know about.'

'I only discovered her identity this afternoon, so I've had no time to check anything.'

'This is a long shot, but I wonder if she's one of Plunkett's escorts.'

Lottie shook her head. 'I showed him her photo and he said no.'

'When did you see him?'

'Long story, and now isn't the time for that conversation.' She was too tired to go down that awkward road with him.

'Okay so. Back to Pine Grove. Maybe she wanted to buy a house. I can check with Charlie tomorrow.'

'Okay. Get gloves on, and we can go through the box together.'

They settled into the task, removing each item, shaking the pages to see if anything fell out, then scrutinising it. Most of the leaflets were in Polish, but there were some old tourist brochures too.

'Had she a laptop?' Boyd asked.

'I don't know. Unless it's in the suitcase, but the caretaker didn't mention one. Why?'

'Because if she had, I'm sure she could have looked all this stuff up online.'

'I wondered about that myself,' Lottie said. 'She could have used her phone, too, which we don't have either. We'll go through the suitcase when we finish with the box.'

'This is all rubbish as far as I can see.'

'But why did the caretaker keep it? I was thinking maybe someone else packed up her things. I'll ring him in the morning.'

'If someone else packed the box, why didn't they take it?'

'Maybe they found what they were after and left the rest hoping it would be destroyed.' She thought for a moment. 'There's no sign of her passport. They might have taken that.'

With no more interesting discoveries in the box, they put it to one side. 'I'll get Garda Lei to read through everything tomorrow,' Lottie said.

'Good idea.' Boyd hefted the red suitcase up on the table, and pulled back the rusted zipper. The case was packed with clothes. Simple and cheap. Like the stuff Lottie's girls wore. It didn't help the argument that Aneta might have had money.

'Judging by these sizes, she was an awful lot thinner when she died.' She held up a T-shirt. 'Someone took that girl, held her and starved her for months.'

'Doesn't bear thinking about.' He was going through a bundle of jeans, searching the pockets, turning them inside out. 'Hold on a minute. There's something here.'

'What is it?' Lottie dropped the clothes she was checking.

'I don't want to rip it.' He slid the paper out of the jeans back pocket and laid it on the table. 'A photograph. It's like it went through the wash. It's all faded.'

'If it was washed, it would be in pieces. It's just old.' She touched the image. 'It's a group of teenagers, male and female, with two slightly older males either side of the group.' She counted the heads. 'And I think two women, one beside each man. Turn it over to see if it's dated or has names. Careful.'

He turned it over. 'Blank.'

'They seem to be on the steps of a building. Do you recognise it?'

'Means nothing to me.'

'I might be clutching at straws here, but it could be Cuan. I read that part of the building burned down years ago. But I don't know...'

'You're tired. I'm tired. Leave it until tomorrow. I can put this lot in my car.'

'Leave it here. I might have another root through.'

'You need to sleep and I'd better head home. Grace will have another canary if I'm any later.'

They both washed their hands at the sink. Lottie wished he could stay. Wished he could hold her for the night to ease the memory of Aneta's emaciated body in a field of birds.

They kissed at the door and she waited until the red rear lights of his car disappeared before she returned to the kitchen.

She sat at the table and looked at Aneta's possessions. The girl's only legacy was the scraps from the box and the cheap clothing from the suitcase. It broke her heart.

————

Rex kneeled on his bed in his dark bedroom and looked out the window. Wrapping the duvet around his shoulders, he gazed over at the spot where he'd seen the woman's body. She had been pretty. But someone had killed her. He thought of the night before he'd seen the body. He'd been looking out his window then too. The car with no headlights had stopped at the lane before the cinema and a man had got out and dragged something from the passenger seat.

Had that been the woman?

Probably.

Should he tell someone?

Probably not.

Life was too complicated in his house to bring a further problem to their door. He got into bed, keeping the duvet wrapped tightly around his body. He tried to sleep, but it was impossible. The images haunted him. Her dirty feet. Her pretty face. Her dead eyes. Giving up on sleep, he got his Nintendo Switch from under his pillow and played Mario for hours.

68

MONDAY

At six a.m., Lottie walked into her kitchen, her coat on over her clothes. It was bloody freezing in the house. The windows had iced over in the night and a white frost glistened on the grass outside. It was so cold her breath hung in the air, a white mist. Inside! She flicked the oil switch again. Not a sound. It couldn't be out of oil already, could it? She scratched her head, thinking. She'd only had it filled at Christmas. Hadn't she? But now the tank must be empty.

She made a coffee and the hot liquid slowly warmed her up. The house was so quiet without Katie and Louis in it. Not that they'd usually be up at this hour, but she always felt their presence. This morning, the house seemed slightly empty. Sean would have to get up for school in an hour. Chloe was in late from work last night, so she'd stay in bed a bit longer. The atmosphere felt depleted.

She was tempted to text Katie to see how they'd got on at Rose's last night. No, leave it for now. She'd call round there this evening and have a heart-to-heart chat. It was time to talk seriously about their living conditions, and about Rose. And then maybe she'd talk to Boyd about pooling resources and see what they could afford. She might even swallow her pride and phone Leo in New York. Maybe. Maybe not.

The first person she bumped into at the station was Garda Lei.

'I want to revisit all the witness statements,' he said. 'I should just say statements really, because so far no one has witnessed anything, but we may have overlooked something. You know what I think—'

'I have a job for you,' she cut in. Lei would talk all day if allowed to. 'There's a box and a suitcase in the boot of my car. Can you bring them to the incident room, please? Be careful with the box, it's disintegrating. Then I want you to check every item thoroughly and catalogue them. Let me know if you find anything of interest.'

'Oh. Right. Sure. Of course. Who do they belong to?'

'Aneta Kobza.'

'Who's she?'

Lottie realised she hadn't updated the team on her discovery. 'Our latest murder victim. She worked at Cuan rehab for a month early last year.'

'Right so, boss.'

She handed over her car keys and entered the general office. The door opened behind her and McKeown strode in.

'You're early,' she said, and almost added 'for a change', but stopped herself in time. No point in antagonising him.

'Decided to leave home early because of the frost, but the main roads had been gritted, so I had no delays.'

'I want you to dig up what you can on an Aneta Kobza. And check if her passport has been used in the last year.' She filled him in on the details and asked him to populate the incident board as he worked. 'See if you can find out anything on her financials. Cuan should be able to tell you what bank they paid her wages into. Check if she had any connection to the escort agency.'

'Will do.'

As McKeown headed for his desk, Lottie heard Boyd talking to Kirby in the corridor. They were followed in by Garda Brennan.

'Martina, any update from Diana Nolan?' Lottie asked, taking off her coat.

'She kicked me out yesterday afternoon. Doesn't want an FLO, so she says.'

'What caused that reaction?'

'She'd been out with her grandson and returned after Detective McKeown had left. I just asked her the question he'd intended asking her.'

'And what was that?'

'Whether Laura had been in rehab. But she got very uptight and insisted I leave. I believe she's not being totally honest with us.'

'In relation to what?'

'I don't know, to tell you the truth. She's been acting weird. I get that people react differently to grief, but something's not quite right in that house. Not one neighbour or friend has visited her. That seems so strange. You'd imagine the place would be overflowing with Tupperware containers of food by now.'

'Have any of Laura's friends called?'

'Not a one. Maybe they were a private family and had no contact with other people.'

'Possibly. Go over what we gleaned from the canvass of their neighbours.'

'Will do,' Martina said. 'When Diana came back yesterday, she began ransacking the drawers in the sitting room dresser.'

'For what?'

'Don't know.'

'Where had she been?'

'She didn't say.'

'I'll go over there now.' McKeown stood.

'No, I gave you a job to do. I'll call round later.'

'Is there anything else you want me to do, besides checking the house-to-house reports?' Martina said.

Lottie thought she caught a satisfied glint in the younger woman's eye at her put-down of McKeown. 'Help Garda Lei in the incident room. He'll explain.'

She filled Kirby in on the latest developments, then began allocating jobs to the team. 'We need to uncover all we can about Aneta. Talk to friends, co-workers, neighbours from Hill Point apartments. If her passport wasn't used, then everything indicates she was missing for almost a year.'

Kirby said, 'And Shannon Kenny is still missing. I spoke with her brother first thing this morning. We need to issue further appeals for information. It's most likely she didn't leave voluntarily.'

'Not good news,' Lottie agreed. 'Do what you can and I'll talk to the super to prioritise it. I also need the exact dates Shannon was in Cuan.' She thought of the photo they'd found in Aneta's jeans pocket and turned to McKeown. 'Would you be able to enhance an old photograph that's faded and creased? I could send it to the tech guys, but I need it in a hurry.'

'I can have a go at it.'

She handed it to him in a clear plastic folder.

McKeown peered at it. 'I'll do my best, boss.'

As she went into her own office, she was glad he was projecting positive vibes for a change. She booted up her computer ready to launch into her day.

69

There was a commotion at the office door. Boyd could not believe who was walking into the office, followed by Garda Thornton.

'Grace, what are you doing here?' His sister had a scowl on her face and Sergio by the hand.

Thornton said, 'I brought her to the interview room to wait while I went to call you down, and next thing I know she's marching out behind me. Sorry.'

'It's okay,' Boyd said, waving the older guard away.

Grace folded her arms and stood her ground. 'I have to go back home to Galway. I brought Sergio to you. He's fed and watered.'

He hugged his son and stared at his sister. 'Did you walk?'

'Well, I don't drive.'

'But why bring him here? I'm at work.'

She gave him a look as if to ask was he stupid. 'I could hardly leave him home alone, could I? You need to look after him.'

'But you agreed to mind him. Why do you have to leave so suddenly? You could have given me some notice.'

Grace's eyes darkened. 'I'm not your employee. I was helping you out as a favour, but now Bryan needs me more than you do. Lambing has started early. I'm going home to give him a hand.'

Boyd tried to get his head around it all as Grace eyed him with an indignant expression.

'Stay until tomorrow at least. I'll drive you to Galway myself. I need to put something in place for Sergio. Please, Grace. One more day, then I'll drive you wherever you want to go.'

'The only place I'm going is home, and I'm leaving now. I have my suitcase packed. I won't change my mind.'

Boyd knew she could be as stubborn as he was at times. The difference being that Grace allowed no leeway. She had her mind made up and that was that. He tried one last time.

'What if I ring Bryan and tell him Sergio needs you more than the sheep do?'

She frowned, drawing a shade down over her entire face like a window blind. 'I know what you're doing. You're trying to emotionally blackmail me. That no longer works. I'm more intelligent than you give me credit for.' She slung her bag over her shoulder and stood, feet apart, as if waiting for an apology.

Boyd didn't want to fight. He glanced over to where Kirby had Sergio sitting on his desk. The boy was playing a computer game on Kirby's phone. What was he going to do?

'Have you nothing to say for yourself?' Grace sounded more like his mother than his mother ever had.

'I agree, Grace, I've been selfish. Go home to Bryan. Let me know how the sheep and lambs get on. Don't keep me out of the loop.'

Her eyes widened. 'What loop?'

'I want to be part of your life. I want to meet Bryan. Okay?'

'Of course you'll meet him. Goodbye.' She went over to

Sergio and shook his hand as if he were an adult. Grace didn't do hugs. A handshake was her limit.

When she'd left, the walls of the office seemed to heave a breath of relief and the air returned to Boyd's lungs.

Kirby came over. 'As the English say, you're in a right pickle, mate. But listen, Amy's at home today. I'll ask her to keep an eye on the lad. She'd be happy to help.'

'You're a godsend. Thanks.'

'I'll call her.' Kirby patted his pockets. 'Now where did I leave my phone?'

70

There was an email from Mona, the Cuan receptionist, waiting in Lottie's inbox, with the dates Aneta had worked there. She cross-referenced them with John Morgan's dates and found that they'd overlapped for one week. She looked up Kirby's notes on Shannon Kenny. Yes, she'd been there then too. Mona's email had no mention of Laura Nolan.

She knew Gordon Collins had visited Cuan last February – the photo in the brochure, and the local paper McKeown had found online proved that – and the date coincided with Aneta's time working there. Was there something about all this she should know? She couldn't put her finger on what it could be.

To complete the link, she needed to confirm Laura's actual dates in Cuan. Irene had intimated she was there when John was but why had Diana not answered Martina about it? She'd have to ask the woman herself.

After struggling into her coat, she drove over to Redwood Court. It was not yet nine a.m. She felt she'd worked a half day already. The curtains were drawn and the house looked forlorn. She hated having to wake the grieving mother, but she needed answers.

She'd rung the bell a few times before the next-door neighbour came out on her step. The older lady was wrapped up in a quilted jacket and woolly hat. She had Tesco bags under her arm as she locked the door. 'No one there, love. Saw her and the young lad get into a taxi early this morning when I was bringing in the milk. Frozen solid in the carton it was.'

'Oh, what time was that?'

'Who might you be then?'

Lottie introduced herself.

The woman nodded, satisfied.

'Must have been seven. I always get up before seven. A throwback to when I worked in Dublin and had to drive to the city every morning. That was before the commuter train. I miss the job, but you know—'

'Did they have anything with them? Bags? Suitcases, perhaps?'

'I didn't notice. They could have had them in the car before I came out. She didn't wave or nothing. Never does anyhow. Just shoved the youngster in the back seat and got in beside him. She had the door shut before I could open my mouth.'

'Thanks, Mrs...'

'Ms Molloy. Never got married. Glad now. Who'd want an auld fella telling you what you can and can't do? Not me.'

She marched proudly down the path in snow boots, which was a bit excessive, Lottie thought, considering the frost was already melting.

'Did you happen to notice whose taxi it was?'

'No, I didn't, but I heard the driver say something about the train station.'

'You've been a great help.'

'I hope she's okay. Such a shock about poor Laura. Not that they ever mixed with anyone around here.' The woman reached the gate. 'I should have dropped in, but what does one say in these situations? I kept putting it off.'

'Did you know Laura?' Lottie hoped her answer wouldn't turn into a saga.

'Know her? No one knew Laura Nolan. Closed book of a girl.'

'What do you mean?'

'She never raised her head or her hand in hello. Like her mother. Always silent. Worked in Lidl. I prefer Tesco myself. Kept to themselves, they did. Then Laura had the baby. I saw her go out a few nights recently all dolled up. Her mother is a bit of a dolly bird herself. Never saw her with a hair out of place and—'

'Okay, thank you.' Lottie felt she'd get nothing concrete from Ms Molloy. Just conjecture and gossip. All the same, she might come in handy at some stage. 'Here's my card in case you think of anything that can help us with Laura's murder.'

She almost ran back to her car before the woman built up steam again.

71

Garda Lei didn't mind being the dogsbody on the team. He loved being busy. Trawling through the dead girl's belongings, which some might see as a little morbid, proved satisfying. Getting his hands dirty. Being involved. That was what he relished. His recent work was a step up from the bike unit. Of course he was only called to work with the team when there was a major crime, but he was grateful for the experience.

'Well there, Lei, how's it going? I've been sent to help you.'

'Hi, Garda Brennan, didn't hear you come in.'

'Jesus, Lei, it's either Brennan or Martina. Keep the formal stuff for when we're in public or in the presence of the head honchos.'

'Oh, right. Great. Thanks. You can help me search this lot. Inspector Parker has already gone through it, but she asked for it to be thoroughly examined. Think you can do that?' He baulked when she rolled her eyes. 'Sorry. Didn't mean to offend you. I forgot you know more about this kind of thing than I do.'

She laughed. 'You're a scream. What are we looking for?'

'Something to give us a clue as to who Aneta Kobza was or

anything to aid the investigation. Gloves too, as this lot has to go to SOCOs.'

She tugged on gloves and a face mask, and opened the suitcase. She held up a bally jumper. 'This stuff is old. It tells me she either hadn't much money, she wasn't proud or she didn't care about her appearance.'

He liked Martina. She was a roll-your-sleeves-up sort of person. As he extracted the magazines and brochures from the box, he remembered the boss's instructions. 'We have to catalogue everything too.'

'Might be a waste of time. Let's see what we find first and then we can draw up a list of anything that seems important. Okay?'

'If you say so.' He wasn't so sure, but Martina was the more senior guard.

He watched her work. She took out each item as if it was a designer piece of clothing, rather than Penneys' past-its-best fare. He admired her for the reverence she afforded the dead woman's possessions. Her fingers traced seams, cuffs and pockets, searching for something hidden.

He had to be as meticulous. He extracted everything from the cardboard box, then searched around the inside of it, his only find a wayward spider in a corner. He turned each page of the brochures and, determining there was nothing of interest, put them to one side. Then he concentrated on the small bundle of papers that remained in a forlorn pile.

Most were typewritten in a foreign language. Polish, he presumed, seeing as the woman was from Poland. Some looked like pages from a CV, but the cover page was missing so he had no name or address.

'Bingo,' he said at last, waving a sheet of paper.

'What did you find?' Martina wiped her hands on her trousers, even though, like him, she was wearing gloves. 'Treasure, I hope.'

'One page of a bank statement. Dated 31 December, year before last. She had the sum total of five hundred zloty in her account at that time.'

'Is it her account?'

'It must be. That's her name and an address in Kraków. It has an IBAN. She must have come here after that.'

'She might have used the statement to open an Irish bank account. She'd have needed an account for paying rent and for her wages. We should get it from Cuan.'

He had an idea. 'Give me a minute.' He googled Hill Point for details on how to rent an apartment. 'She'd want at least a grand for the place she was living in, and unless she came into money after that bank statement, she didn't have it.'

'Maybe she had cash, or opened an Irish account.' Martina went back to the clothes. 'Catalogue the statement anyhow. The detectives can delve deeper. Anything else of interest?'

'Nothing that I can understand. Most of it's in Polish. I'll check it on Google Translate.'

'We haven't time for that,' Martina said. 'We're supposed to be looking for a clue to Aneta's life, to what happened to her and why she went unreported as missing for a year.'

'It's easy to fall through the cracks. So many people have no one in their lives to care about them. I always wonder—'

'Lei, it's our job to find out why she was taken and who killed her.'

He breathed out, the elated feeling dissipating quickly. There had to be something else.

72

Irene Dunbar hadn't slept a wink, and no amount of foundation could make a difference to the deep black rings sagging under her eyes. She nodded at Mona, and went into her office, kicking the door shut. She paced the floor with her phone in one hand and her takeout coffee in the other.

Should she call him? Would it make any difference? Three people with links to Cuan were now dead. And what about Shannon Kenny? The early-morning news had run a plea for information about the missing girl. All four were mid to late twenties, so they had to have other crossovers in their lives besides a stint in rehab. The gardaí had made the connection to Cuan very quickly, and she knew she was about to come under scrutiny from them and her board.

She put down her coffee, ready to make the call, just as Mona entered without knocking.

'Sorry, Irene, but I can't stop thinking about Aneta. We should have enquired when she failed to come back to work. There was that incident the day the donors were here last February. Do you think something about them freaked her out?'

'How would I know?' She hadn't meant to sound bitchy, but that was exactly how her words came out.

'Well… you talked to her afterwards. She was a nice girl. A good worker. Imagine if she went missing back then and was held somewhere all that time. It doesn't bear thinking about, does it?'

Irene sat down and tried to think of a reply that would get Mona out of her office before she threw the coffee across the room.

But the receptionist wasn't finished. 'I sent the email to the gardaí with the dates Aneta worked here. Also the dates confirming when John Morgan was resident.' She must have seen the shocked expression on Irene's face, because she added quickly, 'That's what the inspector asked for. I wonder if I should send over Laura's dates too.'

'Why in heaven's name would you do that?'

'Because it might all be linked.'

'Linked to what?' Irene clutched the coffee cup so tightly the dark liquid splashed over the rim.

'To Cuan. I remember listening to a true-crime podcast once and—'

'I've calls to make, Mona. Don't send anything to the guards again unless I say so. Do you understand?'

'Of course. I was only trying to help.' Mona slouched out of the office leaving a cheap tangy perfume trail in her wake.

Irene waited for a moment, then took three deep breaths before once again picking up her phone. She had a feeling the house of cards on which she'd created a successful business was about to come tumbling down.

73

Lottie sent McKeown to the railway station to see if anyone remembered Diana and her grandson, and failing that, to check the CCTV.

He returned quickly. 'No one remembers seeing them, but I did a quick check of the camera footage. You can't see them getting out of the taxi, but I caught them heading inside the station. I lost them after that. The platform was busy. Commuter time.'

Lottie pulled up the rail timetable as she spoke. 'Where was she going? Dublin or Sligo?'

'She only had a rucksack and a handbag,' McKeown said. 'No suitcases.'

'And you have no idea what train she was getting?'

'She was in time for the seven twenty to Dublin. But the thing is, she could have got the bus to Sligo.'

Tapping furiously, Lottie found the bus timetables. But Diana might not have taken either a bus or a train. She could have got into a car or doubled back into town.

'And you couldn't see the taxi?'

'No, sorry. I only had a quick look. Do you want me to go back and check further?'

'Leave it for now. I don't want to take you away from your other work. We can do it if it becomes necessary. Did you have any luck on the bearded guy in Fallon's?'

'No, they wipe their CCTV every Sunday morning.'

As he left the office, Martina's words came back to her about how Diana had been ransacking the drawers in the sitting room dresser. What was that all about? Was Diana running away? If so, what did she fear?

A call came to the incident room from Danny's Bar following the appeal about Aneta Kobza. Boyd headed down there. He'd had a quick word with Charlie at her office to see if Aneta had ever expressed an interest in Pine Grove. But there was no record of it.

He'd talked to Amy on the phone when he'd left Charlie's office to see how Sergio was getting on. She'd told him the boy was a dream and she was delighted to have the company. Feeling a bit better, he hammered on the pub door. It wasn't yet opening time.

Andrew, the bar manager, brought him in and bolted the door behind him before leading him through the dark lounge.

'The garda press office shared her photo on Instagram about a half-hour ago,' he said by way of explanation. 'When I saw it, I knew I'd seen her somewhere. I've a great eye for faces. I'd make a good bouncer if I wasn't the bar manager.' He laughed.

'When did you last see her?'

'It must be nearly a year ago. Around Valentine's Day, that's why I remembered her. Striking-looking woman in a red coat.'

'What exactly do you remember?'

They'd stopped at the end of the bar. Andrew took a key from a ledge and opened the door, switching on a light.

'She went off without her coat. Left it behind. Her prick of a date seemed to disappear, probably hooked up with someone else, and she just upped and left. I noticed the coat on the back of a chair and brought it in here. I was sure she'd be back the next day to claim it. But she didn't appear and I forgot all about it until I saw the photo. Beautiful girl. My wife would kill me if she heard me. Now where is it?'

'Why didn't you report it to us at the time?'

'It was just a coat left behind in the pub after a boozy night. Sure you'd be knee-deep in shite for a year if I reported them all.'

'True.' Boyd got the point when he saw the stack of coats and jackets, jumpers and cardigans piled high on the floor at the back of the storage room.

'It's here somewhere. Probably down at the bottom. We used to send this stuff to charity shops, but it's not been done for ages.'

'How can you remember her coat after so long?'

'It was unusual. Red, with a white furry thing around the hood. A bit like Santa Claus. Ah, here we are.' As he hauled out a red coat, the pile toppled over. 'Fuck. Now I will have to do something about them.'

Boyd took the coat. It was made of shiny red material, like a raincoat. The white fur trim was stained where it met the zipper. Possibly from make-up or fake tan. He patted the pockets.

'There's something in here.' He extracted a phone. Samsung. Older model. It was dead when he pressed the on button, obviously, after a year in storage. And it might not even be Aneta's. He checked the rest of the coat. A few torn tissues in the other pocket. A tear on the elbow. Nothing else of note.

'Thanks, Andrew. I'll take it with me.'

'I'm sorry now that I didn't do more at the time, but we're so busy all year round. Not enough hours in the day. You know yourself. How was I to know she'd end up dead?'

'I don't suppose you remember who she was with?'

'God, no. Probably just some dick who didn't care enough about her.'

Poor girl, Boyd thought. No one seemed to have cared about her.

'Any CCTV from back then?' he asked hopefully, but that hope was dashed when Andrew stared back at him.

'You're joking, right? Not a hope in hell. We wipe it weekly.'

'Would you be agreeable to look at photos to see if anything jogs your memory?' Boyd had no idea what photos he was even talking about. Maybe John Morgan, Gordon Collins or Greg Plunkett. The workmen from Pine Grove, perhaps.

'Sure, but I honestly don't recall him.'

'Do you remember anything else from that night?'

'It was jammers. I only remembered her because she was beautiful and because of the coat.'

Boyd got a refuse sack from Andrew and bundled the coat into it. It might yield nothing. Then again, it might be a critical clue. His shoulders drooped as he left. A suitcase, a box, a Santa coat and a phone. All that remained of Aneta Kobza's life. No one had cared enough about her. Now it was his job to care.

75

Boyd sent the phone up to Gary in technical, who began searching for a charger to fit it.

'Do you think it's Aneta's phone?' Lottie asked.

'It was in the coat pocket.' Boyd held up the red coat. 'It's well worn, and cheap. It looks like something she'd wear, don't you think?'

'Maybe. But anyone could have owned that coat. Is this Andrew guy to be believed? Could he have something to do with her disappearance?'

'I doubt it. He was being helpful.'

'He was only helpful after her photo was released.'

'No, Lottie, he was genuine. But I can do a quick check if you like.'

'Don't waste time on him if it's unnecessary. I'll get the super to release a statement. This guy Aneta was with might come forward.'

'You sound sceptical, but it's a good idea. What about Greg Plunkett? Do you believe him when he said Aneta wasn't registered with his escort business?'

'McKeown checked the database and her name doesn't

appear on it. If it turns out she is on it under a different name, then the killer could have targeted these young women thinking they were sex workers.'

'That leads us back to Plunkett,' Boyd said. 'No one else has access to that database, do they?'

'Not that we know of. Did his background check throw up anything?'

'He hasn't come to our attention before now.'

'John Morgan is the anomaly.' She scratched her head, remembering how badly her hair needed a cut. 'He may not be linked to the two dead women at all. He wasn't killed in the same way. But still...'

'The other connection between them is Cuan.'

'Yes, and I don't know what to do, Boyd. Someone killed two young women and a young man, and probably abducted another woman. And they all were in that rehab centre.'

'Agreed on that point.'

'But Laura and Shannon were registered with Plunkett's agency,' she said. 'I'm still not ruling out that activity as a motive for a sick killer. However, we need to find Aneta's family.'

'If it's her phone, it should give us some information. Was there anything on her CV about her prior to coming to Ireland?'

'No, it was skimpy at best. I'd like to know why she came here and why she picked Cuan for work.'

'She got an apartment handy enough, so she must have had it all worked out before she arrived. And according to Garda Lei, she'd need about a grand for a deposit.'

'The caretaker said she paid cash.'

'So she took cash out of her Polish bank account. There was only five hundred zloty – that's about a hundred and twenty euro – in her account before she travelled. Speaking of which, how did she get to work? Cuan is twenty kilometres away.'

Lottie reached for the phone. 'I'd like a word with Ms Dunbar,' she said, dialling.

'It's Mona,' she mouthed to Boyd before she resumed listening. 'Oh, well maybe you can help me, Mona. How did Aneta get to and from work?' She listened a while longer before saying, 'I might drop out that way later. For formal interviews. Unless you'd like to come to the station?' She winked at Boyd. 'I thought so. I'll ring beforehand to let you know when we'll be there.'

She hung up. 'Irene isn't taking calls. But Mona says Aneta had no car and she thinks she may have got lifts or taken a taxi now and again.'

Just then Garda Lei bustled into the office without knocking. 'You'll never believe what I found in that cardboard box from Aneta Kobza's apartment.'

'Go on, what did you find?' Lottie said. She saw he was holding something with a bad crease down the middle. 'What is it?'

'A photograph. You're going to want to see this.'

'Today, if possible.'

'Sure. Here.' He handed it across the desk with a triumphant smile.

Lottie studied the photo.

Standing in what looked like an Australian bar, pint in hand, was a smiling John Morgan.

76

'I want Brenda Morgan in here, and I don't care how much she objects. She's staying at the Joyce Hotel. And I want to talk to Irene Dunbar. Gordon Collins too.' Lottie paced the tiny space behind her desk. 'Let's work in the incident room, where we can breathe. Get copies of that photo, Garda Lei, and bring them in too. Good work.'

McKeown waved his iPad as he trooped into the incident room behind them.

'I got Aneta Kobza's financials from Poland. I had the IBAN from the bank statement found among her possessions, so I was able to fudge the truth. They emailed over the full year's statements up to the December before she came to Ireland.'

'And?'

'A regular monthly sum was transferred into her account. I converted it. Around a thousand euro a month.'

'From who?'

'Don't know. I rang her bank again. The money was sent via a transfer from a London bank.'

Boyd said, 'Where did it all go? She hadn't much left in the account per the statement.'

'She must have withdrawn it or spent it,' McKeown said.

'Did the money continue to hit the account monthly?' Lottie asked.

'Yes.'

'How do you know that?'

'The clerk on the phone checked for me but wouldn't send me up-to-date statements.'

'It could mean that whoever's sending it didn't know she had moved or that she was missing.'

Boyd said, 'Unless it's someone with enough foresight to know we'd eventually check and this is their way of feigning innocence in her disappearance.'

'A disappearance no one reported,' Lottie countered. 'What about her family? Why wouldn't they report it?'

McKeown said, 'I'll have to dig a bit further.'

'We need to go through that mobile phone. Garda Brennan, can you check with Gary upstairs?'

Martina was back within two minutes. 'Met him on the stairs. He got the phone partially charged. It's Aneta's, and the PIN was 1234, if you can believe that.' She handed Lottie the phone with the charger dangling from it.

'Okay. Let's have a look.'

Lottie plugged in the phone in case it died, and opened the texts. 'Only one message on it. Fourteenth of February, to Cuan, telling them she was taking the day off. Nothing before or after. That's odd. Why would she delete them?'

'So there's nothing to or from her date?' Boyd asked.

'Not on text anyhow. I'll check her calls... Shit. She either didn't call anyone, or she deleted the log.'

'Gary can check it,' Boyd said. 'He should be able to restore deleted stuff.'

'But I need to know now.' Lottie couldn't help her impatience. Shannon Kenny was still missing, possibly taken by Aneta's abductor and murderer.

She opened Aneta's contact list. 'She only had two contacts. Cuan, and Ragmullin Estate Agents.'

Boyd leaned his head to one side. 'I talked to Charlie Lennon earlier. She could find no record of Aneta requesting a viewing of Pine Grove. But she did say they don't log calls unless a request is made.'

'Damn.'

'She didn't recognise Aneta from her photo, but it's possible she never visited the office.'

'Maybe Aneta had the brochure because of John Morgan. She had his photo.'

'But Morgan wasn't working at Pine Grove back then. He was in rehab.'

'Aneta worked at Cuan,' Lottie said. 'Why had she got his photo stashed away? She has no photos on her phone, which is odd for a young woman. She has to have had another phone.' She glanced at the incident board with the images of the three dead people plus Shannon Kenny. 'See if Aneta was on social media. We need to trawl Shannon's social media too and get access to her phone records via her provider. Kirby, you do that and ask her brother about it. Martina, tell Gary I want Aneta's phone forensically examined for anything deleted and whatever else may be there.'

'Will do.' Martina took the phone back.

McKeown said, 'I couldn't find Aneta on any social media platforms. I could go through Shannon's social media. I'd be more up to date than Detective Kirby. I'd know what to look for.'

Kirby bit back his retort, for which Lottie was grateful. She eyeballed McKeown.

'You have CCTV to finish, plus we need Aneta's Irish bank information. Follow up that warrant. Okay?'

'Sure,' he said, without sounding even close to sincere. 'It's a bit odd Aneta has no family contacts listed on her phone.'

'Yes, it is,' Lottie said. 'So there *must* be a second phone.'

Garda Lei said, 'We went through everything in the suitcase and the box.'

'Maybe whoever abducted her had her keys and took the phone and anything else that might have incriminated them.'

'Should we examine her apartment?' Kirby said.

'It's been totally redecorated. New furniture, too. We're lucky the caretaker hadn't dumped the suitcase and box.'

Garda Thornton, the desk sergeant, put his head around the door. 'Is no one answering a phone? Brenda Morgan is downstairs. She's spitting fire, I may as well warn you.'

'Thanks.' Lottie looked at her team. 'You know what you have to do. We need to find Shannon Kenny too. Please, please get me something.'

She followed Thornton out, hoping they caught a break soon, otherwise she herself might break.

After speaking with Brenda Morgan, Lottie was no further on. All she'd gleaned from the grieving mother was that Brenda was gunning for Collins. She'd flatly denied anything to do with the money going into Aneta's account and had no idea who she was. Then she played the 'speak to my solicitor' card, which infuriated Lottie further.

Her mood didn't improve with the news that Gordon Collins wasn't at home, nor was he on the building site at Pine Grove.

'We need to speak to him,' she told Boyd.

'He's probably visiting his ex-wife and daughters in Dublin. Or something...'

'Or something? Why isn't he answering his phone? Why doesn't the site manager, Patrick Curran, know where he is? Jesus, Boyd, if Collins is behind these killings, we've let him slip through our fingers.'

'Don't get ahead of yourself. He has no reason to think that we suspect him of anything. We don't even know if *we* suspect him yet.'

'I know that, but Aneta's face was all over the news and social media this morning. What if that spooked him?'

'Perhaps,' Boyd said. 'He clammed up when we showed him her death-mask photo.'

She inspected the copy of the photo they'd found of the group on the steps of a building. 'This building could be Cuan years ago, before the fire. The facade could have been altered in the rebuild. Maybe that's why they need the big donations from the likes of Collins.'

'You're really stretching that fishing line now.'

'One way to find out. Let's pay a visit to Irene Dunbar.'

Boyd drove them to Cuan and expelled a low whistle when they reached their destination. 'It's impressive. What are the fees like here?'

'Expensive,' Lottie said.

He parked the car. 'How would Laura Nolan and Shannon Kenny be able to afford them?'

'Hadn't thought of that.' She mentally kicked herself. Had someone helped them out financially? 'We can ask. Hope you brought that photo.'

He tapped the folder he carried under his arm. 'I have all we need.'

Mona buzzed them in.

'Hi, Mona,' Lottie said. 'This is Detective Sergeant Boyd. We'd like to talk to Irene Dunbar.'

'I told you on the phone that she's in meetings all day,' Mona said.

'We still need to talk with her. Otherwise I'll have to get an arrest warrant for her.'

'I'm only doing my job.' Mona's lips turned downward. She wiped crumbs from her mouth, smearing her bright red lipstick, then balled up crusts in tin foil and threw them into a bin behind her. Was it lunchtime? Lottie felt she could eat the crusts herself.

'Maybe I can help you, if you tell me what it is you want to know. I emailed over everything you asked for yesterday.'

'Thanks for that, but I want to talk to Irene.'

Sighing loudly, Mona pressed a button at the side of her glass prison. 'This way.'

She tapped in a code on a keypad and led them down the short corridor. She knocked, and when there was no reply, she opened the door. The office was empty.

'Oh, Irene must have left.'

'Wouldn't you know if she had?'

'Not necessarily. She often leaves by the rear exit.'

'You said she had meetings all day. Here or elsewhere?'

'Phone meetings. She's trying to rally the board, because there will be fallout. You know. Because Aneta worked here.'

'And don't forget, Mona, two other murder victims and a missing woman had connections here too.'

'That's not public knowledge.'

'Not yet,' Lottie said, trying to stem her growing annoyance at being given the runaround. 'Where would Irene go?'

'I honestly don't know. I can give you her home address and mobile number.'

'Thanks.' Lottie looked to Boyd. He didn't seem to have anything to add, so she asked, 'What are the fees like here?'

'The day care is covered by the health service, and they subsidise a portion of the costs for residents if they undergo means-testing.'

'You don't necessarily have to be wealthy to be admitted, then?'

'Not really, though we have a waiting list.'

'Would Laura Nolan and Shannon Kenny have qualified for the subsidy?'

'I'd have to check.'

'I'm sure you've looked at their files since my visit yesterday.'

'Right. Okay. Laura and Shannon's stays were subsidised.'

'What about John Morgan?'

'His fees were paid in full.'

'And do you know why Aneta wanted to work here?'

'No.'

'She seemed to walk into a job the minute she arrived in Ireland. Is that usual?'

'There is a vetting process all employees have to go through.'

'But Aneta bypassed that,' Lottie said, reading between the lines.

'I don't know anything about hiring staff. Someone must have put in a word for her.'

'Who would that be?'

Mona dropped her head. 'All I know is that Irene would insist on a warrant for that kind of information.'

'Do you really want to work for a woman like that?' Boyd asked.

'She's a great boss. Built up this place single-handed over the years. You know it burned down about thirty years ago? Irene saved it from ruin. She fundraises and fills out tons of grant application forms. She's done nothing wrong.'

Lottie stood at the window of Irene's office. She noticed a worker driving a sit-on mower on the lawn.

'The day Aneta had her breakdown, for want of a better word, there was an event here for financial donors. How did that work?'

'They had a meal, then a guided tour. We were trying to attract new funding.'

'Do you have the names of those who attended?'

'Their photo was in the local paper, but I'll get you the list.'

'Do you know what exactly happened with Aneta that day?'

Leaning her hands on the back of the visitor chair, Mona

took a deep breath. 'The donors came into the common room to view it. There were only a few people there, all of whom had given consent. Then suddenly, Aneta started shaking violently, as if she was having a fit. She was a blubbering mess and nothing we did could stop her crying. I was about to follow the touring party but came back to help. I didn't know what else to do, so I got someone to bring her to Irene's office to wait for her there.'

'Did Aneta say anything about what had sparked it?'

'She could have, but she was speaking in Polish.'

'Who was in the party that had just left the room?'

Mona bit her lip. She starting listing names, then stopped. Lottie recognised a few of them. Local business people. 'Go on.'

'We also had family members visiting.'

'Who?' She glimpsed Boyd idly flicking through the manager's desk. Mona didn't seem to notice him.

'You already know Gordon Collins was there.' The receptionist twisted her hands into each other and bounced on her heels like a child who'd done something wrong and been caught out. 'He'd been talking to John Morgan.'

'Collins wasn't family.'

'I know that. You're confusing me. He's a donor.'

'Back to family members... Why were they there?'

'Just visiting.'

'Who were they?' Lottie was sure Mona was holding something back. 'I'm sure you've checked it out.'

'Okay, okay. Laura Nolan's mother was here that day.'

'Diana Nolan?' Boyd looked up as he lifted a letter-opener.

Mona took a step towards him. 'Don't touch anything on the desk, please. But yes, Diana Nolan.'

'Did Aneta interact with her?'

Mona gave a wry laugh. 'I don't know. You're persistent. You've got more out of me than I meant to say.'

'One final thing. Were any of Shannon Kenny's family here? She has a brother, George.'

'I met him once or twice. But on that day I don't think he was here.'

Lottie had one last glance out the window. The guy on the lawnmower had disappeared. 'Why are you having the grass cut in January?'

'What?' Mona frowned at her like she was mad. 'What has that got to do with anything?'

'I was just wondering,' Lottie said.

Even Boyd gave her a funny look then.

78

Shannon felt too ill to do any housework, but she had no choice. She dropped a plate and watched as it smashed to smithereens. Unable to stop the tears, she slumped onto the floor and buried her face in her hands. She felt a squeeze on her shoulder. A small hand. Magenta.

'I'm sorry. I'll clean it up,' Shannon said, but as she tried to stand, she fell back down again.

'Don't be sitting there when she gets home. She's in a bad humour and you really don't want to make her worse.'

Shannon wondered if Magenta was spying on her in order to report back to the woman. At this moment she didn't care. She just wanted something to take down her temperature, and to sleep in her own bed.

Her hands trembled like mad and she figured it was withdrawal from alcohol. That reminded her of her time in rehab, her withdrawal from drugs, when John had made it bearable. Now he was dead. Laura too. Shannon had never properly bonded with her because Laura seemed to be stuck-up. Or, now that Shannon thought about it, maybe she was genuinely shy, or perhaps afraid. Whatever it was, both Laura and John were dead and she was being held captive in this... what? It felt like a prison, with all the locks and bolts on the doors and windows. How could people live this way?

Eyeing Magenta, gauging her mood, Shannon ventured, 'Can you tell me about the woman who was here before me?'

The child sat down on the floor beside her. 'I'm not supposed to say anything. But I'm bored. Are you bored?'

'Kind of. Tell me about her.'

'She was sad, and talked funny. They called her the stupid foreigner.'

'She wasn't Irish?'

'I heard him saying she was a *damn Polack*. I don't think that's a nice word.'

Shannon had a feeling the girl didn't know a whole lot else about the woman. 'Tell me about your mother. What's her name?'

'I don't even know if she's my real mother. She's so mean.' Magenta chewed on her fingernail.

'What's her name?'

'Can't tell you or I'll get beaten.'

'I won't tell anyone. You can talk to me.'

'Nope.' Magenta paused and Shannon held her breath, hoping. The child continued. 'She is very careful, but he might talk if you're nice to him. He killed the last one, you know. The sad foreign woman. He stabbed her.'

Shannon shivered and felt her fever spike, though she was chilled to the bone with fear. 'How do you know he stabbed her?'

'I crept down the stairs and saw him do it. But she was no use to them by then anyhow. She was... what's that word? Delirious, I heard them say.'

Desperate to keep Magenta talking, Shannon was about to ask her about the locks and bolts on the front door when she smelled him. A weedy, manure-like smell. It was so pungent that when he came in through the door she tasted it on her tongue.

Picking the broken crockery off the floor, she put out a hand to Magenta.

'What's going on here?' he growled.

'I fell over. She's helping me up,' the child said.

Standing, Shannon smiled her thanks. The child glowered. An act to fool him? Totally confused, she took the rest of the plates off the table and put them in the sink. This time without letting them drop. She almost passed out as he came to stand behind her.

'Don't even think about it,' he whispered in her ear, 'for all our sakes.'

Then he disappeared into the bowels of the house.

It took a few minutes for her breathing to return to normal and a glass of water to get rid of his smell where it had clogged her throat. She'd love a real drink. Something to knock her out of this nightmare. Then, she swore she'd never touch a drink again if she made it out alive.

79

After the meeting in the incident room, McKeown went back to the CCTV footage and his search for the boy he'd seen. The job had fallen by the wayside, but he felt it was important to locate him because he'd been close to Laura Nolan's crime scene the morning her body was discovered.

Superintendent Farrell had refused to publicise the image, but McKeown felt differently. If he found the boy, he could determine if he was a witness or not. He'd worked late the night before and he'd been in work early, and then the bank stuff had taken up all his time.

He busied himself with footage from behind the cinema, where the complex backed onto the sprawling Moorland housing estate. Had the boy come from there? The households had been canvassed for information, but nothing had shown up in the resulting reports.

Running his hand over his head, he was beginning to think it was a waste of his time. He yawned, and was wondering about having lunch when he heard the boss's computer pinging in her office. The door was open. She and Boyd were out. Might be important. No harm in having a look.

She'd left the device unlocked. Bad practice, Inspector, he thought.

He spied the email icon with new mail from the lab. Clicking it open, he scanned his eyes over the text until he came to the summary, where the data was presented in layperson's terms.

The clay found under Laura Nolan's fingernail and on her neck was a match for soil deep in the stab wound on Aneta Kobza. It was not from any of the crime scenes. This confirmed they were looking for the same killer for both women.

Another unopened email caught his attention. Toxicology analysis for Laura had returned negative for narcotics with a small amount of alcohol. There were no results for John or Aneta yet. Too soon.

He pulled up the SOCO report on Laura Nolan's crime scene and read through the account of the footprints that had been found there. The smaller set had to be from the boy he'd seen on the CCTV footage. He needed to find him.

He turned around when he heard Martina enter the office.

'The very woman. Fancy coming on a wild-goose chase with me?'

'I wouldn't go on a tame one with you. What are you doing in the boss's office?'

'Christ Almighty, what's wrong with everyone around here these days?' He grabbed his coat and left before she had a chance to throw another barb his way. He'd get someone else to accompany him.

———

Kirby found himself and Garda Lei commandeered by McKeown to accompany him to the Moorland estate. Once he'd seen the child on the footage, he knew the image was too grainy to put out to the media yet. They had to use the shoe-leather approach first.

'Why do you think the witness hasn't come forward?' Kirby asked. He had a weird feeling that the tall, bald detective was on to something. But he would never give McKeown the pleasure of admitting it.

'The fact that it was a child, maybe?'

'Maybe.'

'But let me tell you this, Kirby, I have kids and they talk all the time. If it's something new to them, they won't shut up about it. It's cute until it's annoying.' McKeown divided up the estate between them.

'We only have a vague description to go on,' Kirby continued to protest. 'Hardly a description at all, and who's going to admit their little boy was out alone at that hour of the morning?'

'If we don't knock on doors, we will never know.'

'At least Lei is in the mood.' Kirby noticed the young guard rapidly going from door to door with the grainy CCTV image in his hand.

Separating from McKeown, he began his own knocking. After twenty minutes, he realised the quest was verging on pointless. Most people, those who were at home, said they couldn't make out anything on the image. Their children wouldn't be out at that hour anyhow. And so on.

He decided to work towards the end of the row before giving up. Ringing the next doorbell, he waited. No answer. He moved across to the front window to have a peek inside. The curtains were drawn, though it was still bright out. Maybe they'd been left like that since morning.

He was about to walk back down the path, having written the house number in his notebook, when he heard the door being opened. A kid of about six or seven. Still in his pyjamas. Big round brown eyes looked up at Kirby.

As Kirby hunkered down to the child's level, he tried to read what was in those eyes.

Fear? Or relief?

80

Lottie munched the chicken fillet roll. Boyd had run into Millie's garage for it and then parked on double yellow lines outside the town park. He got that she needed space to think, away from the station. Her waistline wouldn't thank him, though.

'Explain to me what's going on, Boyd.'

'You've a dribble of mayonnaise on your chin.'

She wiped it with the paper napkin. 'Happy now?'

He smiled, and the hazel flecks in his eyes twinkled. She couldn't help grinning. Boyd had a way of alleviating her tension with just a smile. She felt an urge to dump her sandwich and kiss him, but her rumbling stomach objected, plus it would be unprofessional.

'Irene Dunbar isn't at the office or at home, nor answering her phone, so where is she? And where have Gordon Collins and Diana Nolan disappeared to?' she asked. 'Have they all gone to ground and is it a coincidence?'

He leaned back in his seat and stared out the windscreen. 'Let's talk it through. What have they in common?'

'Pine Gove? Or Cuan?'

'My money is on Cuan and the financial donor event last year.'

'I agree. The day Aneta broke down, they were all there. Plus Laura, John and Shannon.' She swallowed a bite of chicken and savoured it. 'We have to up our public appeals for information on Shannon's whereabouts.'

'I'll check if there are any updates when we get back.' He pointed to the end of the roll she'd put into the wrapper and reached over. 'If you're not finishing that...'

'Would you take my grave as quick? Go on, I'm stuffed now.'

As he ate the remains of her food, she focused on the murders. 'We need to examine what the motive might be. However warped it is, three young people have been killed. There's still a question mark over whether John Morgan was murdered by the same person, but we can connect all three, plus Shannon, to Cuan. But that was a year ago, so what has triggered their deaths now?'

'Concentrate on Aneta for a moment. She seems to have disappeared shortly after that day at Cuan. Irene Dunbar should be able to shed light on the reasons behind that, wherever she is. I believe it's significant.'

'Okay,' Lottie said, 'but why wait a year to kill her, dump her body and kill Laura and John? And possibly abduct Shannon.'

'Laura's murder could have been unintended. Maybe she was being abducted and something spooked her abductor and he killed her. Then he took Shannon.'

'If we agree the same person is the killer, surely it has to have something to do with Aneta. It's obvious she was held somewhere, abused and starved. Why?'

Boyd said, 'Back to your first question. Why kill her now? And what caused this murder spree to start?'

'Maybe we need to look at the Pine Grove connection too,'

Lottie said emphatically. 'We found the brochure among Aneta's possessions. Laura was interested in buying a property there but was turned down for a mortgage. John Morgan worked for Collins and his mother had bought a house there. I can't figure it out...'

'And how does Shannon fit in? Is she the anomaly or the final link? I think one or all three, Collins, Dunbar and Diana Nolan, may provide the answer.'

'We should issue an alert for them,' she said.

'Might be difficult.'

'Yes, since they haven't done anything wrong that we know of. But they are persons of interest and we need to talk to them,' she insisted.

'See what the super says.'

'I will.' But she didn't hold out much hope for a positive response. 'I was wondering why Diana didn't answer Martina when she showed her Aneta's photo. She may have seen her at Cuan.'

'We can ask her when we locate her,' Boyd said. 'And don't forget Greg Plunkett and his escort business in all this.'

'I'm not forgetting him. I don't think he's a killer, though I have to accept that Shannon and Laura were registered with his agency. I know we can't find Aneta on the database, but he or his PA could have purged the records before we came asking the real awkward questions.'

'Plunkett is worth another look then.'

'Yes, but Boyd, I still can't put my finger on a motive for all this sorrow and death.'

'It will come. Once we turn over every stone.'

'That reminds me, we need to review whatever door-to-door reports we have from around the area where Aneta's body was found.'

'Why dump her out there in the arsehole of nowhere?'

'So that she wouldn't be found easily?'

'Exactly.'

'Maybe the killer slipped up,' Lottie said, with more hope than conviction.

81

Katie had the phone in her hand with Jackson's contact details open on the screen. Or Greg's or whatever the hell he called himself. Granny Rose was sleeping, while Louis was doing a jigsaw, though she knew he was really watching television. She had hoovered and dusted the house, then tidied her gran's clothes away. With a chicken roasting in the oven, she was at a loose end.

Things needed to be clarified with him, but at the same time she wondered if she wanted to do that at all. Conflicted, she was about to put the phone back in her pocket when a sharp knock rattled the back door. If it was Greg, she was angry enough to kill him. But how could it be him? He didn't know where she was or where her gran lived.

Opening the door, her mouth dropped open. Had she subconsciously manifested him to appear? She said nothing, waiting for him to speak.

'Eh. Ehm. Hi, Katie. I'm sorry to barge in. Your sister, the girl who works in Fallon's – Chloe, isn't it? She gave me the address. She said to go to the back door. Here I am.'

'I don't believe for a minute she'd tell you. She knows all about you.'

'I get that, but she was prepared to give me a chance, and though I don't deserve it, I'd like you to do the same.'

Katie thought if she had a euro for every time she figured she was going to kill Chloe, she'd be rich by now. She struggled to get a word to come out of her mouth.

'As I'm here, can I come in?' He sounded unsure.

'On condition you tell the truth this time.' And against her better judgement, she led him into her gran's kitchen.

He was seated with a mug of coffee, which she'd reluctantly made for him. She noticed he didn't touch it. He just ran a finger up and down the chipped ceramic. He looked gorgeous in a navy polo jumper and dark blue denims. His leather jacket seemed new. She hoped her gran stayed asleep a little longer, because she could do without interruptions this time.

'Say what it is you've come to say.'

'You're not making it easy.'

'You don't deserve it.'

'Point taken. I'm sorry. I was afraid to tell you my real name. I thought if you googled me, you'd find out that I run a dating agency, as well as being a photographer. I know it all sounds seedy, but I made good money and I'm on the verge of buying my own office space.'

'Do you want a medal for all that then?' She paused, wanting to shove him back out the door. 'My mother said you run an escort business, and when I think of escorts, the first thing that pops into my head is sex workers.'

'It's nothing like that. It's like online dating.'

'I think you're delusional, Greg. Is that even your real name?'

'Yes, it is. I sometimes go by Jackson when I'm out. It's my middle name.'

'Why are you even here?'

'I like you, Katie. I've made a hash of things so far... I'd like us to start again.'

'Not a hope. How did my mother know who you were?'

She noticed how he bit his lip. Was that what he did when he was making up another lie?

'She met with me as part of a murder investigation.'

'I gathered that much. She's investigating Laura Nolan's murder. What has that got to do with you?'

He looked at the table, unable to meet her stare. 'Laura was registered with my agency.'

'Okay. Go on.'

'And there's a girl missing too. Shannon Kenny. She was also registered with me.'

It's getting worse, Katie thought. 'I didn't hear that name mentioned last night.'

'No, but you will the next time your mother lets fly about me.'

She had to smile. 'I thought she said another name... Anita or something.'

'Aneta, yes. She has a foreign surname. I didn't recognise her photo and I double-checked everything this morning. She wasn't registered with me.'

'What if she used a fake name? Like you,' Katie said, creaking her neck to one side.

'I do my best to vet everyone.'

'Mm. Maybe one of your male clients is behind the murders.'

'It's possible, isn't it? I've given everything to the guards. Didn't even wait for a warrant. I could get into trouble with GDPR, but I'm getting out of this business now. I can see how it can be abused. I'll be concentrating on my photography.'

'Did any of the women ever complain about being harassed?'

'No, not one. That's why I can't understand how the guards are targeting me.'

'Are they, though?' she asked. 'The investigation team has to gather all the relevant information about the victims to identify the killer. And if a murder victim happened to be an escort, then it's the first place they'd check.' She wondered why she was defending her mother's job.

'Do you think there's a chance for us?' he asked.

'Not a chance in hell,' she said. A sudden sadness nestled in the void in her chest and replaced her anger. 'Not yet, anyhow.'

'What do you mean?' He leaned closer, an eagerness in his eyes. Should she be afraid?

'I'm caring for my gran and my son at the moment. I haven't the time or energy to be thinking of meeting with you.'

'But maybe there is a chance. Soon? In the future? Sometime?'

She grinned despite herself. Greg Plunkett had a way about him, and she understood how he could manipulate girls. Maybe manipulate was too strong a word, but he was a charmer.

'There might be a chance, Greg, if you're not a murderer.'

He smiled, and then appeared crestfallen. His eyes darkened as he looked up from beneath his long lashes. 'And what if I am?'

She pushed back her chair so quickly that it hit the stove and knocked an empty saucepan onto the floor. The sound reverberated around the kitchen and Louis ran in.

'What's the noise?' he asked.

'It's okay, sweetheart,' Katie said. 'Just a pot.'

'You must be Louis, young man,' Greg said.

'I am, but I'm a boy, not a man. You're silly.'

'I suppose I am. I better be off. You have my number, Katie. I was joking a second ago. Honestly. Please, call me.'

He left without another word, and she had the feeling he would not let her go that easily. Could he be a killer? Was she going soft? Or was he who he said he was? Just a photographer?

Rose sauntered into the kitchen. 'What's all the noise? You'd wake the dead.'

Katie lifted up Louis and smiled at her gran.

'Don't see any bodies rising up out of the floor here,' she laughed, and ruffled Louis' hair.

82

There was no way Kirby would enter the house alone. He indicated for Garda Lei to join him. Lei was good with kids.

The child brought them into a cramped living room. A dining table with six chairs at one end, and a tatty cream leather couch piled with cushions at the other. A flat-screen television took up most of one wall, the only item that looked any way new. Kirby perched on one of the dining chairs while Lei sat on the couch beside the boy.

'Rex, you say your name is?' Kirby said. The child nodded. 'Where are your parents?'

'Work.'

'Okay. Shouldn't you be at school?'

A shrug.

'Are you often home alone?'

A nod.

'What age are you?'

'Seven.'

Kirby thought of Sergio, who was eight. There was no way on earth Boyd would leave him home alone. 'Do you not have friends you could stay with when your mammy and daddy are at work?'

'Not really. They'll be home soon anyhow.'

'What's your mammy and daddy's names?'

The boy shook his head. He wasn't telling.

'What's your surname? Rex who?'

A shrug of a shoulder but again no answer.

'Okay.' Kirby glanced at Lei and hesitated. Should they wait for the parents? It might be nothing. The kid might not have seen anything. He might not even be the kid they were looking for. But he had to go for it and suffer the consequences later.

'Rex, I don't want to scare you…'

'I'm scared of nothing.'

'Good. I'm wondering if you were out early last Friday morning? You know, before your parents got up?'

The boy dropped his head and bit his lip. 'I'm not supposed to do that.'

'You're not in any trouble. I think you can be a big help to us. How does that sound?'

'Is it about the woman?'

Kirby felt his heart beat a little faster. 'What woman would that be?'

'The dead woman lying on the ground at the cinema.'

'Jesus.' He had the word out before he caught it. 'Yes, Rex. I'm wondering if you saw her?'

He looked towards the window with its heavy curtains drawn, blocking out the natural light. 'She was just lying there. She wouldn't talk to me because she was dead.'

'Okay. Good lad. What did you do?'

The boy leaned his head to one side and looked at Garda Lei beside him. 'Are you Chinese?'

'I'm Irish, but my grandparents are Chinese.'

'That's so cool.'

Kirby nodded for Lei to continue the conversation, all the

time fretting that they should not be quizzing a child without his parents' knowledge. But hadn't they left the lad to fend for himself?

'You're such a brave boy,' Lei said. 'How would you like to help us find out what happened to the poor lady?'

'Can I go in a squad car? With the sirens on?'

'We could arrange that for you sometime, if your parents allow it.'

Rex dropped his head and fiddled with his nails. Kirby noticed they were clean. The boy appeared well cared for, but he wasn't at school and was home on his own.

'They'll say no,' Rex said eventually.

'Why would they say that?' Lei asked quietly.

'They're always fighting. I'm just a nuisance.'

'No you're not. You're a great kid and you're able to help the guards.'

'Really?'

'Sure you are.' Lei inclined his head towards Kirby without verbalising his question. Kirby nodded.

'We'll need to call your mam or dad now,' he said, 'to see if it's okay to talk to you.'

Rex sprang up quickly.

'You better go,' he said. 'Mammy will kill me for letting you into *this* house.'

The way he said it, Kirby figured the child did not like his home. 'Why do you say that? Did you live somewhere before?'

Rex sat back down and curled up into himself. 'Leave me alone.'

Kirby felt they had to leave, even though the child was a viable witness. Should he call social services? He didn't know what to do, but the boss would.

'Don't worry, Rex, we're going now. We'll come back later when your parents are here. Okay?'

The brown eyes bored into him. 'Don't tell them I let you in. Don't tell them. Please.'

'I won't say a word.'

Out on the pavement, Kirby saw McKeown storming towards them.

'Here comes trouble,' he whispered to Lei.

'Where did you two lugs disappear to?' McKeown's face was purple, incandescent.

'We found the boy,' Kirby said.

Staring from one to the other and back again, McKeown threw his hands in the air. 'Where is he, then?'

'He lives in there, but we need to wait until his parents come home to question him.'

'That's a load of bollox. Phone them. What are their names?'

'Rex wouldn't say.'

'Who the fuck is Rex? The dog?' The top of McKeown's head looked like someone had set a match to it.

'No. The kid is called Rex. That's all we know.' Kirby eyed Lei with an expression that told him to say nothing.

'How do you know he's the kid we're searching for if he said nothing?'

McKeown wasn't stupid. Kirby toyed with what to tell him. 'Look, we need to speak to the boss first. Okay.'

'What did you do, Kirby? What the fuck did you do?'

'I need to talk to the boss.'

He waddled down the path, waving his phone in the air. He headed towards where McKeown had parked the car. A few neighbours were pulling up in theirs. There was no sign of anyone going into the house where Rex sat on his cracked cream leather couch. Alone.

83

Lottie was hammering on the door of the Right One agency when she heard a car pull up across the narrow street. She turned to see Greg Plunkett getting out of it. 'The very man.'

'What do you want with me now, Inspector? I've been coop-erative.'

'Just a word.'

'A word? Harassment springs to mind.'

'We can talk here or at the station. Up to you.'

He slowly opened the door, then led Lottie and Boyd up the stairs.

'Alone today?' she asked.

'I gave Cathy the day off. Hope that's okay with you, or should we have asked for permission?'

'No need to be smart with me,' she said.

When Plunkett was seated behind the desk, Lottie ran her hand over the filing cabinet, leaving behind a streak in the dust.

'Greg, we need your help with our investigations.'

'Okay. What can I do for you?'

She wondered why he'd lost the belligerent tone of a moment ago. 'I like that attitude.'

'Yeah, well, I thought you were here to warn me away from your daughter.'

'That too, but now's not the time.' She felt Boyd's eyes boring into her. 'We've been looking at what links our murder victims. And you know what? We keep returning to you.'

'I gave you everything. Do you want my blood too?'

She ignored his gibe. 'Aneta Kobza.'

'She wasn't on my books. I told you that.'

'Did you ever take her photo then?' Lottie leaned over and slid Aneta's photograph onto his desk.

'No.' He paused and glanced down at the image, then up with a faraway stare. He was remembering something. She fought down an urge to shake it out of him. He said, 'Maybe I did, you know. Hold on.' He tapped his computer awake. 'I didn't notice it before. I did some work for the local rag last year. Their photographer was on maternity leave. Seeing the photo up close, there's something about that girl's face that's familiar but not at the same time. I have an eye for beauty.'

Lottie rolled her eyes and turned to Boyd. He shook his head. Keep your mouth shut, he was silently telling her. The air in the small office was stifling, and she held in a sneeze.

Greg said, 'Yes! It's her.'

'What's her?' Lottie edged over behind him. A tight squeeze.

He pointed towards the montage of photos on his desktop screen. 'It was a fundraising thing out at Cuan last year. That's the rehab place close to Delvin. Do you know it?'

'Go on.' She tried to keep her heart in her chest and not in her mouth.

'I took a lot of photos. Only one or two made it into the paper, I think. This one was of some of the staff.' Clicking an icon, he zoomed up the photo. 'That's her, isn't it?'

Lottie leaned over his shoulder. 'Have you any more photos from that day?'

'Loads. I'll put them on a USB for you. Give me a minute.'

'Is it Aneta?' Boyd asked.

'Yes,' Lottie said. 'It's different from the photo printed in the paper. Just put everything from that day on the USB, please.' She wanted to get out of the stifling office.

'Sure thing. You're as prickly as Katie.'

'Leave my daughter alone.'

'That's up to her, isn't it?'

Before she could retort, she felt Boyd's hand on her elbow. She kept quiet then and waited for Greg to hand over the USB stick.

When she had it, she said, 'We'll be in contact.'

Back in her office, Lottie read through the email from the lab. The clay found under Laura Nolan's fingernail matched the soil in Aneta's stab wound. It was possible that the killer had transferred it. It had to be that, she thought, otherwise how could the soil have got into the wounds, since it appeared not to be from where the bodies were found? The same killer was involved. She tried to read through the analysis, but it was way too technical for her brain.

Then, in the summary, she caught something she could understand. There was a trace of tomato seeds in the soil. Had it been used to plant tomatoes at some stage? Or was it an anomaly? They still had to link John's murder to the two women's deaths.

About to insert Greg Plunkett's USB stick into her computer, she glanced up to see Boyd at the door.

'Shouldn't you get that checked for a virus before you put it near your computer?'

'Boyd, if there's a virus on this, our system should be able to kill it, otherwise it's not worth the money the department forked out for it. Okay?'

'I don't know why you're so hung up about the photos. We know Aneta was working there that day. It makes sense that she'd have been caught in at least some of the press photos, even if they weren't printed in the paper.'

'We need to identify everyone in them. As far as we know, this is proof of one of the last times anyone saw Aneta Kobza.'

'She may have been around after that.'

'She was, because she went out on Valentine's night, and then puff! Gone. So until we get an eyewitness or some other verification, this is what we have to work with.'

'It's diverting our focus from the other victims.'

'If we solve the mystery surrounding Aneta, why she was taken and where she was held, I reckon we solve the other murders. And we'll find Shannon Kenny alive. I believe Aneta was held somewhere for almost a year and Shannon could have been taken to replace her.'

'What about Laura Nolan?' Boyd countered.

'She either fought back, or something went wrong and he killed her shortly after abducting her. It's the only explanation I can come up with until we get evidence to the contrary.'

'Where does John Morgan's murder fit in?'

'I don't know yet, but he was in Cuan when the others were there, so it fits in somewhere.'

'Okay.' He looked unsure as he edged out to the general office.

She called him back. 'I'm forwarding you this lab report. It mentions soil transference. Can you talk to someone at the lab to find out where this soil might have come from?'

'Sure.'

After sending him the lab report, she slotted the USB into the computer port. The icons loaded one by one. There were 105 photographs. The date was two days before Valentine's Day last year.

Her phone vibrated and skidded across the desk. Kirby. You may wait, she thought, as she opened the first image.

———

Kirby felt bad leaving Garda Lei at Moorland with orders to notify him when Rex's parents arrived home. But it was imperative that he get McKeown out of there. He was liable to say the wrong thing and terrify the child into silence. He could also get them suspended for entering the house and speaking to a seven-year-old child without his parents being present.

'It's a right balls-up,' he admitted to Lottie when he got back to the station.

'You can say that again.'

'I should have called social services.'

'You should not have interviewed a child without parental consent. This is serious, Kirby.'

'Would you have done any different?'

She thought for a moment. 'In the circumstance, I'd have done the same. The child might help us identify Laura Nolan's killer and in turn save Shannon.'

'I spoke to her brother earlier. George is a wreck. Her nephew, Davy, keeps asking for her. We have to get her home safe.'

Lottie nodded slowly. 'What possible motive can someone have for killing those young people?'

'When we catch the bastard, we can ask him.' He took his hands out of his pockets awkwardly and stifled a yawn. His phone beeped with a text and he checked it. 'Lei says Rex's parents are home. The McGoverns.'

'Okay, I'll go over there and see if they'll allow us to talk to their son.'

'Am I in trouble, boss?'

She shrugged. 'Possibly. I won't tell anyone, but I can't

vouch for McKeown. Might be time to do a bit of sweet-talking in that direction. Or buy him a pint in Cafferty's.' She looked at Kirby. He knew he was one of her favourite people. 'But I can't say what the McGoverns will do when they find out.'

'I don't hold out much hope of sweetening McKeown up. There's not enough sugar in the world for that.'

'That might be the case, Kirby, but I have every faith in you.'

———

Lottie threw a lingering eye at the photos she had saved to her computer and wondered if the answer to everything was contained among them. But first things first. They had a witness. She grabbed her bag and coat and left the detective patting his pocket for his elusive cigar.

84

The first thing Lottie noticed about the Moorland estate was how close it was to the rear of the cinema complex, even though it was ringed by hedges and fenced off. The second thing was the affluence it presented. Two-storey houses, all painted the same pastel yellow, with large ground-floor windows on either side of smart grey doors. The third thing she noticed was that the McGoverns' house didn't fit in. The walls seemed sad, the door in need of a rub of a cloth to wipe away dirt and dust. All the windows had their curtains or blinds drawn tightly. Keeping something out? Or in?

Before knocking, she did a hasty Google search about the estate.

'I don't believe it.'

'What?' Lei asked.

'Moorland was built by Gordon Collins.'

'He seems to have a finger in every pie in this town.'

'Too many pies for my liking, or maybe I'm jealous because I can't afford to buy a decent house.' As she raised her hand to knock on the door, she spied a small camera bell, so she pressed that instead.

Muffled sounds came from within before the door opened. The man who stood there had dishevelled hair and a taut jaw. Angry?

'What?' he growled. Definitely angry.

'I'm Detective Inspector Parker, and this is my colleague, Garda Lei. We'd like a minute of your time, if you don't mind.'

'What's this about? I've only just got in from work.' He patted down his unruly black hair and straightened his tie before tucking his creased white shirt into navy suit trousers. She spied the corresponding jacket hanging on the stairs.

'Mr McGovern, is it?'

'Yeah. Benny. What's this about?' He kept his hand firmly on the door, blocking entry.

'We're investigating a murder and talking to everyone on this estate. It won't take long at all.'

'And that requires an Inspector? Waste of resources.' Relenting, he opened the door wider, with an audible sigh. 'You better come in.'

Lei shut the door behind them as Lottie followed McGovern into the sitting room that Kirby had perfectly described. It seemed the family might have been able to afford their house, but furniture was another matter. Not that she was in any position to criticise, with the state of Farranstown House. She tugged off her jacket and pulled down the sleeves of her white shirt, which had travelled up her arms.

Benny sat at the dining table before Lottie and Lei joined him.

'This is a lovely estate,' she said. 'New, is it?'

'We're here five years. More like a lifetime with all the problems we've had.'

'Oh, why is that?'

'Where do I start? Everything from day one was wrong with it. Cracks in the walls. Condensation in the bathroom. No vents in any room. Bad workmanship all round, and that bastard

Gordon Collins gets away with murder. I've sent more solicitor's letters than I can count. Anyhow. That's not why you're here. How can I help you?'

Lottie banked the information about Collins. 'We're investigating the murder of Laura Nolan. Her body was discovered in the grounds of the cinema complex on Friday morning. Close to this estate.'

'I read about it. Terrible tragedy for the young woman's family. This town isn't safe to walk around in daylight, let alone at night.'

She noted the inherent criticism in his tone but chose to ignore it. 'Did you hear or see anything suspicious, Thursday night into Friday morning?'

'No. We're usually in bed early. Both my wife and I work out of town, and our son goes to the school down the road. I'm sorry, I heard nothing.'

'Okay. Can I speak with your wife and son?'

'Brigette is picking up a takeaway and groceries. Rex is only seven, so he can't help you.'

Lottie eyed Lei, who gave a subtle nod to let her know it was true the woman had left the house. 'Even so, I'd like a quick word with Rex.'

'Why?' McGovern pointed at Garda Lei as if just realising he was there. 'You were here earlier, with a fat guy. Got a doorbell alert on my phone and I'm sure it was you I saw. What right had you to barge into my home?' His faux-compliance had evaporated.

Lottie figured he had been cooperative thus far because he knew he was in the wrong regarding his son; now she caught his anger. 'You're aware that leaving a seven-year-old home alone is a matter for social services, Mr McGovern, aren't you?'

He looked like he'd been punctured. 'What do you want?'

'I believe your son might have crucial information to assist us in our inquiries.'

'I warned him time and time again not to open the door. You should know better than to interview a child without parental consent. I might make a formal complaint to your superintendent.'

'You're within your rights to do that, and I will inform social services,' Lottie said. Was McGovern a habitual complainant? 'I need to speak with your son.'

'My wife isn't here and... I don't know...' He faltered.

'Just a few minutes. That's all I ask.' She leaned forward with her most sincere expression.

McGovern stood. At the door he yelled, 'Rex. Sitting room. Now.'

Lottie felt a surge of rage at the way he had called out, but dampened it down when the boy entered the room. His eyes betrayed a sense of sadness. Like the outer walls of the house, she thought. Did this despondency ooze outwards from those who lived within the walls?

'Hi, Rex. There's nothing to be scared of. I only want to have a chat with you.'

The child looked up at his father and nodded. 'Okay.'

'Sit wherever you're comfortable.' She watched the boy perch on the edge of the couch. She moved from the dining chair to sit on the opposite end.

He turned to face her. Dressed in Superman pyjamas, he had fluffy socks on his feet.

'Rex, you spoke with...' she thought 'colleagues' was too formal for a child, 'my friends earlier. You might be able to help us. Can you do that?'

'If you want. Whatever.'

'You told them you left the house real early on Friday morning and walked up towards the cinema. Is that correct?'

'What the hell are you talking about?' Benny McGovern jumped up.

Rex glanced at his father, his eyes open wide. 'I only went for a walk 'cos I couldn't sleep.'

'Mr McGovern, Benny, please.' Lottie waited until the man sat back down. 'Now, Rex, you said you saw the woman's body. Is that right?'

'She was all alone. I sat on the wet grass to talk to her. I knew she was dead because she wouldn't answer me.'

'Okay, Rex, you're doing great,' Lottie said. 'Can you tell me about her?'

'There was blood on her top and she had no coat. Her feet were muddy so she mustn't have had shoes on. The grass was all wet.'

'Did you touch her?'

He recoiled into the cushions. 'No. No way. Gross.'

'Don't worry, I wouldn't either. What did you do then?'

'Just sat there to mind her until someone came to help her.'

'And did someone come?'

'Yeah, the guy who works in the coffee shop, and I ran off and hid behind the bushes, and then the guards came and I went home.'

McGovern came to sit on the arm of the couch beside his son. 'You went to school, Rex, didn't you?'

Rex bit his lip. 'I was too scared to go.'

'Did you not notice your son missing that morning, Benny?'

The man's cheeks flushed. 'Me and Brigette, well, we'd had a big argument Thursday night so I went off to work in a huff. I didn't look in on Rex. He usually gets himself to school anyhow. It's only down the road. Practically next door. We start work at eight.'

'Where do you work?'

'I'm a manager at Tesco in Gaddstown, and Brigette works for a hair salon in Maynooth. We're both on the road early.'

'And Rex gets himself up, fed and out to school?'

'Brigette gets his breakfast ready and calls him down. But it seems Friday morning was different. It's probably because we were rowing the night before.'

'About what?'

'Money. What else wrecks a marriage?'

Lottie nodded, but she felt uneasy about how Rex was being left to fend for himself. She'd been guilty of that from time to time after Adam died, but her children had been teenagers then, not seven-year-olds. She brought her attention back to the child. He turned his pale face up towards her, his sad eyes swimming in tears.

'Are you all right, Rex? Do you want me to stop asking questions?'

'I don't like it when they fight. It's noisy and makes my head hurt. That's why I was looking out the window the night before and I saw...' He trailed off.

'What did you see?' Lottie asked, noticing Garda Lei taking notes. Good.

'Will I get in trouble for missing school?'

'No. You're doing great. Just tell me what you saw that night. Was it the night before you found her body?'

'Yeah. A taxi was stopped down by the trees on the road and a man got over the wall carrying something. It looked really heavy. Like a big bag of stones.'

'Jesus, Rex!' His father jumped up and pulled the boy to him in a hug. 'Why didn't you tell me or your mother?'

'You were angry with each other. I didn't want you to be angry with me too.'

Lottie noticed a tear escape from the boy's eye. She itched to wipe it away; to comfort him.

'Rex,' she said softly, 'it's important that you tell me more about that night. Do you know what time it was?'

'Well, there were no lights on outside the cinema and it was real dark, so it had to be after it closed. I don't know what time it closes. Can you check?'

'I can. Are you sure it was a man you saw?'

'I think so. He was able to carry her. Well, I didn't know what it was until the next morning, but it had to be someone very strong if he carried the woman over the wall.'

'Can you describe him?'

'It was dark and he was bent over carrying her.'

'Did you see where he left her?'

'Right where I found her, lying in the long grass with no coat or shoes. It was so cold. I was going to put my jacket over her to keep her warm, but there was no point, was there?'

'You did well. What did the man do after he left her there?'

'He ran back to his car. He must have driven off but I didn't wait to see any more because I jumped back into bed. The shouting got louder and I knew Mam and Dad were coming up the stairs.'

McGovern kept his head lowered but squeezed his son's shoulder in apology.

'About that car,' Lottie said. 'You mentioned it was a taxi. How did you know that?'

'It had that sign on top. But there was no light on it.' A crease of worry furrowed Rex's little brow. 'Maybe I made a mistake and it wasn't a taxi at all. Don't those learner driver cars have a sign like that too?'

'Yes, but at the time you were sure it was a taxi, is that right?'

'Yes, because Maggie, a girl in my school, she comes in every day in a taxi. It's so cool.' He hesitated. 'Can I go back to my game now?'

'All this is very useful and you're a brave boy, Rex. Thanks for your help. I have one last favour to ask you.'

'Okay.'

'It's important that you tell the truth and—'

'My son always tells the truth,' Benny interjected.

'I'm not doubting his word, but it's essential to our inquiries that I ask this question.' She waited for the father's consent, and when he inclined his head, she engaged the boy's eyes. 'Rex, you're not in any trouble, but I need to ask you this. Did you take any souvenirs from the body or from the area where you found the woman?' She had to ask because of a similar incident at her last investigation.

'No, no way. I never touched her or anything. I just felt sorry for her. I don't tell lies.'

'That's totally fine. I'm so sorry, but in my job sometimes I have to ask unkind questions.'

His shoulders relaxed. 'That's all right.'

She heard the front door open and shut and an anger-fuelled rant preceded the entrant. 'There's a bloody car blocking the drive and I had to park— Oh! Who are you?'

85

The frustrated woman dropped two carrier bags of groceries and a McDonald's takeout bag on the floor. Without even unzipping her long black coat, she glared at Lottie and Lei as she noticed her son's tear-stained face.

'What have you been doing to my son?' She rushed over and lifted him off the couch. He was too big for her arms, even though he'd looked tiny seated.

Lottie did the introductions.

Benny said, 'They're finished and just leaving.'

'Finished what?'

Lottie gathered up her bag from the floor. 'Your son could prove to be an important witness in my current investigation. He's a little trouper. You should be proud of him.'

'Who are you to talk about my son?'

'Brigette. Leave it.' Benny stood and patted her shoulder. She shook him off.

'What investigation?' Her eyes narrowed with suspicion.

Fetching her coat from the back of the chair, Lottie said, 'Your husband can fill you in. But first I'd like a final word with you both. Without Rex present.'

Benny took the bags of shopping and ushered Rex out of the room. Brigette unzipped her coat and marched around like a lion in a cage. She still had her salon tabard on, and blue jeans with black runners.

'I'm starving, so could you please hurry up,' she said as her husband returned.

'I think you need to look into your childcare arrangements,' Lottie said. 'Rex should not be left on his own.'

'What are you talking about?'

'Your husband will explain. But I may have to inform child services. For now, I want to show you both a selection of photos. You might have seen these people in the news this week, but I need to know if you recognise them outside of that.'

'Go on then,' Brigette said, her body taut.

At the table, Lottie asked Garda Lei to show the photos he had with him.

One by one he laid out the images of their victims. Laura Nolan. John Morgan. Aneta Kobza. And Shannon Kenny.

The two adults shook their heads.

Brigette said, 'I saw that first girl's photo on the news the other day. She was murdered close by, wasn't she? I don't know her or any of them.'

Benny said, 'Is she the woman Rex found?'

'What are you talking about?' Brigette snapped.

'I'll tell you later, Bri. Now isn't—'

'I want to know what this is about. Now!'

'Brigette,' Lottie said calmly, 'your husband can explain but I am up against a killer's clock. So I need answers, not questions.'

'A killer? Is Rex in danger? Oh my God.'

'No, he's not. But it might be no harm keeping his knowledge under wraps for now.'

'What the fuck?' Brigette flipped. 'Rex knows something about a killer? Is that what you're telling me? And you say he's not in danger? For God's sake...' She swung around the room looking for something to punch, Lottie surmised. The woman picked up a cushion and flung it back on the couch. 'It's a fucking nightmare.' She levelled a pointed finger at her husband. 'Everything has been a nightmare since you made us move here.'

'I've a final question,' Lottie said, not wanting to get caught up in their row. 'Rex mentioned something in passing. It could be construed that he didn't like this house. You said you're only living here five years.'

'I didn't hear him say that,' Benny said.

'It was earlier, when my colleague was here.' She glanced at Lei.

Brigette sank onto the couch. 'You were here earlier too? Why didn't anyone contact us?'

'We didn't want to spook you,' Lei said.

'You're doing a fine job of that right now.'

'This other house,' Lottie said. 'Tell me about it.'

'We moved here before Rex was three,' Benny said. 'He loved our old house, but it was too far outside Ragmullin for schools and our jobs. I was working in town then. So we moved when this house came on the market.'

'Biggest mistake of our lives. That Gordon Collins should be behind bars.' Brigette clutched the cushion tight to her chest.

'Rex misses the countryside and our old garden,' Benny said.

Satisfied, Lottie moved to the door. 'I'll leave you for now. I want you to put proper childcare in place or I'll have to report you to child services. And please keep an eye on Rex. He may have bad dreams about his experience. He needs your support.'

'I'll have bad dreams about this too.' Brigette got up, flung down the cushion again and bundled out of the room past Lottie.

'I apologise for my wife,' Benny said. 'We are under huge financial strain. If we can help you in any way, let me know.'

'Thank you, and give Rex a hug from me.'

'I will.'

She followed Lei out the door. She realised the sadness she'd felt in the house was emanating from a financially stretched and worried family. But it did not excuse their actions. No one should leave a seven-year-old to fend for himself.

86

The team gathered in the incident room when Garda Lei and Lottie returned from the McGovern house. She knew she should report them to child services, but she had enough on her plate as it was. Hopefully they'd learned their lesson. She'd get Lei to keep an eye on them.

She outlined her visit before barking out orders.

'Garda Lei and Detective Kirby, contact every taxi firm in town. I want to know which firms were working on Thursday night, plus the names of their drivers. I also want their clock-in and out times.'

Boyd said, 'Maybe it was a cab customer, not a driver, that the boy saw carrying the body.'

'Didn't think of that. That could be problematic, but see if we can get details of taxis that took that route on Thursday night.'

McKeown entered the fray with his tuppence worth. 'Do we even know for sure it was a taxi that the boy saw?'

Lottie thought about that for a moment. 'He seemed to be certain it was, because a girl, Maggie something, gets dropped to school in one every day.'

'Some kids have the life of Riley,' Kirby said.

Boyd checked his phone. 'Time's getting on and I should go pick up Sergio.'

'Give Amy a call,' Kirby said. 'She'll be able to keep him a bit longer.'

Lottie turned her attention back to McKeown. 'You scrutinised the CCTV in that area. Why didn't this taxi or car or whatever the boy saw show up?'

'I found the kid, didn't I?' he said petulantly.

'I'm not criticising. I'm only asking.' Why was she even apologising? She was his boss, for God's sake.

McKeown looked at Lei's photocopied notes, yet to be typed up. 'The kid says it was parked under a tree. We need to find that tree and search the area. There was a power outage at the soccer club, so that's why the car wasn't picked up on their CCTV.'

'Take Garda Brennan with you and carry out a search of the area.'

'It's getting late,' Martina said, immediately displaying unhappiness with her pairing.

'Take a quick look for now. If you find anywhere that appears suspicious, cordon it off until morning.'

'Sure,' the young garda said sulkily, snapping shut her notebook.

Lottie scanned her own hurried notes. 'The lab report on the clay? Anyone got any bright ideas on that?'

'Lab technicians are doing further tests,' Boyd said.

'Keep on to them,' she said. 'Also, will you do a background check on the McGovern family, please? They mentioned complaints they've made against Gordon Collins. I want to be sure that's true. I don't like coincidences.'

'Will do.'

Garda Lei put up his hand. 'Can I make a suggestion?'

'By all means,' Lottie said, and flopped onto a chair by the incident boards.

'This has to do with John Morgan, and I know we haven't mentioned him but I... ehm... just...'

'Everything is on the table, Lei. Go ahead.'

'Right. Okay. Well, Benny McGovern said he knew we had been at his house earlier because of the camera doorbell. We got some footage from the Pine Grove residents. I think we should check it, especially the devices from those who live close to the show home. We might catch something of John Morgan or his killer.'

Lottie stood. 'Have we not done that already?'

McKeown said, 'With Laura's murder there was a lot to go through and I haven't got to it yet.'

'Morgan's murder was a few days ago,' Boyd said, 'but how can a doorbell camera help us?'

'Most are linked to the customer's phone,' McKeown said, 'and the images get backed up to the cloud. Depending on the camera's zoom range, we might catch something.'

'As soon as you can, I want you to check it. Now, has anyone anything else to add?'

A group mumble and chairs being pushed back told her it was time to finish up.

'Shannon is still missing,' Kirby said.

'I'll go talk with her brother.'

87

The sky was dark by the time Garda Martina Brennan and Detective Sam McKeown arrived at the cinema complex. The lights spread a russet hue over the area like an old blanket. They parked at the cinema and walked back down past the area where Laura's body had been discovered. With the crime-scene tape now removed, all that remained was a forlorn spread of wilting flowers and the sentiment of regret and sorrow.

Walking in silence along the outer wall, McKeown looked over at the football clubhouse and then at the path ahead of him.

'It's madness doing this at this time of the evening,' Martina said, and marched on ahead. She was angry at the boss for pairing them together and she had nothing to say to McKeown, therefore she'd say nothing.

'We're in work mode, Martina, no point in giving me the silent treatment. I'm not going to jump you.'

'Fuck off, Sam.' So much for keeping her silence. 'You think you're the bee's knees when you're really nothing other than a shithead.'

'Have it your own way then.' He took off in long strides, leaving her trailing behind. Suits me just fine, she thought. The end of the boundary wall filtered into bushes and shrubs. That was when she noticed a break in the hedge, perhaps a car width. It seemed to be a man-made lane leading to the Moorland houses.

'Hold up,' she shouted at McKeown's broad back, but he kept on walking.

Pulling on a pair of gloves, she took her torch from her belt and headed into the small laneway. The ground was muddy, and there were definitely tyre impressions in the soil. She moved in further along the grass verge where the rutted tracks were more visible. Glancing up, she noted the gap ended about fifty metres from the main road. A short cut into Moorland. Made by pedestrians. Had the killer local knowledge?

She left her torch on the ground, its light shining out over the tracks, and snapped a series of photos with her phone.

Glancing behind, she saw McKeown staring at her.

'What are you doing up there?' he said.

'Go back to the car for tape.'

'For what?'

'This area needs to be cordoned off. There are tyre tracks here, but a lot of them have been trampled on by pedestrians.'

'This isn't on any map that I've seen.'

Jesus, did he have to question everything and everyone?

'It's man-made.' She kept her tone neutral, trying hard not to yell at him. 'Or person-made, whatever you want to call it. We need to cordon off the area until we can get SOCOs out here, and that won't happen until morning.' She showed him the photos she'd just taken.

McKeown rubbed a hand over his stubbly chin. 'If it was used by this taxi killer, whoever he is, how did he know about it? It's not visible if you're driving by.'

'He could live around here.'

'We've canvassed all the houses and found nothing, but, well, good work,' he said, his tone grudging. 'I'll wait. You go get the tape.'

She snapped her torch to her belt and marched off, leaving McKeown behind, a looming shadow in the dark.

88

Irene Dunbar had attended an unscheduled meeting with the Health Service Executive about funding, and once that was over, she'd returned to the office. She'd been glad of the meeting, as she could concentrate on work and not on the other stuff. As she entered the main door, a disgruntled Mona came round the desk to meet her.

'Irene, there you are. You never answered your phone. You can't just go off like that and leave me with all this.' She threw her arms upwards as if the roof was about to fall in on top of them.

'All what?'

'Kitchen staff grumbling, therapists, clients, not to mention the guards.'

Irene straightened her back, instantly on alert. 'What did they want?'

'The therapists need the main group room fumigated and painted. There's mushrooms growing out of the ceiling. The cleaners refuse to do it. Say it's a health hazard and—'

'That's part of the old building.' Irene tried to keep her voice even while her heart was beating double-time.

'Yeah, but we give the impression on our website and our brochures that this is a refurbished state-of-the-art facility.'

'I'll get on to someone in the morning. What did the guards want?'

'Asking how clients can afford the care here.'

'What did you tell them?' The hairs sprang up on the nape of her neck.

'I explained about the subsidy system. That information is in the public domain, so I wasn't telling tales, if that's what you're insinuating.'

'I'm just trying to find out what the bloody guards wanted. Was it that woman again? Inspector Parker?'

'Yes, and another fine-looking thing.'

'Mona!'

'Sorry. They asked about Aneta and how she got the job so quickly after arriving in Ireland.'

'And?'

'I mentioned we have a vetting process, but they twigged that that would take time, so I had to tell them someone must have put in a word for her.'

'You what? Jesus, Mona, no. That's against regulations.'

'Me telling them, or you actually doing it?'

Irene detected the scorn lacing the receptionist's words. 'I suppose you told them who spoke on Aneta's behalf.'

'No, I didn't, because I have no idea. It's not written down anywhere.'

'Good, good.' Irene took off her gloves and tugged at a stray tendril of hair that had come loose over her ear. 'I'll be in my office.' She made towards the door.

'Oh, they also wanted to know what sparked Aneta's outburst that day and who was in the vicinity when it happened.'

'Suppose you told them?'

'I told them what I knew, which wasn't much. What's going on? Is Cuan mixed up in these murders?'

Irene stopped. 'This place has nothing to do with those murders. It's a coincidence. Did the guards say something to plant that idea in your head?'

'Not at all.' Mona strode into her cubicle and began banging the keyboard. As Irene entered the code to leave the reception area, the other woman added, 'I think they were on a fishing mission. They even asked why we cut the grass in January.'

'You could be right they're fishing, but I can tell you, this river is dry.' With that, she left Mona to her work.

Once she was in her office, Irene flopped onto her chair. She turned her hands into fists and twisted them around her eyes. She had to stay strong, because this was going to get a whole lot worse before it got any better. She'd overcome adversity before; she would do so again. She took off her coat and got to work.

89

George Kenny seemed fraught and fidgety. His eyes were red-rimmed and his clothes needed changing. A sweaty smell surrounded him.

'I can't believe Shannon was hooked up to an escort agency.'

'Do you know of anyone who would want to hurt her?' Lottie asked.

'Hurt her? How? Do you know something?'

'No, I'm just trying to get answers.'

'Shannon was her own worst enemy. She abused herself with drugs, but I don't think she'd touched any since her stint in rehab.'

'Do you know of anyone she was friends with in Cuan?'

'I don't recall her talking about any of the residents.'

'Can I see her room?' She wanted to look for herself even though it had been searched and Kirby had seen it too.

'Go ahead up,' he said, 'I'm trying to get fluids into Davy. He has chickenpox. Never rains but it pours.'

'I can sympathise with that sentiment.'

Upstairs in Shannon's room, she recalled Kirby's notes. It had been tidied. No clothes on the floor and the bed was made.

She ran her hands under the pillows. Nothing. She lifted the side of the mattress. Nothing. Then the other side. It was a waste of time and she'd known that. But still she'd hoped she might find something. Back downstairs, she found George with a bottle of Calpol in his hand.

'Did Shannon ever talk about wanting to move out?'

'All the time. She liked to annoy me.'

'She ever mention Pine Grove?'

'Not that I recall. Jess might know. They were thick as thieves.'

'She was interviewed already but can I have her number?'

'Jess? Sure.'

She hoped the girl might be able to give her an insight into Shannon's life and in turn a clue as to where she was.

Outside, she called Jess and arranged to meet in a half-hour.

It was early evening and Fallon's was quiet. Chloe hadn't arrived for her shift yet. Good. With a coffee by her hand, sitting in a nook, Lottie waited for Jess to arrive. She really should go home and prepare dinner. Instead she phoned Sean and told him to rescue something from the freezer and she'd be there in an hour. She had to talk to Jess herself to see if there was anything she'd left out when she was interviewed by Kirby.

The pub clientele were mostly after-work office workers, and the tone was low. Tired, like her, having a drink before facing home. She thought back to the time when she'd have fortified herself with a glass of wine too, but now it was either Diet Coke, coffee or tea. Safer.

A young woman muffled up in a warm jacket and knitted beanie approached and stood by the table. 'I'm Jess. You must be the detective who rang me. I saw you on the telly once.'

'Please sit down. Can I get you anything?'

'I'm fine, thanks. Have you any word on Shannon?' She

removed the jacket and hat, and sat, crossing her jeans-clad legs. Her face showed signs of strain and her eyes were hollowed in her face.

'I'm sorry, there's nothing yet. I'm hoping you can help me.'

'I told everything to that other detective.'

'I know you spoke with Detective Kirby, but you may have remembered something since then that might help us.'

'You sound desperate.'

Lottie had to admit it. 'We are.'

Jess leaned forward, elbows on her knees, her hands supporting her chin. 'I've been over it in my mind a million times. There's nothing else.'

'What can you tell me about Shannon's time in rehab?'

'Poor Shannon was in a bad way back then,' she said. 'Rock bottom. But she was good after it. Really good. I was so happy for her.'

'How was she recently?'

'I think she was fed up living with George and his girl-friend. They use her as a babysitter, childminder, whatever. He works from home and is around all the time. Shannon found it hard to get a minute to herself, so she started going out. She was fixated on getting herself a man. Maybe that's why she joined that agency. She went there to have photos taken with the daft notion she could break into modelling. I told her they only want eighteen-year-olds, but the next thing I know she's an escort.'

'You didn't approve?'

'It's a glorified sugar-daddy service. Not that she had much success with it, and now... I can't believe someone would take her.'

'Let's go back to when she was in Cuan rehab. Did you visit her there?'

'Once, and it was enough for me. She was in the horrors. You get worse before you get better, they say, and it's true.'

'Afterwards, did she talk about her time in there?'

'Not really. But she mentioned John Morgan, the guy who was murdered. She said he was a good friend to her.'

'Friend?'

'Yes. Not a sexual relationship, if that's what you're thinking.'

'Did she keep in contact with him afterwards?'

Jess scrunched up her eyes, pondering the question. 'She never said.'

'Who else did she talk about who was in there with her?'

'She didn't like the manager. Irene something. Shannon said she was like an old-fashioned headmistress. She even had one of the staff in tears at some important event. Shannon said it was awful.'

Lottie sat up straighter. 'Can you remember anything she said about that incident?'

Jess picked at the cuticle on her thumb. 'The Irene one was putting on a big show to attract funding and she had invited a load of hobnobs from town. Then this poor girl lost it and was in hysterics. That's what Shannon said.'

'Did she say who it was?'

Jess shook her head. 'If she did, I can't remember.'

'Okay. Anything else?'

'She knew Laura Nolan.'

'Shannon did?'

'No, well, yes. I remember her saying this Laura comforted the girl who freaked out.'

And now those two were dead, Lottie thought. 'How did Laura know Aneta?'

'Who's Aneta?'

'We believe that Aneta Kobza is the young woman you were referring to.'

'I heard that name somewhere. Maybe Shannon did mention it.'

Or Jess had heard it on the news but wasn't making the connection. Not yet. 'So tell me more about Laura and Aneta.'

'That's all. Oh yeah, Laura's mother was there that day and apparently she left in an awful rush, right after the incident with this Aneta. Shannon said it was bizarre.'

Interesting, Lottie thought. Diana had run off too when she'd heard Aneta was dead. What the hell was she missing?

'And you definitely don't remember Shannon saying anything about what caused the incident?'

'Nope. I was only half listening to her. I'm sorry now. Shannon's a good person. And that escort thing worried me. Maybe it was because she was trying to get enough money to move out. Which is a bit mad really, considering she spent every cent she got on nights out.'

'Did she mention where she wanted to move to?'

'She had big notions. She loved the new houses down at Pine Grove. I remember her saying that if she won the Lotto that's where she'd live. Can you believe she even went to view the show home? Talk about annoying yourself when you haven't a euro in your pocket.'

'When was this?' Lottie leaned forward.

'Oh, I don't know. A few months back, maybe.'

'Did she meet anyone there?'

Jess widened her eyes. 'Oh! You mean John Morgan. He worked on the site, didn't he? And he's dead now. Fuck.'

'Did Shannon say she met him there?'

'I don't know. I remember having a laugh because she said the estate agent was up her own hole. Then again, Shannon thought that of most people who had a good job while she hadn't two cents to call her own.'

'Okay.' Lottie needed to check with Charlie Lennon to see if she remembered Shannon. 'Here's my card. Please mull over this conversation, and if you recall anything else, call me. Day or night.'

Jess's eyes filled with tears. 'You think Shannon is dead.' A statement, not a question.

'I believe she is alive. I'm going to find her.'

'Promise?'

'I don't make promises, but I will do my level best.'

'Thank you.' Jess took the card. She shook Lottie's hand, hustled into her jacket and left.

Lottie pushed away her cold coffee. The noise level was increasing around her and the smell of wine and beer threatened to make her run to the bar for alcohol. The investigation was so slow, but at least now Shannon was linked to Pine Grove, however tentatively. The Venn diagram was beginning to close in on the vital intersection. She hoped she could shut it tight before anyone else died.

90

Boyd knew he should really leave to pick up Sergio from Amy's, but he wanted to have a quick look into the McGovern family. They didn't appear on PULSE, so that was a good sign. For the family. Not for him. The PULSE database was a mine of information, but it had nothing on the McGoverns.

He put the couple's names into Google. A piece with a photo from the local paper popped up. Benny and Brigette, standing outside Gordon Collins's site office at Pine Grove, holding a solicitor's letter that they were attempting to deliver to him. In the article, the reporter listed their many complaints, including sinkage, crumbling brickwork and dampness. Bad for Collins, Boyd thought, because Moorland was a relatively new estate. Then he checked where the family had lived before. After more trawling, he found that they'd had a house outside Ragmullin, just as Benny had said. But what spiked his interest was the location.

The house was seven kilometres from Ragmullin, in the townland of Drinock, about two kilometres from where Aneta Kobza's body had been discovered.

'What?' Boyd said aloud.

Could Benny or Brigette be somehow involved in her death? But Rex had inadvertently given them an alibi for Laura's murder, and it was likely the same person had killed Aneta. The couple had moved house five years ago and were in a legal battle with Gordon Collins. Was he the link? Had Collins something to do with their old property?

He glanced at the clock and jumped up. He had to leave to pick up Sergio. All this would have to wait until tomorrow.

———

Before finally heading home, Lottie decided to check if Diana Nolan had returned. There was no sign of the nosy neighbour, Ms Molloy, as she got out of the car. The Nolan house was still locked up.

She walked around to the rear. The garden was neat, with a tidy lawn, a small trampoline and a sandpit. She wondered where Diana had taken her grandson. Did she not want to help find her daughter's killer? Or did she know what had happened? Worse still, was she involved?

The curtains on the back windows were open. She cupped her hands, peering in. All the cupboard doors appeared to be open, and at least one drawer was pulled out. Had Diana done this? Martina had suggested that Diana had been looking for something. What, though? A passport, to flee the country? But they'd checked, and Aaron Nolan did not have a passport and Diana's had not been used recently. Nothing made sense.

'What could you be searching for that you'd ransack your own home, Diana?' Lottie muttered.

She tried the handle. The door was locked. She upended stones and flowerpots around the door, but no luck. Same at the front door. Maybe the neighbour... Could she put up with the babble to see if she had a spare key?

She rang Ms Molloy's doorbell and braced herself.

'How can I help you, Inspector?'

'I'm wondering if Diana Nolan ever gave you a spare key to hold for her?'

'God, no. Told you, that woman hardly spoke to me.'

'Ah, that's grand. Sorry to have bothered you.' Lottie made to walk away.

'Hold on. Laura and her boy got locked out once and had to wait ages for her mother to come home. A few days later, Laura called round. She gave me a spare key to hold on to for emergencies, and asked me not to tell her mother. I don't think she spoke two words to me before or after that day.'

'Can I borrow the key, please?'

'Do you need a warrant to go in there?'

'Not if I have the key. I'll bring it back to you. Promise.' Promise? Jesus, Lottie, get a grip, she chided.

After a sermon about not losing it, Ms Molloy handed over the key and Lottie gratefully escaped.

It was dark, the streetlights throwing shadows, and she found it difficult to insert the key in the unfamiliar lock. Once inside, she switched on the hall light. A fold-up buggy stood at the end of the stairs and a pile of coats hung on hooks on the wall.

She checked the kitchen, where she'd seen the disturbance from outside. Now that she was here, the mess didn't look quite so frantic, but it was evident that someone had been searching. Apart from the open cupboards and drawers, the room was relatively tidy – just a couple of mugs in the sink. The fridge held some food, so did Diana intend to return?

The sitting room was similarly dishevelled. Cushions from the armchairs and couch were on the floor. Dresser drawers hung open.

Upstairs, she entered Laura's room. It looked almost the same as when she'd had a quick search on her visit after her murder. In the stillness, the room breathed loneliness and sorrow; its occupant was never returning. She closed the door softly and checked the other rooms.

In Diana's, the trail of destruction was more frenzied than downstairs. Clothes hung off hangers in the wardrobe and draped out of drawers. Two boxes were open on the floor, with paperwork strewn around. She kneeled to inspect them.

Among the many bills, invoices and calendars, she found a set of house deeds. She snapped off the elastic band and opened up the yellowing parchment, mentally crossing her fingers. But the deeds turned out to be for the house she was now kneeling in. She put them to one side and continued to delve into the box without making any earth-shattering discoveries. Had Diana found what she'd been looking for and brought it with her?

She shoved the papers back in the boxes and sat on the floor looking around. She could not put her finger on what had made Diana flee. Before getting to her feet, she noticed a corner of something sticking out from behind the bedside cabinet. She eased it out with two fingers. A single page folded over in three. It was old and creased. Spreading it on the floor, she discovered it was a birth certificate. When she read the baby's name, and then the date of birth, she frowned.

'Who are you?' It made no sense.

She wondered if this might tie everything together, or rip it all apart.

91

Feeling she was on to something tangible, Lottie wished she could work longer, but she was exhausted, and she'd already punched in far too many hours. The dead needed her, but her family needed her more. Despite their falling-out, Katie's face brightened with relief when Lottie arrived at Rose's house.

'I know we fight and argue, Mam, but we need to talk seriously about Gran's care. With Betty away last week, I think her condition deteriorated. It's not good for her, being alone. Louis has been great, and when he's around, she perks up. But she confuses him with someone from her past. She called him Eddie earlier. Wasn't that your brother who died when he was little?'

'Yes, and you're right.' Lottie took off her coat and slumped onto a hard chair. 'I was about to look into getting her a live-in carer, but then I latched on to Betty. She's good for Rose, but Betty has her own life and I can't be relying on her all the time.'

'It's a tough one.'

'True. How were things today?'

'Gran is very confused. She cried for an hour. Then she fell asleep on the chair by the stove. Eventually I got her to lie down. I don't mind looking after her, but I could be saying or doing things wrong.'

'Don't worry. You did brilliant. Head home and I'll stay with her. Sean is cooking dinner.'

'Really? Sean? No, it's fine, I'll stay. I've plenty of our stuff here and Louis is content enough. You're wrecked, Mam. A decent night's sleep would do you good. We can discuss Gran's care when you finish with this case.'

'About Greg—'

'Not now, Mam. Go on home.'

Lottie hugged her eldest child, then, without waiting to see her mother or find her grandson for kisses, she left, bone-weary and brain-tired.

———

Amy opened the door to Boyd.

'Hello there. Sergio is in the sitting room,' she said, hobbling on her crutch as she led him into the kitchen. 'I wanted a quick chat with you.'

He wondered if she was about to decline minding Sergio the following day. If so, he'd have to ask Chloe or Katie. They always obliged when he was stuck, but he needed to sort out a permanent arrangement for his son, at least until he started at the school.

Amy made two mugs of instant coffee and placed one in front of Boyd. 'Milk?'

'A drop. I'll get it.' He opened the refrigerator and dashed it into his mug before returning the carton.

'I know it's none of my business,' she said, 'but do you think Sergio might need therapy?'

'He is in therapy.' He wondered what had sparked Amy's comment. 'Why do you ask?'

'He kept talking about his mama. He misses her, Boyd. I

know you were divorced and you had a fraught relationship, but your child is hurting. Badly. He seems to blame himself for her death.'

'It was a car crash. Nothing to do with him. He knows that.'

'He's eight years old and—'

'I know what age he is…' Boyd stopped when he saw the hurt flash across her eyes. 'I'm sorry, Amy. I didn't mean that the way it sounded. Yes, you're right about his mother. He spent most of his life with her. I hope he doesn't think my reticence to talk about her is me blaming him in some way. I'd have thought the therapist would have addressed it with him by now.'

'A therapist can only do so much. You need to be open and honest with him.'

'I've given him so much attention. I've been with him constantly and I'm only a few days back at work…' He let his thoughts drift. Where was he failing?

'When you were with him day and night, he probably didn't dwell too much on thoughts of his mother or her death. Now that you've returned to work, he has more time to brood over all that happened. He almost died. He's harbouring trauma. I know what that's like. You need to talk to him, Boyd. Be more open with your son.'

He was only half listening. 'I wonder if Grace said something to him. My sister is liable to say anything.'

Amy shook her head wearily. 'You're passing the buck again. You need therapy yourself. You've been through a lot. Your cancer. Your complicated relationship with Lottie, and then there's your ex and all the trouble associated with her.'

'How do you know so much about my life?'

'Larry likes to talk.'

'I should have known he wouldn't hold his water.' He grinned and she returned it. 'I agree with you, Amy. I need to face up to all that's gone on in my life and what I want for my future with Sergio. And with Lottie.'

She sipped her coffee before continuing. 'Talk to him, Boyd. Don't be a closed book to your son.'

'Okay, and thanks. I think I needed that pep talk. Where's Kirby the snitch anyhow?'

She laughed. 'Sergio is showing him how to use a PlayStation controller.'

'You have a PlayStation?'

'No, but Larry phoned Grace when I agreed to have Sergio. She'd gone back for her suitcase so she brought the device over in the taxi before she left for the station. Now there's a wise woman if ever I met one.'

'Grace?'

'Yes. She's not afraid to express in words what she feels and thinks. There's a lot to be said for being so open.'

'My sister has no filter and she breaks my heart, but I love her.'

'Grace is honest with herself and is happy with her lot, and with Bryan. It's a lesson for us all, don't you think? You can't go it alone.'

'I agree. Thank you, Amy.' He instinctively gave her a hug, then wondered if that was the wrong thing to do. 'I hope you don't mind, but I was being open and expressing my feelings.' He winked.

'No need to mock.' She slapped him away playfully. 'I appreciate the gesture. Now go get your son and rescue Larry. I'm sure his head is fried with all that technology.'

92

Diana hugged her grandson sitting on her knee, tablet in his hand, watching a cartoon on YouTube. She'd ditched her phone and bought a cheap one with cash. She'd rented a car with more cash and driven to a holiday home village at Doon Lake, miles outside Ragmullin. She'd paid cash to the owner at the door. She hoped being dropped at the train station was enough to throw others off her scent. She needed time to think on her next move, knowing she was still too close to Ragmullin.

The house took for ever to heat up. She was cold to her bones, mainly with fear. Everything was her fault. Her beautiful daughter was dead. All because of her and the choices she'd made. She'd kept the secret buried for thirty years and now it was in danger of being blown wide open. Maybe it already had been. And there was more than her own safety at stake. Laura's death proved that.

She wept uncontrollably, her tears dampening Aaron's hair. Her daughter was dead. Murdered. What had it gained, only loss and sorrow? A gaping, empty void into which Diana was unable to stop herself sinking.

She'd been so careful. Too careful maybe, too regimented, to a point where her daughter found it difficult to grow. To be her own woman. Had it started when she got pregnant with Aaron? Had Diana's loud cries been the catalyst to send Laura into the depths of depression, only to soothe it with illicit drugs and end up at Cuan?

Or was it the fact that all her impositions had driven Laura to seek out a place of her own? And then to be turned down for a mortgage. But Pine Grove! Anywhere but there. Anyone but Gordon Collins. That man! She shivered as she thought of how he used to strut around Ragmullin displaying his wife and daughters like trophies. Diana was sure he was the root cause of all evil. She'd tried talking to him, but that had been a disaster.

And he was involved in everything, including Cuan. She'd nearly choked that day when she'd seen him there. But that was quickly superseded by shock when she spotted the young woman. With her thin hair brushed back, her jawline sharp, her eyes so familiar that she wondered how anyone could deny her existence.

But she had. Diana Nolan and others had denied her once before too. The old memories surfaced and she'd almost run from the room. She did run eventually, leaving Laura behind. And that, Diana firmly believed, was what had caused a spree of murders almost twelve months later.

She hugged her grandson to her chest so tightly he whimpered. She had tried to protect a child thirty years ago and it was obvious she had failed. She had failed to protect Laura too. She had to protect Aaron at all costs.

This time, failure was not an option.

93

The fear was real now. Terror swept through Shannon's body like a blazing fire. She sat alone in the small room – her cell, she called it. The woman had taped her mouth and tied her hands to the bed. She wanted to scratch the pulsing spots sprouting on her body. She needed to relieve the itch. No salve had been offered. She had to suffer.

Her situation was impossible. That word burned and burned without fading. *Impossible*.

The house seemed quiet. Had they all gone out? She knew *he* went out at night. Prowling. Hadn't he abducted her on her walk home from the pub? Didn't he have a taxi sign on the top of his car? That was why she'd got in with him. Dumb bitch.

A door opened and shut somewhere within the house. Sounds were muffled. The room must be padded, she thought. A footstep. Outside her door. The bolt being drawn back. A key in the lock. The door opened ever so slowly.

Shannon hoped it wouldn't be the woman. She disliked the constant darkness in her eyes. The dread she caused in her soul. The fidgeting hands when she talked, as if she wanted to throw something at you and would do so if she had anything in her hand to throw.

But perhaps it'd be him. With that browbeaten look he wore in the house. The persona the night he took her was totally different. He was like two people in one body. That was the only way she could describe him if asked. And she knew who manipulated his various transformations.

Or maybe it would be little Magenta, with her soft voice and menacing eyes. The voice that could turn loud and nasty in an instant. The pair had moulded the little girl into something terrible, and though Shannon thought Magenta was her only hope of escape, she realised she was just as terrified of the child as she was of the other two.

She missed her nephew, Davy's soft hand in hers. Missed pushing him on the swing in the park. She even missed her annoying brother. She missed her old life so much, a life she hadn't respected or cherished, and it made her want to cry and cry and cry.

The door opened a crack and someone slipped inside. A shimmer of light shone in from the hallway. A lighter sort of darkness. And then she was plunged into the pitch blackness as the door closed. A soft footstep on the floor. The rustle of clothing. The sound of a breath close to her ear. The smell of something dead. Not being able to see who was so close to her magnified her fear and defencelessness.

She'd have screamed if she could.

But she was powerless in every sense of the word.

94

Gordon Collins knew he shouldn't have left his home that morning. It made him look guilty. Now that he was back, the house felt like a prison. The walls seemed to draw in on him, consuming him, even with the magnificent glass doors and the kitchen blinds left open. Should he ring one of his daughters to come stay with him? No, he might be putting her in danger. Was he in danger? He wasn't sure, but he did need Dutch courage to get through the night.

Opening a bottle of Kilbeggan Irish whiskey, he poured a generous measure, swallowed it, then poured another. He turned down the lights and sat in his Eames lounge chair in the dark, sipping and staring out at his shadowy garden with the lake somewhere in the distance. He wanted to ask himself where everything had gone wrong. A rhetorical question because he could pinpoint with precision the date and time. He sensed the growing knot in his stomach, the rapid beating of his heart and the rising heat in his face.

Draining the glass, he flung it at the triple-glazed floor-to-ceiling window. The Waterford crystal shattered. The reinforced glass pane did not.

'Angry, are we?'

The voice behind him startled him more than the splintering tumbler.

Jumping up, he swivelled round, steadying himself with his hands on the back of the moving chair. 'What the fuck? How did you get in?'

'You gave me the code, remember? Or have you just marked me up as another proverbial notch on your bedpost.' She laughed. It was forced, with an underlying sinister tone.

She had a child with her. This caused him to momentarily baulk, but eventually he found his voice. 'What do you want?'

'I want to know what you're up to. Killing all those people.'

'I did not kill anyone and you know it.'

'Oh Gordon, I know nothing of the sort. They all had a connection to you. I really don't think you can talk yourself out of this one. *You* killed them. And I'll make sure the guards believe it.'

He felt perspiration bubble up on his forehead and trickle down the creases on either side of his nose. He knew she was smart, and now she was dangerous. 'There's no evidence of any such thing.'

'There's plenty of evidence.'

'Then go to the guards, why don't you? Or is there a reason you have to barge into my home making daft accusations against me?'

'You bankrolled that slut in recent years. Oh, I know. She told me. Have you no conscience? No sense of right and wrong?'

'I think you're the one without a conscience.' He threw her words back at her. 'Don't forget I know all about you and what you've done. I won't hesitate to use that knowledge if you dare come near me or enter my home again.'

'You're in no position to threaten me. I know everything.'

'You only think you do.'

'Oh, and what is that supposed to mean?' For the first time there was a wobble of uncertainty in her voice.

'Exactly what I said.'

'I can say you had John Morgan killed. He was found on your fucking site after all. And I know about you using the escort agency. How low do you go?'

Her words burned a hole in his brain and his heartbeat trebled. How did she know about the escorts? He had a fake profile; that Greg Plunkett couldn't vet a paper bag.

He strode across the room, intending to grab her and push her back out the way she'd arrived. But he stopped when he caught sight of the child's wide eyes; only then did he see the knife in the woman's hand.

'Hey, no need for violence,' he said, forcing his voice to be calm. 'We can work this out.'

'That's always your answer. Working things out. But look at the mess you've made.'

'I'm serious. This time I can make things right.'

He sincerely hoped she believed him.

If not, he was a dead man.

95

TUESDAY

The birth certificate tingled Lottie's hand. She knew she'd had no right to enter Diana's house, let alone take anything, but the woman had disappeared with her grandson and needs must.

The creased yellowing document made no sense. The names of the child and the mother meant nothing to her. No father was included on the cert. It was dated thirty years previously. She searched the names on PULSE without success; similar negative result on Google. Two phantoms to add to the mystery of the murders and disappearances.

Kirby was with SOCOs at the lane beside the Moorland houses. The warrant for Laura Nolan's financials had been executed and the bank submitted them that morning. McKeown was working his way through them, having given up trying to enhance the old group photo found among Aneta's possessions. He'd forwarded the photo to the tech guys. Lottie hoped the photo or the financials yielded a result, because she needed something to happen soon.

She went in search of Boyd. 'I need to get out of here.'

'You've only just arrived,' he said.

'I can't settle. Let's see if Gordon Collins has reappeared.'

Boyd drove and she leaned her head against the side window. 'How did Sergio get on with Amy?'

'Brilliantly. He had no objection going there this morning.'

'She works in town, doesn't she?'

'Two mornings a week. She mentioned she can take them off this week to look after Sergio.'

'Kirby hit pay dirt when he met her.' As they drove along the narrow road to Collins's house, she noticed a thick plume of grey smoke in the sky. 'Is that a fire?'

'Gosh, it could be.'

At the turn in the road, the way ahead was blocked by a fire engine. Boyd parked up on the grass verge and Lottie jumped out, running as fast as she could towards where the smoke grew thicker, clogging her throat. At the open gate, she paused. There was frantic activity, with a glut of firefighters spraying water on the house.

'Where's the owner?' she asked one firefighter.

'Hey, you can't go any closer. It's in danger of collapse.'

'Is there anyone inside?'

He shrugged and continued his job.

She eventually found the fire officer in charge.

'Ambulance is on the way.' He was crouched beside a man blackened with smoke, wrapped in a foil blanket. 'But we need to move him further away now.' He turned to Lottie. 'Can you help me?'

She grabbed one elbow while the fire officer got hold of the other, and they hauled the man to his bare feet. She had to squint through the smoke as they moved off the lawn and onto the road to await the ambulance. There they sat him on the grass verge.

'Can you stay with him?' asked the fire officer.

She nodded her assent, and he went back to the burning site.

Sitting beside the shivering silent man, she asked, 'Can you tell me what happened?'

To her surprise, he began to cry. Loud, gut-wrenching sobs. They scared her more than if he'd pulled a knife on her.

'What is it?' She looked back at the inferno that had been his home. 'Is there someone in there?'

He was convulsed with tears and couldn't or wouldn't answer.

Boyd appeared, tugging on his coat. 'What the hell?'

'Find the fire officer in charge. Tell him to make sure there's no one inside.'

Boyd took off, and she returned her attention to Gordon Collins. He turned his head towards her. His tears had washed some of the soot from his face.

'I'm finished. I've destroyed everything and everyone.'

'What happened?'

'It's gone. Everything I ever loved is gone. She has destroyed me.'

'Who are you talking about?'

But he lowered his head and sobbed softly as the ambulance siren wailed in the distance.

———

SOCOs were as busy as ants in the lane by Moorland, but so far they had nothing to report to Kirby. He stood a little away under a tree and lit a cigar before doubling up coughing. Maybe Amy was right. He should give up the blasted things. He quenched it and stuffed it in his pocket as Grainne Nixon approached.

'Got something for you.' She held up an evidence bag.

'Might be nothing to do with the Nolan girl's murder, but it's worth checking.'

He inspected the contents of the clear bag. A page from a child's reading book. 'It could have been dropped by a kid taking a shortcut to school.'

'Yeah, it could, but there's a speck of what looks like blood on the corner. It's possible it came from the car that transported Laura's body,' Grainne said. 'Turn it over.'

He did. There was a name printed in biro on the top right corner of a title page. 'Maggie. Name means nothing to me. Where exactly did you find it?'

'Embedded in a tyre rut. We've taken impressions. It's really soggy, but it was sheltered by the bushes. It might be possible to extract DNA from it.'

He photographed both sides of the page with his phone and handed it back.

'Thanks, Grainne. I better show this to the boss. Buzz me if you find anything else.'

96

Working his way through Laura Nolan's bank statements, McKeown didn't discover anything to alarm him. The only inward payments were her pay cheques. No maintenance from Aaron's mystery dad. Her outgoings were mainly for food and clothing. No big mystery uncovered.

'Waste of time,' he mumbled as he put the statements to one side. He eyed his workload and decided to spend some time on John Morgan. He'd start by checking the footage from the Pine Grove doorbell cameras which he'd neglected.

As he loaded the first file, McKeown saw that they had only downloaded the day of Morgan's murder and the day before. It would have to do for now. He began with Friday, the day of the murder.

Some of the doorbells had their lenses focused out onto the footpath in front of their houses. He quickly became bored with people walking dogs and a few kids running to and from school. He then watched the feed from the house situated next door to the show home.

John Morgan walked by, hands in the pockets of his yellow hi-vis work jacket, and disappeared. McKeown immediately pulled up the images from the house straight across the road, only to find the zoom didn't stretch further than their gate.

'Damn.' He had no way of knowing if Morgan had entered the show home, which was the first at the entrance to the estate, or kept on walking.

Returning to the feed where he'd seen Morgan, he restarted the footage. The images only appeared when someone triggered the camera. He watched, waited, watched. John Morgan did not reappear. McKeown reached the conclusion that he had either entered the show home at ten a.m. Friday morning, or he'd gone on somewhere on foot and not returned to the estate via that road. There was another entrance direct to the working site, but his body had been found in the house later in the day. Was it logical to assume he went in and never came out?

He fast-forwarded to the same afternoon and saw the boss and Boyd arriving at Pine Grove. He watched them exit their vehicle. The show home was out of range, but he knew they'd entered it.

He did not see the estate agent arrive. It was feasible she had parked her car either across the road or on the main road before going into the house. Maybe that was why Boyd had parked where he did. He still expected to see her arrive. She'd have to be asked, if it became relevant.

He went back to the day before Morgan's murder and started the footage from another house across the road. As he watched, shortly after eleven a.m., he found himself staring at a woman he recognised.

'Holy shit!' He jumped up to go tell the boss, but discovering that Lottie was out at the scene of a fire at Gordon Collins's house, he returned to his desk and studied the stilled image on the screen. With his heart beating too fast, he clicked start and watched the images unfold.

Diana Nolan was looking all around her before walking towards the show home.

Was she meeting someone? If so, he didn't see anyone else in the area.

He ran every piece of doorbell footage, then started checking and rechecking all the CCTV footage. He came across something from a back garden camera trained on the alley that ran behind the houses. Shit, why hadn't he checked this already?

He watched as Gordon Collins entered the lane and disappeared directly at the back gate to the show home. Had he been meeting Diana Nolan? The times matched.

He checked the same camera for the day of the murder, knowing now that he'd fucked up. He hadn't run this footage at all as he'd been concentrating on Laura Nolan. There was nothing he could do about it now. He held his breath as the camera was activated by movement.

The woman walked decisively along the lined-up bins and disappeared at the back gate.

He exhaled in a loud whistle.

97

Propped up on a trolley in the corridor of A&E, Gordon Collins was physically reduced in stature. While he awaited treatment, the triage nurse had covered his hands in temporary dressings. He was coughing up black phlegm; otherwise he didn't appear to be injured.

'They've left me here to rot,' he said with self-pity, staring at his hands.

'You were lucky to get out before you burned to death.'

'Lucky? My house is gone. All my beautiful things, up in smoke.'

'Things can be replaced.'

He exhaled a raspy breath. 'I suppose so.'

'How did the fire start?'

'I don't know, do I?' A tinge of anger crept into his tone. 'I was asleep until the smoke woke me up. I raced down the stairs. The kitchen was in flames. I couldn't find the fire extinguisher because it wasn't hanging in its usual place. Someone did this to me. To my house. The bastard.'

'You believe someone else started it maliciously?'

'What do you mean by someone *else*? Do you think I did this to myself?' He held up his hands. 'You're crazy.'

'You said earlier, "she has destroyed me". Who did you mean?'

'I... I never said that.' He doubled over coughing. More black phlegm lingered on his chin.

'You did.'

'I must have been raving.'

'Can you tell me about Aneta Kobza?'

After wiping his chin with his elbow, he said, 'Who?'

'The young woman we found dead Sunday morning. I think you knew her.'

'What?'

'You reacted badly to her photo.'

'I'm not used to looking at dead people.'

'You know who I'm talking about then.'

'You're putting words in my mouth.'

'Someone was paying her a grand a month.'

'Nothing to do with me.'

'It came from a London bank.'

'Still nothing to do with me.'

'I believe you use a London bank for some of your business ventures.' This was hearsay based on Brenda Morgan's recent interview.

'What are you suggesting?'

'I have a host of suggestions, but I'd prefer if you told me the truth.'

'I am telling you the truth.' His cadence displayed the grit of a businessman used to getting his way. Used to lying.

'You're fudging it, Gordon. You're involved in these murders either directly or indirectly. Let me tell you what I think.'

She paused, waiting for him to object. He merely nodded for her to continue.

'You were paying Aneta Kobza to keep quiet about something. I don't know what that was, but it was possibly some underhand deal that she knew about. Then she decides to come to Ireland and scares the shit out of you. Or maybe you scared her that day in Cuan at the financial donors' event. She freaks out, and then she's abducted and doesn't reappear for a year. When she does, she is starved, abused and very dead. Am I warm?'

He shook his head, leaving a sooty smear on the white pillowcase.

'We found John Morgan's photo among her possessions.'

'I know nothing about that.'

'Why were you paying her?'

He set his mouth in a thin line. Then his demeanour shifted to one of melancholy as he made his admission. 'Aneta was my daughter.'

'Shit.' Lottie leaned against the wall and blew out her cheeks. 'How? When? Shit. I'm so sorry for your loss. Did she always know, or did she find out and then blackmail you?'

'She found out because someone told her. Aneta was the result of a regrettable indiscretion years ago. She was placed for adoption very soon after she was born. After her adoptive parents died, maybe someone who wanted to destroy me told her. Or else the adoptive parents knew and had told her. It doesn't even matter, does it? I transferred a maintenance amount to keep her in Poland, but she wasn't satisfied. She came to Ireland to seek out her birth mother because I wouldn't give her that information, and I'm not giving it to you either.'

'Why not?'

'I was threatened. My fucking house was torched. I nearly died in it.'

'I don't understand.'

'Inspector, I never killed anyone, but I have a fair idea who is behind the murders, and I've been warned, so I'm keeping my mouth shut.'

'I could arrest you for impeding my investigation.'

'Arrest me then. I'm done talking.'

He closed his eyes and clamped his lips shut. Lottie noticed another dribble escape the side of his mouth and trickle down the cleft of his chin. Collins was helpless, and despite herself, she felt sorry for him.

'If you have a change of heart, contact me, but I'll be formally interviewing you when you're well enough.'

He gave no indication that he'd heard her. She left him there, lying on a trolley in the overcrowded A&E corridor, and wondered what this new information meant to the case.

———

The smoky smell had adhered itself like glue to his suit, skin and hair. Boyd desperately wanted to take a shower, but he hadn't time. He felt in his bones that the investigation was gearing up. The burning of Gordon Collins's house had added a new dimension. The fire officer had told him there was evidence of an accelerant having been used. Boyd doubted Collins had done it himself. The man had appeared besotted with his house. Someone was trying to kill him. Or warn him. Had Collins murdered three people and abducted Shannon? Was he missing a crucial tell?

He'd driven out to the field where Aneta's body had been found. He wanted to get a feel for the area again, especially after discovering the McGoverns had owned a house in the Drinock locality. He imagined Collins's fingers were all over that transaction. What did it mean, if true?

Breathing in the fresh country air, he studied the landscape. Someone had to have driven along the road, stopped the car and carried her body to the field. Why this field? It was about two kilometres from the McGoverns' old house. Was that a coincidence, or were they involved? Small-town living meant people had connections all over and coincidences were rife. The McGoverns had it in for Collins because of the defects in their current home. They appeared to be a hard-working, if struggling, couple with a young son who had inadvertently witnessed the disposal of Laura Nolan's body.

He scanned the horizon. He couldn't see any houses from where he stood, though the land was flat. The spires of Ragmullin Cathedral were just about visible in the distance. All around him was farmland. The farmer who'd found the body had been cleared of any involvement without shedding light on why his land had been used to discard the young woman's body.

Boyd surveyed the area again. Was it opportunistic, because this was somewhere far enough away from the actual crime scene to be deemed safe from detection? Or was it close enough for someone in a hurry?

Back in the car, he pulled up the McGoverns' old address on his sat nav and out of curiosity, drove towards it. The house was listed as an old Protestant rectory dating from the nineteenth century. The road narrowed the further he drove until it was nothing more than a lane. He reached a closed gate, which he estimated to be at least ten feet high. He stopped the car and noticed an intercom on the pillar to the side of the gate. The house was not visible. Walls and trees surrounded it. Was it just an old rectory that was now someone's abode, or was it something much more sinister?

He wasn't going to get answers outside the wall, and he needed more information before he went pressing an intercom on a whim. He decided to return to the station to check the property register. His humour didn't improve when he realised he had to reverse five hundred metres, praying he didn't meet a tractor.

98

'I'm not sure about this, Kirby,' Lottie said as they exited the car outside the school. It was a sprawling mishmash of interconnected buildings located on a small hill a few hundred metres from the Moorland houses.

'Well, you said you remembered Rex mentioning a Maggie getting a lift to school in a taxi.'

'But still... Let's see how far we get.' She shook out her arms, trying to dispel the smoky smell, as Kirby entered the school showing his ID.

The grey-haired school secretary played her role like a Rottweiler, insisting they could not come further onto the premises without an appointment. 'Child protection and safety are paramount.'

With her patience skating on the thinnest of ice, Lottie flashed her own ID, her finger under the word *Inspector*. 'It's imperative that I speak with the principal. He can come out here to talk if we can't enter.'

With a strangled sigh, the woman punched a number on the phone.

'Mr Cohen, two detectives are here to talk to you. They don't have an appointment.'

She raised an eyebrow at his reply and a buzzer beeped on the door beside Lottie. She entered a long, narrow corridor lined with closed doors and little coats hanging on hooks. A young man appeared and gestured for them to enter his office.

'Sorry about Belinda. She's good at her job.'

'She could use better manners.' Lottie could have bitten her tongue when she saw his crestfallen expression.

'I apologise, but we have to be careful. I was physically assaulted twice last year by irate parents. Sit, please.'

He slumped into a tattered swivel chair behind an over-flowing desk, his face drawn and haggard. He couldn't be older than forty, but stress lines feathered his eye sockets and mouth. His shirt needed the rub of an iron and his tie was as askew as his blonde hair. 'What can I do for you?'

'We need some information about a pupil.'

'Not sure what I can tell you, but fire ahead.'

'We're investigating a series of murders and the abduction of a young woman. During our investigation, we found this page from a school book.' She passed over the photocopy Kirby had arranged, the original already dispatched for forensic examination. 'You can see the name Maggie printed on it. We need to talk to this girl.'

'Why do you think she's at my school?'

'Rex McGovern attends here, and he told us about a Maggie who gets dropped to the school by taxi. We're hoping you might enlighten us.'

'Even if I wanted to, my hands are tied. We have to protect our pupils and—'

'Mr Cohen, I need to know if this is from your school.'

'It could be, yes.'

'You know who this Maggie is, right?'

He tapped his computer. 'Yes.'

'I need her full name and address.'

'I'm sorry, I can't give—'

'This page was found close to a crime scene. I need to speak to Maggie.'

'That's impossible. She's not in school this week. Chicken-pox, the text said. It's rife at the moment.'

Lottie opened her mouth to protest further, then hesitated. She'd recently heard of someone having chickenpox. Think. Yesterday. George Kenny had said his son had it. Was he connected to this Maggie? But Davy was too young for school. Was there a link?

'I'll be back with a warrant, Mr Cohen. And if this Maggie comes to harm or the missing woman turns up dead, I will hold you responsible for not giving me the information I've asked for.' She knew she should have toned it down, but feck him.

'You're bang out of order, Inspector. You should leave.'

'I want her full name and address,' Lottie pressed.

'Inspector Parker,' Kirby said, 'I think we should go. Now.'

'I'm sorry,' Mr Cohen said. 'Really sorry.'

99

Garda Thornton called Lottie to one side as she entered the station with Kirby.

'Charlie Lennon is in Interview Room 1. You wanted to see her.'

'Great, thanks. I need to shower and change my clothes, but feck it.' She spied Boyd coming in the main door. 'Boyd, you're with me. Work your charm. She likes you.'

'Who likes me?'

'Interview Room 1. Let's go.' As they walked, she added, 'Do I smell as bad as you?'

'Why are we...?'

His question petered out as McKeown came trundling towards them waving sheets of paper. 'I found something. You have to see it.'

'Can it wait? I want to interview Charlie Lennon now. I have to see if she remembers Shannon Kenny viewing Pine Grove. Jess said... What is it, McKeown?'

'You've Charlie Lennon in there?'

'Yep. Why?'

'Look at this first.'

. . .

The interview room never had enough air circulating. Constantly stuffy and too hot. Lottie assumed it was designed to make suspects sweat out a confession. Outside, the weather was cold, but inside she felt totally overdressed, and the smoky odour travelled up her nose. She tugged off her sweater, balled it up on her knee, and rested her hands on the table, calming her breathing in order to face off Charlie Lennon.

Originally she'd wanted to find out if what Jess had told her last evening was true, but after McKeown's discovery, the interview had taken on a new importance. As she handed the folder to Boyd, she noticed that her nails were clogged with soot.

'Hello, Charlie,' Boyd said politely. 'We're recording this interview. You're free to leave at any time. We're just after some information.'

'That's totally fine. I want to help if I can. It sounded urgent when I picked up the message from my answering service this morning.'

She smiled sweetly, but Lottie noticed how quickly the expression disappeared from her face when Boyd lowered his head to switch on the machine.

Charlie was dressed casually while still managing to look like a model: denim jeans, her white shirt immaculately ironed, a sweater tied loosely around her shoulders. Her hair was loose, slightly damp from a recent shower. She looked twenty-six rather than forty-six. Must be Botox, Lottie thought.

'We appreciate you helping us out.' Boyd had the charm offensive in spades. 'We need to ask you about last Friday afternoon. We met you around half three at Pine Grove to view the show home. What time did you arrive?'

'Oh, I was there earlier than that. I had a chat with Patrick, the site manager, in his office.'

'Do you know what time that was?'

'I've no idea. Sure, it's days ago now.'

'Did you meet or see anyone else at the site office?'

'I can't recall. Gordon Collins may have been there, or maybe that was after... you know, after we found the body.'

'And did you see John Morgan that morning before we found him dead?' Boyd was so polite, but if Charlie professed not to remember one more time, Lottie thought she'd slap her.

'Not that I recall.' Charlie's lips were pursed and she no longer looked like a model. There was something simmering beneath the surface, Lottie was sure of it. Time for her to jump in.

'What was your relationship with John Morgan?'

Slowly Charlie turned to face her. 'Relationship? I had no relationship with him. He was just a lad working on the site.'

'But you must have met him when you were in and out to the site?'

'I dealt with prospective clients there. On occasion I met with Gordon or Patrick.'

'Really?'

'What's that supposed to mean?' Charlie was unsettled, Lottie could hear it in her tone.

'I find it hard to believe that when you were around the site, you never passed the time of day with John or had a chat.'

'I didn't say that. I said that I cannot rec—'

'Yeah, yeah. You can't recall.' Lottie folded her arms and leaned back in her chair.

'I don't like your attitude, Inspector,' Charlie snapped. 'I'm here of my own free will and I think I'd like to leave now.'

Boyd interjected. 'Charlie, I'd appreciate if you could hold on. We've just a couple more questions.'

'Okay, sure.' The saccharine smile was plastered back in place.

'We went through a lot of camera footage around Pine

Grove. Can you look at this?' He slid a photo from the file and slid it across the table. 'This is you, Charlie.'

'Looks like me.'

'Do you know where that is?' Boyd asked.

'Yes, it's the lane by the back entrance to the show home.'

'Do you see the date and time?'

'I'm not blind.'

'That's the morning of John Morgan's death.'

'So?'

'So,' Lottie piled in, 'you never told us you were there that early.'

'Well, this makes it obvious I was.'

'What were you doing there?'

'Probably making sure the house was presentable for viewers.'

'Did you open the front door to anyone?' Lottie kept her eyes glued to Charlie's face. Would she spout 'I don't recall' again, or was she clever enough to realise they knew exactly who she'd let into the house.

'Oh God!' She clamped a hand to her mouth. Too dramatically for Lottie's liking. 'I remember now. There was a socket loose in the kitchen. I rang the site office and this young lad came to fix it. It must have been John.' Her face was contorted in confusion. 'Does that mean I was the last person to see him alive? Other than his killer?'

'Seems so.'

'Gosh, I left him working there. If you have the footage of me entering the house, you will have it of me leaving the same way. Was the killer caught on camera too?'

Lottie wondered if McKeown had run the footage on both the rear and front of the house for the entire day. She hadn't asked and he hadn't said.

'I'll check your story with the site office. Who did you speak to there about the socket?'

'Might have been John himself, but I can't recall now.'

After a pause, Lottie decided to forge ahead.

'Did Shannon Kenny ever view the show home?'

'Who is she?'

'She's missing, presumed abducted.'

'You think she also viewed Pine Grove? I'll have to check the office diary. One of my colleagues might have dealt with her.' Charlie looked from one detective to the other, confusion knitting her brows into anxious curves. 'What's going on?'

'Her friend says you showed Shannon around sometime last year.'

'I can't remember everyone off the top of my head.'

'You've that many prospective buyers, huh?'

'Not everyone who views intends to buy.' Charlie looked pointedly at Lottie. 'Some people like to snoop. Time-wasters.'

Lottie bristled at the dig.

Boyd laid two more photos on the table, Shannon and Laura. 'We're trying to find a link between the victims. Pine Grove is our best bet so far.'

Lottie kicked him under the table. This was not the time to show their hand.

Charlie shook her head. 'This is awful.' She pulled Laura's photo towards her. 'I seem to remember her. She was moaning about how expensive it was. A definite time-waster. Never saw her again. That's why the name didn't ring any bells with me.'

'And Shannon?' Boyd pointed to the girl's photo.

Pursing her lips, Charlie shook her head. 'I'm not sure at all. I'll let you know later, once I'm back at the office.'

Lottie took the folder from Boyd. She slid out Aneta's photo. 'What about this girl?'

Charlie hesitated, glancing at the photo. 'You showed me this already, and I checked. As far as I know, she didn't view the house.'

'She had a Pine Grove brochure in her possession.' Lottie

had to be careful. She couldn't relate what Gordon Collins had told her about his relationship to Aneta. It needed to be verified, and anyhow it had nothing to do with Charlie Lennon.

'That doesn't mean anything. Those brochures are everywhere.'

'She was working at Cuan rehab centre.' Lottie passed over another photo. The group photo taken by Greg Plunkett on donor day. 'That's you there.'

'Yes. It was a big shindig. Gordon asked me along. He said there'd be wealthy people there and I might be able to do a little scouting for sales.'

'Mm...' Lottie played it as if she knew something else. 'You never told us you were there.'

'Did you even ask?'

Good question. Lottie glanced at Boyd, who shrugged. She pointed to a young woman standing in the background of the photo. 'That's Aneta.'

'The dead girl?' Hesitating, Charlie considered the photo. 'I've no recollection of her being there. I was more interested in people with money.'

Lottie clenched her fists under the table. Christ Almighty, but the woman was grating on her nerves.

Charlie said, 'Are you done? I want to leave now.'

Nodding her assent, Lottie waited for Boyd to sign off for the recording and switch off the machine.

'Thanks for all your help,' she said.

Charlie stood and tightened the sweater at her throat. 'I'll help in any way I can, but I don't like your tone, Inspector. I've done nothing wrong.' With that, she left the interview room.

Lottie and Boyd turned to each other.

'What are we not seeing here?' she said.

100

When her bonds were released, Shannon had to use every bit of willpower not to tear at her face and torso. She was covered in tiny blistered spots. Magenta was the same. The kid was home from school again and in a foul mood.

The woman was presumably at work and the man had gone off after locking them in. He'd checked all the windows and doors before he left.

'I wish I was in school,' Magenta said. 'I like school. But I have to pretend there.'

'Pretend about what?'

'Who I am.'

'What do you mean?'

'I'm Magenta here and Maggie there. It's a bit shit.' The child scratched at a spot until it bled. Shannon did nothing to stop her.

'Why have you two names?'

'How would I know?'

'Do you know their real names too?'

'Are you joking? Of course I do. But you can't trick me into telling you.'

'I'm not trying to trick you. I need to get out of here, and you do too. This is not normal, what they're doing to us, to you. All the doors chained and locked. Tying me up and taping my mouth shut. Can you not see how wrong it is?'

The girl continued to scratch the same spot then stared at her bloody finger. 'I kind of like it. It's like a big adventure.'

'How long have you lived here?'

'Years. We came on a boat over the sea. Then we got a bus and then a car. A nice man gave her a car and this house. I think it's cute.'

Jesus. Shannon could think of a lot of words to call the house, but cute was definitely not on the radar. 'It's horrible.'

'You're not very nice,' Magenta said, her eyes darkening. 'I know where she keeps the knife. Don't move.'

Shannon's hands shook uncontrollably. She glanced around trying to find some way to get the fuck out of this nightmare. She wasn't waiting for the child to return with a knife to taunt her, maybe kill her.

She rooted in the drawers, though she knew the one with the knives was padlocked. In the top cupboard she eyed the mugs and glasses. A glass. She could smash one and arm herself with a shard. But could she hurt a child? Like fuck she could, if it meant protecting herself.

She took out a pint glass and smashed it against the ceramic sink, hoping the noise didn't carry to wherever Magenta had gone. Extracting the longest and sharpest piece from the sink, she palmed it, careful not to cut herself.

'I wouldn't if I was you.' The voice came from the doorway. It was low and menacing. Turning round, she was totally wrong-footed by the person standing before her.

Before she could raise her hand to wield her makeshift weapon, she felt her body on fire and sizzling, and she dropped to the floor.

101

The holiday cottage was so cold when Diana woke up, her breath hung in the air. She'd wrapped every available blanket around Aaron. At least he was cosy and snoring. She made herself a mug of coffee and held it between her icy hands, warming them.

After switching on the television, she scanned the limited channels until she found the rolling twenty-four-hour news service. It was currently on sport, so she had to sit through a recap of the previous night's Premiership loss by Manchester City to Liverpool before the feed rolled on to the headlines.

Sitting forward, she watched smoke billowing in the distance behind the midlands news correspondent. A drone flew over the site, showing the devastation. The coffee caught in her throat and she spluttered it out over her hands. Gordon Collins's house. What the hell?

She read the subtitles, not daring to turn up the sound in case it woke Aaron. The images showed an ambulance screeching off followed by an unmarked garda car, blue lights flashing on the grille. Was he dead? The subtitles didn't mention any fatalities, so he must be okay.

This was getting too close to home. She'd lost her daughter. Gordon his house, if not his life. His protégé, John Morgan, was dead. Aneta was dead. And another girl was missing.

She'd have to go back to Ragmullin. She knew the person behind all this would make sure she was blamed if it came to it. She had to tell the truth.

Once she'd made up her mind, a calmness descended. She'd tell all, bury her daughter, then leave for ever.

As she switched off the television, there was a knock at the door.

She stood, frozen, mug in hand. No one knew she was there. Get a grip, Diana. It had to be the house owner. She peeked out the window. A car was parked beyond the hedge, an unlit taxi sign on its roof. What was this about?

She went to answer the door.

102

Lottie gathered the team in the incident room and fetched Superintendent Farrell.

'There's a strong smell of smoke in here,' Farrell said, loosening the elastic on her tie and taking a seat at the front of the room.

'I was with Gordon Collins at the fire and then spoke with him at the hospital,' Lottie said. 'I received word that he's having an operation on one of his hands and I haven't had a minute to pee, never mind wash myself or change my clothes. Boyd smells worse.'

He sniffed his sleeve.

Farrell blanked him. 'Hopefully we can wrap things up soon and find Shannon Kenny. Alive. We have enough grieving families. What had Mr Collins to say for himself?'

'Without beating around the bush,' Lottie said, 'he claimed Aneta Kobza was his daughter.'

A cacophony of *oh* and *what the fuck?* went up among the team.

'And?' Farrell said, the only one in the room nonplussed.

Lottie detailed the conversation she'd had with Collins.

'He was paying Aneta to stay in Poland after someone informed her he was her father. But she still came to Ireland searching for her mother. I suspect Diana Nolan may be her mother, because of the old birth cert I found in her house. It names a girl, Magenta McCabe, born thirty years ago. It has to be Aneta who was then adopted. The mother's name on the cert is Christine McCabe. Diana could have used a fictitious name.'

Boyd said, 'Someone didn't want Aneta to find her birth mother. It's hard to get a handle on it.'

McKeown held up the old photograph taken outside a building and the one of John Morgan. 'These two photos were in Aneta's possession. They must be key.'

'But why would she have John Morgan's photo?' Kirby asked.

'According to Charlie Lennon,' Boyd said, 'John Morgan was Collins's protégé. Maybe whoever sent it to Aneta wanted to point her in that direction.'

'But Aneta knew Collins was her father,' Lottie said.

'You're right.' Boyd conceded. 'Was someone jealous of the attention John got from Collins?'

'All three victims had a connection, however flimsy, to Pine Grove,' Lottie said. 'As did Shannon Kenny.'

'And all are tied to Cuan.' McKeown pointed to the old group photo. 'Gary worked on this photo, and I've determined that it definitely has a younger Gordon Collins and Diana Nolan in it. Maybe we should try to trace the others.'

'Hold on a minute.' Superintendent Farrell got up to examine the photo. 'That's Irene Flood. She married a Dunbar from Athlone. I played golf with her.'

'She runs Cuan rehab now.' Lottie felt a rush of excitement. 'We'll interview her again. She might be able to shed more light on the photo.'

'If she's not involved herself,' Boyd said. 'She's slippery as an eel.'

'We need to find Diana,' Lottie said. 'Last known to have been left at the train station by a taxi.'

'Talking of taxis,' McKeown said, 'I've contacted all the taxi firms in town and no one remembers picking up Laura Nolan last Thursday night.'

Garda Brennan raised her hand. 'What was the upshot on the page with the name Maggie found by SOCOs at the lane?'

'It's been sent to the lab but we may wait awhile for DNA results. We got very little from the school. A warrant is being drawn up to get the girl's full name and address.'

'She could be crucial,' Kirby said.

'Or she could be nothing to do with anything,' McKeown said.

'Will you give over?'

'I want answers, not speculation,' Superintendent Farrell snapped. 'Have you got hard facts or evidence?'

'Apologies in advance, but I've more speculation,' Boyd said. 'The location, that field where Aneta's body was dumped, bothered me. Rex's parents once owned a house in that area. They're in a constant battle with Collins over the state of the house they now live in...'

'Where are you going with this?' Lottie asked, surprised. This was the first she'd heard of it.

'I drove to their old house earlier. A rectory that's now a bloody barbican. Huge sliding gates with an intercom. Totally surrounded by trees and ten-foot walls. Garda Lei, did you find out who owns it?'

'I searched the electoral register, but no one is listed at that address. Then I checked the property register. Bingo. It's in the name of GC Construction.'

'Gordon Collins,' Lottie said. 'Did he buy the house from the McGovern family? He doesn't live there, so who does?'

'No way of finding out unless we knock on the door,' Boyd said. 'If we can get to the door, that is.'

'We could ask Collins,' Farrell said.

Lottie said, 'Don't know when he'll be fit enough to interview and we haven't time to wait. I'll head out to this rectory with Boyd.'

'Hold on.' Farrell's tone was stamped with authority. 'What has that house got to do with anything?'

'It's two kilometres from where Aneta's body was found,' Boyd countered. 'She was missing for a year, though no one realised it. A secluded, fortified house like that is as good a place as any to hide someone away.'

'Conjecture.' Farrell wasn't backing down. 'Didn't I say I want facts and evidence?'

'With all due respect,' Lottie said, 'Gordon Collins seems to be slap-bang in the centre of everything so far. He told me he was in rehab thirty years ago. He fathered a child, Aneta, who was put up for adoption when she was born. He was sending her money but then she arrives here and shortly afterwards disappears. It's possible she was being held in that house.'

'You think he killed his own daughter?' Farrell was incredulous. Lottie didn't blame her. Still...

'If she was getting close to something he didn't want revealed...'

'But why kill the others?' Farrell asked.

'We've established that they all had some sort of connection to Pine Grove and they were all in Cuan at the same time last year.'

'So were a lot of other people.' Farrell wasn't giving up.

'Can I add something else into the melting pot?' McKeown asked.

'You might as well.' Lottie slumped onto the nearest chair. She felt her phone vibrate in her bag by her feet. She prised the bag open with her foot and glanced at the screen. Katie. Not now, she whispered.

McKeown said, 'I revisited the Right One database to verify the clients' alibis in person. One of the men who provided an alibi early on was not resident at the address given. Never lived there.'

'I thought Greg Plunkett background-checked his clients,' Lottie said.

'He said he did,' Boyd said.

'Obviously he didn't do a good job,' McKeown said.

'I agree it's suspicious that the man gave incorrect information.' Lottie stood, ignoring her phone, which had begun to vibrate again. 'Maybe he has a wife and kids. However, we need to find him.'

'That's a waste of time when we have a host of other leads to follow,' Kirby countered. 'What's so special about this guy?'

McKeown's head reddened as he looked down at his tablet and back up again. 'He was on a date with an escort on Valentine's night last year. And... shit. I'm only realising something now—'

'But—' Kirby began.

'Aneta wasn't registered with them.' Lottie looked to McKeown to see where he was going with it. 'Or was she?'

'She could have faked an identity.'

'Seems Plunkett wasn't as diligent as he claimed.' Lottie got up and paced in front of the boards, aware of Farrell scrutinising her. 'What's the name of the girl he met?'

McKeown's face was puce now. 'Magenta McCabe.'

'Holy shit.' She pointed to the board. 'The name on the birth cert I found in Diana Nolan's house.'

'Staring me in the face.' McKeown shook his head. 'Sorry, I fucked up.'

'Good God,' Farrell said.

'We need to—' Lottie was interrupted by a harried Garda Thornton rushing in.

'There's another fire. Out at Doon Lake.'

'Let the fire service deal with it.' Farrell stomped towards him, arms flapping. 'Nothing to do with us.'

'I think it might have.'

'Go on, then.'

'One of the holiday cottages is on fire. The owner says he rented it to a woman and a little boy yesterday morning.'

'Christ,' Lottie gasped. 'Diana and her grandson?'

'We don't have a name...' Thornton said, backtracking.

'Boyd, come with me.'

103

'Well, we can't blame Gordon Collins for this fire. He's still in hospital.' Boyd stood surveying the smouldering mess. A small bungalow reduced to concrete and ash. 'I'm sick of smoke.'

Lottie approached the fire officer, who'd also been at Collins's house. 'What can you tell me?'

'Accelerant was used. You can smell it from here. Petrol.'

'Anyone inside?'

'Not that we found so far. According to an eyewitness, there was shouting earlier, and when she looked out, she saw a taxi driving away, right before the place went up.'

'So no bodies?'

'I can't be sure until the fire is fully extinguished. Too dangerous for my crew to go on site yet. Another hour maybe.'

She joined Boyd, who'd been talking to the owner. 'Well?'

Boyd checked his notes as the other man quivered, biting his nails. 'Rented to a woman and a boy. Cash. No names. Rented for the week.'

'Did you get any ID?' asked Lottie. The man shook his head. 'Feck's sake.'

'I reckon it was Diana and her grandson,' Boyd said.

'If so, how did they get here?'

The man pointed to a grey VW Golf that had miraculously escaped any damage and made his way to talk to the fire officer.

Boyd visually inspected the car, tried the handle. Locked. A decal on the windscreen showed it was a hire car. 'I'll check with them.'

'It has to be her but what's she up to?'

'You think Diana torched this place as well as Collins's house?'

'I don't know. Why didn't she take the Golf? Why get a taxi?'

'If we've to go checking taxi drivers again, we're back to square one.'

'Hold on.' Lottie approached a woman with a dressing gown over her shoulders. She was fully clothed underneath but was shivering. 'Miss Farnham?'

'Yes. I called 999. I hoped there was no one inside.'

'Did you see the taxi?'

'Yes.'

'Tell me what you remember.'

'I heard shouting. A woman. Maybe screaming. By the time I looked out, I saw a taxi heading up the road and the fire had started next door.'

'Can you tell me anything about the car? Colour? Make?'

'It was just a taxi. Had the sign on top, unlit. Dark coloured car, maybe black. I can't think straight.'

'Any numbers or letters on the sign?'

'I couldn't see. It was almost gone round the corner by the time I looked out.'

'But it was definitely a taxi?'

A shrug. 'It had the sign.'

'Okay, thanks.'

Lottie went back to Boyd. 'Wherever Diana went, she didn't go voluntarily. The witness heard screams. There's no

CCTV out here, so that's a dead end. I think we should pay Irene Dunbar a visit.'

'You think she is involved? Or that Diana went there?'

'Not necessarily. But I want to ask about that old fire at Cuan. Gordon Collins's house burned down, and now this holiday let. Our murderer could have started out as an arsonist.'

Her voice authoritative, verging on domineering, Lottie marched past Mona. 'Open the door.'

There was no stalling or protestations this time. Lottie, followed by Boyd, rushed into Irene Dunbar's office.

The woman jumped, hand to her heart. 'What's going on?'

'You tell me.'

'I've no idea what—'

'Enough.' Lottie slapped the photo found in Aneta's possessions down on the desk. 'I want to know the names of everyone in that photo.'

'It... looks ancient.'

'Try thirty years old.'

Irene fell back into her chair. 'What do you know about it?'

'I said—'

'Okay, okay.' She picked up the photo. 'Some people just want to dig up the past when it's best left buried.'

'Who do you mean?'

'Aneta. She kept digging and wouldn't give up.'

'Did you know who she was?'

'Not at first, but she couldn't deny her looks. She was the image of her... when she was young.'

This confused Lottie for a second. 'Who? Her mother? Who was her mother?'

Irene dodged the question. 'There were shades of her father in there too. The ruthlessness. The doggedness.'

'You mean Gordon Collins?'

'You know about it then.'

'Just that he was her father,' Lottie conceded.

'Ask him about it.'

'I can't. His house was burned down and he's having an operation.'

'God Almighty. Is he okay?'

'He should be.'

'You'll have to talk to Diana.'

'She was burned out of her rented accommodation.'

Irene turned her head frenetically, gulping. 'They'll come for me now and burn me out too. Dear God, what did we do?'

'You tell me.' Lottie sat in one of the chairs. Boyd did likewise. They sat in the silence. No sound of a lawnmower outside today. 'Go on, Irene.'

'She was a first-class manipulator. Manipulated all of us, especially Gordon. When she got pregnant, we tried to help her. God, we did. She just sneered. Stamped her foot and laid down the law. Then this place went on fire. Half of it was burned down. I knew it was her, but I couldn't prove it. And Gordon... Poor Gordon. He's been making donations he can't afford, because he feels responsible, and perhaps he's afraid I'll tell. I'd never tell. I value my life too much.'

'I'm lost, Irene.' Lottie side-eyed Boyd to confirm he felt similar confusion.

'She was at the event here last year. I nearly died with shock. I thought she was still in the UK. I had no idea she had come back. Then I found out she'd been working in Ragmullin this five years. I'm afraid that when Aneta got upset that day, I admitted who her mother was.'

'Who are you talking about?'

Irene darted her finger towards a girl in the photograph without touching it, as if it might scorch her.

'Name her for me,' Lottie said, returning to her earlier question.

'I fear her more than I fear the law. She's a chameleon. Her face could tell a hundred different stories in one hour. You never knew who you were going to meet.'

'We have alibis, albeit weak, for everyone in our investigation,' Lottie said, half thinking out loud.

'What about her sidekick?' Irene said.

'Who?'

'He keeps his eyes stuck to me every single day since I discovered she'd returned.'

'And who is that?'

'The gardener here. She forced me to take him on. Claimed she knew all sorts of things about me that would ruin me if made public. I've nothing to hide. I did nothing wrong. Not in recent years, anyhow. I helped back then. What we did was a mistake, and she couldn't reveal that old secret without implicating herself. But I know she'd twist things so badly that I'd never be able to hold my head high in public again.'

'What's the gardener's name?'

'Probably not his real name. And I pay him in cash. Her stipulation. No money trail. Clever bitch.' Irene's body sagged, as if the revelations had sucked the life from her.

'His name?'

'Thomas McCabe.'

Lottie wondered if he was related to Magenta McCabe, the name on the birth certificate. He had to be. 'Do you know anything else about him?'

'No. He says nothing. He's good in the greenhouse, I'll give him that.'

'Do you sow tomatoes in a greenhouse?'

'Why on earth...? Yes, but why?'

'Doesn't matter. How does he travel to and from here?'

'He drives a taxi. I reckon it's bogus.'

'Did he transport Aneta to work?'

'He wasn't here back then. He started shortly after she left.'

Lottie thought over what Irene had said about Aneta and her features like her young mother. She visualised the various photos on the incident board, the dead, the witnesses... It came to her in a flash. She stood and walked over to Irene, looking down at the seated woman. 'If I say who I think the woman is, will you confirm it?'

'I suppose so.'

Once she said the name, she got the nod from Irene that she'd been expecting.

104

Boyd parked the car outside the monstrous sliding gate at the old rectory. 'I think we need to wait for reinforcements.'

'They'll be here soon,' Lottie said, 'but we don't even know what we're dealing with yet.'

The leafless trees were black with birds, sitting in groups on branches, cawing loudly. 'A murder of crows,' she said.

'As long as there are no more murders, they can caw there all day long,' Boyd said, handing her a Kevlar vest. He tightened the Velcro on his, while she did hers.

'This is the address we have for our suspect, the gardener, and it's the same address we got just now from the school for the child Maggie. She's home with chickenpox. Shannon's nephew, Davy, has it too. So it's probable that Maggie got it from Shannon.'

'Speculation. The incubation period is at least ten days.'

'And we found a page from her school book where we suspect the taxi stopped the night Laura was killed.' Lottie studied the forbidding gate and walls. 'I hope I have the energy for this. I'm starving.'

'Did you eat today?'

'I meant to tip home for something... Oh shite. I never called Katie back.' She'd just leaned into the car to get her phone when a massive sound cut through the air, flattening her to the seat. 'What the...?'

'That's an explosion,' Boyd said, crouched by the open door. 'Stay down.'

'We need to find out what's going on. Shannon could be in there.'

Lottie righted herself, forgetting about calling Katie, and stood staring at the impenetrable gate. 'Is the wall too high to climb over?'

'Yes. We have to wait, Lottie.'

'Fuck that.' She checked her weapon was loaded and set off around the wall. 'There must be a way in.'

'This is madness.' Yet he followed her.

The walls were crawling with ivy and creepers. Trees the entire way. When she came to what she thought was the rear of the property, the wall was even higher. Another explosion rang out, knocking them both off their feet. They fell to the ground, more from the noise rather than any flying debris. Lottie's fall was cushioned by Boyd.

'You okay?' She couldn't hear her own words or his reply. The blast had deafened her.

She got to her feet and turned to him. Blood gushed from the back of his head, darkening the grass. He'd landed on a jagged rock. 'Boyd!'

'Don't shout. You'll alert them.'

'And a fucking big explosion won't? You're bleeding.'

'It's a scratch.' He struggled to his knees before standing. They buckled and he leaned on her shoulder. 'Let's wait for the others in the car.'

'You go back. I have to see what's going on.'

'Not on your own. I'm dizzy, Lottie. Seeing double.'

'I'll walk you. Come on.'

When she had him seated in the car, she looked up the lane. No sound of a siren yet. 'Stay there. I won't be long.'

'Don't be stupid.'

'They're in there destroying evidence. I can't let that happen.'

She slammed the car door shut. Knowing Boyd was in no state to follow her, she took off at a run, back the way they'd walked.

She had to get inside.

105

He walked in small circles around the blackened garden, his decimated sanctuary. His shed was gone in a bomb of smoke. The petrol had done its job on his car out front too, but the next blast hadn't been strong enough to dint the outer walls. He regretted ever learning how to make bombs with fertiliser.

'Why can't we just leave now?' he said. 'Why do you have to destroy everything?'

'Evidence, idiot,' she snarled. 'If we're to disappear again, to start over, we can't leave clues. We've done it before. We can do it again.'

'I'm tired of running. Tired of killing for you.'

'Want me to put you out of your misery? I can easily do it.'

'Like you did to John Morgan?'

'He was too clever for his own good,' she snarled. 'He knew what he was doing with Gordon. A man with only daughters needs a surrogate son. A man who disowned his first daughter. Bastard.'

'But why kill John?'

'Because I couldn't risk that he knew about me and Aneta.'

'No one knew—'

'Collins knew. Morgan was in rehab where Aneta worked and he was close to Collins, ergo... Use your brain, if you have one. They had to be dealt with.'

'You got them good and proper.'

'Yes, but that fucker Collins survived the fire.'

'By killing Aneta we should have ended any threat from him.'

'You should have seen his face when I told him how I starved and abused her for a year, and he thinking she'd returned to Poland. I'll treasure his look of incredulity for the rest of my life.'

'What are we going to do with the others? We can't take them with us.'

'We will take Shannon to care for Magenta and Aaron. But I've something very unpleasant planned for Diana.'

'You killed her daughter, is that not enough?'

'*You* killed her, you fool. You couldn't even do that right. I wanted her alive. You're such a hindrance. Maybe you need to die too.'

He worried that he'd said too much. He thought he'd mastered the art of keeping his true thoughts suppressed in front of her. 'You need me. You've always needed me.'

'No I don't. Since those horrible things were done to me, since he raped me when I was only sixteen years old, I've *needed* no one. I have to use people to get me what I want. How else do you think I got you registered on that escort site and pointed you to those I wanted? I paid Cathy in the Right One office to allow me access to the database. I forced Irene to give you a job at Cuan so you could report back to me. I have manipulation down to a fine art.' She paused. Her face took on the darkness that terrified him more than if she held a knife in her hand. 'And you know what? I don't need you any more.'

'You need me to kill the woman.' He turned to look at Diana trussed up like a turkey on a chair behind them.

'I will take pleasure in watching you end her useless life. She colluded with Gordon to take my child away from me and—'

'You agreed to it all,' Diana said, the tape loosened on her lips. 'You said you didn't want her growing up to remind you of Gordon Collins.'

'Shut up, woman.'

'You were going to burn her alive!'

'I said shut up!'

'If you're going to kill me, do it now. I can't bear to listen to your lies any longer.'

'You will suffer first. Perhaps you'd like to see your grandson in pain as you die. Fetch him for me.' She pushed him and he staggered from the room.

He didn't like this. She was supposed to love him. But did she even know how to love? She'd taken everything from him, from everyone. And he'd been complicit. A weakling. Was now the time to stand up to her? But fear burrowed its way deep into his groin and he almost cried out.

As he made his way to the room where they held the children, he wondered if he should just keep walking. Out the front door. Out the gates. Up the lane. Across the fields. Keep going until he had put enough distance between them to feel safe for once in his life.

At the front door, he hesitated, long enough to hear a crash and two gunshots from somewhere behind him. Where had she got a gun from?

He backed away from the door without unlocking it.

Something was very wrong.

———

Both knees of her jeans were torn and she'd ripped her jacket sleeve up to her shoulder, but Lottie had succeeded in climbing the wall despite the cumbersome Kevlar vest. A fallen tree, its trunk rotting, had given her the leg-up she'd needed. The crows had departed in a flurry of noise, but she was masked by a multitude of branches that swept low over the wall.

A car was on fire towards the front of the house and some sort of shed smouldered at the rear wall. The scene confirmed that she was in the right place. Someone was trying to cover their tracks while getting ready to escape.

Dropping down the other side of the wall, she heard sirens in the distance. She lay flat on her stomach and crab-crawled across the slabbed ground towards a solid back door. Rising, she glanced in through a darkened window. A slit at the bottom of the blinds revealed what she'd suspected.

At the door, she found there was no handle, only a lock for a key. She pushed, but it was secure. She fired two shots at the lock and kicked the door in, crying out with the pain shooting through her foot before ignoring it. The next door was easier to kick in, and she flew through it into the nightmare scene.

'Drop the knife, Charlie.'

'Like hell I will.'

Charlie Lennon, still dressed in her designer jeans, her shirt creased and stained with sweat and smoke, stood behind a tied up Diana Nolan, holding a knife to her throat. The skin had already been nicked and a trickle of blood ran down Diana's neck. Her eyes were wide with terror, and though she was bound, her right knee bounced uncontrollably.

Lottie forced herself to stay calm. 'You've nothing left to gain by killing another woman. Especially with a witness present.'

'I killed no woman, you delusional bitch.'

How many times had Lottie been called delusional in her life? The word pulsed red-raw anger through her veins and she propelled herself across the space and hit Charlie in the side of her head with her gun before the woman could react. She drew back her arm to thrash her again, but stopped. Charlie was knocked out. Not dead. Pity.

'You okay, Diana?' She bent to untie the rope.

'Leave me. He's gone to get Aaron. Find him.'

Taking handcuffs from her belt, she secured Charlie's hands behind her back and left her lying on the floor as the woman moaned, regaining consciousness.

She listened at the internal door. All was quiet. Too quiet.

She depressed the handle just as the door opened, knocking her back across the kitchen. Banging her head against the corner of a cupboard, she slid to the ground. She heard Diana scream as a tidal wave of darkness crushed her and she gave herself up to the darkness.

The hospital was quieter than earlier that day, when she'd been there with Gordon Collins. It seemed like a lifetime ago. Lottie's head felt as if it'd been split open with a mallet, though she'd only needed five stitches. Her black eye and bruised cheekbone would fade. Her damaged foot would heal in time too. Boyd had had ten stitches on the back of his head, and he had concussion. War-wound comparisons would abound once they were back at work.

She glanced over at him on the bed by the window as he slept. Amy and Kirby had agreed to keep Sergio for a few nights so Boyd didn't have to worry about his son. On the other bed, Diana Nolan was sitting up drinking a cup of tea. Aaron was in the paediatric unit being assessed physically and psychologically. Easing herself off the bed, Lottie winced at the torn ligaments in her foot as she hobbled over to sit beside Diana.

'I'm sorry,' the older woman said. 'I should've told you about Charlie, but I was scared witless. I knew what she was like as a teenager, and that made me terrified to challenge her.'

'Why had you got a birth certificate for Magenta McCabe at your house?'

'That was Aneta's birth name. She found the certificate among her adoptive mother's things when she died, and she gave it to me for safe keeping that day I was visiting Laura in Cuan. She recognised me from the photograph. She recognised Charlie too, at the event. It was like seeing her own reflection, she said, and she was petrified. Though when I saw Aneta's death photo, she looked nothing like she did that day. How could a woman be so cruel to her own flesh and blood?'

Lottie wasn't sure of the full story about what had happened all those years ago. 'We believe Maggie L is Charlie's daughter. We had Charlie's DNA on file, as she was present when John's body was found. We're not sure if Thomas McCabe is the father. Waiting for DNA analysis on that.'

'He's Charlie's stepbrother.'

'Really?' Lottie wondered what that dynamic had been like. 'He's not talking. The armed response team were a little too forceful when they broke through the front door. He's in an induced coma.'

'And Charlie?'

'In custody. Talking very little, though Detective McKeown and Superintendent Farrell are doing their best with the interviews.'

'Such a fucked-up family.'

'Aneta was registered as Magenta McCabe on her original birth cert. The mother's name was falsified, but why wasn't Gordon Collins named? He claims he was Aneta's father.'

'My head hurts thinking about it.' Diana put the cup on the tray and pushed it away. 'Who knows how that woman thinks. Charlie claimed Gordon raped her when she was sixteen. Said he treated her like a prostitute. I don't believe that was true. She twisted facts all the time. Twisted people into knots with her warped mind. He believed her when she said she was pregnant by him. He said it happened once. He was vulnerable back then, as was I. He was in Cuan rehab for addiction issues and I was his girlfriend at the time. I hated him after everything that happened. Maybe Aneta wasn't Gordon's at all.'

'Could Thomas have been Aneta's father?'

'No, he was only ten years old then. I don't believe Charlie was that warped.'

'A DNA test will confirm it one way or the other.'

'Inspector, how did Charlie come to have such a big house out in the countryside?'

'I've to talk to Gordon Collins about that.'

'She used everyone she came in contact with.'

Lottie sighed. 'The more I learn about her, the more I'm convinced she was a dab hand at exploitation. We'll talk again, Diana. Take care.'

After a torturous walk along the corridor and up in the lift, Lottie reached the ward where Shannon was recuperating. Davy was sitting on her knee, with George standing by the foot of the bed. The days of incarceration had not been kind to her.

George took his son in his arms. 'We'll go get juice, Davy.' He mouthed thanks to Lottie and left her alone with Shannon.

'How are you feeling?'

'Worse than rehab.' The young woman attempted a laugh. 'I owe you a huge thank you.'

'Doing my job.'

'She would have killed us all. She told him she'd take us with them, but I know she was too self-consumed to take baggage while she made her escape. I can't get my head around how she hated her own daughters, both Aneta and Maggie.'

'I believe Charlie is a classic sociopath. I have to get more information to understand her relationship with Aneta. From what I've learned so far, she was forming Maggie in her own image.'

'I get that she was moulding the child to be like her.

Magenta... Maggie had found her knife in a scabbard. I truly believe she was about to kill me until Charlie tasered us both. Where is the girl now?'

'Child services.'

'What'll happen to her?'

'She'll need psychological rehabilitation. After that, who knows?'

'Who cares?' Shannon pursed her lips glumly. 'No, that's wrong. It's bringing me down to their level.'

Lottie took her hand and squeezed it. 'You'll need therapy after everything you've been through.'

'I've had my fill of therapists.'

'At least confide in family or friends. Talk to Jess, if you feel George is a step too far.'

'Jess is a star.'

'She is. Lean on her for support.' Lottie pondered whether Shannon had suffered sexual assault, but didn't want to ask. Didn't want to add to her trauma. The doctors would confirm it later. 'Did you view the house at Pine Grove with Charlie?'

'I did.'

'Did you not recognise her when you'd been abducted and were living in her house?'

'I thought she seemed a bit familiar, but then again, I was more interested in the house than in her when I viewed it. Those days in captivity were endless, and every time I looked at her, she was like a different person.'

'Charlie's a narcissist as well as the classic sociopath. A chameleon who manipulated everyone. A person I would not like to meet on a dark night walking home alone.'

Shannon smiled weakly. 'And I just happened to walk home alone and meet the one she manipulated the most.'

'Thomas is not an innocent in this. Take care, Shannon.'

107

THREE DAYS LATER

Lottie sat with a dejected Gordon Collins in the show home kitchen. He'd moved in temporarily with Brenda Morgan's blessing, as he was now homeless.

'I was duped by Charlie. Taken in by her.' He ran his hand through his hair, then grimaced with pain. The skin grafts on his bandaged hands were still healing. 'I didn't understand it, all those years ago, but I've read up about her type since. She was only sixteen, but she was on a mission to escape her life, her stepfather. He ran Cuan back then and she claimed he was violent towards her, but perhaps that was another lie, and I was her escape route. I was damaged, struggling with my addiction, easy prey. I'm not excusing my actions of thirty years ago, but I understand them more clearly with the passing of time.'

'Explain,' Lottie said.

'Things really began to unravel behind the scenes when I took John Morgan under my wing last year. I think Charlie saw me giving him something I never gave her. Respect and time. She was insanely jealous of him. And of me. She had manipulated me into acquiring and then giving her the old rectory house. She inveigled money from me to get into the estate agent business and forced me to give her the contract for selling my flagship housing project. She threatened to expose my actions of thirty years ago. She even installed her stepbrother, Thomas, at Cuan to spy on Irene Dunbar.' Collins took a long drink of water before continuing.

'Irene was a young secretary at Cuan back then. She joined forces with us after the facility partially burned down. She helped Diana with the baby's adoption. We had to be careful, and when Charlie returned to Ragmullin, I believed that she was working her way back into our lives in order to control us all over again. As if her actions three decades ago wasn't control enough. She wanted to destroy us all.'

'Did you realise what had happened with Aneta?'

'I'd assumed she'd gone back to Poland, but now I know better. Charlie took Aneta as a slave because that was her ultimate control over another human being, next to killing them. She took great pleasure in telling me how she'd mistreated and murdered her. She didn't see her as her own daughter, only mine. And I had to be punished. Plus, she was insanely jealous of my mentorship of John. Her cruelty had to be shared to bring me down further.'

'How long were you in contact with Aneta?'

'I couldn't tell you too much before. I was terrified you'd go straight to Charlie and then she would target my daughters. When her adoptive mother died, Aneta found her original birth cert and some old papers. She tracked me down and I kept in contact with her. I sent her money. We talked on the phone. Long conversations. I told her about my girls, sent her photos, and we discussed my marriage troubles. She was interested in my life; a good listener.' He looked wistfully out the window. 'I spoke to her about John, and how he was going into rehab. I emailed her his photo because she seemed interested. She must have had it printed, as you found a copy. Why did she do that, I wonder? Maybe she wanted to bond with me through him, but I honestly don't know.'

'Why did she come to Ireland?'

'She wanted to know who her birth mother was. I kept putting her off and didn't realise she was here until that event Irene ran at Cuan. And then Aneta disappeared. Like I said, I assumed she'd gone home. I continued to send her an allowance but heard nothing further from her.'

'Why didn't Charlie target your ex-wife or daughters?'

'They could have been next on her list. Who knows how her warped brain works.'

'I'm trying to understand why Aneta went to work at Cuan,' Lottie said. 'She had an old group photo, which was taken around thirty years ago on the steps of the facility. Do you know when it was taken, and why?'

'That was the night of the fire. The night that led to all our lives being scorched for ever more.'

108

THIRTY YEARS AGO

The flames had not yet taken hold of the entire building. Cuan's facade was a red and yellow tableau. The heat reached out to them as they stood under the trees to one side. The day had started off like any other, and they had gathered on the steps with friends who were there that day, for a photo. And then Charlie had morphed into what they'd all suspected. A demon.

Gordon could not believe what he'd just heard from her lips. 'You can't be serious, Charlie.'

'I'm very serious. I started the fire and I will burn her in it if you don't take me away from here and marry me.'

'But I can't. I'm going out with Diana.'

'You should have thought of that before you raped me.'

'Rape? What are you talking about? We had a one-night stand. That's all.'

'It's the same thing in my eyes. You used me as a whore, like my stepfather did. He ran this place like a tyrant and betrayed my mother by fucking me like he did his prostitutes. I had to live here with him, seeing all that. Seeing my mother die of a broken heart. Now I'm burning down everything he worked for, his stupid safe harbour, Cuan. Hah!'

'You're insane.' He turned away.

She caught his sleeve and pulled him back forcefully.

'Don't you ever, ever say that to me!'

'What is wrong with you?' He tried to twist out of her grip, but there was no escape. She seemed possessed of an inhuman strength.

'Me? I'm a sixteen-year-old abuse victim. You're the one with the addiction issues, not me. So who will people believe when I tell them you raped me and got me pregnant?'

His resolve faltered. 'It was consensual.'

'I am sixteen years old!'

'You told me you were eighteen. You followed me like a puppy until I gave in. You're like a disease, Charlie. You need help. Cuan is no use to you because you're addicted to causing pain. You and your lapdog brother.'

'Stepbrother. Call him what you like, but he is not my blood.'

'He's still your lapdog.' He tried to sound brave, but he felt only fear in her presence.

'I'm burning fucking Cuan with your brat of a child in it. Do you not realise how serious I am?'

'I do.' The voice came from behind them, and he turned to see Diana walk from the shadows. 'I'll take the child and you can get on with your life.'

Charlie sneered. 'Oh Gordon, you need your heroic *girl-friend* to bail you out. You're not a man at all. You're a mat.'

He caught Diana's eye and shook his head, but she moved forward.

'I want to help you,' Diana said. 'I understand you don't want the child holding you back. Give her to me and I will make sure she's cared for. We'll find a family to rear her. Then you can be free.'

'I'll be free if I throw her on that fire.' Charlie's laugh sent

an avalanche of terror down Gordon's spine. He forced himself
to reply.

'But when her bones are found, she will be linked to you.
You don't want that, do you? Spending the best years of your
life in prison?'

He caught the look in her eyes. The calculations going on
behind their bleakness. The realisation that this was a way out
lit them up like the flames beginning to burn out of control.

Eventually she spoke. 'I'll need money. You can pay me to
leave the country. Me and Thomas. And I never want to see
that child again. Never!'

'Where is the baby?' Diana asked.

Charlie turned to the tree trunk beside her. 'Come out.'

Ten-year-old Thomas stepped forward carrying the
newborn wrapped in a blanket. Charlie didn't touch the baby,
just indicated for Thomas to hand it over to Diana.

'Here's her birth cert.' She held up a folded page. 'I put my
mother's name, Christine McCabe, on it instead of mine. The
stupid woman took my stepfather's surname when she married
him, but I still have my father's surname, Lennon. This child
will never be traced back to me. That cert must go with her
wherever you take her. I don't really care what you do with her,
but I never want to lay eyes on her again. If I do, you and
everyone you care for will pay. And so will she.'

109

The prison interview room was bleak, but somehow Charlie
Lennon brightened it up when she walked in. She had not yet
acquired the greyness of skin that often plagued prisoners. Her
eyes shone manically, and Lottie prepared herself for the lies to
follow.

'You're in a world of trouble, Charlie.'

'Oh, I don't think so, Inspector.' She sat while Lottie started
the recording device.

'You killed Aneta, Laura and John. You abducted and
imprisoned Shannon. All that before I even get to what you did
to Diana and her grandson.'

'I think you'll find that Thomas is the culprit, not me.'

'You like blaming others, don't you?'

'What's that supposed to mean?'

'You said your stepfather abused you, but from my
enquiries, though he is long dead, Michael McCabe was a
good man. He ran the Cuan centre with care and attention
and—'

'Ever hear the saying "what goes on behind closed doors",
Inspector?'

'Yes, and that's what you are, a closed door. But I will open you up and get a confession out of you.'

'Have fun trying.' Charlie laughed and swung her hair over her shoulder. 'I hear you have a lovely family. And a grandson. If I was you, I'd be more concerned with them than with me.'

An ice-cold shiver travelled the length of Lottie's spine. She shook it off. She could not allow herself to be spooked. She had to play to Charlie's narcissism.

'I must admit, I admire how you were able to command such adoration and compliance from Thomas. He would do anything for you.'

'He's still a ten-year-old at heart. Easy to mould.'

Charlie didn't seem to realise her admission. Lottie felt she had her snared.

'You were so young to have to care for him. It must have been difficult for you.'

'Not at all. I had his inheritance after his father died.'

'Why did you return to Ireland five years ago?'

'Magenta. Maggie to you. I wanted her to grow up in my home country.'

Lottie wasn't buying that. Charlie had come back to wreak havoc on those she believed had wronged her. 'She is your daughter and Thomas's?'

'She has nothing of him. I made sure of that.'

'She's a child, and you were moulding her to do your work like you did with Thomas, is that right?'

'She was turning out just fine until that Shannon bitch wormed her way into her brain. Making her question things.'

Lottie noticed Charlie was so self-consumed she didn't even ask where her young daughter was now.

'It was clever how you used the escort agency to lure the girls.' Come on, Lottie thought, tell me how you did it.

Charlie glowed. 'I'm a genius. That Cathy one hadn't a clue what I was at. All she wanted was money. Shallow individual.

Once I had control of the site, it was easy to set the girls up with flakes and fakes. I knew where they were and all I had to do was set Thomas on them.'

'He says it was you who took Aneta last Valentine's night. Why?' She had spoken with the broken murderer. His injuries were healing, but she knew he never would.

'I couldn't afford for him to fuck it up. I disguised myself, but I should have burned her in the fire all those years ago and then she wouldn't have come back raking over the ashes.'

'How did she learn about you?'

'She found out about Collins after her adoptive mother died. And next thing I know she's working at Cuan, the one place on earth I hated with a vengeance. Collins should have kept his trap shut.'

'Gordon didn't tell her about you. It was Irene.'

'I should have known!' A cold glint crept into her eyes. 'She worked for my stepfather back in the day. I didn't realise she was involved so deeply.'

'Didn't you know that Diana and Gordon asked for her help to get Aneta out of the country thirty years ago?' Lottie hoped that by goading Charlie she might crack.

'Such a manipulative clique.'

She almost laughed at the irony. Charlie was so caught up in recounting her own genius, was she even aware of all she was revealing? Probably, and she didn't care. That scared Lottie.

'When did you realise Aneta was in Ireland?'

'When I saw her at Cuan that day. I knew who she was instantly, and she knew me. It was like staring in a mirror. I couldn't let her be free. I enjoyed beating her down, but she became a burden. She had to be replaced. It was ingenious on my part to take Laura from Diana. But that idiot Thomas lost the run of himself and killed her.'

'What did John Morgan ever do to you?'

'He started asking the wrong questions. Gordon couldn't

keep his mouth shut, asking him about Aneta when John was in Cuan. When Laura died, one thing led to another and John accused me of being involved. He went down like a ton of bricks.'

'And you had the perfect alibi. Us finding the body while you were present.'

'Worked like a dream. For a while.'

Lottie could see Charlie was itching to ask how they'd eventually found her, but she wasn't going to reveal it. The little boy, Rex, who'd once lived in the rectory, had to be kept safe, and she had no idea where Charlie would end up. Hopefully she'd be in prison for a long, long time. But who knew what manipulation and coercion the woman could wield from behind bars. And that terrified Lottie more than the dark demon eyes staring across the table at her.

A FEW WEEKS LATER

It was Valentine's night and Lottie had her family all under the same roof, for one evening at least. Dinner had been a success, with no arguments between Katie and Chloe. They appeared not to be talking to each other anyhow. Sean had agreed that Sergio could sleep on a fold-out bed in his room. Won't be much sleep there, Lottie thought, but at least the noise-cancelling headphones were doing the trick.

She had stripped her bed again, because she thought it smelled of smoke even weeks later, and stuffed the linen in a pillowcase for the launderette. No way had she the energy for washing, drying and ironing. She missed Rose for all that. The old Rose. They used to fight and argue, but Lottie discovered that she missed her. Was the real Rose in there any more? She looked at her knitting at the kitchen table. Her head bowed, concentrating on each laborious stitch. Gone were the days when her fingers would fly with mesmerising speed of wool and needles, while she simultaneously read the newspaper. It was all so sad.

As she climbed the stairs, a set of fresh sheets and pillowcases under her arm, she regretted not having cherished her mother more. With each step she resolved to make more time for her going forward.

Katie followed her up. 'Need help?'

'Sure.'

As they tucked the sheet under the mattress, Katie said, 'I'm sorry, Mam, for being so bitchy.'

'I just worry about you. I hope Greg is now banished from the scene.'

'Uhm, not really. I'm meeting him for dinner next weekend.'

Lottie paused, pillowcase in hand, trying not to let her jaw drop. 'Is that wise? You know he is being investigated by our vice unit.'

'Probably not wise, but I like him. He's been shattered by Cathy's duplicity and he's abandoning the dating and escort side of his business. Wants to concentrate solely on his photography. So he says.'

'So he says?' Lottie raised an eyebrow.

'Yeah, I know, but he's kind of cute and he likes Louis.'

'He met Louis once, that I know of.'

'That you know of.' Katie winked.

Trying not to show her exasperation, Lottie plumped up the pillow with extra force. 'He's a lot older than you too. And don't forget he dated women using a false name.'

'Not everyone is perfect.'

'You're right there.' She'd have to relent. 'Promise me you'll be careful.'

'Promise. Favour? Can you talk to Chloe for me? She thinks it's a bad idea.'

'Why don't *you* talk to her?'

'I tried. She snapped my head off.'

'Sisters.'

When they'd finished making the bed, Katie threw her arms around Lottie in a hug. 'Thanks for being you, Mam.'

'What does that mean?'

Katie grinned and left the room, closing the door behind her.

Lottie flopped onto the pristine bed, wishing she could sleep for a year. The door opened slowly and Boyd stuck his head in.

'Can I join you?'

'Please do.' She scooted over and patted the space beside her.

'I could do with a hug and a kiss,' he said. 'It's Valentine's after all.'

'I could do with a long sleep and breakfast in bed in the morning.'

'Your wish is my command.'

'Great, and here's the hug and kiss you wanted.'

He grinned. He still had a monster-sized plaster on the back of his head, which would have been comical if his injury hadn't been so deep. He was suffering from headaches and looked thinner, if that was possible.

'We're two old crocks,' he said, before pressing his lips to hers.

She felt an awakening in the pit of her stomach. An intense tingling that was beautiful before it was replaced by a moment of fear. 'Did you lock the door?'

'Give me a minute.' He got off the bed. 'You don't have a key in it.'

'Push the cabinet up against it.'

'We really need our own place.'

'Where are we going to find somewhere to fit a family like the Waltons?'

He laughed and lay down beside her. His phone chirped.

'Don't,' she warned.

He checked the screen. 'It's Grace. I better—'

'Go ahead.' She fluffed up the pillows and raised herself onto one elbow, close enough to hear, staring at the contours of his face, the glint of gold in his hazel eyes like flint sparking a fire. Fires were dangerous, as their investigation had demonstrated, but this one was exciting.

'Hello, Mark. This is Grace.'

'I can see your name on my screen.' Boyd smirked, and Lottie pulled the pillow over her face to smother a laugh.

'I know you're laughing at me, Mark. It's not funny.'

'I'm not laughing. What's up?'

'What would be up? You're so silly. I'm sitting down. Are you listening to me?'

'I am.'

'I thought you were too stressed when I stayed with you last month. Your living conditions are not ideal. That apartment is too small. It's not healthy for a young boy. He needs a garden to bring his friends over to play.'

'He hasn't got any friends yet.'

'How could he have friends when he has nowhere to bring them to? You're a very stupid man, Mark.'

'I suppose I am.' He winked at Lottie. She tried not to giggle.

'Listen, Mark,' Grace said. 'Myself and Bryan... and don't say with a Y or I'd clobber you if I was there...'

'Go on.'

'We made a decision. It's a surprise for you and Sergio.'

Boyd muted the phone and turned to Lottie, 'She can't be moving here, can she?'

'Bryan with a Y won't leave his farm,' Lottie whispered.

He unmuted the phone. 'What decision, Grace?'

'Bryan and I are buying a house in Ragmullin.'

'What about his farm?' Boyd's eyes widened in horror.

'If you keep interrupting me, I won't tell you.'

'Okay. Sorry.'

'We can sell Mother's house and share the proceeds, but this house will be for you and Sergio. And Lottie too, if she wants. If I gift it to you, you'll be fleeced with tax, so it will have to be in our name. Mine and Bryan's. We can draw up a rental agreement, and when I die, which I hope isn't for a long time, it will be yours. Then again, I'm much younger than you, so you'll probably die first. I'll make sure it goes to Sergio in that case.'

'Why would you do this? Or Bryan?'

'He has money he wants to invest and I told him my family come first. He's not my family yet.'

'Can I think about it?'

'Why would you want to think about it?'

'It's a bit of a shock.'

'You never even said thanks, Mark. You're not very appreciative of your generous sister.'

'I love you, Grace. And thank you.'

'Settled then. Say hello to Lottie. I know she's there with you. Bye.'

Boyd turned off the phone and left it on the bedside cabinet. 'How could she know you're with me?'

'She's cleverer than her brother.'

'She continues to surprise me. We'll have to discuss this. I don't want to end up living with Bryan.'

'Not even a Bryan with a Y?'

'Now you're making fun of Grace's surprise.'

'Can I surprise you for a change?' Lottie asked, sitting up.

'You can try?'

'First, I need a shower. Care to join me?' She hauled her T-shirt over her head.

'I'll need a shower cap for my wounded head.'

'That is something I'd pay to see.' Lottie laughed until the tears ran down her cheeks.

'It's not funny.'

'It is, but you know what? Feck the shower.'

'I second that.' He pulled her down on top of him.

She felt the taut lines of his body through his clothes right before she began to take them off him. She didn't even notice the drip, drip of water from the leaking ceiling. That could wait for another day.

A LETTER FROM PATRICIA

Hello, dear reader,

I am so pleased that you have read Book 14 in the Lottie Parker series. I hope you enjoyed *Her Last Walk Home*, and if you want to keep up to date with all my latest releases, just sign up at the following link.

www.bookouture.com/patricia-gibney

Your email address will never be shared, and you can unsubscribe at any time.

If you enjoyed the read, I'd be so pleased if you could post a review on Amazon or on the site where you purchased the eBook, paperback or audiobook. It provides me with great encouragement and I'm so grateful for the reviews received so far.

If you have already read the other Lottie Parker books, *The Missing Ones, The Stolen Girls, The Lost Child, No Safe Place, Tell Nobody, Final Betrayal, Broken Souls, Buried Angels, Silent Voices, Little Bones, The Guilty Girl, Three Widows* and *The Altar Girls*, I thank you for your support and reviews. If *Her Last Walk Home* is your first encounter with Lottie, I hope you will find time to read the previous books in the series. You can also connect with me on social media.

Thanks again for reading *Her Last Walk Home*. I hope you will join me again for Book 15 in the series.

Love,

Patricia

facebook.com/trisha460

x.com/trisha460

instagram.com/patricia_gibney_author

ACKNOWLEDGEMENTS

I want to start by thanking you for reading *Her Last Walk Home*. I hope you enjoyed it, and the series to date.

My days hidden away from the world pounding my laptop are made easier with the support of my family. Thanks to my children (young adults now), Aisling, Orla and Cathal, for being with me on this journey. You are amazing young people and I am so proud to be your mam. And life is never dull with my grandchildren giving me their own view on the world. Love you all.

Though writing is a solitary business, it takes a team of people to get a book published and out in the world. As ever, I want to take this opportunity to thank them.

My agent, Ger Nicol at The Book Bureau, has been with me since day one and I'm eternally grateful for her wisdom and friendship and her tireless work on my behalf. Thanks also to Hannah Whitaker at The Rights People for sourcing publishers for foreign translations of my books.

I absolutely love working with my editor, Lydia Vassar-Smith, and am forever thankful for her editorial expertise and advice. This one is for you, Lydia. Head of Publicity at Bookouture, Kim Nash, has always been in my corner, so thanks to her and her team of Sarah Hardy, Noelle Holten and Jess Readett. Thanks also to Mark Walsh of Plunkett PR for his work publicising my books that are published with Hachette Ireland.

The Bookouture team is professional in all they do. Thanks

Lizzie Brien, Mandy Kullar, Alba Proko, Peta Nightingale, Jen Shannon and Melissa Tran.

I'm delighted once again that Jane Selley is my copyeditor. Jane's expertise is invaluable to me and my work.

Sphere Books and Hachette Ireland bring my books to you in English-language paperback. Thank you to all involved. Special thanks also to all my foreign translation publishers for producing my books in their native languages, and thanks also to the translators.

Michele Moran has been the voice of my books since *The Missing Ones*. I'm delighted with Michele's excellent narration and for bringing my words to life in the English-language audio format. Thanks also to the team at 2020 Recordings for your work on *Her Last Walk Home*.

I'm grateful to have my sister, Marie Brennan, helping me along the way with first reads and proofing. Thank you, Marie.

Thanks to each reader who takes the time to post a review, as this is encouraging for me as a writer and it also helps other readers discover my books. A massive thank you to hard-working book bloggers and reviewers who read and review my books. I appreciate the time and effort this entails.

Thanks also to all the booksellers and librarians who continue to support my work and the work of other writers by bringing the books to readers in towns and villages everywhere. Also, the support of other writers is so important, and I am thankful and blessed to have them in my corner. I try to repay their kindness whenever and wherever I can.

Special thanks to Róisín, Amma Massage, for ironing out all the knots in my shoulders from being hunched over my laptop writing this book.

Thanks to those in the Gardaí who have helped me along the way. Just to note that I fictionalise a lot of the police procedures to add pace to the story, and any inaccuracies are my own.

Once again, dear reader, I'm sincerely grateful to you for reading *Her Last Walk Home* and I hope you will continue to join me on this amazing journey. It won't be too long until we are back in Lottie's world once again.

Thank you.

PUBLISHING TEAM

Turning a manuscript into a book requires the efforts of many people. The publishing team at Bookouture would like to acknowledge everyone who contributed to this publication.

Audio
Alba Proko
Melissa Tran
Sinead O'Connor

Commercial
Lauren Morrissette
Hannah Richmond
Imogen Allport

Contracts
Peta Nightingale

Cover design
Tash Webber

Data and analysis
Mark Alder
Mohamed Bussuri

Made in United States
Orlando, FL
27 October 2024

53160251R00276